You Are the Reason

THE HEART OF MORELAND MANOR:

BOOK ONE

ENDORSEMENTS

Fans of Mary A. Felkins will not want to miss her latest contemporary romance. The evocative Southern mansion needs as much restoration as the hearts of the two protagonists. Themes include: success (or lack thereof) does not measure a person's worth; and my personal favorite—overcoming fear by daring to dream. I love a good reunion romance, and Felkins does not disappoint. The chemistry between Everley and Gabe is palpable.
—**Lisa Carter**, Carol Award-winning author of *Under a Turquoise Sky* and *The Christmas Bargain*

Author Mary A. Felkins is off to a strong start in her Heart of Moreland Manor Series. In *You are the Reason*, readers meet Everley, a woman who is meant to shoot for the stars but has anchored her feet firmly to safe, solid ground. Most of all, she's unwilling to open her heart to love again. But circumstances—in the form of a will, a house renovation, and the undeniable attraction between Everley and Gabe, the contractor restoring Moreland Manor—won't allow Everley's life to stay the same. By fulfilling her mother's dream will Everley rediscover her own? Thanks to Felkins' dynamic characters, I'm anticipating the rest of the series!
—**Beth K. Vogt**, Christy Award-winning author of the Thatcher Sisters Series

Do you believe in second chances?

When Everley Scott's well-ordered life is interrupted by the needs of a house she's inherited, she's none too happy. Add the man her deceased mother chose to bring the house back to life (a dying wish) and her life is turned upside down. Can't she get rid of the place and be done with it? But majestic Moreland isn't going down without a fight. Not if restoration expert Gabe Bellevue has his way. Unfortunately, Moreland isn't the only thing that needs restoring and Everley, the girl he lost his heart to in high school, isn't making things easy. Can an old house with hidden secrets give each a second chance at what matters most? Find out in *You Are the Reason*.

A fresh new voice in fiction, Mary A. Felkins's *You Are the Reason* has all the charm and sass everyone loves in a romance!

—**Kit Morgan**, *USA Today* bestselling author

You Are the Reason

THE HEART OF MORELAND MANOR:

BOOK ONE

MARY A. FELKINS

PUBLISHING THE POSITIVE
Plymouth, Massachusetts
A Christian Company

COPYRIGHT NOTICE

Cover and Interior Design: Derinda Babcock, Deb Haggerty
Editor(s): Steve Mathisen, Cristel Phelps, Deb Haggerty

PUBLISHED BY: Elk Lake Publishing, Inc., 35 Dogwood Drive, Plymouth, MA 02360, 2021

Library Cataloging Data

Names: Felkins, Mary A. (Mary A. Felkins)
You Are the Reason—The Heart of Moreland Manor: Book One / Mary A. Felkins
370 p. 23cm × 15cm (9in × 6 in.)
ISBN-13: 978-1-64949-454-2 (paperback) | 978-1-64949-455-9 (trade paperback) | 978-1-64949-456-6 (e-book)

Key Words: Christian romance novels; Christian romance series; New Orleans fiction books; Historic home restoration; Christian contemporary romance fiction; Inspirational fiction; Christian fiction books for women

Library of Congress Control Number: 2021950696 Fiction

DEDICATION

This book is dedicated to my husband, Bruce, who first introduced us to Madewood Plantation Bed & Breakfast in Napoleonville, Louisiana. The memories made during our blissful stays are the reason I hold the beloved architectural marvel close to my heart.

ACKNOWLEDGMENTS

Deb Haggerty, Editor in Chief, who believed in the series and offered it a home.

Cristel Phelps, managing editor, who generously answered my questions as a new author to Elk Lake Publishing, Inc.

Steve Mathisen, editor, who worked to strengthen readability, establish factual accuracy, and adjust descriptions in consideration of the reader.

Pattie Frampton, contemporary romance author of *Repossessing Christmas*, my craft partner who assisted in story construction and cheered for my characters as if they were her own.

Kathy Geary Anderson, historical romance author of *The Trouble With Jenny* and *Songs in the Storm*, an incredibly efficient and thorough beta reader.

The My Book Therapy Huddle group, fellow authors who cheer and pray for one another daily: Dalyn Weller, Kathy Geary Anderson, Geralyn Beauchamp, Pattie Frampton, and Linda Jo Reed. Love and appreciate y'all!

Rachel Hauck, NYT best selling author, whose creative genius inspired the spark of an idea for this story during the Deep Thinker's Writer's Retreat (DTR) in 2017.

Kariss Lynch Dickerson, Sally Jo Pitts, Pamela Snowden, Tammie Edington Shaw, and Gracie Booth

Wursthorn, writer friends who contributed ideas when this story was initially taking shape during DTR 2017.

Carol Cantrell, Board Certified Tax Law, Estate Planning, and Probate Law, and Emily Cantrell, senior associate for a Charlotte law firm, who contributed information related to loans and financial constraints, as well as tax advantages of owning a house of this magnitude. Like my heroine (and very unlike me), these two women love numbers. Grateful the apple didn't fall far from the tree.

David Salzburg, film producer and president of High Road Media Inc. A seasoned veteran of the entertainment industry, David inspired the idea to include a Civil War war widow in this story. His creative input led to a drastic change in the heroine's—and Moreland's—backstory.

Angie Johnson, manager and head of hospitality at Madewood Mansion, Napoleonville, LA. Her enthusiasm for and knowledge of the house exceeds anyone I've ever known.

Jenny Dyer, House Coordinator, Louisiana Landmarks Society and Lindsey Reno, Louisiana and Special Collections at Earl K. Long Library, University of New Orleans, who provided information regarding historical facts and document collection on Madewood.

Wendy Blanton and David Thompson, residents of Chicago who helped craft the heroine's story world.

The ladies of Tuesday's prayer group at Corinth Reformed Church, Hickory NC. Ever thankful for their faithfulness in prayer and enthusiasm for me and Christian fiction.

Sandy Schronce, friend, prayer partner, and author of The Promise: Joy Through the Brokenness. When she says, "Don't let Satan steal your joy," she means it.

For we are God's handiwork, created in Christ Jesus to do good works, which God prepared in advance for us to do.
Ephesians 2:10

CHAPTER ONE

If ever there was a house that could make a widow out of a girl, it'd be Moreland. And if ever there was a girl least likely to embrace the inheritance of said house, it'd be Everley Scott.

A widow.

Why invite trouble?

The elevator to the third floor of Vance and O'Connor, Certified Public Accountants, pinged and opened, ushering Everley past two potted plants clinging to life near a distressed credenza and down a long hardwood hallway. The scent of heated air roused her senses. Seated at her mahogany desk, she sipped her coffee, cringing at the acrid taste.

Everley craved order and logic like a cup of creamy, French roast coffee and beignets from the renowned Café du Monde in her hometown of New Orleans. It had been five years since she left and moved to Chicago, a city boasting its own unique flavors, but she still desired the familiar—the known.

That which was predictable. Manageable.

She awakened her laptop. First order of business, check email before scheduling a site visit to a new client. Her cell buzzed.

Serenity.

Hands paused over the keyboard—anxiety surged. This could only mean an emergency. Her sister knew never to disrupt a workday. Particularly a Monday morning when emails in her inbox spilled like blue ink down the computer screen.

"What's wrong?"

"Moreland."

Okay, next subject.

"How's business in the French Quarter?"

"My bakery is thriving. Which is more than I can say for Moreland."

Disquiet finger-tapped along Everley's skin. "Clarify."

"There's talk about having it razed, Evers. To suffer the fate of others like Belle Grove."

"Old as it is, that house is mine. No one has the legal right to demolish it."

"They most certainly can if you still haven't secured a deed restriction prohibiting its destruction."

"I thought Mom was going to take care of that."

"She was. But she didn't. And being that you've all but abandoned her generous gift, it's vulnerable, working its way back toward being an eyesore, destroying all Mom's progress."

Not a far stretch.

"I've kept utilities going." Defense soaked her tone.

"So, you're letting it die a *slow* death. Putting the house on life support."

"For someone named Serenity, you sure aren't eliciting any of it on my account."

Memories of Mom's sobs over the insurmountable challenge of restoring Moreland began to taunt. An icy chill slithered down her spine to rival the winter air.

Releasing a rescue breath, she spun in her chair, gaze landing on Moreland's enlarged photo on the wall behind her. The lush landscape and gleaming shutters set like black buttons on a crisp white tuxedo shirt. Intricately carved, gold-washed wood framed its historic charm. Only proper for what was, admittedly, an architectural marvel.

The Polaroid Dad had taken of their impulsive 'as is' purchase—a Greek revival which sold for well below market value—managed to find its way onto Everley's nightstand. Mom's denial was never convincing.

"The grass is overgrown, and weeds have pretty much swallowed the azalea bushes," Serenity continued. "And you know how much color they add come March."

Back to routine.

Tap, tap, tap. Delete, delete, delete.

The subject line from the new client caught Everley's eye. *Documents attached*. Finally.

"I hear typing. Are you even listening, Evers?"

"Yes, yes." With upward of 75 percent of her brain on numbers, the remainder given to the antebellum house strategically tucked in a gentle bend of Bayou Lafourche edged by sugar cane fields. "How would you know the condition of the lawn?"

"I stop by at least once a week. It's still ... special and worth restoring."

"Good that someone's got their eye on the place."

"Heaven help us if the good Lord ever blesses you with a child. Moreland needs more than a weekly nod." Serenity's demands clawed at Everley's insides.

Virtual images flashed of Serenity on Moreland's massive porch watering limp, thirsty shrubbery—picnicking beneath the mossy, great oak dominating the front lawn. Establishing a forever bond with an undesirable estate.

Upholding Mom's whimsical dream.

No, her oversized art project ... now left to Everley.

Crazy. Nonsensical. Wasteful.

Everley propped her elbow on the armrest, fingers clenching her cell. "I'm already paying the utilities and several thousands in property tax, due by year's end. I don't need the added burden of restoring thirteen thousand square feet of trouble, bearing one hundred fifty years of who knows what behind its walls." A fixer-upper on steroids. "What was Mom thinking leaving Moreland to me?"

"I've been asking the same question since she died six months ago."

Her younger—and only—sister still smarted at the fact she'd not been Mom's choice, though Serenity'd managed to command Dad's attention for eight years before he died.

"I mean, I *am* the one who wants to champion the place." Serenity jabbed. "And have the geographical upper hand to do it."

Unhindered and fearless, Serenity had marched confidently in the direction of her dreams and opened The Pear Tree Bakery and Coffee Shop in the heart of the French Quarter. And therein lay the difference—Serenity fed her imagination while Everley, a young war widow after only two years of marriage, had starved hers.

Serenity's world of vibrant color held no appeal to Everley, a woman who viewed life through a monochromatic lens.

The mere fact that Serenity thought nothing of conducting baking wars in college with Owen Walker, today a defensive end for the New Orleans Commanders, testified to her frolic through life.

Serenity's 'Go big or go home' mantra suited her like frosting on a cupcake.

Anyway, Everley had her eye on another prize—making partner in the firm of Vance and O'Connor. A logical next step in her career and, now, a means to maintain distance from the burden of Moreland Manor.

"What crazy person takes on a project like this?" Everley took a swallow of her now cold, stale coffee.

"Mom did. Dad agreed."

Right. Mom had help. Until she didn't.

"Mom let her dreams get ahead of common sense, the cost more than she could bear."

More than I can bear.

Like the cost Everley had borne seven years ago, marrying Kyle Scott, a guy who'd chosen to enlist in the Marines and chase after bad guys in Afghanistan. She never saw the career shift coming. And Kyle hadn't seen the IED.

The heartbreaking but predictable fate of a dream chaser.

Computer now dozing, another of Moreland's grainy images intruded—this one in black and white. Dwarfed at the base of a column stood a woman in a high-waisted dress, hair swept inside a tilted slouch hat. A house of such magnitude—one left without consistent homeowners for over one hundred fifty years—wouldn't be ignored easily.

The spectacle stirred recall, a documentary created several years ago by a band of exuberant, stargazing historians. Emotive music accompanied the narration.

She graces the property like a priceless pearl adorning a lady's neck, and her interior chambers hold a wealth of mystery. Stories pulse behind those windows that stir the soul and heal the heart.

"Or crushes it to dust."

A practical solution rose to prominence. "Why can't Lettie keep the place up?"

"You fired her."

"I did?"

"Yes," Serenity growled low. "Mom's faithful house manager of how many years? Cast out. And the sole reason Moreland's pear trees produced fruit year after year."

Delete, delete, delete.

The scent of Lettie's fresh-baked, sugar-crusted pear and cinnamon muffins worked its way through her memory. She drew in a breath, tasting them again.

"Okay. So, poor decision."

"Among others."

Everley huffed. "Such as?"

"Taking a job in Chicago, leaving Moreland to fend for itself."

"It's a house, Serenity. A house." *A widow-maker.* "You refer to Moreland like it's a living, breathing ... organic thing, capable of feeling."

"It does. All houses are memory keepers."

"Moreland wins top prize on that account."

Born to and raised by the same two people, Everley and Serenity shared a love for warm, sunny skies, antiques, art, coffee, and pastries, but the similarities ended there.

One who worked to forget. One who reveled in remembering.

Sisters Rational and Dreamer.

"It was an accident, Evers." Serenity's voice swooped low, turned granite.

The past shuddered through and made her dizzy.

Delete, delete, delete.

"Avoidable," she bit back.

"Not everything in life fits into neat little columns and balances out."

"I get paid to see that it does. Look, I've got deadlines to meet, clients to contact, site visits to schedule."

"You're obligated to take care of it. Mom said so in her letter."

6

Stooping to sisterly childishness now.

And the letter mention. Not like Everley could ever forget the booming tone of Mom's lawyer as he read her dying plea, inked on Dazzle Me Art Gallery letterhead. Wrinkled in places as though Mom wept while detailing her sentiments.

A weighty sigh streamed out. "All right, Serenity. I'll get in touch with Lettie, figure something out."

"Don't bother. Lettie works for me now. And, lest you forget, you *have* to hire that restoration guy Mom specified."

Everley's cheeks quirked into a forced grin. "Right. That guy."

Audits stockpiled in her brain. End of the month. Need to close the books for Mason Family Practice, be precise, timely. Secure her position as a partner.

"I anticipated pushback," Serenity said. "So I have a solution to save the place."

No doubt she did. A lemonade stand, perhaps?

Serenity's voice lifted to a dizzying altitude, jet-fueled by optimism. Somehow making others believe two plus two equaled five, tossing logic and reason to the wind.

"I follow MidDay Media on social media, the film production company for *Fixed Up Right*."

Where was she going with this? Breaths thickened in Everley's throat as Serenity's solution unfolded.

"In response to their publicized interest in a historic house project, I shared your story ... you know, Mom's letter, the reno specialist, and guess what?"

"They laughed out loud, deemed the place a hot mess, and politely refused."

Please, *please?*

And where was that critical email Phillip Vance had mentioned? A client to make a girl in pursuit of becoming a partner shine like the noonday sun.

"The Senior Director of Development at MidDay, Don Barnhart, is interested in filming the restoration to pitch a pilot to H2H network for a series idea." Serenity squeaked excitement through the phone. "With strong viewer interest in their favor, MidDay is seeking houses rich in history and architectural charm. Stories over projects."

Moreland had a story, all right. It just wasn't one Everley cared to tell. Leave it to a dreamer to pull strings behind the scenes, disrupt the status quo, and flip predictability on its head.

Words scrambled to form a sentence. "There *is* no restoration ... this is far too—"

"Evers, admit it. Your story—and it *is* yours—has intrinsic value, creates a compelling reason to invest in the house, and adds to viewer appeal."

The dreamer in Serenity was like a horse inside the gate. At the sound of the starting bell, she was unstoppable.

"We could use this opportunity to benefit a local charity—something like what the NFL does for food banks and stuff. Or to help Walker's Kids Sports Camps. Mom and Dad would love that."

Everley worked tease into her tone. "Owen, huh?"

"Don't read into it, Evers. Walker has done a lot of charitable things over the past year. His foundation has poured millions into various philanthropic projects. If you had even one social media account, you'd know this. But this conversation isn't about me ... or Owen, for that matter. It's about what you're going to do when Don Barnhart contacts you and wants to film on location."

The weight of responsibility scooped air from Everley's lungs. On her top-ten list of things she hated, exposure ranked number three—right behind surprises and tardiness. "How do you expect me to take on something of this magnitude when I don't even have a contractor?"

"Wrong. You've got *the* contractor."

Gabriel Michael Bellevue.

In her letter, Mom claimed he'd been named after angels. When she died, the secret as to how she'd come across that little tidbit died too.

Tension rumbled over her forehead. "Serenity, I need to oversee Moreland's restoration like I need a migraine."

"Call him."

Agenda: Restore that albatross to its former glory.

And be rid of it.

Amid the mimicking songs of mockingbirds in the sprawling oak, Gabe Bellevue stood inside the meager shade cast by the gables of Mrs. Beasley's nineteenth-century, cottage-style, clapboard house. Not exactly the contract of a lifetime, but demand for historic restoration had slowed to a crawl in the last year, and he was in no position to be selective.

From the start, attention to detail, zero tolerance for mistakes, and a client-comes-first mantra built his business, G&R Historic Restoration Specialists. Allowed him to escape the plague of repeated paternal failure and bring honor to the Bellevue name. *Some history wasn't worth repeating.*

One boot propped on the bottom step at the base of the porch, Gabe tipped a water bottle to his mouth, an eye lasered on Randy who claimed a plank of wood and was hovering the saw's teeth over it like a surgeon prepped for open-heart surgery.

"You sure you've measured accurately?" Gabe said.

Face shaded, Randy stilled his grip on the saw. He straightened slightly, slung a labored gaze at Gabe. "Ten years in business together, and you still doubt my ability to accurately measure a piece of wood."

"It's special-ordered for this job."

A blustery exhale left Randy's lungs. "I know."

Sweat beaded along Gabriel's back. "Just making sure this gets done right. Wrong cuts lead to failure, and that's not an option."

"Well aware, Bellevue. You've been telling me that since high school. And we've yet to have a dissatisfied client."

"There's still Mrs. Beasley."

A puzzled stare clouded Randy's face as he brought his wrist in a swipe across his forehead. "Who's that?"

Frustration fumed. "You're standing in front of her house."

Randy glided his stare along the property. "I thought she said 'Measly' as in the insufficient sum of money she wanted to dish out for all the work we're doing to this place."

"Until she hands me a chilled glass of fresh lemonade, served with a satisfied smile, I'm not convinced she'll offer a stellar review."

Gabe tugged a waded red bandana from his back pocket, swiped it across his forehead then stuffed it back in. The last plank fit snug along the edge of the porch. Galvanized nails secured it flush against neighboring planks. He stood and pressed his boots against it, bounced on the balls of his feet. No movement. Silent.

Perfect.

Gabe clapped Randy a high-five. "Success!"

The crunch of tires on gravel turned Gabe's attention toward the drive shaded by a cluster of arching oaks. Mrs. Beasley's driver exited the town car, flashed a smile beneath his chauffeur cap. Dressed in a black suit, he strode to the passenger side and eased her to standing.

Gabe followed her scrutinizing gaze as she scraped it over the symmetrical façade, tracing the triangular pediments surmounting a four-bay porch enclosed by a white-washed railing.

A wicked shimmy surged beneath his skin at her tongue cluck, uncertainty curdling his stomach.

"Everything all right, Mrs. Beasley?"

Please, God, say yes.

In a calculated turn, she stuffed her fists inside the pockets of her sweater and fixed a piercing, gray gaze. "Why, I should say not."

Disquiet seared Gabe's lungs, landed in his throat, scorched it dry.

So long, lemonade.

Her palms floated in an upward sweep as though pronouncing a benediction. Or his last rites. "I only wish ..." Her voice rang bright, crinkle lines deepening around her mouth. "I'd called you sooner."

Satisfaction rose on her face to match the sun's brilliance dribbling over a partially shaded lawn.

A steady stream of restrained air blew past Gabe's lips.

Her cheeks rounded. "What a fine job you've done."

A breeze whisked past, cooled the last of his simmering angst. "Pleasure's ours," Gabe added, his breathing slowed to healthy rhythm to suit his thirty-one years.

"Can I interest you men in some lemonade?"

An exaggerated grin inched across Gabe's cheek, which he promptly slung at Randy, who then turned to nod at Mrs. Beasley. "Yes'm, Mrs. Meas—er, Beasley. We'd love some."

Good save.

Her driver escorted his charge along the steps to the front door. The faint smell of mothballs, aged wood, and fresh paint wafted over the lawn.

"All right, King Midas," Randy said. "We got accolades and an offer for lemonade, but the project took too long. We went over budget. And you can't seem to find it in your heart to let the good lady ... who's not hurting for money ... know she owes us two days extra labor."

The rebuke spit like rusty nails and poked holes in his ego. Because people came first.

A stiff breeze chilled the sweat along his arms. "If too long gets it done right, then so be it."

"This was our last job, boss. The Cantrell House at the university is still in the discussion stages, and we need a solid deal *now*. If that means speeding things up, taking modern projects, I say, we do it."

"The deals we've landed are due to quality craftsmanship, my charm, and business savvy." Hand to his chest, Gabe dipped his chin.

"Too bad your pride can't be cashed in."

Brandishing his bandana, Gabe snapped it across Randy's arm, added a hard glare.

"No one's arguing with your ability to bring in business," Randy said, nursing his arm. "As for charm, I'll leave that to the ladies to determine. We've got to work on efficiency. Maybe add to our crew."

"Big Ben, Charlie, and Ryan are plenty enough."

"Whom you let go early today. Just to be nice."

"They were tired."

"And I'm not?" he shot back. "We can't afford to turn business away for lack of muscle. And I, for one, don't relish working twelve-plus hour days like we've been doing."

Disquiet screeched inside Gabe's brain, clawed at his ribs.

"I'm missing family time with Summer and the girls, and no doubt you're missing Jill. Or, no, wait. I got this." He raised a palm and then pointed at Gabe. "Ashleigh."

"Neither."

A disgruntled laugh spilled out. "What happened to Ashleigh? Or Jill, for that matter?"

"We broke up." No, Gabe ended it. Both times.

"Ah, man. They were lookers, too."

"Yeah, well, outward beauty fades. I need depth."

A woman of strength, unshakable.

Someone to believe in me.

"Yeah, but you cast a girl off like a pair of worn-out shoes."

A deafening rumble quaked inside his brain, struck a match behind his eyes. He turned a hard stare at Randy. "If the shoes don't fit, a guy needs to find himself a pair that do."

Randy collapsed one of two worktables, hefted it into the company van, and turned to Gabe, expression granite. "According to Summer, Jill was pretty busted up when you broke up with her."

Slam.

"She left the Children's Advocacy Center board meeting to go bawl her eyes out in the bathroom."

That stung.

"She didn't pass the Champ test. Neither did Ashleigh." Or ... well, names of previous girls had faded to nothing, buried in history. "At first growl, it's over." Gabe hefted another worktable, hands clamped at each side. Since taking in Champ, the yellow Labrador—a hurricane rescue— several years ago, no woman had succeeded in evoking anything milder than a canine snarl. "Anyway, I've got Carmen."

One hip cocked beside the van, arms tightly crossed, Randy tilted his head. A deep notch formed at his brow. "Um, who?"

"Carmen Murdock."

"Tell me she's no relation to financier Warren Murdock, CEO of Murdock Enterprises?"

"His daughter."

Murdock's only daughter and prized possession.

Randy clapped a palm to his forehead, squeezed his eyes shut.

"Just hear me out." Gabe flipped palms up, defense coloring his tone. "I met her in Jackson Square a few months back, outside the entrance to St. Louis Cathedral. She was alone and crying."

"So?"

"Score a minus five for compassion, partner."

"At least I exercise discretion. I don't think there's anyone you wouldn't pick up off the street."

Fair assessment. But this providential encounter came with her daddy's promise of financial backing ... endless opportunities ... maybe the coercion to give marriage to Carmen serious consideration. It had never been his character to put a girl's heart at risk to save his hide. But the mighty Warren Murdock had a sizable project in the works—refurbishing a neglected low-rent district for use by business professionals—and suggested Gabe's company would be awarded the job. Truth was, he genuinely cared for Carmen.

"Carmen was on a riverboat when her date tried to take advantage of her," Gabe said. "When she refused, he stole her purse and left her stranded at the pier. Murdock had the guy charged with larceny, got him fired. Basically, ruined him."

Randy shook his head slowly. "How quickly one bad decision can take a man down."

The reality inched far too close.

"While I'm all about networking with someone of Murdock's prominence, did you consider the risk to us if you make a wrong move with her?" Randy pressed his tone prickly. "You'll incinerate our business if Daddy Murdock retaliates."

The unsolicited warning shredded Gabe's reasoning. Fear snatched a response.

Randy's brows hitched in challenge. "A thousand bucks says you haven't introduced Carmen to Champ."

Without question, his beloved dog would seal Carmen's fate by way of raised hackles and menacing growl. Not entirely the kind of girl a guy brings home to his momma … even if his own had been no prize, walking out on Gabe and Dad back in high school, fed up with Dad's shortcomings. Mom had scattered family unity across the front lawn of their mobile home. Before that had to be sold off, too.

Randy's level stare, rife with judgment, singed Gabe's cheeks. "Is it that you don't believe you can snag a girl with character?"

Anger widened the divide between them. In tandem with the growth of Gabe's business, scads of women had been in hot pursuit. All too eager to please. Not that he would allow things to enter the red zone anymore. Overcome by a fit of conscience last year, rumblings had surfaced from Adam Carmichael, Gabe's spiritual mentor. Prompted him to crush sexual carelessness and resolve to hold off until marriage.

He gave the van door a robust slam. A chortle rumbled in his throat.

"I didn't have to go dumpster diving to find Summer. We met at—"

"I know. Church." Gabe drew a haughty gaze to the sky. "But that won't guarantee a heavenly matchup either. And a man shouldn't have to go through hoops to capture the heart of a beautiful, God-fearing woman."

Randy's nod of understanding thinned the wall of defense. "The real question is, where's your faith? Once you and God are walking in step, he'll bring the woman of his choosing in good time." His tone softened like butter on the front porch of a Louisiana farmhouse, the wisdom equally rich. "You aren't likely to discover what you have no intention to find."

Doubt burned inside his chest. "Not sure this divinely appointed woman you speak of would attach herself to someone hauling generations of father failure." The ache in his heart bled into his tone, rendering it tenuous at best.

"We've all got wounds, boss. Junk in the trunk. God's grace cleans it out."

The words rippled across his soul like a pebble over still water. Only sorry excuses explained why he'd stiff-armed God, allowed his heart to gather dust. Carmen's sultry gaze emerged in his brain. Good woman enough, undaunted by an undesirable family story. What little he'd shared.

"While we're on the subject of fathers, how's your dad doing?"

"Dunno."

The front door whined. Gabe turned to see Mrs. Beasley handling a beverage tray, two tall, ice-filled glasses balanced on top.

Mounting the steps, he took the glasses. "Thanks, much, ma'am." Sticky liquid dribbled over his fingers. The scent of sugar-sweet lemonade soothed his soul.

Pale sunbeams broke through paunchy clouds and branches, caressed the lawn. Her twinkling eyes drew into half-moons. No greater payback than a satisfied customer. One who'd referenced Gabe as the can-do man. Nothing like Dad.

His cell rang. Unfamiliar area code. Not unusual, though. Potential clients inquired from all over. "Yep?"

And then the low, delicious laugh of a feminine voice. "I must have the wrong number. I was looking for house restoration specialists."

"That'd be me."

"Historicals, specifically. Really old ones—pre–Civil War."

Intrigue had Gabe pressing the phone to his ear. Randy stepped close, leaned in.

"You've got one that needs restoration?"

Please?

"I do, actually. My name is Everley Scott."

Gabe's breath caught in his lungs. *That name.* Once-in-a-lifetime, refreshingly unique and assigned to … the numbers girl.

High school crush.

And you answered with … *yep*?

Loser.

"I'm calling from Chicago. I own a house. Quite large, actually. It's near Bayou Lafourche and was left to me by my mother, Marigold Lewis, and doggone if she didn't insist I employ your company to complete its restoration. Isn't that the most ridiculous thing?"

The derisive laugh gnawed at him a bit.

Still, it *was* her. The girl who did crazy things to his seventeen-year-old brain. The reason he believed in love ever after. The shy, smart girl who needed someone to tell her how truly wonderful she was.

Because now, it seemed, she'd taken the name Scott.

If only he'd mustered the courage back then.

CHAPTER TWO

Though gruff and unrefined, Gabriel Bellevue's voice held unshakable confidence, enthusiasm, and the hint of a smile. It dispelled images of a unkempt creeper in dire need of a shower, a cigarette bobbing at the corner of his mouth. Although, the fact that he'd detailed Mom's résumé—particularly her notorious mile-long swim across the Mississippi in her teens and appointment by President Nixon to the Presidential Advisory Committee for the Arts—was unsettling.

Conspiratorial, even.

"My understanding is your momma scaled walls to acquire that Howard Gallagher masterpiece you're honored to possess," he said. "Must have wanted it something awful."

"An understatement."

Dream chasing. Costly business.

"When Marigold Lewis spoke, people listened." A feathery softness filtered into his tone. "I realize it's been a while but, uh, sorry for your loss."

"Thank you." The effort it took Mom's chosen one to spit out a condolence suggested it didn't come easily or regularly.

"What'd you need done to your place?"

At his assignment of ownership, she winced, though she was equally critical of her inability to answer his question. "Honestly, I have no idea. It's been vacant since last fall, my mother's belongings either sold or in storage. My sister lives in New Orleans and tells me complaints have arisen, and some want it razed."

"No way. Not that historic jewel. You kept utilities up at the place?"

"Yes." Even on her dime, Everley couldn't bear to leave it completely lifeless. Nothing good would come of reducing current market value. Goal—invest in restoration, sell for three times the value, invest capital gains in a high-performance stock with a positive trajectory, and call it a day.

Any mention of the remote—and absurd—possibility of an on-site production company might send him scurrying. No sense allowing a non-issue to put the project at risk and upend her agenda.

Back to the reno guy. "If you would, I'd like an estimate of what you think is needed. But just the basics. Enough to list—"

Something of a triumphant—*Whoop!*—sounded through the phone. And then ... "Severson, I do believe we've landed the big one."

Ah, it must be the sidekick noted on the G&R website she'd perused while looking for reasons to drop this deal. But the positive reviews and awards featured in the sidebar urged her forward.

"My partner and I will take a look-see and shoot you an estimate."

"Oh no, you don't, sir. Not without me." She made no excuse for the severity of her tone. "Mom was very specific. I don't want just anybody handling this place."

"I assure you, ma'am, G&R isn't just anybody." His tone stiffened. "You'll be hard-pressed to find a superior contractor to handle a Gallagher—especially one certified by the state of Louisiana. I assume your momma knew that, or she'd not have been so particular with her wishes."

Wishes, shmishes.

Were it not for the bird rasps and rush of street traffic through the phone, she'd have imagined him easing into a chair, ankles crossed on a desk as he coddled victory.

"Listen, I'm snowed under here for the next few days." She activated the weather app on her phone, pleased to find snowfall would ease midweek. A succession of winking sunny days predicted for New Orleans mocked. "Let's meet at the property this Friday afternoon. I'll email the address. Will 2:00 work for you?"

"Sure, that'll do."

The casual air of this so-called master craftsman grated. A psychedelic chemo drug had to be coursing through Mom's veins when she penned her dying wishes.

"Contact me by Wednesday if you can't make it. I can only afford an absence for a twenty-four-hour window."

"Gotcha. No doubt you'll be eager to return to what appears to be a wicked winter in Chi-town."

If that was a smirk she heard in his voice, he'd better wipe it off before their first encounter, or she'd do it for him.

Insufferable man.

Even after all these years, Moreland's gallant emergence from the majestic grove of oaks and pines along Highway 308 still sucked the breath from Everley's lungs. Its stately, white ionic columns hewn from indigenous material, five-bay upper and lower galleries created a picture-perfect symmetry. An almost inescapable pull. The architectural design of a genius.

Purchased by a crazy lady. *Now left to ... me.*

Mom and Dad, eccentric souls known as Marigold and Peter Lewis, owners of the Dazzle Me Art Gallery. Products of the Woodstock era. Lovers of art, impulsive. Whimsical dreamers, both of them.

Schoolyard taunts still gonged through her memory.

Your parents are whacko, you know that?

She knew. And had locked a willingness to dream inside a virtual trunk, clasped it shut. Found solace in numbers. Logical, predictable, and unchangeable.

"Pull up along the drive, please," Everley told the shuttle driver who could easily pass for Louis Armstrong.

He returned a nod, humming the shrill jazz piping from the radio. Made her yearn for the French Quarter brew and fresh-baked goodness at Serenity's bakery that awaited after this obligatory meeting at Moreland.

Loose gravel crunched and popped as he eased onto the property, the drive ending near a screened-in porch off the south wing that faced a nearby wall of trees. And, okay. Moreland's regal façade lacked luster. Its careworn smile didn't quite reach the windows, a lone black shutter hanging like a lopsided bowtie. The roughly trimmed, colorless lawn provided an ideal home to weeds.

Relatively affordable fixes. Fertilized grass, new shrubbery, maybe a pink Dogwood tree ... paint here and there ...

Exiting the car, a swish of mildly warm air swept over her face. The humidity rapidly frizzed her red mane which she clenched into a neat top knot, patted loose ends. Shrugging out of her coat, a caress of cool air ran along her arms. Her feet marinated inside her boots—garb better suited to her Chicago home.

While she continued her assessment, urging herself to care, the driver gathered her overnight bag. A speck of midday sunlight punctuated his dark eyes peeking beneath a black brimmed hat. She collected her bag, tipped generously, and returned his wave as he pulled from the drive.

It was precisely 2:00.

EVERLEY: I'm at Moreland.

SERENITY: See what I mean?

No doubt, Serenity's addition of two sad face emojis was intended to layer guilt.

Taking guarded steps, Everley crossed the patchy lawn, a wild array of field grasses bearing evidence of uneven seed distribution. Still a distance from the fissured cement steps, she paused, her gaze steady on the blistered door, the precarious shutter. One swift wind and ...

The look of betrayal glowered back—prickles scaled her spine, emerged on her skin. Steam of annoyance hissed. "I'm here, aren't I?"

Bag set on the steps, Everley noted the faint tic-tac-toe marks she'd etched into the veranda using Dad's whittled stick. He'd out strategized her each time they played, a frequency with which she could count on one hand.

The hum of a motor spared her from a pitiful stumble down memory lane. She turned to see a royal blue van marked in gold lettering to hail the arrival of ...

"G&R Restoration Specialists, LLC," she whispered, squinting.

A ladder rack outfitted the top. The driver parked beside an unruly hedge that hugged the south wing and blocked the windows.

"Eight minutes late." She slipped her cell into her pocket, tamping down the buzz of irritation.

A hefty Ford truck pulled in beside the van. The driver unfolded from the truck, shut the door, and joined the van driver. They strode her direction, pausing to tip gazes at the house. Lustful grins stretched wide as though they were seasoned Navy pilots mesmerized by a P-3 Orion.

Easy, men. It's just a house.

The shaggy guy on the left wore boots and faded jeans—a short-sleeved, plaid shirt opened in front to reveal a snug white T-shirt beneath which hid lean, solid muscle. Deduct two points for lack of professionalism. The wind had its way with his free-flowing, burnished blond and brown hair parted in a jagged line down the middle. At his cool, lanky saunter, his hair whipped loosely aside his sturdy, defined face.

An apprentice? Gabe's sidekick? Randy something ... Severson, was it?

A good thing. Because, in his shadow to the right, ambled the star of the show, Gabriel Michael Bellevue, owner of Mom's chosen operation. Clearly, the reason for the exceptional rating on the website, though his stride held less confidence than the scraggly counterpart. Unimpressive musculature, far less calloused. Shorter by a few inches and sporting clean-cut, wavy dark brown hair, collared company shirt, and cargo pants. Minus holes in the knees.

Gabriel thrust out his hand.

She took it, noting a brilliant set of blue-gray eyes. Clammy palms, but a reasonably firm grip. "Pleased to meet you, Ms. Scott. You've got a real gem here."

She hooked a studied gaze on a fully enraptured Gabriel who wasted no time ambling toward one of the fluted columns like a bee to honey. He rapped at it with his knuckles, ran his eyes along the length of it.

In the silence, she directed her attention to Sidekick, who stood several feet in front of her. A remarkably contemplative gaze stayed on her. Studying ... recall awash on his angular features. Her fingers itched to run a comb through his unruly hair. How in the world had Mom reconciled this unlikely pair as the only reputable reno business in town?

Mom's prime choice was a dirty, denim clad, bohemian, wild child.

But handsome. *Very.* An appearance to fit the cover of an outdoor supply catalog. The intensity of his amber stare heated her skin. Her breath hitched, radiating heat along her exposed neck and stirring a low boil of interest.

Smile lines appeared in his tan, shadowed face, elongating the grooves aside his mouth, and softened his demeanor. Cheap labor, she reasoned. This was good, considering she'd not budgeted for any of this. Why invest in something that cost more to maintain than it was worth and held no value to its owner?

He brushed his hands along the front of his shirt and offered his hand, his grip as strong as the muscles cording up his arm. Okay. First impression score upped to a six and a half. Maybe seven point three for enigmatic eyes.

Snap out of it. Business!

"I'm Gabe."

That voice. Wait. Hand frozen in his, she flicked her gaze back to Gabriel Bellevue, still lingering near the veranda like a love-sick teen.

Confusion scrambled her brain's circuitry, unraveled logic.

A sudden check in her spirit glued her boots to the hard earth. She released her hand, her half-lidded stare shifting between the two, a forefinger swishing like a windshield wiper.

Gabe, or no ... Randy? ... wandered back over.

Concentrating her gaze, she felt a deep notch form at her brows. "You're ..."

The predicament had her clenching her jaw. "Tell me I did not just crawl out of a snowstorm for this?" she murmured. Risk assessment, risk assessment.

Mom!

Challenge gathered over unrefined Sidekick's brow, deepened his amber gaze. "Is there a problem, Ms. Scott?" He tilted his head and stood straight, adding to his, oh maybe, six-foot, two inches, a muscled chest bowing a little. The voice that matched, that's right, Gabe Bellevue.

With effort, she tore her gaze away from his torso to gather her wits. "No. Of course not," she sputtered out. She switched a subtly scathing stare between them. "I suppose you'll meet my mother's expectations." The effectiveness of sticking packing tape on the doomed Titanic.

Gabe—now she'd come to learn—took two stiff steps. "I plan to exceed them. Shoddy workmanship belongs to the competition. And just to be clear. Where historicals are concerned, I don't renovate. I restore. There's a difference."

Cocky confidence intensified the unique mix of olive and brown in his eyes. The set of his jaw and pronounced dimples quickened her pulse.

And you thought his partner was the big kahuna.

Given that the rugged contractor was—she now recalled—yesterday's pretty-faced boy of Landry-Walker High—hair length far exceeding basketball regulations— the identity conundrum was an easy mistake. She'd never considered herself qualified to have gotten, well ... this close, indulged in his scent of fresh pine and cotton. It'd have been impossible to squeeze in among the cheerleaders who encircled the star player at the game's end.

A treasonous tremble zipped down her arms. She laced her fingers in front of her, assumed the bearing of an heiress on a mission. "Well, then, let's take a look around the place."

What was it about a girl that could cause the solid foundation of a man to quake, threatening to fissure his best laid plans? Walking the perimeter of Moreland and the whole of its interior, Randy took notes while Gabe dictated, identifying areas of wood rot in support beams, peeling paint, and cracked and flaking plastered walls. A thirteen thousand square foot challenge to be sure, but child's play when stacked against the rustling in his heart in the presence of Everley Lewis. No, make that Scott.

In all the universe, there had been only one girl who'd caught Gabe's eye, nestled her way into his heart. But during the span of thirteen years, between high school and now, she'd married.

Belonged to another.

The timbre and clarity of her voice told of one well-practiced in articulating her point. Defending her cause, pursuit of purpose.

Or hiding a hurt.

When dating other women, Gabe had always matched them up against her. The standard. The only one he ever really wanted. Time passed, fear unable to thaw, and she'd moved away.

His loss. Maybe the greatest.

And now talk of proposing to Carmen had hitched itself to conversations with Warren over dinners at fine-dining restaurants. In the months he and Carmen had dated, he'd come to genuinely love her. To enter a covenant otherwise was stupid. But regret seeped into his pores at Everley's unexpected intersection in his life, doubt murmuring in his ears.

Mattered not that he'd been a star on the court. He only wanted to be a star in Everley's eyes. Mistakes could harm his business, but this fiery woman, determined and intelligent, had the power to crush his heart.

Does your husband appreciate the value of what he has, Ms. Scott?

His brain switched compartments, back to needs assessment. For one, an aging roof in need of replacement, and a twenty-four-inch thick brick exterior its only insulation. Even with extensive plumbing and electrical penetrations, Gabe would suggest the installation of mineral wool between the floor joists in the crawl space to enhance energy efficiency. The dead critters would need a different resting place.

Returning to the front lawn dappled in sunlight, an overarching oak to their right and the house in front, Gabe turned to Randy. "Aside from obvious issues, she's a beauty."

His body responded at Everley's tantalizing floral scent. Something like ... he sniffed again. Gardenia, maybe?

Had she always smelled this good?

A withered sigh suggested Moreland's heiress staunchly refused to see the value and embrace the place as momma intended.

"Her double-sash windows appear to be painted shut and rotting in places, given they haven't been cared for. Once I restore them, she'll get a twinkle in her eyes." Gabe said. "Like most old homes, she was designed with repair in mind rather than to have her parts replaced with substandard, modern materials."

In the space of a year or so, Moreland would sing, the pleasing smell of fresh pine and cedar wood, plaster and paint sweetening her rooms. New beams would straighten her posture. Water would course through her veins, cool air and heat distributed through her lungs. New landscaping would dress her up pretty. And she'd be bone dry because a dry house was a happy house.

Above all, she'd need people to enjoy her again.

Abandoned for several months, Moreland begged for an aggressive, loving touch. From the best.

"We'll run the numbers, give you an estimate in the space of a week," Gabe said.

Everley nodded rapidly, the look of one in a rush.

Randy smiled his goodbye, turned to Gabe. "I'm off, boss. We'll talk this through at the office." He turned to shake Everley's hand, offered a parting wave to both, and headed toward the G&R van.

Gabe turned to meet Everley's stare.

"Thanks for meeting me here," she said. "I'll wait to hear back from you."

He took her offered hand—skin soft in his grip. Way better than he'd imagined. Before she turned toward the drive, he winked. The ghost of a smile he detected as she turned to go suggested it'd stirred something.

Unbidden, his heart lurched past the client-contractor boundary and landed at her back. "I voted for you."

Emotion he'd locked away for years now spilled onto the lawn at her feet.

Wow, Bellevue.

She stopped, turned slowly, and tilted her head. The half-lidded stare and abrupt tone bored a hole in his chest. "I'm sorry, what?"

"Cheerleader. Landry-Walker High School. Darn shame you didn't win."

No backing out, you idiot.

A desperate curiosity claimed her face, eased her forward.

Shoot. She didn't know him. Maybe never had.

He narrowed the space to only a few feet, captured her gaze. "You're Everley Lewis. Graduated the year after me."

A line appeared between her umber brows, gaze shifting feverishly. The spark in those emerald greens amid the dawn of a smile hinted at the stir of viable memory.

What he would give to loosen that cinnamon hair of hers. Loosen the stiffness.

Enlightenment filtered into her gaze.

"I'm the reason our basketball team made it to the finals with my three-pointers and unstoppable defense. The winning shot to snag the state title."

Dial it down.

Recollection inched the corners of her lips. "The go-to guy on the court."

Hard fought rep—and she'd remembered. This was good.

Score! And the crowd goes wild ...

Man, that gardenia.

She traced his face with her eyes. "Your, uh, hair."

Head tipped back, he laughed, if only to avoid indulging in her perfume again. Soft, sensuous. Desire sizzled beneath his skin. "Coach made us keep it short."

Anything to maintain killer status. To fit in.

A disturbing reality surfaced on her creamy face, all elbows against the friendly exchange. Through shuttered lids, her gaze darkened, drained of humor.

"Hold it." She shoved her fists into her waist. The look of keen awareness filtered into her eyes. "Are *you* the reason my mom insisted I only hire G&R? Because New Orleans *does* have alternatives."

Second best. Destined to fail.

Her glare grazed his shoulder and pummeled the side of his truck before moving back to him.

Don't. Reject. Me.

He shrugged, winked. "Guess your momma knew excellence when she saw it."

A scathing breath whisked from her lungs. "Or how to shovel a heap of guilt on my shoulders."

That hurt. This client-contractor relationship wasn't gonna be easy. If he didn't blow it, he'd secure the biggest deal ever.

He followed her stare as her eyes traced the roofline, a weighted gaze looking for a place to dump its burden. She trekked it along the prominent gable then directed it at him. "It amazes me the ability some have to keep talking long after they're gone."

Angst churned inside, prickled beneath his skin. Heart on the loose again, he met her stare, managed to hold it steady. "Like I said, I voted for you."

The dazed expression of this cheerleader hopeful blinked a hint of gratitude, lips forming a feeble grin.

"Thanks."

Not the shower of appreciation he'd hoped, but Moreland's heiress was bent on fulfilling an obligation, looking nothing like she wanted to be stuck collaborating with a Bellevue.

CHAPTER THREE

"Correct email address assured, attachment added, and ..." Gabe sucked in a breath, finger frozen over the keyboard. "Send."

Factoring in the magnitude of the Moreland project, the estimate had been calculated in record time, although Gabe sent it three days after he'd promised. Wherever possible, he'd minimized costs, though flat out refusing to scrimp on quality. A Bellevue always got the job done right. At least, this one had. An unfortunate legacy was harder to shake than a demon clamped to a drunk.

Sinking into his chair, Gabe tore his gaze from the screen. Doubt jabbed. Would Everley accept? Janet Calloway, his account manager, had scrutinized his estimates in painful detail. If he'd over or underestimated costs, she'd have said something. This contract would elevate his reliability rating above the competitors.

Make me fail-safe.

But life had taught him to do the next thing. To sidestep stupidity, so a guy doesn't start looking like, well, Dad. With effort, Gabe loosened his grip on the Moreland project and mustered courage to leave the outcome to God.

Could he trust him to engineer this thing?

White paneling brightened the interior of G&R headquarters marked by large windows on either side of a beveled glass door front. The formerly dark, dated space was located several blocks northeast of the famed French Quarter. Shafts of sunlight highlighted black-and-white tiled flooring. Another set of beveled glass doors led to the entrance of Gabe's office off the lobby.

Kourtney Young, a history intern at the University of New Orleans, sat in the front office adjacent to his and took calls, greeted clients in the lounge. The establishment of front-end space created a wall behind which he could play king of the castle.

"Hey, Severson."

Ambling from his nearby office, Randy stepped in wearing a royal blue G&R T-shirt, the logo monogrammed in gold.

"What's up, boss?"

"You sure the figures are accurate for the Moreland job? Three hundred fifty thousand seems a might steep."

Randy tossed him a hard glance. "Will there ever come a day when you don't question Janet's math?"

"No."

"You've got no one better than Janet to assess these figures. For all she does, she's way overdue for a raise."

"Got that right." Janet's muffled, gravelly voice sounded through the adjoining wall. But as a single woman with independent adult children, she didn't share the same financial challenge as Randy and took pride in regaling Gabe with the merits of marginal living and thrifting mind-set.

The underlying mirth in Janet's tone untangled knots in Gabe's shoulders and drew a grin.

Champ ambled in, nails clicking the tile. His mouth stretched to a yawn.

Randy bent to scrub his ears. "Ah, man's best friend has risen from slumber and graced us with his presence."

The welcome sound of a phone ringing at Kourtney's desk unwound a thread of tension. "G&R Historic Restoration Specialists. Best in New Orleans. How may I help you?"

Scooting from the desk, Gabe sounded a sharp whistle and patted his leg. "Here, boy." The beloved pet crossed over and sat at Gabe's boots. Snout tipped up, a glint of overhead light played in his cocoa eyes.

Gabe bent to scratch beneath his neck, fur coarse and thick. Metal tags from his collar clinked together. He cupped his head, fixed eyes on the prized pet, and spoke in a near-silent whisper. "How's my best friend?"

From his stance in the doorway, Randy sounded a fake cough. "Sorry to break up an intimate moment, but have you actually sent the cost sheet to that saucy Chicago woman?"

A challenging gaze drew Gabe's brow in a tight notch. He sat upright and bored a stiff finger into the desktop. "You mean, the soon-to-be client for the highest profile and largest project we've ever had. Which we've needed, and I've prayed for."

It didn't cost Gabe a cent to offer a prayer. All the better if God were listening.

"Settle down, boss. To me, she's nothing more than a means to maintain Ainsley and Madison's private school, ballet, and piano lessons."

Venting a noisy exhale, Gabe snatched the folder marked 'Moreland-Scott Project,' rose from his chair, and crossed over to a metal filing cabinet that held hard copies of digital records. He slipped the folder inside, shutting it with more force than necessary, and turned to Randy. "To your question, yes, I sent it." Concern drew Gabe's gaze toward the floor. "Let's just hope it's well received."

"She's got no choice but to hire us." Randy's tone sounded as though they'd cornered a fawn.

"You're wrong. She does have a choice."

What he'd remembered of shy, sweet Everley Lewis from high school shattered at the stiff and impersonal alternative that'd stood on the property a week ago. A woman of strength who now held his golden opportunity in her hot little hand. In the space of a few minutes, his high school crush double-dribbled across his expectations and missed an open shot at simple kindness. No matter. It wouldn't be long before he'd be offering Carmen a ring.

In a splendorous show of gratitude, Warren had gifted G&R a five-figure investment, attached to verbal assurance he'd never suffer for lack of work. The unexpected windfall enabled Gabe to acquire a sizable, steel-paneled workshop and warehouse to store equipment, historic windows, doors, and hardware he'd snagged at antique shops and auctions.

A month ago, Gabe had joined Warren for upscale dining at Ben's Seafood and Grille, owned and operated by Gabe's friend and former client, Bryan J. Carlyle, an executive chef, cooking show host, and owner of Carlyle's Cajun Cooking School.

"Bellevue." Warren had spoken through a haze of cigar smoke, methodically rotating the rim of his cocktail glass. "Priscilla and I are indebted to you."

All because he'd happened upon their only daughter.

A date gone wrong. What cad wouldn't stop to assist?

Warren had leaned forward, censure filtering into a steely gaze. "So long as she remains happy—as she is now—you can count on my continued support." He drew long on his cigar, lips pursed in slow exhale. "You get my meaning, of course."

Of course. A man had to do what he had to do to be somebody in the eyes of the successful. *To fit in.* In which case, exhuming his secret desire for Moreland's heiress had no place in his busy schedule—which ...

Once Randy stepped out, Gabe returned to his desk, the presence of white space on the scheduling document upping his pulse. "Special K, did we ever hear back about the chancellor's home?"

The contract would fill the space of at least three weeks.

Through the door, Kourtney's welcome answer floated in. "I just got the e-signature and am printing it now."

Papers in hand, Kourtney breezed in wearing cuffed jeans and white high tops. She wore her long, straight chestnut hair parted down one side, gathered over her shoulder opposite the G&R company logo.

"Here's the hard copy." Her cocoa-colored eyes shimmered through metal-framed glasses. "They want interior and exterior restoration." She fingered down the paper. "Upgrades in the guest and master bath and *yada, yada, yada*. Details are all there."

"You're the best, K. Remind me to give you a raise." Gabe leaned back, lacing fingers behind his head, and crossed one boot over the other atop his desk.

"Don't think I won't. College isn't cheap." She folded her arms in feigned demand, giving her hair a swish for emphasis.

Majoring in history and minoring in business, Kourtney was articulate, resourceful, boundless in energy, and in need of a job to carry her through the spring semester and two grueling summer sessions. At the Pear Tree last January, she'd flipped her gaze up from an open textbook and readily offered Gabe her hand, confidence twinkling through lenses. "It's Kourtney. With a K."

Just the kind of sunny persona Gabe wanted on his team. Business thriving, he loved to give others a leg up.

But Dad had done the same.

At what point did generosity become a man's downfall?

A week after Everley's return to Chicago, and she still ached for the warmth she'd left behind. But nothing else. The past was the past for a reason.

Cable-knit tights were no match for the sudden whip of icy wind through the lobby of Vance and O'Connor. In her office, Everley shrugged out of her coat and sat to read email.

The G&R email popped onto the screen.

"Finally."

Click to open and—

"Whaaa—?" The estimate read like a bad CAT scan. "That clown has got to be kidding."

Leaning in, she squinted to assure she'd read accurately.

She had.

"How am I supposed to pay for a restoration bearing a price tag of …" Another glare. "Three hundred fifty thousand dollars?"

The money Mom had squirreled away would cover … divide, multiply, subtract …

Less than 8 percent.

"That loathsome treasure hunter," she muttered. "He and his partner probably worked the place over, invited nonessential contractors desperate to get their hands on a historic landmark. Scrounged for every scratch and ding, tacking on unnecessary costs."

She shoved from her desk. The wheels of her chair caught on her area rug, tipping her backward. Her boots dangled over the floor.

Thunk! When her head connected with the wall, Moreland's ostentatious frame rattled. Profanity rumbled inside her throat, threatened to spew across the room.

Angling her head, her coworker, Margot Ziegler, rapped on the open door. A spark of intrigue rose in her large, dark eyes that were set like polished river stones against an ivory complexion.

On the tail end of a huff, the storm of irritation slowed to a brisk, woolly wind.

A slanted grin drew up the sides of Margot's deep red lips. "I see you missed your classes at charm school again."

"Shut it, Zeigler, and help me out." Her fingers clutched to the armrests. She kicked her feet alternately.

Delivering restrained laughter, Margot sashayed over delivering the pizzaz and electric presence to match Liza Minnelli. She could easily double as a model for a women's business magazine in her tailored pantsuit, dark pumps, and fashionable pixie style do that showcased her deep forehead.

The last of a pastry disappeared into her mouth before she proffered a helping hand. "What I want to know is ..." *Tug* "does this so-called clown have a brother." Margot's grin turned sultry.

"I see you've lowered yourself to eavesdropping, something they discourage in said charm school."

"You were shouting, Ev. Anyone within a mile could've heard you."

Clunk. Everley massaged her head, then mindlessly brushed at her jacket and skirt.

In the doorway, Tyler Allen appeared. Everley's boyfriend in the most literal sense—a friend who was a boy. She'd summed up their relationship as comfortable, non-threatening. Safe. Both committed to the status quo without any investment of the heart.

No matter Tyler's GQ cover qualifications, a short stint modeling men's athletic wear, she'd kept her heart guarded behind a firewall. Sure, Tyler emitted masculine charm, but it hadn't held his previous marriages together. And Everley? One shot at happily ever after was enough, thank you very much.

Over the last week, Tyler had been out of town, untangling legal matters associated with the firm. A Harvard law degree added value to his CPA status and, uh, put him in the running for partner. But unlike him, she needed it. Another reason to stay firmly planted in Chicago, far from past history.

Catching her gaze, Tyler stopped abruptly, took steps backward, and entered. Tax accountants on the west end of the building rarely crossed paths with the auditors on the east side—oil and water. Tyler managed to mix them amiably.

A typical light glinted in his blue-grays. Hand on the jamb, the muscles of his upper arm flexed against his crisp white button-down. "Morning, you two."

"Morning." Everley and Margot answered in stereo.

He moved his gaze to Everley. "How was your trip to …" He circled a hand of feigned interest. "Louisiana. To visit family?"

"Informative."

Margot dusted her palms together. "Time to get back to work." She directed a half-hitched smile over her slender shoulder before exiting Everley's office.

Tyler approached Everley's desk. The hint of desire skated over his features. "Glad you're back."

At his provocative tone, the walls closed in, squeezed the breath from her lungs. That wasn't how they rolled. She broke the magnetic pull of his stare. "So am I."

"We'll catch up at Milano's tonight." A hint of question lingered in his voice.

"Right. It's Friday."

"Meet you at 6:00?"

"Right."

Always. The. Same.

Snug behind the steering wheel of her car outside Milano's Deep Dish at Old Town Triangle, Everley awaited Tyler's arrival. The late afternoon voicemail from a Bryson Cox, who'd identified himself as MidDay Media's Vice President of Development, had her shivering more than the early spring cold snap. Her brain added a new column, labeled it risk.

Ridiculous risk.

At the authority in his voice, she took an influx of air. Wherever Bryson ranked against Don Barnhart, she reasoned Bryson had more sway. A subtle moan rose to her throat, rumbled out. "An invitation to becoming overwhelmed."

Like Mom.

The memory of Mom's wrenching sobs inside her bedroom rose in heated swirls, hissed in Everley's ear. A young daughter, helpless to do anything about it. Long before cancer took Mom's life, her "it'll be so much fun" house project had taken several swings, leaving her emotionally exhausted at times.

Two gloved hands on the wheel, she drew in a staggered breath, released it slowly while the image faded to black and hushed. Time to incline the full of her attention to the palpable interest expressed by a reputable media executive whose job description included discovering hidden talent and rich story. In no time, he'd sniffed after Moreland like a shark to blood, no thanks to Serenity, who'd masterfully wielded her social media prowess to garner public interest in Moreland, layering sentiment like frosting on a cupcake.

Everley, the puppet. Serenity, the puppet master.

Eyes squeezed shut, she shook her head. The thought of Italian food soured her stomach. A fresh wave of doubt crept in. Why had she given Moreland a wink and coaxed absurdity? One quick return phone call should squash the idea, have them in agreement that this was nothing if not ridiculous.

Plucking off a glove, her finger hovered over the screen. "All right, play cool. No way he'll answer. I'll just leave a message—"

It rang. Once. "Who's this?" The voice on the other end was stony, punctuated by urgency, and upheld a veil of caution. Of course. A busy man. Certainly not waiting around for an anonymous girl from Chicago—procurer of stupid ideas—to call.

Her heart leaped. Intelligent words surfaced in her brain, found her tongue. "Is this Bryson Cox, MidDay Media?"

"Who am I speaking with?"

Hackles raised at his abrupt tone—she emphasized ownership, tinged with authority. "This is Everley Scott, owner of Moreland Manor in Louisiana."

"Oh, right, right." Enthusiasm thinned the fortress of defense to mere inches. "Sorry for the hesitation," he laughed, lowering the draw bridge. "It's just, I get dozens of marketing calls, and I rarely ever answer unknown numbers. Providentially, I answered yours."

Thanks ever-so-much, Providence.

Several yards away, Tyler emerged from inside the restaurant, glanced left and right, his expression humorless as though he'd been waiting hours. Pulling the phone away, she noted his text on the screen.

TYLER: Already here. You?

As she unfolded from her car, a biting chill rolled off the distant Lake Michigan, slicked through her coat, bored into her bones. She waved at Tyler while directing a steady voice into the phone. "My understanding is you have interest in capturing Moreland's restoration? For a pitch to a network?"

Slicing through icy air, she stretched her arm high to capture his attention, waved it like a windshield wiper as she navigated through cars toward the entrance.

"I do. I'd like to meet with you to discuss logistics, assess the viability of the project from our perspective."

"Certainly. But I live in Chicago. My job only allows narrow margins for travel outside client visits." The clarification should raise her asset rating to equal, if not exceed, his. Not to mention, she was closing in on Tyler, whose handsome face had morphed into a frown, having checked his cell twice.

As she neared, Tyler's vexation dawned into a welcome grin.

"Chi-town, huh? I didn't realize you weren't local. I assumed you lived within reasonable proximity of the house."

Angst stabbed her chest.

A beat of silence, Bryson's heavy sigh rifting through the phone.

The sound of a *wah-wah-wah* decrescendo clanged inside Everley's head.

"But I did grow up in the area ... know it really well. And my sister still lives in New Orleans ... the house belonged to my mother ... and she left it to me ..."

Desperation had her babbling—all for what was, at its core, Serenity's rogue idea.

"Our Emmy-Award-winning team here at MidDay has sold numerous episodes to various networks. We deliver non-formulaic stories with authenticity and heart. Unscripted, broad stroke, high concept. Character-driven programming, specializing in the unexpected."

In matters of the unexpected, she'd easily earn a PhD ...

And story she had in spades, along with a high-profile production company on the other end of the line.

"H2H is a sucker for stories like yours but needs to hear language that makes sense from a sales point of view," Bryson explained. "Featuring the restoration of a storied manor house is something we believe our audience wants. The on-site design series we sold last year resulted in a measurable rating hike. Your mother's letter with specifications as to who she wanted to restore the place has our attention."

The letter. The contractor. Both like cords tightening about her neck, cutting off her air supply.

"We'll need to discuss how this would all be monetized. The cost to renovate is, unfortunately, quite exorbitant," Everley asserted, every word nailing her to this reckless decision.

"We pay out location and talent fees and have procured initial funding from investors. We'd pay airfare and ground transport for the first meeting and a per diem to cover additional expenses each day you're on location. Most aspects of the contract are negotiable. Should there be irreconcilable differences, we'd each have the option to walk away without breach of contract. Of course ..." He gave a churlish laugh. "That rarely happens."

Spoken like he'd read from a script.

To have caught the roving eye of a media company willing and able to fund the cost of Moreland's restoration—even if only a small percentage—stayed her wobbly feet to the precipice of risk.

Shoot for the stars, Everley Orion!

But would Gabriel Bellevue even agree to this craziness? Would the media exposure for his company be enough to lure him in front of a camera?

"I'd have to insure the contractor is willing to have his work captured on film."

"Right, right. Tell you what let's do, Ms. Scott. Send me a brief synopsis—and I mean brief—specifying the intrinsic value of the house, the reason you're compelled to restore it. I'll have our senior producer, Don Barnhart, be in touch, arrange a meeting with the two of you. How's that?"

She swallowed around the knot in her throat, voice raspy. "Certainly. "I can do that, sure, Mr., um ..."

"Cox. Bryson Cox."

The one, the only. Producer of award-winning docudramas, a notable who's who in the TV network industry.

"I'll have it to you ... when I have it to you ... just as soon as I have it to you."

Partner qualified, yet suddenly she'd lost intelligent thought.

Bryson's wry laugh slipped past before he ended the call.

In the wake of madness, she clapped the heel of her palm to her forehead.

Reaching the entrance, she slipped into Tyler's open arms.

"I was worried. You're never late," he said.

"Sorry. I had to return a call."

He released her, angled a stare. "A client?"

"No, actually, an idea to fund some of the reno cost for my mom's house. A huge answer to prayer."

Pulling back, his lips turned upward into a half grin. "You, uh, prayed?" Pity deepened the lines around his eyes, a full smile stopping just short of his gaze as if to emphasize the obvious. Because the last time she'd prayed ... *really* prayed ... was ...?

Now might be a really good time to revive the abandoned practice.

CHAPTER FOUR

With barely a knock, Phillip Vance, the austere and distinguished half of Vance and O'Connor, invited himself into Everley's office Monday morning and shuffled over in his tailored suit and designer lace-up shoes.

Quick. Silence DIY videos. Appear to be engrossed in an audit.

"Just where *are* those accounts receivable for Llewelyn Ortho?" Her intonation held Oscar-winning believability, a crimped forehead for added effect.

Tap, tap, tap. Click and … open.

Incoming messages cascaded down her screen—upped her pulse.

Near her desk, his scrutinizing stare skimmed the rim of his glasses. Overhead light danced off his balding scalp only partially concealed by a bad comb-over of thinning, silver-streaked hair.

Gaze locked on her screen, she established a pose to convey deep concentration. "How was your weekend, sir?"

A wheeze and squeak sounded as he plopped into the leather chair across from her desk. He crossed an ankle over his knee and wound his arms high at his chest. "Splendid. You?"

"Same."

"Dull, then?"

At the derisive snicker, she shrugged and turned her attention to checks and balances.

"It's safe to presume you've already checked email this morning," he asserted.

Getting there. Tap, tap.

"I've assigned you two new clients and forwarded their portfolios. One won't require much fieldwork. As for the other, given their history of risk management weaknesses, you'll need to present several prospective financial scenarios—give that one undivided attention. Naturally, I'll leave everything in your capable hands."

She snapped her gaze to her inbox, eyeing his email.

Click.

"Well, listen, I won't keep my most prized CPA from her work." The cushioned air hissed as he stood to his full five feet, nine inches. "But, one more thing ... we've prepared a bonus for you. It'll be drafted to your account in ten days or so." A pursed smile drew up the edges of his mouth, coaxing reaction. He added a head bob to elicit gratitude as he gathered the front of his suit across a midlife paunch, to no avail.

Fingertips stilled over the keyboard, Everley fixed her gaze.

"In the amount of $4500." Pride rang in his voice as he made the announcement.

In a wild scramble, numbers crunched in her head.

"That represents—"

"Five percent of my salary," she said. "I appreciate that, Phillip."

Perhaps this was God's wink at her decision to respond to the persistent whine of a vacated inheritance.

"Over the past several years, you've continued to be one of our most productive and resourceful managers. A rainmaker. Ideal partner material."

Better than Tyler.

The accolades thawed her from the inside out—radiated warmth throughout the room. Made winter's cloying chill almost bearable.

"Your recommendations to our board last year on fiscally advantageous methods to save us money was spot on," he continued. "Allowed me to hire additional staff, which, in turn, allowed us to extend our client load."

What any responsible person would do. Make life add up. If it didn't, Everley would puzzle over it until it did.

Bearing the pride of a lion, he rocked onto the balls of his feet. A crinkled smile brightened his expression as he moved his hand across the air like a banner. "Can't you just see the signage? Vance, O'Connor, and Scott …" He drew a slow glance in her direction, brow dancing a bit. "Sure like the sound of that, don't you?"

Buttery-smooth happiness coated her insides. "What firmly planted CPA wouldn't?"

After Kyle died, Everley left the jazzy vibe, warmth, and color of New Orleans to take the job in Chicago. Planting roots, she wisely invested in refurbishing a condo in Gold Coast, prime real estate located near bus and subway lines, only a short jaunt to shops on Michigan Avenue and North Avenue Beach. Setting a stringent goal, she'd paid it off in five years while it doubled in value and had no intention—or motivation—to sell. The possibility of partnership gave her every reason to stay.

Everley enjoyed a predictable, routine pace of life and the companionship of a few steady friends, Tyler among them.

Little, if any, disruption.

"As to the bonus," Phillip said, concentrating a pleading stare. "Do yourself a favor and spend it on something fun. Indulge yourself a little."

Um, no. She'd assign a portion to debt reduction then set this little chunk of unexpected windfall aside. Because what if an appliance failed or a pipe burst? Chicago winters, you know. What if her brakes went out or ...

Or you got stuck with an immensely large house that came with Mother's plea to restore its life, a contractor bid extending beyond the constellations?

At Phillip's hard cough, Everley jerked to attention and fixed a shellacked smile to her face. "I'll give it some thought."

Margot appeared at her door and exchanged shallow platitudes with Phillip before he turned to go.

Never one to let a wicked winter dictate her wardrobe, Margot's stiletto heels clicked over the floor to Everley's desk. In one manicured hand, a donut. In the other, a colorful pamphlet that smacked of a travel brochure.

Brows hitched, Everley said, "Is that donut from Scafuri's Bakery?"

Margot pinched off a piece and offered it. "Here."

Everley flinched. "No. Thank you. But offering me one that hadn't already had bites taken out of it would have been thoughtful."

"How quickly you forget the time I blessed you with a dozen of these darlings, freshly baked and drizzled in glaze, and you looked at me like I'd offered you steaming cow patties."

"I was dieting."

Margot assumed a testy stance. "A worthless endeavor. Genetics has blessed you with a figure to die for."

Margot waved the brochure like a winning golden Wonka ticket. "Hey, listen, Ev. I've got the answer." Her mezzo-soprano, sing-song tone carried a hint of rasp from prior years of smoking.

Tap, tap, tap. "What was the question?"

"Change of pace."

"I'm quite happy with my pace."

Life mapped out, arranged in neat columns.

"Time you switched it up and traveled to the Bahamas. End of spring, St. Thomas Island. You and gorgeous Tyler the Tax Man, me and Stephen." Margot's penciled brows wiggled in provocative dance.

"I've told you a thousand times. Tyler and I are just friends."

If love called again, she'd resolved not to answer.

"Fine. But when the right guy takes up residence in that stony little heart of yours, softens it to clay, you'll cave so fast you won't have time to breathe."

"No prospects. Not looking. Don't need the disruption."

No way she'd leak Tyler's chummy sentiments since she'd returned from New Orleans. A man acting out of accord with their status quo arrangement.

Margot gave an agonizingly long head shake, slathering a look of disdain. "I can see the inscription on your tombstone now. 'Everley Scott. Refused to live a dream. Died of boredom. Not one postcard found in her possession.'"

At this juncture, the conversation had shoveled too deep, loosening territory Everley had no desire to exhume. Logic and reason landed on her tongue. "My mom had scads of postcards. Slick cardstock reminders that one has gone somewhere, seen things, and exhausted all her resources."

An impulsive trip to Paris came to mind. Mom—pregnant with Serenity—jetted off with her art collector friend, Bonnie Sue Gaudet, leaving Moreland and one-year-old Everley in Dad's care.

Annoyance twisted Margot's lips. "Or ... it means a girl has chosen not to stay frozen in one spot."

"It doesn't add up."

"Newsflash." Margot leaned back—fingers splayed. "Not everything has to add up. Life's greatest joys spring from the unexpected."

Or life's worst tragedies.

"Didn't your parents ever throw you a surprise birthday party, Ev?"

The neck of Everley's sweater seemed to tighten about her throat like a rubber band. "Yes, my tenth." Tap, tap. "Hated it. A wild pony stomped on the azaleas, a llama spit on me and my friends, and to top it off, the jump house collapsed."

Mom, Dad, and eight-year-old Serenity all the while reveling in the hilarity at Everley's expense.

Delete, delete.

"When will you let loose and enjoy spontaneity?"

Ever since Granny Caldwell Lewis told Everley she was good with numbers, accounting became the inevitable road. Try as they might, Mom and Dad's whimsical approach to life held all the appeal of a poison ivy rash.

"I can be spontaneous."

"And Chicago can be sweltering in January." Margot took a second head shake over to the window, peered momentarily at the bustling view, and released a not-so-subtle groan.

A few errant strands escaped the clasp in Everley's hair and tickled her cheeks. Securing them, she said, "Considering this afternoon's snowfall, we'd better take an early lunch."

Margot pivoted and sashayed back over, her penetrating gaze sparking to life. "Listen to you, breaking routine." Her tone soared an octave. "I wouldn't pass this opportunity for a date with George Clooney."

"Yes. You would."

With a flourish, Everley collected her purse and stood, adding a purposeful bounce. She jutted her chin and pressed a hand to her chest. "See? This is me, queen of spontaneity."

One gallant step forward, and the strap of her purse caught the armrest and yanked her backward.

Thud! The wall caught her fall and sent her arms flailing.

Margot reached to steady her—assistance accompanied by an indelicate snort.

Pain throbbed. Everley massaged the back of her head and glared. "That's a solid fourteen point six on a completely unfunny scale of one to ten."

Restrained laughter heaved Margot's slim shoulders. "Couldn't resist. It's just that when you try to shake out of your routine, you look like you're just learning to walk."

Stifling a scathing rebuke, Everley bent to stuff her purse in her desk drawer and gave it a slam before she stood tall. "Given that unsolicited snide comment, my friend, lunch is on you."

"Happy to bear the consequence. But for switchers, let's take the L-line and try that new deli on Farrell Street."

"It's Monday. We eat at Liazzo's. I get the all-you-can-eat salad bar. You get the French onion soup bread bowl and a Gala apple as a side."

Margot's hands swirled in gesture. "Five years of Mondays at Liazzo's—factoring fifty-two weeks a year—comes to two hundred sixty lunches at the same stinkin' place." Her lanky arms raised in protest. "A little variation won't kill you."

But it might.

"Liazzo's. Spare the coaxing."

A week had passed, and still no word from Everley about the bid. Justifiable reasons spilled into Gabe's mind. Like maybe she'd gotten snowed in, lost internet connection ... a gorilla ate her cell phone?

Friday morning, Gabe gunned his Harley from the parking garage of his high-rise condo and edged past an idle line of cars on Canal Street. A golden sky hovered over commerce, hotels, and eateries that lined the narrow one-way streets forming the French Quarter matrix, a precious gem fastened to a bend in the Mississippi.

Turning onto Chartres, the scent of pastries churned his growling stomach, barely smothering the pungent smell of horse manure and water-soaked street sewage. He motored past cafés, bars, and foot traffic. Shoppers ambled beneath intricate, ornamental iron balconies, a distinct feature of New Orleans French Quarter architecture.

The year before, G&R had performed restoration on a hotel on Ursuline. As a result, travel consultant reviews of the place soared. When he'd discovered the Pear Tree Bakery and Coffee Shop two doors down, Gabe worked out a deal with the hotel manager to park his ride within their courtyard if needed.

Harley secured in the courtyard, he strode past a souvenir shop and came to the bakery.

The spirited owner faced typical start-up struggles when she'd first opened several years ago. Despite slim staff, her place had flowered into a bustling sweet spot for locals. Gabe was a faithful, Friday morning regular.

Outside the brick façade, thirsty ferns hung between the fluted posts of a balcony rimmed in a metal railing. Private apartments sat above the bakery. Storefront windows crowned with a gentle arch held dark panels just below the sill.

A bell jangled above the door. The smell of frosted cupcakes and coffee greeted him. Patrons chattered, and machines gurgled. A variant mix of pottery sat atop floating wood shelving along a cream-colored wall to his right. An arched entryway at the back right gave access to a spacious courtyard and offered an earthy vibe and a trickling water fountain. To his left behind the counter rose an exposed brick wall overlaid with chipped plaster. Wood and cast iron tables sat in the main eating area separated from the kitchen by a turquoise wall along the back that showcased oil paintings and various antique pieces used to display books and the work of local artisans.

Hazy daylight streamed through the windows and warmed a private nook in the front right corner. Near it, an unfinished wood ledge jutted from the wall where several stools cozied beneath it.

The owner, Serenity Lewis, stood at the register. She kept her shoulder-length, honey blonde hair tinted in lavender and parted down the middle. Beneath a pink apron bearing the bakery logo, she wore fitted jeans, a white pullover, and orange Converse shoes. In a manner he couldn't quite figure, she pulled off sophistication and whimsy like no other.

She circled a rag over the counter beside an illuminated case featuring her baked awesomeness—an art gallery of sorts.

"How's it going this morning, sir?" Her customary greeting warmed his heart. Gave solid reason to frequent the place.

"Cut the formality, Hotshot. Call me Gabe. I'm practically family."

She quirked a grin, the pinprick of light dotting a kaleidoscope of blues and greens in her eyes. "For loyal customers, I aim to please."

He slid her a twenty, his customary payment for a pastry and coffee priced just under $8. A mason jar sat beside a vase of lavender roses and bore a colorful label that read Marigold's Dream. Taking it in hand, a few coins clinked beneath some bills. "What's this?"

"A fundraiser to save a house."

"For a Chihuahua?"

"No," she sniped. "It's a historic estate built on what used to be a sugar plantation."

One brow lifted as he set the jar back down. If nothing else, Serenity bred a contagious hopefulness. "Looks like you've got enough for a welcome mat."

"Every penny adds up." She took a slick flyer off the counter and flashed it in front of him.

He took the paper, glanced at it. Moreland's image stared back in all her unmistakable glory. He raised his gaze to study the tresses of Serenity's hair threaded in gold, her pink skin tone, and doe eyes. Her definitively square jawline and straight set of teeth registered familiarity now. The difference—Serenity's slightly shorter frame was sculpted by solid athleticism.

A close match to Everley, although Moreland's heiress had coppery russet hair, a light spray of freckles on her nose, and enigmatic green eyes.

Both undeniably pretty. Then again, not every sibling shared the same mom and pop.

"Tell me about this house," Gabe prodded, stealing another glance at the jar in feigned ignorance.

"My parents, Marigold and Peter Lewis, bought the place in 1978 for practically nothing and spent years working to restore it. After Dad died, Mom continued to pursue their dream up until her death six months ago."

A house he'd been divinely picked to save.

"Sorry to hear that."

She quirked a cheek in thanks. "Part of living is dying."

Serenity poured his coffee, warmed a large cinnamon pear muffin crusted with brown sugar glaze, set it on a turquoise plate, and slid it—with his change—over the counter.

"Here you go."

Gabe slipped the flyer inside his back pocket and stuffed the change inside her jar, adding two twenties ... a tribute to Marigold Lewis. May she rest in peace. And may her firstborn agree to hire him.

Seated at a nearby table, he bit into his muffin and sipped his coffee, reveled in playing the uninformed. "Your mom left the house to you then?"

Rag in hand, she stilled her vigorous swiping. A pinch of pain flashed across her gaze. Enthusiasm waned. "No. She left it to my big sister who lives in Chicago and has no interest in the place. Mom specified in a letter she wanted Moreland restored and specified exactly who she wanted to do the job."

Annoyance rose in her tone.

A gentle swirl of steam wafted from his coffee, the cup hot in his palm. "Why leave it to the disinterested half?" That's right. Coax more intel.

As though begging to spill all, she rounded the counter and claimed the chair opposite him. "Beats me." Serenity's posture went stiff with aggravation. "I would have called the contractor the moment Mom's casket sank out of sight."

The scent of cinnamon and pear whisked up as Gabe took another bite.

Fascination glimmered in Serenity's eyes.

"Fun fact. Mom said film actress Cora Lindenberg once visited Moreland during a publicity tour in New Orleans to launch a new film. Apparently, she shared the love of art and architecture and had previously shopped at Dazzle Me Art, my parent's art store. I've been posting pics of Moreland on social media for months now, sharing the story. People love it!"

Leaning in, her enthusiasm turned relentless.

"Get this. A major production company wants to film the restoration and pitch a series idea to a TV network."

Gabe's breath caught. Everley hadn't mentioned any of this—maybe afraid he'd walk.

Maybe he should.

Would he want his work recorded? What if things went wrong and his reputation came into question? Was numbers girl setting him up to fail to achieve her own end? A fate worse than death.

Her gaze dimmed. "At my insistence, my sister finally called the guy who's supposed to do the work."

From the start, Everley's forced hand saturated her tone. A saucy type cornered by her own conscience—heart dismembered from the project.

He sipped his coffee and peered at Serenity over the rim. "It oughta be someone who knows what they're doing. Not all contractors are what they claim. Especially in matters of historic preservation."

"Believe me, even if Mom hadn't specified, my sister would never hire anyone without having thought it through, researched companies until wee hours of the night, read customer reviews."

A warmth settled inside his chest following the final bite of what'd transformed into a leisurely and informative breakfast.

"Sounds like she's mighty particular."

"To a fault." Her lipped thinned to wry.

Arms crossed on the table, he leaned in.

"Hotshot, it's time you knew. I'm Gabe, the contractor your momma picked."

Mouth agape, she held the look of a starstruck fan. She shot from her seat and grabbed his neck in a hug. When she pulled back, a dazzle had returned to her eyes. "All this time, and I never thought to ask what you do for a living. You're the one who'll save Moreland!"

The admiration drew warmth into his cheeks, an honor fit for a king. Uh, he was no king.

You're a complete screw-up, Gabriel. Just like your daddy! Failed at everything he ever tried.

No. Dad succeeded at one thing. Failure.

Though the words grated like a gavel inside his brain, he countered them. "Trust me. I'll take care of your momma's place."

So help me, God.

Reclaiming his Harley, Gabe stood in the shade outside the hotel as a mid-morning sun inched above the roofline, glistened in a white gold ribbon down the soaked street. Brassy jazz trumpeted through a thickening doubt.

Rebuke from a nearby bar assaulted him. He turned to see a teetering patron in saggy pants belted at his thin waist and swallowed in an oversized jacket. The man clung to the metal post out front. Judging from his careworn face, he looked to be in his late seventies. Silver-streaked black hair sprouted from his head like it'd been cut with dull scissors and licked by a dog. A severe, angular nose protruded from close-set eyes set beneath a furrowed forehead. A thick moustache and gray beard grew around his small mouth. Sunken cheeks suggested age. Or hunger. Or both.

"Motorcycles ain't allowed 'round here," the man chided.

Gnarled fingers gripped each pole as he staggered over, looking like he and Jack Daniel's had gotten an early start on happy hour. His demeanor suggested he'd yet to find happiness.

Swiftly, Gabe engaged the kickstand and steadied the man's stance. Arm around his bony shoulders, he assisted him to a bench outside Serenity's bakery.

He checked the time. Randy had sent a text.

RANDY: At the office. Discuss Cantrell job?

GABE: Running behind. Be there at 9:30

Or so.

Eyes streaked red inside a glassy gaze, the man slurred, "That your swanky ride?"

"Yes, sir. Need a lift?"

A rusty laugh racked his shoulders. He raised a feeble arm toward the bar. "Sure do. Haul me back inside."

"I believe you've had enough, my friend. What's your name?"

"Sergeant Merrill Clark Downing. Just ask Major General Maxwell. He'll remember." The alcohol spewed an angry rage. "I fought with the likes of the devil hisself in Nam. Took a bullet in the leg hauling my buddy into a fox hole."

Merrill's slur trailed to a raspy, acetone whisper, lonesome gaze drawn ahead. "Then, stateside, I found a friend in whiskey ... the wife left me, and my kids don't come round. A daughter, she moved up north ... a son, growed up, too ... has a couple kids I hear ... never met their Grandpa Merrill." Drained of words, he perched elbows on his knees, then sank his head into his palms, grief gurgling at his throat.

"Wait here." Gabe swung open the bakery door and threw his voice over patrons. "Hotshot. Bring me three of those jumbo pear muffins. Cupcakes. Anything."

He locked one eye on the slumped and defeated warrior as Serenity skittered over. In short order, she handed off a warm paper bag dotted with oil. He took it—handed her a twenty. "Thanks. Add the change to Marigold's jar."

Gabe handed the bag to Merrill and sat beside him.

Head lolled Gabe's direction, Merrill's eyes glistened. Words unnecessary, he merely nodded, a weak smile devoid of joy.

For some hit hard by life, thanks came infrequently and cost more than it gave.

"Where's your home, Merrill Clark Downing?"

Merrill's words tangled in a murmur as he grasped the bag like it held the Hope Diamond. "Shelter." One shoulder hitched, he raised an upturned palm. "What's a home anyhow?"

Hopelessness drenched his question. It begged an answer. Because, at heart, home wasn't a place.

"I can tell you what it should be. It's where people do honest work and love and support each other through life's ups and downs. And if that home has a roof when the rain comes down, why, sir, that's an added blessing."

Derision narrowed Merrill's stare. "In all of Nawlins, the good Lord—if he still pays me any attention—sends a preacher man my way."

Gabe laughed. His grandfather Jedediah Bellevue had attempted to make a living as a preacher over in Utah somewhere, putting his wife and five kids under the hardship of little to no income. Hoped to see pennies from heaven for his efforts. Dad said very little rained down. "No, sir. Not a preacher."

A warbly chuckle shook his shoulders. "Then one of those aggravatin' religious types, eh?"

Gabe shook his head. "I just know who created family and have a pretty good idea how he engineered it to operate."

Nothing like the fabric of his own family, ripped at the seams by failure.

Pulling Merrill to a stand, Gabe eased him onto the back of his bike and secured his head inside a spare helmet. Snarled, silvery locks curled along his neck.

"I'll take you to the shelter."

And arrive late to the office. But business could wait. Because God had yet to put anyone in his path that didn't have his holy agenda attached to them. Sergeant Merrill Clark Downing from a ground offensive in Nam was no different.

CHAPTER FIVE

After Gabe delivered Merrill Downing to a nearby shelter, he and Randy broke for a late afternoon lunch at Johnny's PoBoys near the Mississippi. The river's edge lapped against the railed section of riverwalk a distance from their table and rose to choppy swirls as the Creole Queen paddle wheeler chugged past.

Orange relish oozed from Randy's sandwich when he bit into it. "It's been a week. No word from CPA girl?"

Given Everley's flat response when he revealed that they'd shared the same alma mater, the sweetness of yesteryear had been boiled out of her and hardened her countenance to glazed porcelain.

Gabe rotated his drink between his fingers, his sandwich distorted through the glass. "I'm still hopeful, assuming the sale."

A gruff stream of doubt slipped from Randy's lips. "Maybe we set the bar too high."

"We've cut plenty of cost already. I'm not backing down on our estimate. Any levelheaded accountant would understand that." The chilled spring air pricked along on his skin. A hard swallow of icy liquid cooled the heat in his chest.

If giving business away in exchange for favors was a successful business model, Dad would have made millions. Gabe received another voice mail from him yesterday. Something about reconnecting and a minimal plea to call back ...

"If you want."

He didn't ... despite the distinct clarity of Dad's voice, absent inebriation. Sheesh. He'd almost let it alight on his heart.

"It's all good," Gabe said. "We've landed the Cantrell project, start date the week after next. Our contractors are lined up, materials on order. And Murdock is on the cusp of acquiring a sizable project which he's awarding G&R in the presence of business elite at a big shindig in June on the occasion of his sixtieth birthday."

A shindig that doubled as a surprise proposal to Carmen and the offer of a ring.

Randy's frown belied the fact that he'd dropped all concern. He pulled out his cell and flashed the screen Gabe's direction.

"According to this telling photo from New Orleans' Business Beat, I guess it's sayonara to your most eligible bachelor status," he chided.

Gabe's eyes traced the image. It featured him with a megawatt smile, head tilted against a swooning Carmen, one arm slung around her shoulders. The neckline of her beaded, deep red dress plunged to dangerous depths.

Voice amplified over the din of a husky steamboat, Randy read aloud. "Gabriel Bellevue, owner of G&R Historic Restoration Specialists, spotted at a social event, getting cozy with Miss Carmen Murdock, daughter of CEO Warren Murdock. Keeping pace with steady business ratings, his love life has also soared to great heights as it appears one of New Orleans's hottest tickets has taken himself off the market."

Admittedly, Carmen was stunning, easy on the eyes, and touted a family social status that flashed dollar signs and lured like tantalizing offers on Bourbon Street.

Gabe hitched a shoulder. "We like each other. It'll be a good matchup."

Good. An enemy of the best.

Never mind that Carmen had pressed Gabe repeatedly for sex. So far, he'd managed to put her off, clinging like super glue to his commitment to hold off until he'd taken a wife.

"Listen, Gabe. Me and my dog like each other, but that doesn't make for happily ever after."

Gabe straightened, gaze stilled on Randy. "What about Everley?"

Confusion knit Randy's brow, sandwich midway to his mouth.

"You said her name. Happy Everley after."

"No," Randy said, lips quirked in a sidelong grin. "I said happily ever after."

Impulsively, Gabe thumbed the image of Moreland on his phone, enlarged it, and zoomed in on her columns crowned in intricate ionic scrolls. At his first visit to the property, he'd shoulder-shoved his weight against each column, found them indomitable, the second-story colonnade a sheer marvel. Even in the face of neglect, the whole of the house was enchanting. Regal even.

Uncertainty churned, scooped air from his lungs. Under his command, would generations of father failure wreak havoc, or would Providence enable him to breathe life into her again?

"Considering Louisiana's storms and historic flooding in the mid-1870s, Moreland is mighty tenacious."

"Who'd you say built it?" Randy pinched a napkin between his fingers.

"A man from North Carolina by the name of Colonel Marshall Robert Thompson. In an effort to outclass his brothers, he sought to add to his fortune in Louisiana agriculture in the Mississippi River valley, a slick businessman with an eye for profit. Moreland served as the manor house."

"You ought to get Kourtney to search Moreland's history up through to the time the Lewis's got their hands on it."

"As luck would have it, she's already been assigned a research paper on Louisiana estate houses built during the 1800s."

Unswerving certainty deepened Randy's gaze. "That, partner, isn't luck. It's divine intervention. Moreland must have something it wants you to know."

The scent of rain lingered, clouds unfolding in swags. "Whoever had the privilege of ownership before the Lewis's took her in 1978 maintained it like a bunch of medicated toddlers with paintbrushes, hammers, and saws," Gabe said. "Demolition by neglect."

Made worse by Moreland's current owner.

Ire sizzled hot in his soul. For all Everley's intelligence and beauty—no matter how nice the package—it hadn't served Moreland well.

You're the one who's gonna save Moreland.

Serenity's prophetic statement tore through him, tapping like needles along his neck. Would prophecy overrule a stubborn heiress? As to Marigold Lewis, he had no need of research to discover her intent. The month before she died, the iconic New Orleans art dealer had contacted Gabe, her voice raspy with disease. Conversation brief and marked by reserve as though safeguarding particular details.

She'd asked about his qualifications, his certification to work on historic homes. Considering her of no significance beyond a potential client, he hadn't made the connection with Everley, Marigold's crazy beautiful daughter, today a woman steeled behind a stony façade and crowned in a head of red-hot warning. An impregnable castle surrounded by a moat meant to drown the fool who tried to scale her walls.

A swat on his upper arm startled Gabe to attention. "Hey, boss. We need to talk about Cantrell's place."

"Sure, sure. It's just that ... this is *Moreland*. She ain't no lipstick job." He widened his hands as if he'd reeled in a ten-foot swordfish.

Can't screw this up.

Leaning in, Randy splayed his palms on the table. "As per usual, our contractors stand behind their work, guaranteed to spec."

And did I mention the possible intrusion of a high-profile production company?

"In the meantime, CPA lady hasn't agreed to hire us, and we're contracted to renovate the home of Southern University's chancellor." Randy rubbed his fingers and thumb together, sniffing the air. "Once they procure more funding, we'll be doing campus expansions and dorm upgrades."

It would do no good to tell Randy the Cantrell deal came via Warren Murdock, the university's most substantial philanthropist. As trustee of The Murdock Foundation, Warren spearheaded the expansion of their library last year to include an archival wing.

Keys in hand, Gabe slipped behind the wheel of his truck, Randy beside him as they drove to the G&R warehouse several blocks from the office. Perusing inventory, they found four refurbished antique windows of equal size. "These should bring a smile to Chancellor Cantrell."

Outside, Gabe and Randy eased them into the back of Gabe's truck.

"I'm clocking out early today, boss. Friday is taco night with Summer and the girls."

"But we've still got to finish sash window installation at Felicity House."

"There's tomorrow."

Tension bubbled in Gabe's chest. He gave the gate a hefty slam. "We're not promised tomorrow. Do right by others today."

Randy shook his head.

Frustration fringed Gabe's brow. "I did not make the cover of Professional Remodeler's magazine last year by living for tomorrow."

"And you'll not make it again if you try to evade the inevitable."

"Meaning?"

"Mistakes, Gabe. Mistakes."

"So what you're saying is, you can walk away from unfinished work and sleep like a baby?"

A wan smile dimmed Randy's gaze as he jutted his chin toward his van. "Family awaits. See you tomorrow, boss."

Awaiting Gabe? His tools and his dog.

After a long week at a new client's site and a condo encased in snow, Everley willingly spent Friday night inside. Yesterday, Tyler had flown to Florida for an extended weekend to celebrate a fraternity brother's bachelor party.

All good. Because tonight's episode of *Fixed Up Right* awaited. Living vicariously from the safety of her sofa, she'd be free to tear up at the final reveal. She always did. Because a fixed-up house made dreams come true.

For dreamers.

When the show ended, she'd call Gabe to state her case against his ridiculously inflated bid. Being she'd received his email a week ago, he had to be wondering about her decision. And then she'd segue to MidDay's interest, brace for a sure and certain rebuttal. A man of his caliber probably wouldn't be willing to expose his workmanship to the scrutiny of the public eye. He struck her as a man who shunned intrusion, a thin veil of caution behind his magnetic, cedar brown and honey-gold gaze, though all together comfortable in his own skin.

Intense and inscrutable, shrouded in an invitation to solve the mystery of him.

Distinct grooves in the planes of his grizzled face—superior confidence—magazine-worthy smile put to use on New Orleans' Business Beat and all-around good looks.

From a strategic standpoint, he'd easily capture the heart of viewers. Help her endgame. If he were willing. Which he probably wasn't.

A reckless and costly idea.

One fraction of her thoughts gave way to wonder what he'd be doing on a Friday night anyway.

Then she wondered why she wondered.

The scent of last week's DIY painting project still lingered, the main living area of her condo now coated in dazzling white. Functional, logical, artistic expression. An economical way to conceal the past. A skill rightly learned during long weekends with Mom and Dad as they fussed over Moreland.

Crossing the hardwood floor, she activated the fireplace. She'd chosen purely functional seating, upholstered pieces in solid colors. The glass and metal framework of coffee and end tables tied textures together in geometric, pleasing lines. The midcentury modern décor held nothing of the antique appeal she preferred, but the space called for a clean, urban look. Anything to maintain resale value—though she had no intention of selling.

A flat-screen hung above a row of mustard-colored modular storage units adjacent to a wall of paneled windows that framed winter's reckoning, the evening sky drained of color.

She slipped into gray sweatpants and a Commanders sweatshirt, number ninety-one slicked across the front. A purchase Serenity made two years ago after Owen moved from the Rams in LA to New Orleans to sign a six-year contract with the Commanders.

A purchase Serenity then promptly mailed to Everley.

"If you really don't want it, Serenity, why didn't you give it to Brooke or donate it?" Everley had asked.

"No reason it can't stay in the family. I just don't have any need for it."

The fact that the shirt arrived carrying the distinct scent of Serenity's perfume belied her unwillingness to admit the obvious ... Serenity had the unstoppable defensive end on her radar. And she may not have been as unimpressed with his current stats as she'd alleged.

A great matchup, honestly. Both living big and unafraid.

Lounging on her leather sofa and snuggled inside a blanket, Everley powered on this week's episode which featured Seth and Hilda Gardener's Alabama home, their contractors tackling the Victorian built in the early 1900s. At the end of the hour, their smiles beamed, gazes misty, the restored house all smiles behind them. "Our home has new life!"

Hilda choked at the onslaught of emotion.

Everley patted her eyes. The swell of envy constricted her throat. Her cell rang. It was Serenity. Probably hadn't come down from the moon since Everley told her of MidDay's interest.

"What did Gabe say about the MidDay deal?"

Um …

She gave a hard sniff and muted the TV. "I was just about to contact him. But you understand that if he refuses, both deals are off, and I list Moreland as is."

And be forever haunted.

No, sweet Everley. Momma didn't find Moreland. She found me.

Silence hung.

Everley registered the hum of bakery equipment, the heat of Serenity's annoyed breathing in opposition to the happy ding of the bell over the door.

"But Mom left you money."

Naïve girl. Still no good with numbers.

"Enough to cover one room. There are twenty-three, which includes all main living spaces and bathrooms."

"Hey, it's a start."

Always the optimist.

Freed herself to live the dream, a visual for an unleashed spirit. Everley used to believe the dancing sunshine that constituted her younger sister would at some point rub off. To date, it hadn't. But she loved their talks. They infused life and light, chased shadowed places.

"I bet you a million he'll go for it," Serenity said. "Call me when he does." Another happy ding. "Gotta go, Evers."

The strength of Serenity's optimism delivered a tantalizing fragrance of frosting, French roast … familiarity.

Outside, shards of icy rain pecked at the glass. As a chill invaded her bones, the tease of Louisiana's gentle mid-March warmth stirred a craving.

"Yeah. Me, too. Drowning in audits up here."

Because this was Everley's life.

Predictable.

Safe.

Routine.

"Love you, Evers." Said in marked sincerity like she knew Everley's heart needed reminding.

"Love you, too."

Love they had in common.

Everley's thoughts drifted to the small, varnished pine box Mom had purchased at Vestiges of the Past Antiques in Napoleonville when Everley was in middle school. The Dream Box—as Mom had called it—sat lifeless on the shelf of Everley's bedroom closet. Inside it, Mom's letter, among other sentimental keepsakes.

Drawing in a resolute breath, she claimed the box and sat on her bed. The lid squeaked when she raised it.

Yes, there it was.

Slipping the letter from its envelope, Mom's inked plea wafted upward, mingled with a trace of peppermint and lavender. It gathered volume and aroused memory, her wishes specific, jarring—like the onslaught of another Chicago snowstorm.

Only this time, Everley gave undivided attention to each word, gems strung like a necklace, and inclined her heart to Mom's airy, carefree view of life ...

> *Everley, my dear,*
>
> *If you're reading this, it means I've made my passage into eternity, the place God has prepared for me. No need to shed tears on my behalf. The accommodations here are heavenly.*
>
> *I'm hopeful for a reunion with your Dad, this man of my heart who'd wandered from our marriage bed a wee bit after you were born. But the assignment of one's eternal destiny isn't mine to give.*

A heart that forgives is a heart that is free.

Our quest to visit every continent during our lifetime sputtered to a stop when he died. But four of seven is nothing to sneeze at.

As you know, I've entrusted Moreland Manor to your care.

Deep within her aged wood, brick and plaster and paint, a voice from the past calls. I've heard it, a call to unleash love from places too long denied, bound by pestilent fear.

Love. It's as unyielding as the grave. Somewhere in Song of Solomon, I believe?

It's unfortunate that this persnickety cancer put the brakes on my forward motion. And just as I was making progress on the front entry.

First impressions, you know.

That being said, it's my express desire you will see to Moreland's complete restoration and that you employ none other than Mr. Gabriel Michael Bellevue, owner of G&R Historic Restoration Specialists, to handle all needed repairs. A man named after two celestial beings must be elected by divine design.

In the natural, his qualifications are superior—a New Orleans native highly sought after for historic restoration who has received numerous recognitions in the industry. Perhaps you remember him?

Once he's restored Moreland, I invite you to imagine the possibilities ...

Local artisans from your father's and my art studio could use a gallery to display their craftsmanship.

A Cajun restaurant?

A bed and breakfast for lovers, young and old!

Remember my mention of film actress Cora Lindenberg who paid Moreland a visit while passing through town? Think Hollywood, movie sets, cameras, drama.

Release the dreamer insider you, Everley Orion!

Once Moreland is restored, you are free to indulge in the treasure she holds. I urge you to incline your heart and listen.

Follow her direction, and she will lead your heart home.

Until then, may you always reach for the stars. Now that I'm in company with their Creator, they are an incredible sight to behold!

Love and squeezes, Mom

In labored exhale, she stuffed the letter inside the envelope, rendering it mute.

"Great Scott. What have I done?"

The weight of Moreland's aged wood and brick pressed her shoulders to a slump. Why couldn't life function like numbers? They all behaved with known predictability. Two and two always equaled four. Being overwhelmed by an immensely large object did not a happy girl make.

Mom insisted it had. Till her very last breath.

Where was God in all of this?

The demand rumbled from stony places inside her soul, her mind a calamity.

God owns everything ... the moon, the stars. Calls them each by name.

Or so claimed Dad as the blush of a Louisiana dusk yawned, the sun a sinking orange orb. Like Mom, he was a stargazing eccentric, weekends wrought by Moreland's endless to-do list.

Logic tipped the scales against Everley's faith, creating an unreconcilable mess. A weary whisper drifted from the rise of a familiar ache in her heart. "Oh, God, this is impossible."

With a snap, she shut the box, the sting of a pinched finger surging up her arm. She bit her lip against an expletive. Time to end this nonsense and inform Gabe she had a sister on the loose who'd pulled strings to resurrect Moreland. Full divulgence on social media.

And MidDay had taken the bait.

CHAPTER SIX

Gabe should have warned Carmen long before swiping his key card at the door to his condo after their dinner at Bryan J. Carlyle's highly touted Cajun Cooking School.

"Not a fan of dogs?"

Carmen recoiled at a sharp bark that struck the other side of the door. "Is that …"

"A dog." He flashed a smile.

She answered with a grimace, arms in a knot at her middle.

Bigger smile. "He's real nice."

To the right girl.

The lock disarmed with a hard click. When the door opened a crack, Champ's shiny snout shoved through. Gabe blocked the space with his leg and glanced down. "Back off, boy."

Please don't bite.

A few incessant barks ensued. "Hush now and be nice."

"Sounds awful," Carmen said in vexed displeasure. "Can't you tie him up first?"

Inching through the door, Gabe flipped on the light to see Champ's raised hackles. He bent to nab Champ's collar and countered his forceful pull with a tug.

Eyes rounding, Carmen stumbled back, hands clapped to her mouth in a hard gasp.

"He's harmless. Really." Gabe waved her in, the strength of his best friend thrashing his arm, nearly taking him down.

Head shaking, she lifted her brows and folded her arms. "Me or ... that dog."

His lungs sank in a weighty sigh. "C'mon, Champ," he whispered in the canine's perked ears. "Give it time. You'll warm up to her."

Say, in about a decade.

Despite the playful demonstration of ball toss and retrieval, Champ easing on the show of teeth, Carmen insisted man's best friend be relegated to the corner before they watched a movie.

Slain by Champ's whimper and forlorn eye shifting, Gabe slid the dog bed near his feet. Carmen stiffened and created space.

One more reassuring scrub behind Champ's ears, and he surrendered, snout resting on his paws.

Seated beside Carmen, Gabe clicked the remote, and she snuggled into his shoulder.

His cell vibrated at his hip. "Yeah?"

"Hello, Mr. Bellevue? This is Everley Scott."

At her voice, he jolted, heat curling down his neck. "It's Gabe."

"Sure. Well, the reason I'm calling—"

"Don't be long, wild man," came Carmen's love-drenched purr.

Gabe's conscience fired hot at what had to sound like he was a zookeeper taming a ravenous cougar.

"Is this a bad time?" Everley said, tone a blend of considerate and annoyed.

Perhaps the worst.

"No time like the present. When did you want to go forward on the project? I need to place material orders."

Her tone went frosty, sarcasm seeping through the phone. "Assuming the sale?"

"I see no reason not to, given your momma has entrusted you with her baby."

A big one.

"The problem is financing. Unfortunately, your price tag is far more than I'd expected."

Eyes squeezed shut, he worked to release tension. Sticker shock rarely worked in a contractor's favor. She hadn't called to seal the deal. Meticulous to the core, her resistance to assume responsibility as heiress threatened to cut the mooring of this deal and cast it out to sea.

"Did you hear me, Mr. Bellevue? The cost, while undoubtedly worth every cent, is prohibitive."

"I heard you. And Mr. Bellevue is my father." The sour note delivered a warning.

Carmen tugged on his arm. "We need to get the movie started. I've got an early rehearsal at the theater tomorrow."

Roused, Champ sat up, sounded three sharp barks.

"Back off, Champ! Let Carmen alone."

One dissatisfied canine. Apparently, not a fan of theater.

Between a pawing girlfriend—whose hands roamed dangerously along Gabe's leg—and a haughty heiress, his brain knotted, the disparity between the two women clear as fire-glazed glass.

Everley sounded a sigh. Probably massaging her forehead ... figuring a way out.

"Are you sure this is a good time?"

"It's fine." Drawing a notch at his brow, Gabe waved a staying hand at Carmen, who slunk into a churlish pout, gave attention to her cell.

"Mom left an amount designated for Moreland's restoration, but it covers less than 7 percent." Reticence quivered through Everley's tone. "If I'm to go forward, I'll have to take out a loan to assure I can satisfy your payment schedule, which would require I put Moreland up as collateral—that is, if I even decide to go through with this."

"You'll figure it out."

"Your confidence is admirable."

"I speak truth. But, uh, in the meantime, I've got other project inquiries and need to give them my availability."

Half true.

Shoot. He hadn't meant to deliver his response with finality. If cornered, Moreland's lioness might shred this deal to pieces, despite her momma's wishes to the contrary.

"Listen, the initial reason for my call is, well, crazy, really." The ghost of a chuckle floated through the phone.

"I have yet to be put off by crazy."

"I may be the first."

Yes, in fact, you are. First love. A ceaseless, unforgettable longing. The reason and motivation for everything. The swell of yesterday's matchless desire rose within him and collided with the present.

"Even if it involves your work being filmed by a production company?" The tail end of her tone rang high.

Here came the wrinkle. He paused to take a breath. "I'm listening."

"A MidDay Media producer contacted me regarding Moreland and my obligation to hire you to restore it."

Breathing labored and contemplative, his heart hung suspended from a fragile thread.

"Would you be willing to have a media company film your work?"

Since Serenity's mention at the bakery, he'd allowed the idea to simmer. Carmen snaked her arm across his hips and tugged. "C'mon, hot babe," she whispered in a throaty whisper.

Disparity widened like the Grand Canyon, threatening to shove him off the precipice of an impossible decision.

"They want to use the footage for a pilot to pitch to a network."

At what point had Orderly Everley gone to bat for wild ideas, this one registering a plus-five on a scale of one to pretty darn risky?

"Do they pay out?" he said.

"Yes. Which is the only reason I'd entertain the idea. We'd each be given a talent fee and other perks. I could help you negotiate for sponsorship by supply companies in exchange for advertisement. Or something."

Hope resurfaced, gathered strength. A thread of resistance snapped. He cleared his throat. "What exactly is my part in this film gig?"

At that, Carmen sat upright and turned. Intrigue claimed her gaze. "Film?"

He drew her back to his shoulder, stroking her head to tame interest.

"My understanding is you'd do whatever it is you do. Only difference being we'd have interview segments where I'd share the essence of Mom's letter, the sole reason for Moreland's restoration, and you'd be featured as the guy who's bringing it back to life. The film crew will capture footage of us—my involvement, your involvement. Two distinct roles, client and contractor."

"I'll need to run this by Randy ... pray he'll be agreeable to the idea."

His voice trailed.

"You're asking me to pray?"

"I meant that I will pray he'll be agreeable." He fished for a response to see where she stood in matters pertaining to God, to faith. "But, uh, pray all you like, of course."

"Believe me, I have been."

Encouraging.

"To be honest," she added. "I'm not a fan of making this into a public exhibition, but given your cost, I see no other option."

The low rumble of dry laugh climbed up his throat and spit from his lips. "I'm not adjusting my cost."

"I'm not asking you to, Mr. Bellevue. Hence, the reason I've even entertained the whole thing."

"It's Gabe."

As often as needed, he'd reestablish distance from his last name until it'd etched in Everley's mental circuitry.

"At MidDay's request, I wrote a brief synopsis, detailing the heart of Mom's dying wishes, adding remembrances of what she referred to as the widow's calling, a spooky voice she claimed she'd heard at the house."

Interest perked. "That right?"

"I told you, crazy, isn't it?" She laughed. And when she did, a sliver of joy enveloped him like a blanket out of the dryer in the dead of winter. Because really, he'd bet all it'd been a while since she'd laughed. And he'd been graced with the opportunity to enjoy its music.

"Just to be clear, if we enter into this contract, I expect you to act natural but keep things professional. I'll play my part, and you do what you're trained to do."

Spoken like a dog trainer to a pup, toting a warning that dimmed the sliver of sunshine that'd risen between them.

In an effort to dismantle her doubt, he responded with grace and confidence. "Count on it. I'm your man."

Even if God's intended purpose in this deal amounted to nothing more than a means to enable Moreland's heiress to achieve her endgame ... sell Momma's treasure and presumably get back to her hollowed shell of a life up in the Windy City.

"Very interested. Don Barnhart will be in touch."

Obviously, crazy had worked its magic over the weekend.

A highly competitive industry burgeoning with hopeful visionaries looking to capture the eye of a production company, and they'd picked an obscure CPA with no social media accounts to her name.

It didn't add up.

That afternoon Everley met with Leslie Hewitt, a loan officer who approved her for 80 percent of Moreland's appraised value in present condition. As it turned out, Leslie was from New Orleans, frequented Dazzle Me Art Gallery, and shared Mom's enthusiasm for local artisans. "Did you know your mother painted a wildflower scene for me during a difficult time in my life? To this day, it hangs over my mantle."

Thanks to Mom's act of kindness and Everley's fiscal responsibility, divine favor took the form of an interest deferred loan without rigid draw schedules, plans, or schedules.

Friday afternoon, Everley arrived outside Serenity's bakery to meet with Gabe Bellevue and Don Barnhart. Sucking in rescue breaths to quiet her heart, she stood still outside the front door where new signage dangled overhead.

Hand on her carry-on, she reasoned, "It's 1:40. Plenty of time to change out of these sweltering clothes before they arrive."

When she pushed the door open, she eyed the bathrooms near the back. The smell of pastries and coffee and mellow jazz soothed frayed nerves. Walls held vibrant pops of color unique to Serenity's vision of happy spaces which she'd filled with antiques, artwork, and contemporary metal pieces. As expected, an arrangement of Serenity's signature lavender roses sat near the counter. It wasn't a stretch to believe the floral bouquet was intended to feed her imagination that a Mr. Right had sent them—special delivery.

Everley roved her gaze over the smattering of customers. It fell on a man in a white button-down shirt and dark pants seated at a corner table by a front window. Afternoon sunlight pooled around him, highlighting the distinct features of a prominent individual. Sculpted, dusty gray hair and thick brows shadowed a serious gaze. Definitely didn't fit into the laid-back French Quarter vibe.

Time is money hovered in his eyes.

Was he?

Pulling her tablet from her carry-on, Everley squared her shoulders, summoning the relaxed posture of an heiress. The reason he'd come sniffing out opportunity in an unpredictable game of pin-the-house-on-the-oldest-daughter.

Serenity wore a freakishly pink apron over jeans and a long-sleeved shirt. She toted a large muffin on a turquoise plate and skittered toward Everley for a side hug. "Hey, Evers!" Serenity leaned back and gave her an exceptional once-over. "You so rock that pencil skirt."

Serenity breezed over to the man and set the plate in front of him, the fork clinking as she drizzled greetings. "On the house."

Eyes rising slowly from an open laptop, he drew a notched brow gaze. "Reason being?"

"You're Don Barnhart, right? Big-time film guy? Could we get a selfie together?"

She. Did. Not. Everley tugged the collar of her sweater and scratched at her neck.

The younger and more athletic Lewis sister could stay inbounds on a soccer field but utterly failed at relational boundaries. At Don's slow, acquiescent nod, Serenity skirted the table and plopped into the chair beside him. He tipped his gaze toward her raised cell and strained a grin.

"Mind if I post this to social media?" Her eyes danced over the image on her phone.

At least she'd had the sense to ask. Fate only knew why she'd been relegated to stand backstage in this reality drama.

"Anything to generate viewer interest."

When his gaze caught Everley's, his mouth stretched into a white-toothed smile. Hungry to sign off on a deal. The only thing missing was a dorsal fin.

She smiled back. Far less toothy.

Donning her best Maria Von Trapp, can-do confidence, Everley stepped forward with such exuberance the wheels of her carry-on clipped a chair and toppled onto the stained cement with a hard slap.

Sudden silence drowned happy chatter. Glowers pinged against Everley's face, warmed her cheeks.

Serenity managed to detach herself from fandom and scrambled over. They both bent to right the troublesome carry-on and clunked heads.

"Ouch!" Everley moaned, massaging her head.

Given Serenity's chuckle, the collision hadn't fazed her. In fact, her eyes flared in childlike wonder. "I'm so excited about this media gig, I just can't even—"

"Then maybe you should be my stunt double," Everley said in a seething whisper.

"I could totally do that. I'd just need to dye my hair, part it on the side, wear green contacts ... look all serious, methodical, and super tailored."

Truer words were never spoken.

Drawing in a rescue breath, Everley wheeled her stupid carry-on to the counter with the force of a momma putting a child in time out, then navigated the tables, taking breezy steps toward Don.

At her approach, he stood and proffered his hand, a grip firm and purposeful. "Don Barnhart, Senior Director of Development, MidDay Media. How was your flight, Ms. Scott?"

"Uneventful, thank you. And, please, call me Everley." A certifiable whacko. "I hope you haven't been waiting long?"

"No, no. I arrived early, dictated email, returned phone calls."

Over the dome of his muffin, he lifted a glass of red-tinted tea, a sprig of mint and herbs swirling inside.

"You were right. This is *the* place, corroborated by all the locals."

She flashed a wink at Serenity, the creative half of the two.

Strutting to the case that held her fresh creations, Serenity said, "Want a cupcake, Evers? Or muffin?" She smoothed her hand across the display like a game show hostess. Already rehearsing stunt double.

"No thanks. I'll have my usual. Coke Zero. No ice."

Always the same.

Programmed controls. Minimal risk. Safe and predictable.

Everley sat opposite Don, one eye on the wall clock behind him

1:59.

Angst churned into lead in her stomach. Beneath the table, she ran her palms down her skirt and leggings, feet sweltering inside her boots. "Mr. Bellevue should be here any minute."

Or I'll kill the treasure hunter.

Chin taut, Don nodded. One cheek twisted in a strained grin. "First, let me say Moreland's setting is ideal and meets our production standards, given we'll have multiple crew, equipment, and vendor tents in and around the property." He waved his hands in an animated gesture. "You and your contractor possess that authentic pluck we're looking for, the perfect couple for a network seeking unconventional, non-scripted offerings."

Internal sensors blinked. Everley waved a staying hand. "To clarify, I've not hired him yet, and ... how did you draw the conclusion that we're a couple?"

An impish grin inched the corners of his mouth. "You've got an informative sister."

Sounding a restrained moan, Everley slung a half-lidded glare at Serenity, whose show of innocence was unconvincing.

"Then there's the delicious tension fate has played in all this," Don continued, hope bobbing in his eyes, palms rubbing together in opportunity. "The front-end story ... a dying mother's wishes, a cherished family estate holding rich history, and your noble sacrifice to fulfill her desire."

Leave it to Mom to dominate the meeting from six feet under.

"But we do have concerns." Elbow draped over his chair, Don's gaze drained enthusiasm. "Given the estimated nine-to-twelve months minimum time span to complete the work, noting the strict specifications of ..." He peered at the laptop, lifted a reticent stare at Everley. "G&R Restoration, I'm afraid that would put us way over budget."

A language she understood.

"At present, MidDay has no financial margin outside six months and must adhere to production schedule.

Considering the unpredictability of summer weather here, it's a strong possibility we'd need to reassess to hasten production. Should cost overrun end value at any point, we reserve the right to back out with no further obligation." He sipped his tea, peering at her like a rifleman locked his sights on a doe.

Reason enough for a logical sort to make for the door. And was March always this warm?

She gave her neckline a tug, invited cool air. "Are you saying the contractor is a deal breaker?"

"Well, our account executive says—"

At the sound of the bell, Everley angled a gaze toward the door, one eye latched onto Don, who turned to stare at Gabe, dragging in what appeared to be a crusty, intoxicated old man in tattered clothing who delivered the pungent scent of nicotine and alcohol.

Effectively ushering professionalism out the door.

Bye, bye deal.

CHAPTER SEVEN

Hand pressed to her eyes, Everley splayed her fingers, the sight burning a hole in her chest.

Surely this was all a bad dream.

No. This was real—nothing short of a horribly bad circus act, Gabe as ringmaster.

With one muscled arm wrapped around the wobbly man, Gabe drew up a chair with his free hand, set it against the wall near the front counter, and eased the lax man into it. "Sit yourself here." He patted the air as though restraining an undomesticated animal. "Serenity's got jazz going overhead, so listen to the music. I won't be long."

The man raised apple cheeks over a broken-toothed grin, his pallor sallow. His head lolled to the side and thudded against the post that ran along the wall.

Gabe patted him on the knee and stood to full height, shoulders and chest broad. Skilled hands fit to the ends of long arms, chiseled by hard work.

Don's unflinching gaze darkened. He gave his head a hard shake as if attempting to dislodge the vision. A wrinkle of storm clouds gathered across his forehead.

Turning on dusty boots, Gabe's searching gaze met Everley's open-mouthed stare.

"Tell me this isn't the guy," Don murmured from the side of his mouth.

"It's the guy," she admitted through clenched teeth. Mom's choice.

Like a marigold, a rare flower with heat-loving ways.

Everley released a slow breath, momentarily shut her eyes to darken the vision.

Please, God, help me.

Gabe sauntered over in jeans and an untucked, navy button-down marked by gold insignia.

He thrust a firm hand, the manner of one used to making deals. Calloused hands like a trophy, he claimed victory before ink met paper.

Slowly, Don rose and took it.

Everley stood—if only to run interference should a brawl ensue.

"So you're the big chief who's interested in capturing my work on Moreland." Confidence oozed from Gabe's pores, along with every trace of tact, saved only by the pronounced dimples astride an intoxicating grin.

Impossible to like. Impossible to hate.

The full weight of Don's attention focused on Gabe. A tic pulsed at his temple. "Don. Barnhart. Senior Director of Development, MidDay Media."

"Gabe. Owner, G&R Historic Restoration Specialists."

Gabe turned his engaging smile to Everley and offered his arms.

If only to conceal her irritation, she slipped into his firm hug. Even through the thickness of her sweater, her heart fluttered against his solid chest. The scent of lumber and cotton swirled inside her like ribbons. Reclaiming her senses, she stepped back, barely making eye contact. Because if she lingered in his gaze beyond mere seconds, that magnetic pull of his honey-amber eyes would weaken her resolve, making sense of an increasingly absurd idea.

All six-foot, two inches of his frame dwarfed her five foot, seven inches. Hands cupping her elbows, he stood staring, dimples deepening on his shadowed face. At least he'd kept the auburn grizzle closely trimmed.

"Good to see you, girl." His voice swept low, curled up her spine.

A tell-tale click from behind the counter drew Everley's attention to Serenity, who—cell raised—donned a victory smirk before pulling a Houdini act with her phone.

Everley scowled and sliced her hand across her neck in mock warning. "She's really into that instant snappy gram thing." An awkward laugh spilled out as Everley turned to Don, deflecting the breadth of disparity between her and Serenity.

Countenance now bright, Don swiped his phone and flashed MidDay's instant snappy account Everley's direction. "Good thing. It's how we discovered Moreland. MidDay has harnessed the power of social media to strengthen our fan base and used it to scout out new talent."

From the corner, Gabe's stinking side-sick mumbled nonsense. Hypnotized by jazz, he bobbed his head and played the air sax, fingers wiggling as he tapped his oversized combat boot on the floor.

Gabe shot a thumbs up Serenity's direction.

Since when had the Pear Tree become a daycare for the wayward?

While the resurrected form of Louis Armstrong entertained himself, Everley turned to Don. "If I may, I'd like to speak with Mr. Bellevue for a moment."

Don bowed his head, sat down, and sliced into his muffin.

Giving her hair a sharp swish over her shoulder, Everley clamped a purposed hand to Gabe's elbow—refusing the urge to run a brush through his hair—and directed him toward the vagrant whose lids were now shut in an inebriated slumber. Arms limp in his lap, the man's toes peeped through his boots.

Anchoring her stance in front of Gabe, sarcasm fermented to bubbling rage. "I see you made the effort to don your Sunday best, even dragging in a member of the choir."

Nostrils flaring, Gabe returned a fiery gaze. Ire seeped through clenched teeth. "Hold your fire, Orderly Everley. I am who I am."

Darn sure.

She dragged a labored gaze toward the miscreant, pointed a finger, brow raised high. "What is ... that?"

All trace of civility threatened to vanish as Gabe bowed his chest, his jovial self hardening to granite. "His name is Merrill Downing. He's a vet, a friend, and a fellow human being who deserves your respect."

She riveted fists to her waist. "Why?"

"Made in the image of God. Reason enough."

At the rebuke, she tempered her voice to a near whisper before stepping into a no-fly zone, her defenses weakening at the heady scent of masculinity.

"All right." She drained firepower from her tone. "I didn't come all the way from Chicago for a Rocky versus Apollo match with you. Now that you've arrived for our 2:00 meeting, let's discuss business like ... uh, professionals. Don says he has some concerns."

He bowed his head and swept an arm. "After you, Your Majesty."

Seething, she gave her boot a petulant stomp. "It's Everley."

Serenity pranced over. "Hey, Gabe. Here's your sweet tea. We're giving Merrill another dozen muffins today?"

"Yep. Thanks, Hotshot." He took the glass, reached into his pocket, and handed her a twenty. Overpaying by, oh, thirteen dollars.

The knit of Everley's brows unwound at Gabe's compassion.

How did he engage people like that, getting them involved in the care of others? Take notice of the unnoticeable and love so deeply?

It covers a multitude of sins.

Blinking at the thought, she took sobered steps back to the table and Gabe sat in the chair on the other side of Don.

Everley eased into her chair with the grace of a queen, turned to Don. "Sorry to keep you waiting. Now, regarding your concerns?"

Don concentrated his attention on Gabe, who'd only just removed what felt like a longing stare at her before he matched Don's level gaze. "Mr. Bellevue—"

"Gabe."

In deference to Everley's minimal nod, Don cleared his throat and proceeded. "The price tag you've given is $350K for a home likely worth about a fraction of that in present condition."

"It was appraised for six hundred, twenty-four thousand," Everley interjected—and, just as quickly, questioned why she'd come to Gabe's rescue.

"Surprising, honestly ..." Don turned a stupefied grin on Everley before he turned back to Gabe. "Networks don't typically fund homeowners in reality shows, but because we believe this to be a viable project, we're prepared to grant you the expected profit margin you'd typically charge the homeowner if you're willing to do the work at cost."

In whispered murmur, Everley did the math, gaze bobbing as she forced the figures to reconcile. They weren't.

A restrained sigh wheezed out.

"Since we're asking for spotlight interview segments in addition to filming the work in progress, each of you will receive a talent fee of two grand each day on the set."

Pennies, really.

"Everley, in addition, you'll be paid a day rate for property usage. Subject to negotiation, you can set that as you see fit."

Given that Moreland's utility costs and annual property taxes—and a whole host of other expenses—fell to her, the measure of control in the midst of a costly undertaking was a blessing.

An impassive stare climbed over Gabe's face. He rotated his glass with his fingers. "I've already given Ms. Scott my best price."

The old man's snore erupted behind her. She cocked a wild-eyed glance over her shoulder and trailed it back to Gabe, an act of desperation she pulled off with unbridled authenticity. "Considering your generous spirit, I can't imagine you'd pass on a chance to help a damsel in distress." Now she'd sunk to fluttering her lashes, failing in her effort to ignore the effect his rakish hair had on her when it fell along strongly defined features.

In her periphery, Don's head alternated between them as though watching Wimbledon, awaiting a victor, feasting on crumbs of tension.

Gabe leaned forward, tone impassive and throaty. "If said damsel is in need of lightbulb replacement. But my estimate says she needs rotted hardwood removed, salvaged, and repurposed where possible, plumbing and electrical brought to spec, a new roof, window and door restoration, interior and exterior painting, replastering, customized molding—that alone could take four to six months." He swept a hand upward. "Sheesh. And that landscaping."

"Are you refusing the job, then?" Don said.

He concentrated his stare on Everley and drew a hopeful gaze. "Not if she'll have me." Heat simmered beneath her skin before he turned back to Don. "Problem is, your timeline is a heck of a squeeze play, a mighty big deviation from the way I operate." Sparks flew above his clenched jaw, words sawing through. "I don't play nicely when rushed. Historicals have to be handled with care."

Don flinched, shifted in his seat.

Gabe cut Everley a look, tone tinged by a sorrowful plea. "Moreland's no good left unfinished, Orderly."

"Well aware, Mr. Bellevue."

Between rapid heartbeats, jagged edges of despair sawed at her lungs.

"Look," Gabe said, "I'll do what I can within MidDay's time schedule with no guarantee of completion, or you'll need to find yourself a contractor who can perform miracles."

God can do the impossible.

Or so said Mom as she hammered or painted in and around the house, forever humming that same hippie tune.

I live one day at a time. I dream one dream at a time …

Defeat slumped Everley's shoulders.

Haunting whispers of Mom's final wishes wound around her brain and twisted it to knots. How had she allowed herself to hob-nob with an executive producer, talking lights, camera, action in her sister's bakery?

"Enough of this." Everley shot from her chair and gave both men a nod. "Sorry I wasted your time, gentlemen."

With a slam, she shut the virtual lid on that Dream Box, trapping foolish, unreasonable risk inside. And dared anyone to prod her to open it again.

"You lost the deal?" Randy's heated disdain thawed the space of Gabe's office. The criticism socked him in the gut, nearly doubling him over.

He lowered his gaze, mindlessly tracing tiles. "She's refusing to sign. Can't afford me."

"You mean us," Randy barked. "Your decisions—all of them—affect me, the staff, our crew."

A slow boil burned in his chest, steamed behind his ears. The terror of one wrong decision crawled like ink through a sponge. Gabe pivoted toward the wall and threw a fist into it, sending Champ to tuck tail and scuttle into the hallway.

"Settle down, boss," Randy said, tone droll. "There's still the Cantrell project."

"And after that?"

Angst tugged his chin to his chest. The image of an incoming tsunami emerged, the darkness of cresting, inescapable waves intent on destruction.

"Let's hope this connection you've got with Murdock is fruitful."

"It hinges on a proposal."

"What?" he thundered. "When?"

"At the gala in his honor. Riverside Resort and Hotel. Murdock will announce that he's awarded G&R a reno deal and then I ... propose."

Randy's arms raised in frustration. "Ask the man for an advance then. A lead. Anything."

"I've got a media following in the thousands. Subscribers to my YouTube channel are increasing, and I've been featured in reputable trade magazines. We're good."

Like a snowman in the Sahara.

"Yes, but at some point, you've stopped pedaling and coasted along, become dependent on a guy like Murdock who, quite honestly, doesn't need our business. This arrangement is merely a favor because you're a nice guy. If he has a mind to cut us loose, he loses nothing."

At that moment, Gabe ached to talk to his spiritual mentor. In middle school, Adam Carmichael took him under his wing and taught him all he knew, while Dad played a reckless game of attempt and fail.

Adam believed in Gabe. Invested in him.

Blasted car crash. Snuffed the life of one really good man.

Be that good man.

Don't know how.

Sinking into the wall, Randy released a blustery sigh. "Things ain't looking too good for sustaining my family, Gabe. We really needed that Moreland deal."

The thought shuddered through him, weakened his knees. "I'll figure something out." Fear stood at the precipice of ruin, threatened to pull him into its yawning canyon.

Dad lost that fight.

Gabe refused to lose it.

A knock sounded from the entrance door. Champ's bark pierced the air.

Gabe whistled and clapped. "Get over here, boy."

Champ trotted back to Gabe's office and sat at his feet by the desk, poised to defend.

Peering from his open door into Special K's office, Gabe squinted through the frosted glass. At the unmistakably feminine form of Everley, he turned to Randy, tipped his chin to the ceiling, and raised his arms in hallelujah chorus. "Well, now, if that ain't the client of a lifetime."

Randy's eyes clouded with derision. "Not if she only needs you to paint her mailbox."

Gabe took buoyant steps back to stand aside his desk where Champ held himself in admirable restraint. Panting, his lids shifting in eagerness.

Anticipation sifted through him as K ushered her to his office where Everley Lewis Scott now colored the space of his door. Everley's approachable smile froze Gabe's boots to the floor.

High. School. Crush.

He swallowed around a boulder in his throat, pulse racing in the presence of the only one who'd ever held the power to tie his tongue in knots.

"Ah. Orderly," he said, tamping down his nerves. "Lightbulb out?"

Mailbox need painting? *Anything.*

She returned a playful leer, layers of that luscious rusty hair grazing her shoulders. "Funny, Gabe."

His name on her lips sparked arousal.

That and the scent of gardenia. A darn aphrodisiac.

Gabe caught a glimpse of Randy's impish smile, which quickly vanished when she turned to him. "Hi, Randy. Good to see you again."

Kindness claimed her countenance. Tone easy, soothing. Wholly vulnerable.

"And you," Randy answered with a nod.

A canine whine.

Stern eye on Champ, Gabe pointed a finger. "Stay." He walked over to Everley and raised a hand to the jamb, fingers gripped to the casing. "If you need recommendations for another contractor, I'm afraid I can't help you."

"I came to apologize."

Okay. Shoot.

He lowered his arm, now limp at his side.

Idiot.

Behind him, Champ's moan smacked of condescension.

Posture uneasy, she released a fragile sigh. Her engulfing scent crumbled his wall of defensive to dust.

"Can we talk?" She angled a woeful gaze, the look of a girl who'd skittered past a stinking bar on Canal Street bar.

Act pressed for time. He glanced at his cell. "I can spare, oh … about ten minutes."

No. All the time you want.

At the half-truth, Randy's smirk burned a hole in Gabe's stomach.

"I won't be long. I've got a seven o'clock flight to catch." She worked her lower lip between her teeth. Unlike her typical fiercely determined self—very much the way he'd left her at the Pear Tree two hours previous, stomping all over the deal of the century.

"Sure, then."

With a sweep of his arm, he removed the barricade of his body, waved her into his office, and let his eyes roam the view as she walked ahead of him. Time had transformed the shapeless numbers girl into one attractive woman. That air of superiority was pleasantly subdued by girlish innocence. Helpless almost.

Beautiful.

Champ bounded forward.

"Sit!"

At Gabe's command, Champ skidded to a stop at her feet and sat. Mouth parted, no hint of aggression. The endearing rescue panted, pink tongue sagging aside shiny, black gums, a scrutinizing gaze shifting in hopefulness.

"Oh, how cute." Her eyes twinkled to match the pinpricks of light dancing in Champ's sappy eyes.

Champ whimpered, tail wagging.

The entirety of Gabe's family—right there.

Everley glanced at Gabe, a hand poised to pet his best friend. "May I?"

A shiver zipped down Gabe's spine. He exchanged glances with Randy, who turned a knowing gaze away, profile holding the stretch of a smile.

"S-sure. Pet away." Gabe stepped back and widened his stance. Keeping guard, in case Champ had a change of heart.

Everley stooped to scratch Champ's neck who then raised his moist snout, shamelessly begging more.

The shift in Gabe's soul tremored beneath his skin.

She leaned close, rubbing elegant fingers behind Champ's relaxed ears, soliciting a soulful moan to liquify metal. "You're so sweet," she crooned, a dazzled gaze fixed on the love-sick animal. "What's ... uh ..." She ducked to steal a peek beneath his front legs. "*his* name?"

Gabe laughed low. "Champ."

The Bride Finder.

Jealousy zipped through him as her able fingers threaded through Champ's fur, rendering the sappy canine to a near trance-like state.

"Hey there, Champ." Tone playful and tender—undaunted by a full set of canines—she hugged his neck. Her red tresses blended with his coat like strawberry syrup over vanilla ice cream on a hot summer's day.

Cupping Champ's head, she wrinkled her nose and chuckled when he swiped her lips with a slobbery lick.

Lucky dog.

She swallowed Champ in a hug, guarded persona now faded. After one last pat, she stood and brushed her skirt. Her ivory neckline rose over a white blouse that peeked from behind her gray jacket and emphasized her pleasing form.

Perfect, really—if he were looking.

Ahem. Busy, remember? "You wanted to talk?"

"Oh. Right." She glanced at Randy.

Gabe cut him a sidelong 'make like a tree and leave' glance.

A coy grin converged with a smug expression. At the door, Randy jutted a chin and turned. "Gotta take care of some things. Good to see you, Ms. Scott."

"You, too."

Randy's gaze brimmed hopeful before he turned to go.

The afternoon sun cast shadows long, mellowing the walls. Gabe pulled a chair for High School Crush—er, potential client. When she sat, Champ cozied at her feet like he'd reunited with his human at long last.

Gabe perched on the edge of his desk and thrust his tongue inside his cheek. "What's on your mind?"

She tugged the hem of her skirt and wrenched a tremulous fist inside her palm. "Sorry for the way I acted earlier, the things I said about your street friend, your appearance."

Stone-walled places in his heart loosened at her surrendered spirit. "No worries. Merrill's got a heart bigger than the state of Louisiana. Half the time, he's drunker than Cooter Brown and won't remember a thing."

A hesitant laugh puffed out, sounding a might rusty from disuse.

"I wanted to let you know I agreed to MidDay's terms and signed the contract. Set a location fee of two grand a day to ease restoration expenses."

Hands clasped over one knee, he leaned in. "That so?"

Red lips stretched into a satisfied smile, she nodded.

"Am I still a part of that package?"

"I hope so ... if you're still willing to move forward and can agree to the film aspect of things."

More than willing. Desperate for work.

"I've never completed restoration on a manor house in six months. But for you, I'll do my best."

Everley's gentle nod followed a wandering gaze, swallowed by a distant stare before settling back on him. "It would be wrong to entrust Mom's house to anyone else."

"Hate that you've been cornered into this, all because of a letter."

Resolve sparked hot in her emerald gaze. "My decision is independent of that obligation. Anything associated with my name needs to be quality work."

"Good to hear you take ownership."

She fanned a retreating smile, lashes dusting over cheeks tinted pink.

Scrounging for cool, he circled his thumbs as if this were no bigger deal than switching out an air filter. "I'll draft the documents, shoot you an email. E-sig is fine ... given the distance between us."

She unwound her hands and expelled a long stream of air, tapping the heels of her winter boots on the floor as though she ached to slip into a breathable weave.

"I say let's give MidDay the authenticity they're after, and ..." Everley lifted a shoulder in a carefree gesture. "Have fun with it."

Her smile buttered his insides. Sunlight streamed through slats of a partially shuddered window.

She broke their prolonged stare, taking contemplative gaze with her as she leaned to scratch Champ beneath his chin in a manner that suggested she needed the comfort a dog could give. "Time away will consume vacation days, result in significant schedule disruption, but the work needs to be done so I can list the house."

At that, Gabe eased off the desk and pierced a glare. "You're not going to keep her?"

She shifted, ire sparking in her emeralds. "It's just a house."

"*Your* house, Orderly."

"Everley."

"Right," he bit back.

Champ barked.

Gabe shushed his meddling pal.

Because what Everley did with Moreland was her business. He served merely as the hired help.

Gabe's phone buzzed. A text from Carmen, photo attached. Her puckered, sultry gaze, arms cinched at her side to accentuate a buxom chest, shot heat across his neck. He turned the cell over on his desk. "That's my fiancé."

Instantly, he hated himself for attempting to hurt Everley, coddling fantasy that she'd missed out on a great opportunity.

Lines of uncertainty drew around her flustered gaze.

He stole a glance at her left hand. Found it ringless.

With the force of a rocket at lift-off, she stood, lids lowered in scrutiny. "Any reason you felt the need to clarify your status?"

He matched her stance. Hitched his jeans. "Just thought I'd save you from thinking I had ulterior motives here."

A wry smile pasted to her lips. She delivered her response in terse syllables. "On the contrary. Happy for you."

Her struggle to appear indifferent hadn't escaped his notice.

Battle-ready, Champ hopped to all fours and turned a well-deserved snarl in his direction.

"Hush," Gabe muttered, the strength to dominate his best friend withering.

She stepped back, rigid in irritation at what'd sunk to a near catfight. "Thanks for your time, Gabe. I'll be in touch."

He escorted his new client to the front entrance, the open door giving way to a throng of late afternoon traffic. The reedy and organic scent of the Gulf Coast wafted in. Moist afternoon air swallowed his breath.

She eased past him. In slow turn, she caught his gaze and tilted her head. "The cheerleader mention. Why'd you vote for me?"

Reticence claimed his face. "You were chasing a dream."

Gratitude blazed in her emeralds, intensified her beauty. A prolonged stare accompanied her sluggish, backward steps as she graced him with a shy grin, waved a limp hand, and turned to go.

CHAPTER EIGHT

The receipt of Everley's e-signature washed over Gabe like a spring rain over dry earth and flowered hope inside. Per typical fee structure, he'd stipulated 25 percent upfront, 50 percent paid midway, and the balance due at project completion. In an email response to her comprehensive and detailed questions, he explained that he paid his subcontractors upfront and ordered specialized wood from an overseas supplier, requiring cash to cover costs.

"Once I sign the one from MidDay's account officer, we're good to go."

Subject to change, MidDay's wordy terms and conditions and projected six-month production schedule through September included the possibility of project extension should funding be procured.

To Gabe's surprise, Randy agreed to the deal. "Anything to gain exposure apart from riding Murdock's coattails."

Heretofore referenced as *talent*, Gabe would receive two thousand per film day. Highlighted in yellow ...

If talent is found in default of this Agreement, MidDay reserves the right to terminate said contract ... no obligation to render fees thereafter.

Whatever. His fingers just itched to get going.

Because what he'd estimated to take three months at the chancellor's house shrank to two after last week's rapid start, coupled with a client request to curtail several updates. They'd likely complete the project by the end of May.

Early April delivered the usual humid breezes. Mellow sunlight filled a blue sky and blanketed Moreland's lawn. The anticipation of seeing Everley sideswiped Gabe's emotions and stirred up angst. Funny how desire freezes inside a guy's heart until thawed to life by an unexpected encounter. But a man edging near the offer of a ring to another woman had no business giving his high school crush further consideration.

Gravel pinged against the underbelly of Gabe's truck as he pulled into the partially shaded southside drive. He parked behind a silver, two-door rental.

The property teemed with about sixty or so Hollywood types, outfitted with earphones and mics, pointing direction. Cables tethered to film equipment and computer screens snaked over the lawn. Backlighting umbrellas were stationed behind cameras. Food vendors set up beneath canopies near the south wing delivering the savory scent of fried chicken, grilled pork, and shrimp pies.

Randy met Gabe beside the truck. A withered sigh streamed out as he momentarily gazed at the house. Head shaking, lines around his eyes underscored worry.

"Restoring the mighty Moreland will take a miracle," Randy said.

A string of concern pulled tight, threatened to snap. "I'm believing him for one." Gabe crossed one boot over the other in a relaxed slump against his truck, urging his words to reach his heart.

"Unexpected things happen in this business. Material orders are delayed, weather goes crazy, and employees get sick."

The warning finger-tapped down his spine in a wicked shimmy. Is this the kind of shiny deal that sent Dad into an unrecoverable pit of failure? Eyes darting from one opportunity to the next, fiercely determined to build a business without counting the cost.

Fear hissed, threatened to explode. The swell of optimism punched it back. "Janet secured electric and plumbing. I'll bring in Silas for carpentry and landscaping when time comes."

Out on the lawn, Everley stood before a man bearing significance. Nodding and all agreeable at his direction, she wore a fitted, white dress to showcase a nice set of legs. Beside her, a woman pushed Everley's coppery mane from her shoulders and adjusted a mic to her neckline.

Not all redheads could pull off white.

This one can.

He leaned to glance at his reflection in the side mirror, finger-combed his hair, and scrubbed hands down an unshaven face.

The look was roughhewn. Like the wood he handled.

He trekked his gaze across the lawn. Sunlight and shadows layered a colorless palate. The first time out, he hadn't noticed the extent of the bleak landscape. Maybe because his interaction with Everley was equally colorless, the way she stiff-armed the house, a fortress of reluctance squeezed inside cold, professional attire. Something ... *something* stood between homeowner privilege and her ability to care.

Tools at his hips, Gabe ambled over. Her glare measured a solid five on the Richter scale of disapproval and quaked through him.

A mere ten minutes late didn't justify a sour greeting.

For one agonizing second, he considered doing a one-eighty, leaving her—and the once-in-a-lifetime deal—in the dust. Until the forgotten mantra of Dad's wisdom surfaced, urged him forward.

If you're gonna do a job, give it all you got, Gabriel.

The formidable character beside Everley wore a black ball cap, tennis shoes, jeans, and a collared shirt. At Gabe's approach, he offered his hand. "Alex Coleman. Head cinematographer and director."

So, puffed up film guy.

"You must be Gabriel Bellevue." He gave a sharp nod, shading what looked to be glassy gray eyes to match the silver and black ends curling along his neck.

Gabe took his hand in a hard clasp. "It's Gabe."

Thumbs touching, Alex framed his hands and turned toward the veranda. "Josiah Banner is assistant cinematographer establishing shot over there." Turning back to Gabe, he took the posture of a father to a rogue son, tone laced in condescension. "You'll listen to my direction, set up where I need you." A smirk crinkled his gaze. "That is, when you're not, you know, pounding nails and hanging wallpaper and such."

Okay, puffed up and incredibly ignorant film guy.

"As I was telling Everley," Alex said, "you'll simply detail the problems you see from a construction standpoint as she leads you in and around the place. We clear?"

Nerves jangled. He gave his jeans an upward tug and nodded.

Don't screw this up.

Alex turned and motioned to Josiah, who jaunted over. Outfitted with a harness crisscrossed at his chest, Josiah stood beside his equipment, beard dark and eyes shrouded in seriousness. Circling his finger, Alex landed a glance of authority at the rest of the crew behind him, his carriage like one whose mantle was lined with Emmys.

Probably was.

The keeper of the digitized clapperboard shut the clap stick and took steps backward.

Behind them, Moreland's stately columns rose to create a magical backdrop and overshadowed the weathered front door. Light emerged in her lonesome eyes. Hopeful.

You're the one who'll save Moreland.

He turned to Everley. Yesterday's crush now wholly woman. A coy smile sweetened her countenance—caught his breath. Desire's red zone blared white-hot, short-circuited his brain. Shoving caution aside, he leaned in and whispered, "You look good."

Insanely beautiful.

A blush colored her cheeks. She smiled over jittery breath. "Thanks."

Three-point play. Set up, toe on the line. Eye fixed on the basket and ...

Slowly, she broke his stare, invitation coursing into her gaze. "Show you around?"

"Lead the way, Ms. Scott," he smiled back, flashing a wink for show. Or not.

At their interlude, Alex scuttled closer, moved within Gabe's periphery, the look of a fisherman who'd felt a tug on his line.

Everley traipsed the crumbled steps to the front door, its dull varnish bubbled over old layers. As she opened it, the hinges creaked beneath the burden.

Inside, the stillness of death hovered. Echoes of the past gonged. The smell of age, dust, and wood seeped afresh into Gabe's pores. Prodded his urge to fix the broken.

The grand entry featured double parlors to the right, an elegant cross hall to the left, a music room, and a downstairs bedroom suite. Gabe led Everley between two fluted, Corinthian columns that flanked the foyer and gently interrupted a triumphal arch. The hall concluded at a curved, floating staircase.

Behind them, the crew scrambled in. Motioning, Alex directed Josiah to pan the entryway, maneuver the electronic eye along the fissured wall, and up the stairs covered in faded burgundy carpet.

A crystal chandelier dulled by dust hung suspended from an ornamental ceiling rose. Everley tipped her gaze and glanced around. Unrest dimmed her gaze. Rubbing her arms, she shuddered as though something dark had spooked her, aroused unpleasant memory.

He moved a pointed finger along the floor, pressing the toe of his boot. "The pinewood flooring needs refinishing here, planks replaced in several places. I'm guessing there'll be rotted joists."

Plaster flaked above the cypress molding that topped the dining hall entry. A light operator rotated, narrowing the beam to trace Gabe's finger along the wall. "That'll need replastering."

From another angle, the man maneuvered a tungsten light near Everley's head, streaking strands of gold through her hair.

The beam found her eyes and glinted starlight in them. She pinned arms to her ribcage. "Can't you just drywall it?"

To her question, he shook his head. "Plaster is superior. A better insulator, sound blocker. Plus, it can heal its own cracks and pull carbon dioxide from the air."

Her gaze roving the interior, she nodded intrigue.

"That and the National Historic Registry prohibits the use of modern materials in order to assure the original remains intact, particularly the outside."

A girl with her smarts had to know this. The idea she'd play dumb to elevate him emboldened him.

Moving on, she led him to the single-story south wing, which housed a small, working kitchen that adjoined a dining hall and opened to the parlor at the front of the house. A screened-in porch off the kitchen looked out toward the top of the drive and grove beyond it.

The downstairs tour concluded in the two-story north wing that contained a library, immense ballroom, the original kitchen, and service rooms. From there, they scaled the stairs, and he addressed needs within the rooms.

In stealthy movement, the crew padded behind Gabe and Everley, capturing dialogue like crows snatching crumbs.

Costs racked up in his brain on this second pass through. Back at the landing, a weighty breath left his lungs, words rolling off his tongue. "This could end up being more than I originally bid."

She angled a stunned gaze. "Even factoring the 10 percent margin I agreed to for unforeseen issues?"

"Yep." He nodded, parted his feet, crossed arms at his chest. And so wishing he could retract the crass response intended to convey confidence.

Turning with her back to the wall, she sighed against it. A look of desperation tugged at her brow.-"But Gabe. It's already … too much … I just … can't."

Tears glistened. Her chin quivered, the rumble of a sob chugging upward. This wasn't for show.

Ah, no. Please, don't.

Eva, I need you to believe in me.

How can I when your unbridled generosity has priced you right out of business again, Dalton?

Conscience nagged.

He needed this job—one whopper of an opportunity without Murdock's inky fingerprints on it. To restore

Moreland was to restore and protect his name. Rebuild what Dad had messed up.

Silence fell among the crew skittering around them, gorging on raw authenticity. Reveling in unscripted hardship.

A holy presence swooped in. Breezed across Gabe's heart and loosened the grip on grizzly self-determination. He placed his hands low on her waist, held her gaze, assumed the posture of a father to an anxious child. "I'll do whatever is needed, however long it takes, and keep to bid."

The crew crouched, steps nimble and intentioned. An imposing mic hovered between them like a swollen caterpillar on a stick.

Everley blinked, gratitude rounding her gaze. "But … you're worth every cent."

At that, he could've called it a day, her affirmation patching up splintered places.

Believe in me.

Heart thundering, he fixed an unwavering gaze on her face … held it … moved it to her lips. Secret desire burgeoned. If he could hold her—kiss her. What would it have been like? The urge billowed hot inside.

Rendered trance-like, Everley stepped closer. Romantic tension pulsed between them. A tinge of longing alighted in her eyes. Made him forget he was obligated to another. In that moment, he hated himself for not chasing after his crush years ago—the reason behind everything he did back then.

Mmmm, that gardenia encircling her neck …

Jerking him from the jaws of unrecoverable mistake, film guys moved in and raised a floodlight.

Lids flickering, Everley drew back. A disconcerting gaze claimed her eyes. "Let's, uh, go take a look at the north side of the house."

Perplexity had him raking his hands through his hair and returning a slow nod.

For all his ability to fix things, he could not reason how a guy had been privileged to stand close enough to hold someone he had no right to lay claim to but who'd roused invitation otherwise.

At the landing, he smoothed a hand along the railing's wounded wood and offered Everley his right arm. Chin firmed, she looped her arm in his, and they descended.

To her right, Alex skipped past, reaching the entry, gesturing direction to the crew as they made their way outside and around to the back of the house.

He moved a cozy arm over her shoulder.

She didn't resist.

The sun had climbed higher. Shadows stretched to the edge of a grove of magnolia, pine, and oak. A jagged pattern of laid brick led from the back porch and ended before a panorama of wide-open space, the vast acreage covered in field grasses.

Gabe swept his arm over the view. "Thousands of acres of sugar cane were harvested here, once a booming business." Or so said K, babbling off snippets of initial research.

At her shrug of indifference, Gabe guided her back to the front and onto the veranda.

Murmurs rife with dictation, Hollywood maintained close proximity.

A warped plank creaked beneath his boots. How'd he miss this?

Grinning, Everley lightly jabbed his ribs. "Hey. I lost you."

No. I lost you. Years ago.

He clutched his side, faking gunshot wound, and worked up a pretend grimace. A wink disarmed her smirk.

He glazed her pretty face with a lopsided smile, cupped a hand over his mic, angled his head, and delivered a throaty whisper near her ear. "Just studying your place, Ms. Scott."

"Cut!" Alex's bark boomed in Gabe's ears.

Josiah's shoulders sank, disapproval skating over his face. "This is no time for whispers." He chopped the air with his hand.

Everley turned to Alex. "Need us to run that again?"

"No." Alex gave his head a blustery shake. "Up until Gabe went radio silent on us, it's all been terrific." A disused smile emerged over a bristled countenance. "In fact, that's a wrap."

At that, Alex directed Hollywood off the property.

The glow of a job well done dimmed as Everley's gaze went pensive, sinking in dusk's encroachment beyond the highway, amber and lavender hues descending on the fringe of distant oaks.

That something again.

Shoulder flattened against a column, arms pressed to her middle, her tone went all icy. "Just so we're clear, no matter what manner of magic you perform on this place, I've no intention of keeping it."

The stillness of a frozen Chicago morning enticed Everley to break away from number crunching at a client site and give a wink to online historic house restoration. Turned out, Gabe maintained an active YouTube channel featuring tutorials for laymen and professionals.

Yesterday's post, a plea for old window restoration ... "Old-growth wood used to construct historic homes has survived what newer, pre-fab materials cannot." Wrapped in irresistible confidence, worn jeans perfectly fitted to his solid frame, Gabe took sure-footed steps down a front porch and paused to prop his hand against a column. A streak of sunlight caught fire in his bronzed hair. "If you're blessed to own such a gem, do the house a favor and hire a professional who's got an eye for beauty and a drive to restore the broken."

In short order, she became one more among his twenty-five thousand subscribers.

Aside from his propensity to be late and his penchant for strays, Gabe's qualifications left no room for criticism. A quick perusal of his website had her eyes roving down the list of customer reviews.

"It's good to know excellence and integrity still exist ..."

And another. "We've used G&R for our home on several occasions. Never had an issue. Fast, friendly, and efficient service."

Still scrolling. "After my house flooded, Gabe gave me a fair and reasonable estimate. He and his crew worked the entire day and treated the place like his own. He replaced insulation, sheetrock, baseboards, shoe molding, wood flooring. All to spec. No way I'd trust my house to anyone else."

Not sure what possessed Everley to slay Gabe with her agenda to sell Moreland minutes after the first day's filming earlier that week. He'd performed flawlessly, skilled hands smoothed along walls in need of capable touch. But the lingered stare fraught with passion, a lazy arm around her shoulders as they strolled the property, almost playing the role of joint ownership ...

She and Gabe were all wrong.

More so, stirring love's stagnant waters was all wrong. Foolish was the girl who attached her heart to a guy who crawled over roofs for a living like they were basketball courts.

At that, Everley sat hard against her chair and hugged her arms, the boom of her heart demanding attention.

Gabe was the best.

Mom, you knew it.

Guilt churned. Had she been too abrupt, telling him she refused to keep the house?

Yes.

No.

Um, okay, yes.

Uh-uh.

And ... *yes.*

The mental whiplash had her assessing enterprise risk management. Had she lost all reason hiring a full-scale specialist while involving a production company?

Did risk outweigh opportunity?

What might come of two industry professionals chasing different outcomes? One racing against time and constrained by budget against another determined to do the job right however long it took?

To be certain, her contractor had a camera-worthy smile, undaunted by media with enough charisma to upend a convent. But how would she track progress, assure Gabe wouldn't fumble under pressure while a film crew hovered? What if that recklessly kind heart of his stooped to employ poorly educated ruffians? Free-spirited folks, who traipsed through life?

Like Mom and Dad.

Creatures of the Woodstock era, a perfect fit among a rogue gathering of deviates. Scads of pictures Mom had taped to scrapbook pages, dried flowers poking out, gave evidence to the mind-set of these two crazy daisies who were nourished by carrots and water. One photo of Dad showed him barefoot and shirtless, wearing faded bell-bottoms and sporting a grizzled beard. Arms outstretched, his head was slung backward as though worshipping the stars.

Seated cross-legged beside him, Marigold Summerfield Lewis with her stringy, russet hair and flouncy skirt … palms upturned at her knees … a thin-lipped expression mellowed to the point of altered consciousness.

Stoned, Mom had unabashedly admitted, at peace beyond the point of ecstasy.

Maybe some things were beyond internal control and strategic planning.

Like matters of the heart.

The following Saturday, Everley met Margot for an early dinner at Navy Pier on Lake Michigan, spring's temperature reaching midsixties.

"I've seen him, you know." Full lips quirked to elicit a response, Margot's voice was evocative and swiped a cool rush over the table.

A breeze teased through Everley's hair, restrained in a tight knot. "Who him?"

Their waitress approached, a new hire not yet schooled in Everley's usual. "Burger, well done, on a toasted sourdough bun. Lettuce, tomato, pickles. No cheese. A side of fries. Coke Zero. No ice, please."

"Same," Margot said. "Only unsweetened tea. Generous ice."

When the waitress turned to go, Margot flashed her cell, leaned in, and whisper-shouted. "Your contractor. All snuggly with some floozy named Carmen."

Unbidden, Everley's stomach jumped. Thick clouds marched past a blinking sun, shadowing the pier.

The caption told all.

Hearts heard breaking over New Orleans as Gabriel Bellevue of G&R Historic Specialists gets serious with Warren Murdock's only daughter, Carmen. Will she be the favored recipient of a ring?

Everley perused the tantalizing image of a clean-shaven Gabe, hair neatly slicked in place, broad shoulder glued to the glitzy socialite. Her toothsome smile matched the blood-red of her sequined dress, a neckline that plunged enough to make the devil blush. The grasp she had on his muscled arm had to smart, though nothing in his countenance spoke discomfort.

Pronounced grooves beside Gabe's mouth softened the gleam in his enigmatic eyes. Breathlessly handsome looks that should be outlawed and tempted a girl to exhume thoughts long since buried. And darn if she could almost smell the fresh-cut wood and success he delivered.

Further thoughts of Gabe were disrupted when her burger and fries arrived. Uncapping the ketchup, she squeezed, meticulously drizzling the fries ... losing herself in the artistry ... working to forget the unsolicited update. "Interesting."

Margot managed to pluck her stare from her cell, set it down. Fingers laced on the table, she leaned in. "The spark in your eyes speaks of envy. And the guy is light-years from interesting," she rebuffed, brows wiggling in provocative dance. "You two pair up nicely."

Legs crossed, Everley pumped her foot. "Don't be ridiculous."

Palms to the table, Margot prodded. "Don't you believe in destiny? Matches made in heaven?"

In the distance, amber dusk blushed along Lake Michigan's charcoal-glazed surface. A deepening azure sky held winking starlight and a sliver of waxing moon. A beautiful and fearless display of God's splendor. Instinctively, she dipped her head, interlaced her fingers, and shut her eyes ...

May your dreams be bold, and may your faith take you there.

A sharp cough jolted Everley upright. Her gaze collided with Margot's puzzled stare. "What'd you do, go to church on me?"

She responded with a condescending chuckle. "No matter the outcome, I'm selling Moreland once it's market-ready."

"And dishonor your mother?"

A harsh gurgle sounded as Margot sipped hard through her straw.

"Not much she can do about it."

"Listen, Ev, my mother died when I was in college, and she hasn't stopped talking since. A Ziegler family gift, I suppose." Contemplation played at her brow. A churlish giggle bubbled up. "That or I'm being haunted for spreading the rumor in middle school that I was rescued from a rogue band of gypsies."

"It's honorable enough that I've kept Moreland from being razed."

"It'd honor her more if you'd put your heart into it."

A heart duly shielded and bearing chinks of defeat. All because she'd let the promise of forever love woo her to its playing field.

"This venture is merely a business arrangement, Margot. Once Moreland is restored, I'll be able to return to my, my—"

"Boring life," Margot spit out. "Confined to known and measurable parameters."

A sudden rush of cold seeped into Everley's bones, the curl of clouds trudging over the sky, stealing the remainder of the sun's warmth. Going for unperturbed, she pinched a few drizzled fries—now limp and cold—ketchup dribbling down her fingers.

"I think you're afraid to put yourself out there." A sassy smirk punctuated Margot's challenge.

"I'm the one who agreed to allow a film company on the property, a bold move that could cost me a partnership."

"Now we're getting somewhere."

"What's the destination?"

"The truth. The cry of your heart. The fact that you even responded to MidDay tells me you're not as opposed to blending in as you think. I mean, c'mon. You've got TV personalities, high-profile types like NFL great Owen Walker and professional model Laurel James following your story on MidDay social media sites."

They did? Everley glanced at Margot's phone, proffered at the end of a stiff arm.

Facts. Everley was a common girl who fed on obscurity but who owned a house of vital societal interest—*thank you so very much, Serenity!*—that no more blended in than a cop in uniform at an underage drinking party.

"If this project launches a TV series, you'll be expected to attend publicity gigs, your rigid schedule suddenly crammed with junkets at public expense. It might require hiring security. I refuse to believe you hadn't already factored this into your decision."

For two milliseconds, she had. Then promptly ditched the thoughts, labeled them ridiculous, far-fetched, and impossible.

A swift wind slicked off Lake Michigan and scattered a stack of napkins. Scrambling to chase them, facts and reason tumbled around in her head. She took fists of rogue napkins in hand, returned to the table, and stuffed them beneath her plate. "The percentage of pilots picked up is extremely low."

"But didn't you say MidDay already has a network interested in the idea, something about mansion makeovers?"

"That's just sales talk, so I'd agree to the project."

Margot's mustang red nails gleamed around her glass. "No reputable production company films without assurance they can recover their investment. MidDay must have high confidence they can sell their idea. Viewers like you, me, your sister ... we love stuff like this." Her gaze went all dreamy, tone lilting toward hopeless romantic. "A woman seeking to restore a treasured family property, rich with history, stories yet untold."

"Moreland may have stories, but it's nothing worth telling."

"It was built in 1846, Ev. For goodness sakes, it's begging to share. Besides ..." Margot leaned in. "A little bit of online scavenging on my part revealed that you and your mother are not Moreland's only widows."

I hear her, Everley ... the widow's calling.

Everley's heart clenched.

"When you toss in an obligation to work side by side with a handsome reno guy ..." Margot winked. "Networks will be sniffing at this like sharks."

"I'm not in the market for marriage."

Or sharks. And why can't fries be made to maintain warmth and rigidity under the artistic drizzle of ketchup?

Fingers greasy and red, and now she needed a napkin ... and an antacid.

With confusion hitched to one penciled brow, Margot said, "Then what's the point of you and Tyler?"

"We're friends, neither one interested in long-term."

Those deep river stones smiled above a cheeky grin as Margot nodded, all slow and disbelieving. She'd make a superb criminal court judge. "Makes me wonder if it's really marriage you're refusing or love."

Everley slid her plate aside and folded her arms along the table's edge. "I researched this whole film madness. The chance of someone's story—anyone's story—capturing the attention of a production company is very slim. It baffles me why MidDay would choose me when absolutely nothing of the subdued hues of my indistinguishable, colorless life matches the profile."

"Au contraire, Ev. You've got scads of color—a virtual rainbow of promise and possibility. MidDay talent scouts were skilled enough to detect it. The problem is, you're afraid to take brush in hand and paint a pretty picture of your life all because you married a man who chased a warrior's dream, died a hero's death."

A peevish laugh spit out. "I have no fear of loss or death."

"No believer in Christ should." Tongue ripe with lecture, Margot spilled wisdom across the table. "It's living you're afraid of."

Each word—a rusty metal link—connected to form a chain, constricting the pulse of life inside her heart.

So overwhelmed.

CHAPTER ΛIΛE

Awash in the buttery morning sun within the serene space beside the front window at the Pear Tree, Gabe swallowed the last of his Friday muffin and chased it with a sip of fresh brew. He tried to forget Everley's blind disregard for Moreland earlier that week. If she'd ever choose to embrace her inheritance, she'd manage it with excellence, guard it like a copper-headed lioness.

His thoughts meandered to the two calls he'd received minutes before he arrived. The first from Carmen, a need to discuss tonight's event, a widely publicized fundraiser for the New Orleans Museum of Art. A golden opportunity to garner business among high society and network the night away.

The second, Dad. Two attempts in a month. This time, no message. Probably didn't want his request for a handout recorded.

The hiss and gurgle of coffee preparation redirected his attention to Serenity, who served a short line of customers. Beside her, Brooke O' Brien, Serenity's college friend who worked a few days each week while her kids were in school. Lettie Thibodeaux's throaty, soulful hum of "Amazing Grace" from the kitchen rippled over the eating area. A dearly loved, longtime Lewis family house manager and Serenity's recent hire, Lettie's primary responsibility was baking products.

Serenity had collected her hair into a ponytail, strands loose around her face. A pencil nested over her ear. Given the bakery's vibrant atmosphere and a perpetual bounce in Serenity's step, Gabe struggled to believe neither sister had been adopted.

Catching his gaze, she moved with an eager gait toward him. "So, tell me. How'd the film thing go?"

Hope. Excitement. Enthusiasm. Like balloons floating heavenward.

"Fine enough. No doubt your sister's got her take on it."

"She said it went okay."

"Just okay?" That didn't bode well.

"Hey. For Everley, that's a lot. I'm just grateful Moreland is finally getting attention." She drew clasped hands to her chest. "Lord knows, I've loved that place. You'll finish by September, right?"

No, short of a miracle.

"It's gonna take an act of God to restore Moreland in that time frame."

Serenity's hand to his arm in gentle squeeze pumped courage. "I believe you can do it. Heck, Noah got it done with far less equipment and skill than you've got."

That Lewis smile situated directly above their shared feature of squared jawline drew across her lips. Delivered the impossible.

Right words. Wrong sister.

Orderly hadn't picked him. Marigold had. The dutiful daughter was merely bending to her mother's wishes while sometimes looking like she'd bordered on breaking.

From inside his patch pocket, his cell rang. It was Carmen. He raised a finger of apology to Serenity and turned toward the window. "How're you doin'?"

"Never better," she said in a feathery giggle. "I've got the hottest date in town tonight."

"The event begins at seven?"

"Yes, but Daddy says we need to arrive by six for the silent auction. He'll send the limo at 5:30."

A knot formed in his stomach. How could he get all spit shined that early? Beadboard for the Cantrell project needed to be picked up, hauled over, and installed. "I'm on a pretty tight schedule and have to get to a stopping point before I can celebrate."

"No one keeps Daddy waiting."

Head in a vice, his temples pounded. "I'll do what I can."

"Let your contractors do all that stuff."

"Until I give approval, the job isn't done. And the job isn't done until I get a satisfied customer."

Lack thereof had brought ruin to Dad's and Granddad's ventures. God only knew how far back the Bellevue failures went.

At the entrance to Chancellor Cantrell's house, Gabe passed through a plastic drape, waved off a veil of dust, and stood beneath newly installed, vaulted beams. He peered upward along an A-frame ladder in the dining room, gaze connecting with Randy, who stood anchored at the top rung. The smell of fresh-cut white oak rippled through him. The buzz of a circular saw and the zip and pop of nail guns, vibrations behind the walls, soothed his soul.

Linking arms with the Creator. The old, restored to new.

At 4:30, shirt soaked in sweat and jeans coated in dust, he turned to Benjamin 'Big Ben' Calhoun, an ursine, Cajun local. "Let's clean up in here and wrap it up for today."

"Yes'r, boss," came Ben's husky reply.

Turning on his heels, Gabe addressed his team. "Strong work today. Go home and … enjoy your families."

Desire bubbled to a slow boil. Man, he'd love to do the same.

Expelling a satisfied breath, he turned to Randy, peeled off his gloves, and swiped a bandana across his forehead. "I've got an event with Carmen and her parents tonight. You good to wrap things up here?"

Randy nodded and tipped the brim of his ball cap. "Under control, boss. Give my regards to Daddy Murdock," he jested with a jut of his chin.

"Will do."

Dusk blushed the early evening sky in gold and rose, erasing earlier cloud cover. Nearing the museum, camera lights flashed. Cheers and whistles sounded from a gathered crowd.

Sandwiched in the back of the limo between Priscilla Murdock and Carmen—who'd gripped Gabe's arm and wedged herself ridiculously close—he struggled for air, the bow tie at his neck doing him no favors. With blonde locks swept into styled twists on her head, she showcased a creamy neck above exposed shoulders.

Warren's steeled gaze registered warning. He'd have made a terrific FBI agent. Gabe's toes pinched inside tuxedo shoes. What he'd give to be clothed in denim, shirt untucked, and slip back into boots shaped by a hard day's work.

"Gabe, it thrills me to see Carmen so full of life." Priscilla layered her pleasure in airy breaths like he'd resurrected her daughter from a terminal disease. "No telling what would have become of our baby girl had you not intervened after that scoundrel left her sobbing in Jackson Square." She shook her head and clucked her tongue to suggest disapproval.

"Her happiness rests in your hands." Warren's words were like nails piercing pine, lids lowered in scrutiny, the subtext armed with explosives.

A holy frown flashed over the screen of Gabe's mind. He racked his brain to recall when and why he'd justified this arrangement when it didn't align with his principles.

Lids fluttering bashful, Carmen nestled her head into Gabe's shoulder and stroked the top of his hand with her own. "Gabe has *very* capable hands, Daddy."

Priscilla sounded a gasp, her mouth partially gaped.

Oh, way to make it sound as if he'd made himself a straight-A student of Carmen's body when he'd kept things solidly G-rated—despite her attempts otherwise.

Immobilized, Gabe fixed his stunned gaze on Warren, fitting a toothy smile to his lips. He tugged at his neckline then motioned with a circling hand. "Carmen didn't mean that, sir ... she means, you know, I'm really good."

Digging the hole deeper.

Warren bored a critical gaze, leaning forward.

Heart thrumming, sweat beaded at his forehead. *Man, this penguin suit.* "No, no. What I'm saying is—"

Warren raised a staying hand, quirking a grin as though releasing his catch in the ocean. To drown. A tinge of mirth softened his granite countenance. "I get her meaning."

Upon arrival, patrons spilled out of luxury cars ... men in tuxedos in company with ladies wearing shimmery dresses and elaborately coiffed hair, faces colored and smiling.

Ah, my people. The upper crust. The ones who made it.

Failure never allowed Dad to see this day.

Gabe hadn't crashed this party, forced his way in, begged to fit in. He'd become one of them. In company with Warren Murdock, who'd measured Gabe against a near-impossible standard and found him acceptable. Worthy of his only daughter.

Oblivious to the wreckage from which he'd come.

The driver opened the door and bowed to Warren, who edged out ahead of Priscilla. Warren took Priscilla's hand, and they waved at admirers lining a red carpet.

Disregarding the cue to exit, Carmen pressed closer and feathered his ear with a sultry whisper. "Hey, hot babe. Look at me."

The scent of something feverishly exotic haloed her hair. She cupped his face between her hands and pressed full lips to his—a hungry murmur sounding in her throat. Amid camera flashes outside the car, he gave in to her advance, amply supplying a feast for what had quickly amounted to a throng of roving eyes and lenses.

Two cameramen shouldered inside the space of the open door. "Give us one more of those, love birds."

Taking another whopping bite of success, Gabe fed the insatiable crowd and kissed her again, drinking in the limelight. Untangling himself from her grip, he stepped out of the limo and turned to ease her out like a curated museum piece.

Swaggering along the blood-red carpet, he returned a megawatt smile that spurred a succession of camera flashes, waving left and right.

Targeting the entrance, Gabe guided her through the velvet ropes. Before entering, she pivoted to face the crowd and hitched the hem of her sleek gown, exposing a leg through an elongated slit.

"Have you found the perfect match, Miss Murdock?" a spectator asked.

She glanced at Gabe, lips drawn into a foxy pucker. "Most definitely."

"When are you going to tie the knot, Gabe?"

He tucked rogue strands of hair behind an ear. The answer stuck in his throat, slipped past a boulder, and tumbled out. "Soon."

Mid-April, Everley flew to New Orleans and drove to Napoleonville to attend a simple Saturday morning wedding at St. Anne's Church for Ms. Bonnie Sue Gaudet and her sweetheart, Hollis Fontenot. It was only right being that Bonnie Sue was Mom's closest friend—also widowed—and mother to Brooke O' Brien, Serenity's friend and coworker at the Pear Tree.

After the simple reception in the church's fellowship hall, Serenity started the engine to her sedan. Cold air whooshed through the vents, cooling Everley's arms.

Serenity secured her hair in an elastic tie. The tips of her ponytail swished over her neck. The look of the soccer player she'd been in college, toe to toe with the best—an attractive mix of feminine and raw athleticism. "While you're here for the weekend, let's go to Vestiges of the Past," she chirped.

The place where Mom took her two daughters on long summer days while Dad stayed back to hammer at Moreland. The truth was—it was Dad's cussing she'd meant to spare them from. More often than not, choice profanity blustered through like a Gulf Coast storm as he crouched over a broken this or that.

Joy. Unspeakable joy.

"Love to." Everley itched to free her toes from the suede, low-rise heels she'd paired with a fitted coral-colored dress.

"Plus, there's this adorable empty house between Moreland and Napoleonville I want to show you."

"What is it with you and empty houses?"

"Houses are living, breathing things. I can't bear to see them abandoned when they've got so much potential."

"Potential for trouble," Everley muttered. She squinted against the harsh sunlight reflecting off the bumper of the car ahead as Serenity pulled from the church parking lot onto the main road.

"Only for those who've given up on childhood imagination for logic and reasoning," Serenity countered.

"Which pays well."

"Anyway, it's an asymmetrical French Victorian with a wraparound porch, multi-faceted Mansard roof, and turquoise shutters. I could totally see someone converting it into a bakery."

"Would that someone be you, perhaps?"

Dreaming. Always dreaming.

"Why not?" Serenity shrugged and turned another block nearing the antique store. "I mean, the Pear Tree is rock-solid and all, great exposure, but the rent and parking—or lack thereof—is wearing on me. Some of my regulars have disappeared because of it."

Maybe not as thriving as she'd originally conveyed.

"A relocation near Napoleonville makes no sense. You'd lose all your regulars."

"I'll establish new ones. It would meet a need among a community of folks that currently lack a bakery. For the sake of the house, I'd be willing to give it a shot."

"You'd be wise to take on a business partner for a move like that."

Serenity's gaze went focused as though giving partnership consideration.

"But no matter where you establish the Pear Tree, there's no better bakery and coffee shop alternative. Because she's your baby. The dream you chased—and captured." Everley's voice withered. She lagged her gaze out the window to an uncomplicated landscape.

"Thanks, Evers. You've got dreams to chase, too, you know."

"I did. Fell and scraped my knees."

Nearing Napoleonville, a sultry haze within a copper sky covered an endless acreage dotted with farmhouses, the view morphing to simple.

Quiet. Inviting solace.

Promising, even.

As she cruised along, Serenity's hair swished as she bobbed her head to classic rock, singing unhindered and off-key, missing the lyrics 80 percent of the time. A party waiting to happen. Perpetual optimism pulsing through a bright gaze, a trait woven into her DNA.

The two had little in common aside from facial features and a shared love of pastries and antiques. If Mom and Dad had ever had a third child, maybe they'd have possessed a perfect blend of both.

Outside Vestiges, the tepid air whisked aside the remnants of spring chill. Generous sun filled a blue sky, its warmth feathering Everley's cheeks. Sandals, sandals ...

The weathered door creaked beneath a bell ding. Inside, dust motes swirled like pixie dust within a shaft of sunlight that fell over fractured cement flooring. The rich ambiance of yesteryear enveloped Everley, seeped into her pores, inviting her to incline her heart to the past. To stories begging to be heard.

Taking opposite sides of the aisle, Serenity wandered to a trunk of sundry frames, Everley to furniture.

One looking to complete a picture. The other seeking stability.

Repetitive pings drew Everley's attention to her phone. Nagging social media notifications appeared on her screen like pimples. In a move to silence Serenity's yammering, Everley had created an account and established a website for Moreland, ticking off another item on Mom's unfinished to-do list.

Vying for internet space to lure potential buyers was no more than a strategic move, really. One she hoped would serve Moreland well—a valuable piece of real estate that'd captured the roving eye of a production company.

"I see you posted another image of Moreland, the one with me out front," Everley said.

Smiling, proud.

What had once been child's play between them, Serenity had "tagged" her, an insidious ploy to keep Everley glued to her phone.

Follow requests dribbled onto the screen. Those of friends, Lewis family acquaintances, media executives, several of Kyle's military brothers, old house fans. Add to that a few celebrities.

Among her first followers? Gabriel M. Bellevue.

An impulsive follow-back and curious scan of his photos ensued.

A tease of authority played in Serenity's gaze. "You like the updated profile pic and call sign I gave you?"

"The *what*?"

"Oh, for pity's sake, Evers, you, like, live in the Dark Ages."

"So, shed light," she smarted.

Taking Everley's phone, Serenity pointed to Everley's smiling and filtered image. "Following the 'at' sign, it reads, 'Happy Everley after.'"

"You are so pushing sibling privilege here." In short order, Everley reclaimed her cell.

"To build your following, use hashtags like numbers girl, CPA queen, favored heiress. That kinda thing. Get the hype going." Serenity circled her hands in enthusiastic gesture.

Another unsolicited social media tutorial. "Whatever happened to the use of hashtags to indicate a number?"

Skilled at diversion, Serenity said, "How many followers do you have?"

She raised upturned palms.

"The parameters of your cold, hard CPA world are far too small."

"Small is manageable."

"Large is fun."

Right. Sunshine wrapped in skin. Impending storm clouds an opportunity to dance in the rain.

And ... followers?

She glanced at her cell, pride swelling behind her ribs. "Well now, look at that. I've already got two hundred seventy-three followers. How many do you have?"

"Just over seven thousand."

In the space of one breath, Everley's impressive stat shrank to nothing, a drop of water in the ocean.

"Gotta work this thing if you're looking to be in the spotlight."

An intense spotlight that threatened blindness. Bending to loyalty, she'd plunged headlong into a project, miles from routine, and added her face to the lunacy of social media.

Even so, this meant war. "All right, smart mouth. You really don't want to enter the numbers arena with me. Because I'll not only beat your following, I'll surpass it."

Serenity's eyes flickered to an endearing azure. "There you go. Spoken like a Lewis."

Behind Serenity, wood cases ran along the wall, old books and fabric remnants sagging the shelves.

"What's the name of that guy you work with?" Serenity asked.

"Tyler Allen."

Milliseconds ticked.

"I found him," Serenity said. "Tyler the Tax Man."

Intrigue had Everley glancing over Serenity's shoulder. Images stacked in ordered formation like monochromatic tiles. Screenshots of winning scoreboards. Tyler on the golf course. Tyler on his sailboat. Tyler in a tailored suit wearing a stop-traffic smile. And ... scroll, scroll, scroll ... the two of them at the pizza joint, Tyler pulling her into a buddy old pal side hug.

Hashtag, #mysteady

Letters ordered behind a pound sign—he'd labeled her a reliable, loyal soul.

One-dimensional.

Pinpricks of joy filtered into Serenity's eyes, broadening her smile. A sibling push-pull. "I posted this one of the four of us on the front steps."

Staring back, Everley's nine-year-old self was seated beside Serenity, age seven. Behind them, Moreland's front door blinked welcome—or showed the way out. Mom sat to Everley's right, face shaded by an imposing pillar. And Serenity, the chosen recipient of Dad's crushing hug on the opposite side.

Not pictured. Everley resenting Dad's preference for abstract over concrete.

That ache simmered, rumbled to a low boil, and threatened to bubble over.

This trip, she'd refused to visit Moreland. Ignored its petulant whine.

A house you've got. It's a home you need.

She slung a stare at Serenity. "What?"

Hand stilled on an antique wardrobe, Serenity returned a blank expression.

"You said something ... about a house ... a home."

Serenity's forehead wrinkled in a frown. She shrugged, turning her attention back to the piece.

Okay. Travel exhaustion, a girl divided between audits and having committed a mammoth restoration project to a misfit band of contractors. An unknown number-cruncher who'd agreed to share camera space alongside Mr. Dusty Boots—the clutch basketball player of Landry-Walker High who'd never bothered to make her acquaintance.

To know her.

Carefree. Capable. Handsome. Closely trimmed scruff dusting his chin, drawing up in perfect lines to create a pleasing dusky shadow. Carried the subtle scent of pine and hard work …

Enough!

Everley joined Serenity to admire the wardrobe, stress marks and nicks rough beneath her fingertips. "Look at this incredible old-growth wood and chipped paint. Such character."

Serenity's tone hitched in whimsy. "Wonder who made it, what it's heard and seen … where it's been …"

"Maybe it's held pottery or functioned as a wardrobe."

For lingerie.

Romantic thoughts resurfaced, nibbled through reticent inquiry. Indulging, Everley imagined the able hands of the carpenter, sanding the edges, painting careful strokes along the wood … a gift for his love. The scent of potpourri, the mingling of hot breath.

Passion. Throaty whispers of forever love. Secret sentiments shared, penetrating soul-deep.

At a finger snap, Everley's lids shuddered open, cheeks aflame.

Serenity wore an amused smile, one hip cocked. "Wherever your mind traveled, take me with you next time."

I can't go there.

Unhooking a nineteenth-century gown of cream-colored chiffon, Serenity drew it to Everley's neck, pressing the delicately beaded bodice against her waist. She stood beside her in front of the oval mirror.

Eyes fixed on her reflection, Everley gathered layers in hand, fanned them, and pivoted left and right. "I could definitely see this altered to a modern design, fused with French lace, worn to a cocktail party."

"Listen to you, imagining possibilities."

Everley lifted a chin in defense. "Merely expressing an idea."

"No," Serenity said with a rascally grin. "That was dreaming."

At the ping of Serenity's phone, a Cheshire cat grin split across her cheeks. "That pic of you embracing Gabe in the bakery—both looking like you need to find a room. It's gotten a few hundred likes and climbing."

Everley's breath hitched. "Take it off. Now. Before people see it and, and—"

"See that you're in love?"

Mouth agape, Everley cupped her face. Fire pooled in her belly, swathing her neck.

"A picture is worth a thousand—"

Impulsively, Everley snatched Serenity's phone and held it mid-air.

A few robust hops, frantic bobbing, and Everley's hip bumped Serenity's. Gravity sent them tumbling into a display of antique dolls and upset a row of trunks along the wall. One bumped against another like dominoes.

Nearby heads turned and glared.

Silence clanged.

Slowly, they sat upright.

Unruffled by the conundrum, Serenity's eyes twinkled.

Hands gripping an upholstered armchair, Everley stood and dusted the back of her dress. "You're like a Rocky movie. Never know when to quit."

Shoulders shaking, Serenity placed her hand to her middle and gave a little snort.

While they worked to set the trunks and dolls to rights, melancholy churned, bled into Everley's tone. "Don't you feel uneasy—even just a little—when you're there?"

Memory shuddered across a listless gaze, joy draining from Serenity's countenance. A hard swallow bobbed at her throat. Her gaze morphed to an empty stare before rallying to flick a determined gaze on Everley. "No. Moreland gave more than it took. Recreational companionship, working toward a common goal. That outweighed bad things."

If bad were no more serious than a sprained ankle.

The edges of Serenity's lips drew up in a smile. "Like the tire swing in the old oak."

Dancing sunshine again.

Memories sparked. "Playing hide and seek ..."

Pink of delight rushed into Serenity's gaze. "Twirling on the balcony, making believe we were movie stars."

"Fanning ourselves while Prince Charming begged kisses from down below." Everley clutched her hands and drew them to her chest in a fake swoon.

"The lemonade stands ..."

"Who knew there'd be minimal traffic along an obscure highway out front?"

"But we made thirty-five cents that afternoon."

A guilty hand went up. "Confession. Mom gave it to me when I went inside to use the bathroom."

"Oh." Serenity's smile sagged before a light of awareness filtered into her gaze. "Then you 'split' the change, handing me a dime and a nickel, knowing full well I was no good with numbers."

"So, I owe you two and a half cents," Everley answered in jest.

"Don't think I won't haunt you if you don't pay up." Serenity wiggled her fingers like a spook.

Everley startled at the clank of a doll that'd slipped off its perch on the chest. Righting it again, a sobering chill shivered down to her toes, reality the perpetual party pooper. "I should have just found a buyer who'd take the house 'as is' rather than extend the boundary of reason."

"You're too smart to let Moreland go when you could double, even triple, your assets by restoring it first ... best assets being you and the super-hot reno guy."

Hands balled into fists at her side, Everley stomped. "Would you *staaahp*. That man is no more than a rascally contractor, paid to do a job."

The humph suggested Serenity wasn't buying it.

"So when your *contractor* is finished, we could transform Moreland into a restaurant, which I could so manage. Maybe open an art gallery, have tours or whatever." She skidded to a stop in the aisle, grasping Everley's arms, ankles springing again. "I've got it. A bed and breakfast. Imagine how incredible that'd be! And Mom smiles down from heaven."

"She's with Jesus. She doesn't need a house to make her smile."

At that, the two continued toward the exit—one buoyed by a dream, one sinking under the weight of it.

CHAPTER TEN

Satisfaction coursed through Gabe at the sight of the rustic, antique door he'd discovered in the warehouse of Vestiges antique shop. "That one. Right there." He swiped his forehead with the back of his hand. "After structural repair, wood epoxy, and thorough sanding, she'll be a perfect fit for the Cantrell project."

Happy customers make for a secure business.

Fingers curled at each side, he hefted the load away from the wall and leaned its weight against his chest. He guided it into the bed of his truck, secured it, and gave the gate a slam. The sun overhead streamed along the back of the entrance bay, sapping Gabe's energy. That and the pestering thoughts of Everley Lewis. Now Scott. A deeply loyal sort like her wouldn't drop her maiden name.

And deep-rooted crushes never die.

Her momma's unexpected call the week before the obits pronounced NOLA's champion of the artisan community had died left an indelible mark on his brain ...

You're the reason Moreland has hope of life, the best to complete and maintain the work. And that gift to Moreland might also be a gift to you.

Right. The big bad basketball player whose winning dunk earned a title that year. Bubble-headed cheerleaders teasing availability in the parking lot beside his blue Camaro when all along, he'd only ever wanted Everley.

Undaunted by locker room jeers.

The red-haired math nerd? You gotta be joking, Bellevue!

Before the call with Marigold ended, he'd seized the opportunity. "Your daughter Everley and I went to the same high school, Ms. Lewis." Dang, if his voice didn't sound tinny. "How's she doing?"

"Glad you asked," she'd said in palpable buoyancy. "She's in Chicago now. Works for an accounting firm. Not currently in a relationship."

The unsolicited update came packaged in hopeful intention.

The thing of it was, he desired what Everley used to be. Very little evidence remained of the sexy shyness she'd once possessed. The most beautiful flower on the wall, ushered into prom by Miles Stephenson, student body president and valedictorian. Ugly looking thing, all hundred twenty pounds of him. But, hey, Miles had guts Gabe hadn't been able to muster.

Whatever the cosmic reason, Gabe's world had collided with Everley's, if only for the span of a few months. He was the key to satisfying her momma's dream. Once his work was completed, the high school crush would wave him off and deface the lawn with a for sale sign.

None of it mattered. He'd had his chance. Failure dominated.

And now, Carmen.

Entering Vestiges retail area, the aisle narrowed as he wandered toward the checkout counter. Mid-step, he halted at the sight of a woman in an orangey dress, hunched down on all fours, peeking beneath the shelves ... hair shining like copper wires.

It couldn't be.

The woman inched backward, tone rife with aggravation. "Where on earth did I leave it?" She sat on her heels and released a withered sigh.

None other.

Gabe clenched his teeth, forcing back the spit of laughter at her expense.

Draping his ample shadow over her, Gabe stood behind the unmistakable and altogether beautiful damsel in distress.

"Last person I expected to see at a place meant to give life to the past."

Everley gave a horrified gasp and twisted at the waist to face him. Pink tinged her cheeks, jaw slackened. Not one to be caught off guard.

Moving to stand in front of her, he offered his hand. For a moment, she returned a sour glance at his hand like he'd offered a joint. Until the look of gratitude—and a heap of helplessness—crinkled the lines of her eyes, added a deeper vibrancy to those gemstones, and moved her to accept.

With one firm tug, he brought her to her feet, setting a firm grip on her waist to steady wobbly footing, those heels presenting a challenge, it seemed.

Only a sliver of space remained between them, his height dominating hers by inches. She held his gaze, her breathing rapid, making no effort to step out of his hold. That wickedly intoxicating gardenia scent shivered through him, sparked desire. Warmth clawed at his neck and radiated down to his boots.

Guilt unfolded across her face. Slowly, she slid from his grasp and turned attention to dusting the front of her dress.

"I feel so stupid." Her voice went all reticent. "Serenity and I were shopping here earlier, and, somehow, I left without my purse." She softened the self-criticism with an awkward grin.

He pinned a cockeyed grin on her eyes and traced the contours of her porcelain face.

Shirking unease, she broke his stare again. This time, exerting greater struggle.

"Where'd you have it last?"

"Here, on this aisle, I thought." She scanned left and right.

Behind her, a purse rested in shadows atop a stack of fabric remnants. Creating a smidgen more space, he drew in a breath and sidestepped her ... chest to chest ... to claim the purse. "This it?"

Relief slackened her features. She nodded, an awkward laugh amplifying unease. "Not sure how it ended way up there." Her glower burned along the shelving—face wrought with confusion.

A girl, who didn't relish losing her wits, found herself in need.

Helpless.

"Guess a person's got to be willing to look outside the ordinary to find what they're really after."

For the sheer joy of seeing her typically steady bearing unravel a bit, he leaned against the shelf, crossed one ankle over the other, rolled a tongue inside his cheek. She went fishing inside her purse as if assuring everything was in order. "This is so unlike me."

Such a herculean effort to explain a common mistake.

"I guess miscalculations in your line of work could be disastrous."

Coming up from a feigned perusal, she met his gaze, the remnants of the shy wall flower lingering in her features. "Thanks for saving the day, Mr. .... uh, Gabe."

Right. Keeping a safe distance, her involvement just enough to satisfy the wishes of her dead mother. To fake congeniality for the cameras until the final nail is secured.

In a slow bow, he dipped his head at the would-be cheerleader.

Shuffled footsteps and lighthearted conversation from the next aisle pulled Gabe out of a mental pit of despair over missed opportunities.

"What brings you back to town?" The rise of hope had him entertaining the idea he was a subset of her reason.

"A wedding."

Guess not.

"A dear friend of Mom's, Bonnie Sue Gaudet, got married this morning at St. Anne's. Her daughter Brooke and Serenity are good friends and were college roommates. Bonnie Sue was a great support to Mom after Dad died. And when Bonnie Sue's husband died, Mom comforted her."

Mention of death had Everley's gaze dimming to a dull green. A lonesome sigh puffed her cheeks—the look of an orphaned child. Disengaged, a soul shackled by fear. Unwilling to let go.

"Serenity and I love this place."

The hint of a smile, the willingness to indulge in the past, dawned in a glorious pink hue on her face. Her playful countenance held the hint of invitation for him to share her joy.

He did.

The old renewed.

"Mom used to bring us here. Called them 'rescue missions.'" Arms folded, gaze adrift, she quirked a grin. "She'd urge us to choose something new ... well, old, I guess ... things once treasured, cast off for someone else to appreciate." Her chest jerked in a weak laugh. "Rescued by Marigold Summerfield Lewis."

"It's that kind of attitude that keeps me in business."

Curiosity crinkled her brow. "You here for ...?"

"A door for a client." He widened his hands like a fisherman exaggerating the size of his catch. "It's a bit of a drive, but Vestiges has the best selection."

Holding his gaze, hers went pensive as though seeking more than superficial platitudes. Still, she bubble-wrapped herself in numbers and plunged right into business. "Actually, it's providential I ran into you."

"Yeah. How so?"

"I've given a lot of thought to factors contributing to your restoration cost, and I'm wondering if it's not due to things like, well ..." She circled a glance around her. "Over-priced antiques and hardware rather than more affordable parts."

As though she'd slung mud, he gave his head a vigorous shake. "I'm being paid to restore the place to original excellence, not patch it up with cheap substitutes that'll result in a higher cost to replace each time they wear out."

Chagrin twisted her lips, defense clouding her gaze. "I can appreciate that, but your approach is costly. Not to mention your unconventional fee schedule. It doesn't fit the look of other contractors."

Your kind doesn't fit in, Bellevue.

A volatile hiss simmered, expanding his chest. He released a hot breath in a steady stream. "It'll have to fit, Orderly, or you'll need to look elsewhere to get Moreland looking pretty again." Arms clenched at his chest, he moved in close and targeted an icy stare meant to cool her heated breath. "And judging from your finding capabilities ..." He dropped his gaze to her purse, then lifted it to her now peeved expression. "It's in your best interest to keep me around."

At the indomitable presence of Phillip Vance at Everley's open door, Everley silenced her laptop, yanked her attention from Gabe's recent YouTube post, "Six Ways to Stop Demolition by Neglect."

Judging from Phillip's winged brow, Everley's sudden ramrod posture had likely roused suspicion—made worse by a sharp influx of breath at the issue of New Orleans Business Beat resting aside her laptop. The one she'd snagged from Serenity's bakery because Gabe—no, her contractor—graced the cover as last year's recipient of the Independent Business Leader Award of Excellence.

In one swift movement, she rounded her desk to stand in front of it and faced him, attempting a relaxed pose as though she'd expected him.

She hadn't.

"And what brings you here?" The pitch of her voice attempted to mask supreme awkwardness.

Stupid, stupid.

Taking on the look of a leathery old billy goat, sniffing the air for something to chew on, he swung his hands behind him and concentrated his gaze over the rim of his glasses. "Being the brunt of a distasteful email, I'm searching for reasons why you've not submitted documentation for the Llewelyn and Martin Orthodontics audit. But, more so, why you're *here* ..." He stabbed a finger at the floor. "... rather than *there*."

"About that—"

Disrupting her rebuttal, Phillip turned slowly and stepped to her window that framed a dreary cityscape.

Perfect opportunity to covertly flip the magazine over. An unsuccessful move, the troublesome thing landing—*splat*—on the floor.

Unfazed, he said, "If we can't bill the client, we don't make money."

Duh. Accounting 101, sir.

He turned, approached the end of her desk, and arched his fingers on top. "And if we don't make money, Phillip will have to make changes."

Assailed by the smell of stale coffee and garlic on his breath, she leaned back while firming her resolve. "No reason to succumb to communicating in third person, disregarding my ten years of experience."

Evocative, maybe, but she had red hair and didn't hesitate to put it to good use. "Over a week ago, I'd requested a depreciation schedule from Llewelyn and Martin in order to reconcile their financial statements. Meanwhile, I discovered some intolerable deviations in accounts receivable that required more thorough investigation."

He stood upright, answered a hmmph, and stroked his chin. "How is it you justify travels back to Nipperville?"

"Napoleonville, sir. It might interest you to know the little town was named by a soldier who served under Napoleon Bonaparte. In fact, he's buried—"

At his raised palm and blustery head shake, she snapped her mouth shut.

"Sounds absolutely medieval, your inheritance a money pit."

His derisive laugh shifted something in her heart, slashing like knives inside her chest. Never mind the fact she'd believed the same—sweat equity and limited resources wasted on a mess of a place in a dismal little town barely registering on GPS. Why had she suddenly come to Moreland's defense and all but raised a banner over it?

Contracts, that's why. Obligation.

Fix house. Sell. Return to routine.

"I'll contact the client again to push for those documents."

One cheek protruded as Phillip rolled his tongue inside his mouth. "Fine, fine. Partner, remember?" He dabbed a finger in the air.

Never was it more evident why Phillip had been divorced twice, and his present marriage to Joanie, God bless her, teetered on the brink.

A rebuke slithered up, coiled around her neck. Self-control unwound and disarmed it. Good thing. Because Phillip—cheeks the shade of a ripened tomato—appeared to be in no mood to respond rationally to news of her upcoming scarcity over the next several months in order to flash a show-host-worthy smile in the midst of said money pit while Gabe, making exceptional use of his musculature and wisdom, exposed cypress beams and managed his crew.

Becoming one among them. Shoulder to shoulder. Never lording his authority. Equal.

A faithful friend ... kind to the outcast ...

Attractive qualities in a contractor. *And potential partner for life.*

A fragile sigh escaped her lungs, blinked her from a dazed stupor as Phillip turned a one-eighty and disappeared out her door.

Conscience pummeled like jagged stones, the throb of her heart pulsing behind her ears. What began as means to satisfy Mom's request had quadrupled in size. How would she commit to two things and give each her undivided attention?

Be God?

Like bricks hefted to her shoulder, the pursuit of this oversized idea turned her legs all wobbly. But with the final take, Moreland would be market-ready, and she'd send a satisfied Gabe on his way to restore some other old house. Once sold, she'd pay off the loan and settle back into obscurity.

Except that ... Moreland's website boasted a growing subscriber list that'd experienced a 32 percent increase since it went live. Who knew the place had so many souls fighting for it, feasting on images of its progress and occasional photos Gabe had taken and shared with Everley?

Within the hallway, Tyler appeared, assuming the stance of one summoned.

Broaching her open door, he delivered his professional savvy, looking all too much like partner competition. The scent of musk wafted in as he crossed over. "Thought you'd be out at a client site."

Tap, tap. The dozing screen awoke. "Still playing catch up."

He perched on the edge of her desk, fixed a wolfish gaze. "How's my girl?"

Uh ...

The sensuous tone, his hovering posture, the staring. Disquiet rolled through her. He leaned closer, a swift kiss connecting with her cheek.

Drawing back, she pressed a hand to his chest. "Company policy, Ty."

Your steady, remember?

He returned a wink and promptly returned to seriousness. Kiss forgotten.

How'd men do that?

"This house deal you've got yourself all tangled up in ... a committed CPA can't just go ghost. You need to list the place as is and leave it at that."

"I'm sorry. I don't remember asking your opinion, Ty. And that's not the right financial move. Present condition, it's worth half a million. Restored, it could go for well over two million."

"Sheesh. That much for an old house?" A swift wave of his hand suggested her assessment polluted the air.

"It's registered as a national landmark, a wise move on Mom's part. Saves on property taxes. Its restoration requires professional handling."

The best hands in New Orleans.

"Assuring its completion is a necessary, honorable disruption. I don't mind a little change of pace."

Did I really just say that?

A gruff tease erupted. "The Everley I know hates change." He stood and plunged his hands into his pockets. "If I surprised you with a trip to the range to hit a bucket of balls instead of pizza night, you'd revolt."

"That's a fact. And Louisiana is pleasant this time of year. Chicago winters are brutal and far too long."

His brightening eyes reflected the look of a rich Lake Michigan blue when an unobstructed angle of sunlight plunged below the surface and dissipated. He drew in a hard breath as if standing on its frozen shore, relishing the scent of fish amid frigid, static air.

The stillness of death.

She shivered, curling her toes inside her boots. "Napoleonville is actually a quaint little place. I think you'd like it."

His jeering laugh rattled through her.

In a swift movement, he leaned in. "No sense arguing over a piece of property." Ardor tinted his gaze. "Let's eat at London House on the river tonight. I've got an offer you can't refuse."

Her heart lurched. This held weight. Whatever it was had better be worth missing an episode of *Fixed Up Right*. Fourth season. Final episode.

CHAPTER ELEVEN

Pizza night. And yet, Everley found herself ensconced in luxury on the elegant second level of a three-tiered, narrow rooftop terrace of London House. Situated in the heart of Chicago, Hilton's curio collection hotel boasted quintessential architecture, fully restored to chic and modern.

From the vantage point of twenty-two stories high, she took in the sweeping views and peered at the gently angled, greenish-black Chicago River and its famed bridges. A distinctly high elevation where it was presumed everyone aimed to be. Or had already happily reached.

The picture of dashing in his dark blazer and trousers, Tyler hugged her, his grip tight and prolonged. She sat when he pulled a chair at the glazed, black table in the far corner. He took the seat opposite her. To her left, a mounted granite urn faced the Trump Tower rising from across the river. Food and beverage service was situated beneath a metal-framed canopy entwined with greenery. A shadowed, waning moon was pinned to a cobalt sky that reached over residential and commercial high-rises.

Menu in hand, she studied the various offerings of reimagined American cuisine. Seated in stacked formation along the railing, patrons engaged in low-toned conversations clinking crystal and flatware. Chilly winds blustered past, ruffling her linen napkin, slicking her cheeks.

A server in pressed dark shirt and pants arrived to take their orders.

"For starters, the lady will have water—hold the ice—and, I presume ... hmmm ... the kale salad, blue cheese on the side?" He angled his gaze from the menu and raised his brows in question.

She nodded, pleased at his proficiency in remembering her preferences—thus far.

"I'll take a half dozen oysters on the half shell, and she'll have ... let's see ... ah. Faroe Island Salmon with broccolini and so on. For me, the Painted Hills Prime Striploin, Nichols Farm potatoes, and whatever you've got on tap."

The usual. Never mind that the London House bacon burger with red onion marmalade, gruyère cheese on a brioche bun, and a side of hand-cut fries tempted her to try something different ...

Something that didn't require a fork. *Something Gabe might eat.*

"Yes, sir." The server claimed the menus, gave a gentle bow, and returned to inside dining.

Tyler captured her gaze as though prepping a witness, brows inched in scrutiny. "I see you've converged on the world of social media. Even found time to maintain a website for that place."

"Thanks for following me back," she teased, never more thankful Serenity had removed the far too cozy picture of her and Gabe. The one that came off like she had feelings for him.

Ridiculous.

"It's quite the venture capital project you've started." He took his phone and grimaced, thumb scrolling the screen. "Amassed over five thousand followers."

A figure that positioned Everley in close competition with Serenity.

Challenge bled into his tone, the overbearing look of a skilled attorney gathering data—cornering the defense. And she well knew her stats. Watched them closely, numbers climbing like vines along a garden trellis ... 41 percent growth in two months.

Bubbles of what felt like joy fizzed behind her ribs. "Behind the scenes is truly fascinating." She sat upright and fanned her hands in gesture. "They've got these huge cranes called jibs that capture higher elevations of the house. Highly-skilled creatives in every department follow direction like trained soldiers. There are multiple cinematographers working to capture our every moment, recording each take using a digital clapper stick. The key light is the main light set up near us and is placed at a forty-five-degree angle to the camera-subject axis. And they make adjustments depending on whether we are inside or outside."

"We, us." His gaze narrowed to slits, setting off alarms in her head.

"Me. And the contractor."

"Whom you despise." Posture stiff, he set his elbows on the table and tapped fingertips together.

"Naturally. Anyway, the crew spends hours studying multi-screens on what they call switchers ..."

Heart breezy, her insides went all pinkish and buoyant, voice thinned to a near whisper, thoughts of Gabe emerging unbidden. "A joint effort to capture raw, unscripted ..."

Romantic gestures.

Disheartened by her propensity for fault-finding, she hated to consider she'd sandpapered Gabe's ego during their last encounter. If Mom had witnessed it—and maybe somehow she had—it'd earn Everley a smoldering glare.

Another apology was in order.

Tyler snapped his fingers. Twice. "Do I need to be concerned here? Because it sounds like you're enjoying this circus."

Voice tinny, she squirmed beneath the weight of his stare but fought to claim control. "I hear mistrust in your voice."

A cold steel gray claimed his gaze. "What's not to trust?"

Hidden meaning boomed between them.

"You're straddled with a massive project for which you've incurred a substantial debt and have received a mere pittance from this film company to pay it down with no assurance of return on investment," he drilled.

"H-h-hold it a minute." She gave her hand a vigorous wave. "The sale of Moreland will more than pay back expenses incurred."

"Maybe, maybe not. But you're a CPA, not an actress. You've turned this into a media feeding frenzy, your private life ripped open—which involves me." The tic in his cheek jumped, his voice icy.

Artificial light strung along the outer roof ridge glinted off the rim of his glass as he circled it inside his palm.

A wellspring of defense gathered like storm clouds, her temples pulsing. "I'm honor bound to take care of Moreland."

Each proclamation added another stone to the fortress she'd built to protect her venture.

The server brought her kale salad and his order of oysters. Tyler thanked him, then took Everley's hands. "Listen, Everley." His tone swooped low, oratorical skills coming into play. "Your die-hard loyalty is admirable, but let's drop this, okay?"

"Consider it dropped." She reclaimed her now clammy hands to chug lukewarm water, throat parched against the chilly air thickening around her neck. Suddenly, it seemed, London House climbed within inches of the constellations, a dizzying sway seizing her middle.

She pierced the leafy kale on her plate, thoughts adrift to the reason for the switch from pizza to extravagant rooftop dining. "What was it you wanted to discuss?"

Swallowing an oyster, he rolled his shoulders back as if hefting boulders. A hint of nervousness assailed his squared features.

"I've been thinking—"

Mid-sentence, two women in business attire walked past. The first woman skidded to a stop, gaze flared in recognition. The woman behind her slammed with a hard bump against her back.

"Aren't you the one who's restoring the house down in Louisiana?" the first woman said.

Power of the media.

A weak smile drew across Everley's face. "That'd be me."

Tyler sank into his chair and spewed a blustery sigh over the railing.

"How more lucky could we be, Sharla?" the first woman crooned, turning to face Sharla, whose head bobbed in wonder.

"We're huge fans," Sharla said. "Subscribers to Moreland's website, followers on social media."

A few selfies later, and they went on their way, rabid gazes given to their screens.

"Might better get an autograph while I can," Tyler jested, tone incongruent with a humorless gaze.

With cool movement, he reached inside his coat and retrieved a ring box. He gave it a one-finger slide across the table in her direction. Wholly reclaiming her attention.

The breath left her lungs.

I've always wanted to be a Marine. Now's my chance to fight for justice.

But what if something happens to you, Kyle?

I'll be back. Promise.

Moisture stung her eyes. Fragile threads of desire and fear twisted inside her chest, a worrisome cadence of 'yes, no, no ... yes, no, no' clanging in her head.

Crinkle lines formed around his dancing gaze. He gave an awkward laugh. "Don't get all teary until you see what's in it."

Any girl with half a brain knew what a ring box looked like, what it held, and what it promised. Lids partially shut, she pried it open, curling her trembling lower lip between her teeth to see ... a simple pair of diamond earrings blinking back. Quite pretty. Rather small and delicate, light glinting off the angled facets.

He massaged her hands in his, gaze softened all puppy dog-like. "I'd like to take our relationship to the next level."

In one sentence, their relationship was likened to a video game.

"I don't say it often enough, but I love you."

To date, he'd said it once. Tonight was the first. That's what accountants did. Count.

This one counted the cost of loving again—the risk to her heart. The bottom line was that she and Ty didn't love each other. Not romantically anyway. Their relationship held together by way of a shared fondness.

The brilliance of the diamonds caught the light of dimming dusk. "They're beautiful."

He bore the look of a lawyer who'd won a case.

Disquiet drew her gaze toward the swirl of high-rises across the river, staring at, well, nothing. Seeking something. Maybe a measure of heavenly discernment. Uproarious music belted from corner speakers and drowned the sounds of traffic far below. Chatter from an adjacent table clanged as the party of two climbed to six.

Struggling for breath, she gripped the table's edge as though suddenly suspended from the sky, dangling mid-air from a thin thread.

"I know one way you could pay off your reno loan." Optimism laced his tone.

"How?" She snapped her attention back to him—to numbers, reason, and sensibility.

To solid ground.

"Sell your condo and move in with me. Split cost 50-50. See where our relationship takes us." In the space of quiet, he sipped his beer and set it back down. Gaze pinned on her, one cheek furrowed, he awaited a response.

Disdain cinched her forehead. "No, no. I couldn't."

"You could." Seduction darkened his countenance.

"But I won't."

He jerked his head as though he'd been slapped.

Previously married to a highly-skilled Marine, she'd mastered a few defense maneuvers.

"First," she said. "I refuse to sell my place, and second, I'm not into that." She parted her palms over her steaming plate as though calling time out.

"Didn't see the legalism coming."

She balled her fists, championing childhood values. "There's nothing legalistic about demanding respect. To uphold the desire to be cherished and highly esteemed within the confines of a commitment. I refuse to be a means to gain economic advantage."

Chin taut, he nodded slowly. "Sounds like you would consider a permanent arrangement."

At the question, non-question, darned if she hadn't lost her appetite, the scent of blue cheese dressing acrid, the atmosphere delivering a chill that bore into her bones.

Tyler's half-lidded stare stilled on her. Thumb moving along the sides of his glass, he stroked beads of condensation. The look of a slick lawyer with hours of rebuttal left in him who'd conceded to somber silence.

Confusion had her bolting from her chair. Was it disappointment at his gift—one woefully short of a breathlessly romantic proposal? Or her inability to accept an unknown, unpredictable future that required she put her heart at risk again?

Or was he just the wrong guy?

Friends, remember?

She walked past patrons to the far corner and peered down at the snaking Chicago River straddled by bridges. Restless, it seemed, a body of water confined within designated boundaries, doing due diligence to provide passage for boat tours. Inching a weary gaze toward patterned constellations—those ancient storytellers—her thoughts wandered to God.

The Creator. Nothing of confusion. Perfectly ordered and limitless in creativity.

A vision of Mom and Dad on Moreland's front lawn surfaced. The spirited pair sprawled on a patchwork quilt beneath a dazzling canopy of dusk ... stargazing ... sharing dreams while Everley eavesdropped from the balcony, a concerted effort to embrace this same manner of thinking. To let loose, the feel of God's firm grip on her hand.

Reach for the stars, Everley Orion!

A heated sigh streamed out as she heard again Mom's choking sobs after Dad died, desperation swiping those dreamy stars from her grasp, shutting off the light.

The fate of a dreamer.

A fate that'd now threatened to disrupt Everley's perfectly ordered world.

Since the sour encounter with Everley at Vestiges, it was no wonder several weeks passed without a word. But they had no reason for communication outside their contractual relationship. Now that April had drifted into May, the next three-day film gig featuring the two of them was set for this afternoon.

Temperatures climbed to a pleasant sixty-something, with mild humidity. Unseasonably minimal rains were ideal for construction.

The Cantrell project had progressed, although completion—and final payment—hinged on the arrival of one final material order.

Gabe thought it might be time to put the squeeze on Murdock, who'd returned only convenient excuses for why no other viable leads had been secured beyond the promise of an upcoming contract.

"No worries, Gabriel. I'll be in a better position to give full attention to other possibilities after the wedding."

Unease pinpricked along Gabe's skin. At what point had he rested on his laurels and left the hustle to someone else? If God were for him, he had no need to depend on others to carry him along.

From the front lobby, a growl of frustration slithered into his office. "I can't believe this." Kourtney bustled in, ponytail swishing left-right. "My professor moved up the due date for term papers, which means I've only got two months to gather research stuff. Response time from archive staff is super slow. The library charges twenty bucks an hour to access online documents."

"Well, then, get to it, Special K."

"Easy for you to say." Her arms came up in frustration. "You're not a struggling college student working two part-time jobs."

"What other job?"

Nose tipped upward, she bobbed on her feet and assumed a proud pose. "You're looking at the new evening barista at the Pear Tree Bakery. I'd stopped in the other day right when Serenity had to dash off to the bank. Lettie was busy fulfilling an order, so Serenity pretty much left me in charge. I rocked it with the latte machine, introduced a new flavor—Special K's Blend—and when Serenity got back, she hired me on the spot."

"Cool." He rocked back in his chair, fingers laced at his middle.

The landline rang. K tossed a glance toward the lobby. "Gotta go get that." And off she scooted with the spunk of youth.

Future stretched wide. Rich with opportunity.

Envy crept in. Had he reached his zenith? Passed it? If the end goal was to maintain success, then what? Would averting failure bring lasting satisfaction or leave him exhausted? What gain was there in dodging failure merely to prove a point to a generation of Bellevues long since past? Did having a good rep mean he'd really lived or just managed to avoid the crushing blow of defeat?

His phone chimed a reminder. Film at Moreland. Two o'clock.

Detail omitted. See her again.

Hours in, Gabe's contractors had converged on Moreland, all doing their thing. Ground coverings amply draped the floors. He loved the melody of buzz saws and nail guns. Amid the fog of dust and smell of fresh-cut cypress, he crossed through the kitchen, eyes circling inspection through his safety goggles.

A construction company had donated materials in exchange for promo on his website and YouTube channel. Payment to his contractors came, in part, by way of NFL's Owen Walker's financial gift, an abundant thanks for restoring a house for his dad that included handicap access to the front entrance. Owen's father, Harvey Walker, a quarterback hall of famer, had begun to succumb to the ravages of head injuries, and at some point, the man would face limited mobility.

Inside the grand hall, plaster flaked down along Randy's ladder where he stood near the top.

Hand aside his mouth, Gabe said, "Hollywood calls, partner."

"Say hi to our fans, boss," Randy's voice came out muffled through his mouth shield.

He returned a thumbs up and stepped onto the veranda. The panorama caused him to suck fresh air into his lungs. The sound of hard work faded as he stepped toward the raised production tent beside the great oak. Beneath its sprawling branches, sunlight flickered atop the lawn.

Designated interview spot.

Outside air cooled his skin, but sweat clung to his back, his neck. He swiped his face with his bandana and stuffed it back inside his pocket. Working alongside Everley for a common cause was a bonus. Except, the mundane gaze she'd directed his way suggested she remained forever disinterested in said cause.

Warring against the visceral response to those skinny jeans she wore, a casual jacket over a shirt the color of unfinished wood, and open-toed shoes, he worked up disinterest and nodded once. "Everley."

"Hi, Gabe."

The pinch of a friendly grin eased his stance. If only to disarm the effect of her gardenia, he broke the entanglement of a longing stare and maintained his distance.

A makeup artist sporting cropped, fuchsia-colored hair and nose piercings swooped in. Her dark pants narrowed to thin ankles above athletic shoes. She powdered Everley's nose and cheeks, then stepped back to assess her artistry before jogging out of sight.

Smiling broadly, Gabe turned to the director of this gig, Alex Coleman, and dusted ready palms together. "What are we talking about today?"

Alex dragged a gaze in Gabe's direction, his forehead furrowed in disapproval. "Now that you're here ... we need more content to stretch the length of the pilot. Let's begin with a brief progress update, then," he motioned to Everley, "you'll add your comments from an owner's perspective—what's going well, what's not."

Gabe's heart clenched. What would she say? Was anything amiss? Orderly held his rep in her hands, the ability to tear down what he'd built.

A flurry of film crew intruded to finger his hair into place, fuss with Everley's clothing.

At their retreat, Alex bellowed, "We're ready. Quiet on the set. And ... action." He speared a finger at Gabe and took agile steps back.

"Things here at Moreland are shaping up nicely. We've replaced some rotted joists in the subflooring of the dining hall. I've got my electrical team rewiring. It's a wonder the place hasn't burned down before now." At that, he cut Everley a sidelong glance, crimping a grin. "Old wallpaper has been stripped from the main rooms upstairs, and we're replastering where needed."

Satisfaction jetted through him as he detailed accomplishments. From his periphery, he felt her speculative gaze burn like a fire poker.

He angled a glance. She showcased a toothy smile suggesting years of orthodontic work—the appearance of a satisfied heiress. Genuine or not, it made him look good. He swept a hand in her direction. "Ms. Scott?"

In a blink, she turned a smile toward the camera. "I've been impressed with what's been done, but there's still the ongoing issue of getting things wrapped up in time."

Fleeting affirmation morphed into a displeased client who carried the enthusiasm of someone at a budget meeting for the National Sleep Apnea Society.

Made him look bad. Caught on tape.

Eyes locked on the camera, boots planted beneath the shaggy, oversized boom mic, Gabe leaned toward her and whispered from the side of his mouth. "Think you could go easy on me a bit?"

She smacked him with a cocky head waggle. "Nothing supersedes the right to express my concerns. I am the owner, remember? And you are being paid to do the work."

The criticism sliced through his ribs and twisted like a rusty Phillips head. He raised a hand to Alex and swirled his finger mid-air. "Hey, Spielberg, hold up a minute." Slowly, he pivoted to her, gave her upper arm a playful cuff. "Would you relax a little, Orderly? Remember, we agreed to have fun with this."

"Stop calling me Orderly." She widened her stance, plunged fists into her side, donning her best Annie Oakley, fiery gaze a good match with her hair.

"It fits."

The little bit of smile she'd mustered evaporated. Her frame went rigid. "This isn't a home movie, Mr. Bellevue. Viewers are after the facts, and the fact is, this freakishly large house is a wreck, and you're being paid to save the day within an inordinately limited time frame. I have legitimate concerns about how long the job will take."

He eliminated the remaining space between them and met her gaze, an attempt to disarm the spring-loaded glare. "It's story they're after. Let's give it to them. While you're at it, dig up a little affection for the place, all right?"

"We're not here to win an Oscar. And I'm not legally bound to satisfy Mother's wishes. So let me be clear. You were *her* choice, not mine."

The facts pelted him in the face, her forefinger to his chest scouring his ego. Dazed, he shook his head. The rejection turned his heart to thin glass, threatening to shatter.

Retreating from enemy line, he slowly stepped back and bent to pluck a dandelion. He snapped the stem and tossed the severed weed aside. As he rose, his lungs heaved a labored breath. Everything in him wanted to back out of this deal. Refuse to be made the fool.

Refuse to fail.

Filling the space of silence, the murmuring film crew had become intensely preoccupied with their screens.

Gabe superglued his gaze to her unflinching stare. "I got it, Orderly. You're stuck with me. Reasonably sure you can't make that any clearer." His arms flailed. "But maybe if you could find a way to rip your focus from only what you want out of this deal, consider what's best for everyone, and stop making this shindig distasteful."

"*I'm* making this distasteful?" She pressed a palm to her chest. "I told you, act natural. Professional."

"Professional is the reason your momma chose me above all others to tackle this thing."

"Mom and her flighty ideas." Her scathing head shake sawed through his soul.

Sunlight paled inside a gauzy sky. His shoulders sank beneath the weight of insult, the earth rupturing beneath his boots, making way to swallow him whole.

"I thought you might at least consider a haircut or wearing, I dunno, khakis for once."

He stepped close, ignoring the flecks of gold inside her fiery emeralds. "Two things. My hair stays the way it is, and denim is as natural as it gets. Grown from cotton on fields like these." He raked a challenging gaze over her stilted frame. "And if you hadn't bothered to take notice, this ain't a seated talk show in an air-conditioned studio. I'm dressed for the part I was asked to play."

"That's three things."

"Who's counting."

"I am."

"Then you must know life doesn't always line up in neat columns."

"I work hard to see that it does."

"And miss out on a buttload of life because of it," he spit back.

"Don't you Dr. Phil me. I've seen pictures of you at social events, dressed in a tuxedo, in company with prominent people."

She'd researched.

Like a dog who'd sunk her canines into a marinated steak, she wasn't letting loose. "It wouldn't have killed you to consider a little sophistication on film days."

A guffaw pooled in his belly and traveled to his shoulders. Hand to his abdomen, he leaned forward and launched a salty laugh. "You gotta be kidding me."

"I don't kid." Her lips pinched thin.

"No news there."

Momentarily, he glanced away. Exhaustion crept from his toes, slackening his spine. Enough already. Man up.

Don't hammer the truth. Caress with grace.

Laying down arms, he returned a softened gaze.

The blaze in her gaze dimmed. She chewed on her lip, the look of surrender emerging, brows angled with ... regret, maybe?

Compassion seeped into his pores.

Nudged to action, he unknotted her fists and held them loosely. His fingers tingled at the cottony-smooth feel of her skin. She tensed as his fingers roved the length of her arm. Inviting a truce, his tone swooped low. "Hey. If we each give a little effort, I really believe this could be a great adventure."

A long stream of surrender blew through her lips.

When he continued stroking her arms, she eased. Her ghost of a smile almost fooled a guy into thinking she welcomed it, maybe.

Nodding slowly, her tone was devoid of provocation. "You're right. Sorry I overreacted. I appreciate your getting this whale of a house restored, giving me the best price."

A price requiring him to skim the slightest fat off the profit and stoop to bartering with his crew.

Her eyes blinked in awareness, staring down at their now clasped hands. "Clearly, you're the best. I meant no disrespect."

Humility tasted like cotton candy, the delicious respect coating his heart.

Imagine if Mom had uttered even the smallest measure of respect for Dalton Bellevue ... despite his failures. Trusted his goodwill toward her, encouraged him to stand up tall and try again.

But she'd taken the wide road and left him to clean up the financial mess of good intentions.

At the sting of moisture in his eyes, his gaze roamed to Moreland's façade as if her columns could hold him steady.

"Managing two worlds is taking its toll, I guess." She eased her hands from his, plunged a thumb and forefinger into her temples, gaze shaded by an unadorned left hand.

Fingers slender and well-defined. Wholly intelligent, adding and subtracting numbers for a living.

Capturing her enigmatic gold-green gaze, he offered a bent arm. Without hesitation, she turned to stand beside him and took it, tucking her head against his shoulder.

"That's a wrap," Alex pronounced behind them.

Gabe whipped his head toward the nodding camera crew, who lowered their gear and scrambled before screens like ravens over a lawn strewn with fresh carcasses.

"Of what?" Gabe said, tone irked.

"You two. The house." A coy grin climbed across Alex's face as he fiddled with equipment.

Everley took stumbled steps backward, sucked in a breath. "But ..."

Forefinger raised, Gabe targeted the camera. "You mean to tell me you were filming this entire time?"

Looking smug, Alex chomped on gum and gave a few sharp nods. A toothy smile tipped the edges of his lips. "And from my perspective, you two could be our next sensation."

CHAPTER TWELVE

On the third and final day of filming, Gabe observed production as they crawled over the property like ants at a picnic. Vast lines of cables powered everything from electric saws to mega flat-screens.

Draining energy sources from one another.

Two industries mingling, sidestepping each other in a forced dance of opposites.

Morning sun bathed Moreland's façade and graced its columns. At the swish of warm breezes, moss-leadened branches of the large oak swayed like snarls of dangling gray hair.

A chugging engine drew Gabe's attention to Silas Guidry's weathered truck on the drive. Silas unfolded from the door. After him, his son, James, and James's sixteen-year-old son, Quinton.

They were a father-son power team, bound by skill and mutual admiration. At their approach, Gabe pumped Silas's calloused hand.

Inside a leathery, dark complexion, Silas returned a broad smile showcasing a prominent set of teeth with a slight gap between the front two, one tooth covered in gold.

"Hey, my friend," Gabe greeted. "Great progress on those joists in the dining room."

"They's heavy things, but we gettin' it done," Silas said. He turned to James and Quinton, squeezed their shoulders in turn, then gave his saggy jeans a yank.

Gabe tugged on the brim of Quinton's ball cap that crowned a head of coiled black hair, his lean frame barely supporting gray sweatpants. "Shoot hoops with me later?"

Sunlight danced in his eyes, a bright smile to contrast his skin. "Absolutely."

Around the side of the pedimented south wing, Everley appeared, her gait confident, wearing heels better suited to a high-rise office.

Striking. Not unlike an artist's palette in a short-sleeved, spring-green dress with the hemline just above her knees and hair like a free-flowing paintbrush over her shoulders. Stopping at the columns, she glanced up, her expression studied. A hand shaded a roving gaze. The look of a conflicted heiress doing right by her momma, a heart struggling to care.

The sun caught her hair, set it afire, and traced a line of white long her profile. Those alabaster limbs hadn't seen much daylight in the Windy City. Southern exposure would do her good.

Gabe hailed her with a shrill whistle.

Turning, she drew a smile and cut across the lawn. If it wasn't enough that her appearance made his heart flip, the scent she delivered drove him wild. After he took her in a side hug, she created space.

Keep it casual.

He gestured to Everley. "Men, this is Everley Scott, the lady of the manor house."

Silas nodded in a reverent bow. "Pleased to make your acquaintance, Miz Scott." He turned to James and Quinton. "My son, James, and grandson, Quinton."

She took each hand in turn and smiled, a lock of hair loosening from behind her ears. The urge to tuck it into place nearly overtook him.

"My folks tole me our ancestors built the bricks that holds Mo'land together, milled the interior woodwork here on this site." Pride ripened in Silas's gaze and held steady above hollowed cheeks.

Gabe cocked a brow. "That right, Silas?"

History. Full of surprises.

Everley responded with a soft murmur of interest. Natural light tipped her beautiful nose, soft lips, delicate chin. "What do you do for Gabe?" she asked, returning to the safe zone of business, refusing any tug of the past.

"Tend lawns. Primarily a carpenter by trade." Puckered smile rising, Silas clapped a hand to Quinton's shoulder and glanced at James. "I pray these two'll work for Mr. Gabe when these old hands gives out."

Clanking tools plucked Gabe from an infernal yearning for sons of his own. His dusty crew—Big Ben, Charlie, and Ryan—approached. He introduced them to Everley, who grasped each hand in greeting, adding a genuine smile.

Alex walked over and tapped Everley on the arm, infernal purpose marking his gaze as he shifted it between them. "Before you continue the roof installation, we'd like to capture an interview segment with you two. Mics all set?" Gabe tamped down nerves, returning a thumbs up. "Ready."

She scraped a pained glance over the house, drew it to the rooftop, and shivered, arms tightening across her chest like a blizzard had swept through.

At Silas's lead, the father-son trio offered a parting wave before they ambled off.

"See you at the top, boss," Big Ben said.

Intrigue claimed Ryan's expression as he trekked a glance over the buzz of production while Charlie's gaze lingered two nanoseconds too long on Gabe's high school crush.

"I'll join shortly, guys," Gabe said. "Roof tiles and components in the van, along with extra hook blades to cut if you need 'em. Check and re-check your measurements, keep your eye on hash lines between tabs, and six nails per shingle. Aim for a five-inch reveal—"

"We got this," Big Ben assured.

"Taught by the best," Charlie added, attention now rightfully averted from Everley.

"Oh, and Big Ben, check with electrical and see how they're progressing."

Nodding at Gabe, the burly form of the bearded crew chief lumbered his grizzly frame toward the house.

Secured by a tie-out at a distant oak on the north end, Champ pierced the air with a succession of barks.

"Uh, Mr. Bellevue, do you mind?"

Gabe turned to see Alex, thumb and fingers mashed to his forehead, hooded gaze drawn down.

On the driveway, Randy hefted lumber from the back of the van. "Hey, Randy!" Gabe said. "Take Champ to the van and open the window. That way, he can watch her from there."

Everley turned a slow, hard gaze at Gabe, expression rife with reticence.

Leash in hand, Randy scuttled past. In a blink, the crazed canine lunged free like a sprung trap. Ignoring a fierce whistle, Champ sprinted across the lawn, nearly upsetting a tripod. Man's best friend skidded to a stop in front of Everley, encircling her in a happy trot before he claimed a spot at her feet.

In throaty whine, Champ's lids shifted over begging eyes. The presumptuous pet offered a sappy, howdy-do paw. She bent to shake his paw, cooed, and stroked his chin.

A harsh cough pummeled Gabe's cheek. He turned to Alex, who arched a thick brow, face registering heightened irritation.

Randy dashed over, breathing labored. "Guess Champ ... knows a pretty face ... when he sees one."

Treasonous lips couldn't prevent the rise of a grin. "Just get him outta here before all hell breaks loose."

Muscles flexed, Randy dragged Champ by his collar, stopping short to heft the resistant canine into his arms before shutting him inside the van. In seconds, Champ's face popped through an open window, pink tongue sticking out, paws draped over the ledge.

Following a sour thanks, Alex said, "Are we ready?"

A hint of merriment played in the lines around Everley's eyes. Expelling a fragile breath, she smoothed hands down the front of her dress and gave her hair a toss.

Alex raised a limp thumb to the clapperboard guy and nodded at the other camera operators who steadied their shoulder cams.

"And ... action."

Gabe's cell pinged. Smiling at the camera, he answered. "Yep?"

"Hey, Gabe. Kourtney here. Isn't it incredible what I discovered?"

"Um ...."

"You didn't read the papers, did you? The initial findings on Moreland's history." K's enthusiasm took a nose-dive.

"Ease up, little girl. I get paid to fix the past, not amble back around in it."

"You should have read them." Her voice singsonged and smacked of reprimand.

All trace of mirth drained from Alex's face—forehead furrowed beneath the shade of his ball cap. "*Miss*-ter Bellevue." He stretched out the syllables like taffy. "Unless you have the president on the line, this needs to wait."

"Are you at Moreland?" K said.

Alex blustered a frosty exhale.

Josiah folded his arms and looked askance at Gabe, who glued his gaze to Alex. "Uh ... yeah." A lineup of film people joined Josiah in increasingly agitated scrutiny.

"Ms. Scott there too?" Hope soared in K's voice.

"Right beside me."

Felt miles away.

"Ask if I can come out, share my findings, take pictures."

Turning the phone away, Gabe tilted his gaze at Everley and breezed a whispered request. "K dug up some stuff about Moreland, wants to regale us with her fact-finding finesse, come snap a few pics out here. That okay with you?"

"Sure."

"She says sure," Gabe said to K, Alex's smoldering stare singeing his neck.

A happy squeak and jingling keys sounded. "Thanks! See you soon."

An hour and a half later, MidDay paused filming and clustered in front of multiple monitors. Voices of authority leaned in. They scratched chins in thought, gave vigorous nods, pointed left and right, punched buttons, and flipped switches.

On the driveway, dust billowed behind the back tires of K's dull green Camry till it sputtered to a halt. She popped out like toast, papers fisted to double as a cop's baton as she pumped her arms and trekked toward the veranda where Gabe stood beside Everley.

Despite the welcoming look of jeans and a flouncy yellow top, her carriage matched that of a Green Beret, hair secured in a knot like a grenade.

"Hold your fire, K. They're just papers."

"You're wrong. And if you'd read them as prompted by the neon sticky note I attached to the top, you'd know why."

Alighting her gaze on Everley, K's bearing softened, expression breezy. "Hey there, Ms. Scott. Thanks for letting me come out."

Everley smiled. "Good to see you again."

Something of awe alighted in K's gaze as she glanced around at the activity. "I'm totally following your story on social media. So fun."

Pride rippled over Everley's face. The first sign of ownership he'd seen.

Snapping the papers in front of her, K claimed an impassive countenance. The way she cleared her throat, shoulders squared over a puffed chest, she'd make a superb political candidate.

"Built in 1846 at the commission of Colonel Marshall R. Thompson, Moreland is the architectural magnificence of Irish immigrant Howard Gallagher. It served as the manor house for vast acreage owned by Thompson and his wife, Esther Anna. In 1852, yellow fever claimed Thompson's life, leaving the care of Moreland and its acres to Anna. They were childless."

She paused, raising a glance at Gabe. An auspicious grin dawned on her face. "In 1855, Moreland's widow Anna remarried a Louisiana-born inventor, turned lawyer and civil servant named ..." Another glance. "You listening?"

A huff blustered out. "Yes, little girl. Go on."

"Edmund Charles Bellevue."

K's searching stare infused heat, slackened his posture. "A ... Bellevue?"

"One of Moreland's previous owners," K said.

But wait. Denial had him straightening into a challenge. "That could've been anybody."

She shook her head, slipped out a photograph of this Edmund character and flashed it. "Here's his image, ye of little faith." She firmed her chin with assurance. "It took some doing, but I traced his genealogy to a certain Gabriel Michael Bellevue. The only child born to Dalton and Evangeline Bellevue of New Orleans, March 10, 1985."

Awash in sepia, an unmistakable likeness emerged. Edmund Bellevue—arrayed in a brass tacked overcoat, the upright collar embroidered with three stars denoting officer ranking. "A soldier," Gabe rasped out.

"Brigadier General. Referenced 'a hero,'" K added.

Hero and Bellevue in the same sentence?

Moreland's heiress turned an impassioned look at Gabe, urgency claiming her tone as she turned to K. "Go on, Kourtney."

Another throat clearing. "In 1862, Edmund Bellevue left his family to fight the cause of the south, leaving his wife, Anna Thompson Bellevue, their six sons, and a meager number of workers to manage Moreland Manor and its acreage. During the war, Bellevue rose to prominence as a Confederate States Army military leader, ultimately commissioned as Brigadier General in 1864. Unfortunately, Bellevue was severely wounded while commanding a brigade during the Union's downhill bayonet charge in the Second Battle of Petersburg, June 1864. Though Moreland remained a beacon to welcome home her lord, death prevailed, returning only his embalmed body to the family for burial."

Reverent silence stilled the air.

A fragile sigh wheezed from Everley. Gabe claimed her hand.

"War widow," Everley whispered, hands trembling in his grasp.

"You okay, Ms. Scott?" K said.

She gnawed her lip and gestured for K to continue.

"One of Bellevue's fellow officers gave an eyewitness account of him gathering canteens and venturing back onto the enemy battlefield to supply wounded soldiers with water, warm clothing, and blankets. Neither side fired a shot."

Everley tipped her chin, gracing Gabe with admiration. "Benevolent. Even in the heat of battle."

"I, I had no idea." He fisted his hair, raking fingers through it.

"Shoulda read the papers," K muttered. Bearing the authoritative posture of a professor, she flipped the page and continued. "Anna and Edmund's oldest son, William, was a successful banker in New Orleans. He and his wife Abigail stayed on at Moreland, along with his younger brothers. Upon Anna's death, William inherited the home. He employed full-time staff to manage the manor house and keep the grounds. Cancer claimed William's life in 1913. He was esteemed by the negro community, several of whom attended his funeral."

Tucking trembling hands into his back pockets, Gabe drew a slow gaze toward the carpentry tent where Silas and sons sawed at planks. Three generations at work. Peaceful co-laborers.

"The diamond of Bayou Lafourche later passed to financier Ralph Colbert who, after WWI, incorporated modern conveniences." K stopped, lowering the papers. "And so on and so forth."

Through the haze of history, Everley dredged up her piece. "Left empty for ten years, Moreland Manor managed to claim new owners in 1978, Marigold and Peter Lewis ..."

Anguish clouded the sheen of her eyes, voice strained as she wrapped the story in black twine. "Too bad Peter's death left his widow to manage the house on an artist's income while raising their two daughters."

Everley's words trailed to nothing, gaze distant.

Shoot. How he wanted to kiss the pain of tragedy away, bury that wicked memory deep beneath a cement slab, silence the taunting. An endless drip like a leaky faucet. Wicked water seepage behind the wall, crawling ... traveling ... rotting the interior.

Fitting Everley to his chest, Gabe let the feel of her melt into him. Eyes shut, he clenched his teeth in silent prayer. *God, please show her the source.*

Everley's reentry to work the following Monday went about as smoothly as an injured shuttle returning to earth. And just as precarious. Didn't help to discover Gabe and his rich ancestry had upped the value of Moreland from his perspective, twining their worlds. At least Kourtney's discovery would assure excellent craftsmanship—as if he could do less.

On the heels of Phillip's lecture this morning about audits stacking up, she received a terse voice mail from Bryson Cox.

"Call as soon as possible."

A fresh wave of concern assailed her. Likely he'd not called to hail praises of southern Louisiana fare.

On the first ring, Bryson answered, enough urgency in his tone to spike icy apprehension into her chest. "Ms. Scott."

"Mr. Cox. Things going well?"

Please say yes.

Waiting, she brought a knuckle to her teeth. The spit of nail guns and squeal of machinery sounded in the background.

"Fine for someone filming a video for a high school woodshop class project. Which we are not."

Her pulse thudded behind her ears, nerves and muscles twitchy like she'd consumed a triple shot latte. A bolt of lightning broke through the gray sky and speared the horizon.

"According to Alex, who added days to capture footage under the promise of clear skies, Mr. Bellevue has maintained a less than cooperative spirit. Not to mention his dog, Chump."

"It's Champ. The dog. His name is Champ."

There she went again, going to bat for that rascally contractor and his rescue.

Why, for pity's sake? Just why?

"No matter. He's become a nuisance. Sound can only edit so much."

Oh, if only she were free to let Moreland fall into the hands of fate so she could return to obscurity – and before her absences created margin for Tyler to steal the top prize.

And now, Gabe couldn't play nice? She was beginning to feel like a mother of two toddlers. Under duress, she took a flight to New Orleans on her dime to meet Alex and mediate before the whole project went up in smoke. This was, after all, her house. Now that she'd become vested, she'd see the project to the end.

No matter what.

Mid-afternoon at Moreland while still clothed in her work skirt and jacket, the thrum and scurry of contractors

179

calmed Everley's nerves. The welcome sound of progress, forward motion to end goal.

Get in, get out.

Within the shaded veranda, she awaited Gabe's arrival, propping her travel-weary frame against a column. Tapped her toe. Huffed, checked the time.

"Late."

Alex raised his ball cap, tunneled fingers through his hair, and replaced his cap. "Could you find out where Mr. Bellevue is and let him know the timing is critical?"

EVERLEY: Where are you?

GABE: Coming.

The speedy response unearthed a confident smile. "He'll be here soon. He sends sincere apologies for the delay."

Okay, a lie. But he should have.

In the full light of sun, moisture beaded along her neckline and traveled down her back. Ditching propriety, she shimmied out of her jacket, tossed it on the ground, and tugged at her neckline to invite a rush of cool air.

"Tell you what, Everley," Alex said, tone airy as though suddenly struck by new inspiration. "While you're here, let's capture your perspective." Forefingers raised, he formed a frame. "In fact, where you're standing in front of the door is perfect."

Giving Moreland a once-over, its magnificent threshold within the shaded veranda engulfed her. As though seeing its hopeful gaze through new eyes, she allowed the sight to draw her in. Memory tugged. The veranda had once been one of Everley's favorite spots where she could rock in a chair beside Daddy. Until the day Serenity skipped over and coaxed him to push her on the tire swing beneath the great oak. And then the sight of Momma, who'd stood inside a front window, a glint of moisture in her eyes. Sullen cheeks and pursed lips nullified the fact that those were tears of joy.

In a shuddered blink, Everley turned back to Alex. "If we're filming, I'll need to recover travel expenses for coming down."

"Agreed."

"Need me to wait for makeup or whatever?"

"Oh, no, no." He waved a hand. "Capturing your natural look as though you've stepped right out of the office, hopped onto a plane, and arrived here to see about Moreland is fantastic."

Precisely. A mighty big leap out of her office shifted favor strongly Tyler's direction. She gave her hair a quick pat, tucking strands behind her ear that'd come loose from the clasp.

"Start by telling us the vision you have for Moreland once it's completed, incite viewer interest." Alex took nimble steps backward to stand beside Josiah, leaning to glance at the screens.

Quick. Assign a promising future for this place. Assume the posture of a foolish dreamer, a brain oozing possibilities.

"And detail the challenges that come with restoring an estate of this magnitude," Alex directed, one hand circling.

Challenges like, I could lose partner, my job. Get stuck with this freaking house.

At the crescendoing rumble of a motorcycle on the drive, Alex drifted a condescending gaze toward Gabe who swung a lazy leg over the seat and plucked off a sleek helmet, looking all too much like a slow-motion commercial for Harley.

A delicious shiver whooshed through her spine.

The man of the hour ... who'd voted for her.

Stop!

Passing the canopy, Gabe stooped to touch his forehead to Champ's snout and scrubbed the dog's fur. After one more generous pat, he sauntered across the lawn in his usual garb. Jeans—the pair sporting bleach stains, a hole in the right knee—and a white T-shirt. Sleeveless. And sporting a set of sculpted biceps and nicely bronzed tan.

Gaze locked on her, a lopsided grin bloomed across his countenance.

Everley's pulse thumped. As Alex rolled his eyes back to her, she pretended annoyance—a measurably difficult act given the curl of pink warmth weakening her knees and urge to thread her fingers through his hair.

The southern heat and humidity did a city girl's sensibilities no favors.

From the south wing roof, Randy called down. "Hey, boss. Were you able to find a match for the knobs on back doors and more of those flat head, galvanized nails?"

He shot a thumbs up, dimples flanking an endearing smile.

Breathless, her heart stutter-stepped at how difficult it'd become to hate this guy. Wasn't he merely her ticket to unload the brick-and-mortar burden looming over her shoulder?

"Sorry to keep you folks waiting. I stopped to give a fella a lift to work."

The explanation drew a slight smile from Alex's pursed lips. "Now that you're here ... let's stage this a bit differently and film the two of you near that old tree."

Gabe grinned and gave his head a shake. "You'll need to give me, say, two hours. I've kept my people waiting long enough."

Not subordinates. His people.

A gruff, piercing cough zipped through Everley's chest. She whirled to find Don Barnhart assuming a battle-ready stance, arms crossed, his glare-unnerving.

"No. That won't do," Don said, voice baritone with authority. "We've already adjusted the schedule to add days. The sun isn't going to sit still at our direction, and we've got our own end point to reach."

Unknotting his arms, he advanced in slow, calculated steps. "I appreciate the fact that you've got work to do, Mr. Bellevue. That's why you and your contractors ... and we ..." He swept a hand over the crew. "... are all here. But seeing as how we've lost precious time, due to your absence, our production is behind schedule. So, one way or the other, we intend to capture something worthwhile today."

Nostrils flared and eyes as amber-colored glass heated by flames, Gabe moved a few steps closer to Don, towering over the senior director by several inches. He hiked up his jeans and drew in a heap of air. A tea kettle about to blow.

The crew made space, turning to spectators as though watching a bullfight. Everley's problem-solving skills muscled through the tension. She grasped his hand, pumping it a few times.

At her touch, he blinked from a fearless stare and turned to face her, bearing the look of a lion lured from its prey. An ache overcame his gaze, softened the lines around his eyes, and tenderized the toughness of his features.

A man in want of understanding—who needed a champion.

That could be her.

Maybe just once.

Voice gentle, she stroked the flexed muscle of his upper arm with her free hand. "Gabe, you and your contractors have made great progress here today. Impressive attention to detail." She lathered compliments until the tic in his jaw eased.

She caressed a coy smile along his bristled cheek and ran fingers down his arm to clasp the other hand, her sound mind now a ship adrift at sea. "I can even hang around and help out if you want."

Oh, can you now?

Gabe eased his stance, his breath warm as he minimized the space between them and managed a grin. "I'll bet you've got plenty of skills I could use, Orderly."

The innuendo flushed heat through her insides.

As though prodded by a holy branding iron, she raised on tiptoe and kissed him.

She did?

I did.

Fool brain.

Shock registered in Gabe's eyes, quickly replaced by the blossom of a rogue smile, the notch in his dimples deepening. Inviting a girl to take a swim.

"You and me, we could make a good team." His cottony-soft tone cooled the rise of disquiet at the impulsive move. For three eternal seconds, their gazes locked. He searched her face, stilled a gaze on her lips, roamed it down her neck, and inched it back up again. The look and feel of a hero in a romance novel. Only this was real.

Her cheeks flushed, knees almost buckling as her heels sank into the soft earth.

Releasing his rugged hands from hers, he nonchalantly tucked a strand of hair behind her ear in his knowing way of putting things in their rightful place and thumbed the line of her jaw.

Loving. Every. Second.

He gripped her waist, drew her to his chest, and returned the press of a feverish kiss to her lips.

At the richness of his taste, salty from hard work and skin rough against her mouth, a subtle moan reverberated inside her throat. Surrender tugged at her heart. Ached for release.

"And, cut!"

Several victory hand claps split the air. "How's that for interaction between the two, Alex?"

Brain regaining focus, Everley's lids shuddered open. She knit her brow and rounded to face an overly enthused crew.

"Perfect."

The balls of Don's cheeks inched up. He gave a smug laugh and lit a cigarette. "I can smell the money." Taking a drag, the tip glowed red-hot, then faded to black. Through a veil of smoke, the lines of his gray eyes drooped like half-moons.

Hitching a thumb at Gabe, Everley said, "Were you, um, filming when I ... when we ... when *that* happened?"

Alex nodded, tone throaty. "Remember, our goal is to get everyone interacting like they'd do in real life."

She opened her mouth in defense, Mount St. Everley on the verge of eruption. "*That* was not real life."

Hands to her waist, Gabe spun her to face him. He touched his finger to her lips and gently shook his head, his amber gaze disarming her defense. "No regrets."

No, not really. Except she'd acted the fool.

Indulged in a dream.

CHAPTER THIRTEEN

Everley's offer to lend Gabe an elbow to avert a near crisis amounted to hours of sanding, dusting, hauling debris to the dumpster. Trusting his wisdom, reveling in his direction. She'd had to change out of her work clothes for an extra pair of Gabe's boots and oversized company T-shirt, loaners he'd retrieved from the van.

Muscles aching, time to call it quits. Reno work was his business. Not hers.

Then, for heaven's sake, she'd gone and kissed him.

Worse, she'd responded to *his* kiss, a man headed for the altar. Which begged the question ... why hadn't he resisted her advance? Ducked or something?

Two hours earlier, Gabe had excused his crew, staying to assess every inch of the day's work. Presently, he worked upstairs doing whatever needed doing.

Leaving tools where he'd designated, she slipped out of his boots, leaned a shoulder against a column. Dusk twirled ribbons of light and shadow across the lawn. Signs of growth through scarred earth stirred her soul, color returning to Mom and Dad's property.

Her property.

Exercising remarkable skill, Silas, James, and Quinton had cleared overgrowth and unruly shrubs and were set to lace the front wings in hardy Nandinas to pair with existing azalea bushes that'd blossom bright pinks and whites in spring.

No doubt about it. Gabe was resourceful. Add to that, impulsive, presumptuous, provocative. But behind that cocky grin, he possessed benevolence enough to make Mother Theresa look selfish.

Like his ancestors.

In short, he'd laid able hands on Moreland, creating a virtual playground for his imagination.

According to Mom, when she'd first spotted this house from the highway, its countenance dull, cheerless— even spectral—vines choking the columns, she'd jogged through field grasses, twisting her ankle in an unseen rut. Hobbling over, she'd pressed her nose to the front window.

On the tail of a whimsical sigh, Mom's gaze had gone all dreamy, imagining the reality into existence.

A sorry-looking thing, empty for several years. But she found me, Everley, darlin'.

A finding that stole the very breath from Dad and left Mom overwhelmed. If Mom and Dad hadn't exhausted energy and resources trying to revitalize this place, maybe Dad would have kept a steadier footing on the roof.

And maybe in his marriage?

Mom had once shared a pithy piece of history with Everley about when she was five months pregnant with Serenity and left on a whim to Paris with Bonnie Sue. Upon her return, something between her and Dad had been amiss, his sexual passion lacking, the carriage of a guilt-ridden man ... though he'd staunchly denied infidelity.

Had Moreland exacted justice?

"Oh, God." Chin tipped, Everley lifted the feeble prayer toward an ethereal sky of gold, dusky rose, and slate while the horizon swallowed the last traces of daylight. "I feel like I'm crawling around in the dark."

Celestial lights twinkled like diamonds on velvet, heaven's glory rendering her speechless. Made sense how a man and woman could become so starstruck they'd made love beneath them. Unashamed, basking in Creation's gift.

An ideal ambiance in which to conceive a little girl.

She expelled an easy breath. A cool breeze kissed her cheeks and tugged at her hair. Cricket chirps drew her heart to memory's table, inviting her to sit. Taking sluggish steps toward the highway, she reached the road's edge and turned toward the house, awash in splendor.

A vision she'd never seen. Nor cared to.

Subdued moonlight traced a silver-edged roofline along the edifice, glowed along the trellis, and blushed the columns.

"Looking good, girl." The confession ribboned over her soul. Gooseflesh popped along her arms.

If only she could free herself from order and sameness, upend her aversion to change. Because maybe she'd figured things all wrong, the need to keep life in reconcilable columns becoming an idol. Tool guy certainly didn't fit into any of her columns and only added up to trouble.

"Like his kiss …" A buzz of emotion fell on her lips, sprouted a giddy smile, and zinged down her spine. The glittery feel of a girl in love.

The thing of it was, social media made it all too clear the handsome cover man was unavailable.

And you're not on the market.

As the veil of darkness thickened, the image of Gabe's work light beamed inside the colonnaded gallery and whisked her from a slow drag of desolation. A timely reminder she wasn't alone in this endeavor.

And when you get to dreamin', let others in, Everley Orion. The joy is meant to be shared.

Gabe was probably refinishing the refinishing of someone's refinishing until it was to Bellevue spec. A stiff standard to meet. One she appreciated. "What could he possibly be fiddling with up there?"

Through the open window sash, a country tune floated over the balcony, feathered her ears, Gabe's accompaniment drawing a grin. "Huh. A sappy love song."

Striding back, she halted mid-stride at the ping of a text, squinted to read it.

GABE: Look at your house.

A second text, this one a winking emoji.

Cute. But ... why—?

Several yards from the steps, a radiance of light illuminated the house and fell over the lawn. Eyes flaring, she faltered, thudding to her backside. Her bare feet flailed upward. Heart rate rapid, she scrambled to regain her footing. And her wits.

Gabe's solid form appeared at the railing, his silhouette encased in a flare of amber backlight. "You comin', Juliet?"

That husky invitation did nothing to slow her breathing. A ticklish grin claimed his dusky jawline.

Only hired help, only hired help.

Mouth agape, her tongue knotted. She stared long at the roughhewn Romeo before he ducked back through the sash, leaving her heart to freefall, lungs chugging erratically.

Minding her step, Everley quickened steps over the threshold. The illuminated entry scooped air from her lungs, sanded wood cool beneath her feet. Her gaze landed on Gabe's ambling descent on the formerly creaking staircase.

Oh heavens, if the tool guy didn't look all too much like the lord of the manor!

Hand latched in his, she followed his direction around the landing and toward the master suite.

Hand splayed on the sizable door, he eased it open. "Care to take a look-see?"

The sweet smell of polished pine soothed her soul. "I do."

Way to sound like a blushing bride.

She pinched the bridge of her nose and shook her head. *Stupid, stupid.*

Inside the formerly dark and lifeless space—the curator of haunting sobs—her anxiety dissipated. A scalloped string of white lights twinkled along the walls near the ceiling. In the center of an expansive canvas, a fresh linen-scented candle burned inside a jar. A basket sat open, corked bottle peeping out.

On each of two plates sat a cluster of grapes and a variety of cheeses. To her plate, he'd added a pile of french fries, ketchup drizzled over the top as though he'd taken great measure to create the right effect.

Wait. *Drizzled?* To perfection. The way she'd always eaten them.

Her eyes feasted on the magical scene, coaxing her skittish—stubborn—heart to indulge. To trust.

Plopping onto the blanket, he draped an arm over a bent knee and patted the floor. "Join me."

His tone held no question, his stare so intense she jerked her gaze away. Her heart lurched at the burn of his roaming eyes. Turning back, that teasing wink buckled her knees.

Trying for collected, she sat cross-legged near the edge of the canvas, maintaining proper distance. Yeah, right. In the bedroom of a hollowed house, atmosphere saturated with romance now brought to life by a handsome, skilled contractor with a body looking like *that*.

Great Scott!

She smoothed a hand along the floor, the feel of Momma and Daddy's footfall seeping through her fingers, twining around her heart. "It's beautiful, Gabe," she rasped.

"It's what I do, Orderly."

More. *Much more.*

"When the walls were exposed, I had my electrician two-step it and work overtime to upgrade the amp panel. As an incentive, I gave him and his wife a gift card to my buddy's restaurant, Ben's Seafood and Grille." He came to his knees, uncorked the bottle—*pop!*—and poured an effervescent liquid into a flute. "Champagne?"

She nodded, took the flute, inhaled the fruity scent. "Yes, thanks."

"You strike me as a girl who prefers her fries to look pretty but practical—to your way of thinking, I guess."

Reading her thoughts the way he did, the heat of his stare. It had the power to unravel her tightly wound agenda, re-thinking the benefits.

Flute raised, Gabe offered a toast. "To Moreland."

"To Moreland."

As they sipped, their eyes locked. She set down her flute and pointed to one of two prominent windows. "Mom used to kneel in prayer in front of an oval mirror that stood in the corner over there."

"She didn't strike me as the prayin' type."

"She wasn't."

He returned to a lazy posture on his side, propped on an elbow, and donned an expression eager for story.

"After Dad died, Mom tuned more into spiritual things. Praying to Jesus in front of the mirror helped her remember she'd been created in the image of a limitless God and should live life accordingly."

We were created to create, called to a purpose, our life a story we tell the world.

Yes, Momma.

"Do you believe that?"

At the tug of his stare, Everley turned back to Gabe. "What?"

"That God is limitless in creativity?"

"Of course." She took a warm, drizzled fry to her mouth and nibbled, coating her tongue in tangy pleasure.

"Then why won't you live it?"

Heat simmered inside her chest. She straightened—tugged at her ankles. "What do you mean?"

"If you can't make four out of two and two, then you won't even try new things."

"Au contraire, Sir Fix-A-Lot. Just look at me. I'm—"

"Oh, I'm looking at you," he said in a rogue chuckle. Another wink, his cedarwood gaze a hypnotic mix of tease and unfettered desire.

"Seriously. I'm here, miles from where I'm supposed to be, and knee-deep in the unknown. That should tell you something."

That impossible grin, those dimples tempting her to take a dive.

She swallowed another fry and quirked a brow in challenge. "As if exposing my private life on social media, being interviewed on camera … caught lip-locked with someone I hardly know … isn't a risk of epic proportions."

His shoulders heaved in silent laughter. One side of his mouth lifted in a grin. "Whew, your kiss was somethin' else, Orderly," he teased.

As was yours.

Lidded stare meant to maintain ire, she blustered out, "You better pray that mistake doesn't make it back to your girlfriend."

The sparkle in his eyes dimmed, an empty gaze drifting on a trail of thought while she scrambled to douse the passion rolling inside her as mighty as the Mississippi.

Weren't mistakes supposed to feel wrong?

"To my point, life ain't gonna add up all the time." He returned a level stare, a bold attempt to skirt the girlfriend mention. "The way I understand things, God does all the figuring and uses his own measuring stick."

Her posture went rigid. "My life has no need of change."

Disbelief skated over his brow, inciting clarification.

"It makes no sense to invest in something that might not turn out the way I'd hoped and risk losing something of value."

"Refusing to chase after what you want, settling for less than God's very best makes no sense. We're called to invest in eternal things now, even if we never live to see the results of it."

In the beat of quiet, Everley gathered Gabe's words like precious stones, stringing them across her heart. Just how long could she stay hinged to the status quo before the door to desire slammed shut?

"Why'd you go to all this trouble here tonight, Gabe?" Her words floated on whispered breath.

He sat upright, determination ablaze in his eyes. "This was no trouble. I wanted you to see what this place could be."

"I already know what it could be." A widow-maker. "I endured hours and hours of Mom and Dad's babbling about what it could be."

Disdain tinged his voice. "But all you're willing to see is a house in need of repair. The fact is, Moreland was built by masters of house preservation. Men, women, children, and, it turns out, my ancestors lived here. Families bonded by laughter, love."

A chapter of history broke loose. She wielded a defiant gaze. "And they died here."

Frustration marred his countenance.

"Gabe ..." Throat dry, her voice cracked. Anger fumed, unleashed in her tone. "My father died here."

His breathing stilled.

"He lost his footing on the south wing roof, broke his neck mere yards from where we sit."

Moisture swam behind her lids. She bit her lip against the swell of emotion.

"To be sure, that's an awful loss, Everley," he said in a hoarse whisper. "But consider that ..." Voice tender and low, he claimed her eyes. "... Moreland has also persevered through years of hardship and still teemed with life, walls holding over a century and a half of conversations." Inching close, his gaze grew serious. "Babies were born, even conceived, here."

Closer.

One side of his mouth quirked, smile lines beside his eyes deepening. "Probably in this very room."

She belted out an unfettered scoff. "I wasn't."

Interest sparked.

Time to detail the oddities of Marigold and Peter Lewis. She lolled her gaze. "Hiking the Appalachian Trail, Mom and Dad stopped to pitch their tent. Apparently, the sight of the constellations got them all hot and bothered. So they, well ... I was created beneath a wintery sky, the constellation Orion smiling down through a gaping hole in their tent. And thus, my full name ..." With a flourish, she placed a hand to her chest, giving a slight bow. "Everley Orion Lewis."

"That's fantastic." He rolled onto his back and laughed, tiny white lights playing in his eyes. "Everley Orion."

She'd always hated her name. It wasn't normal, certainly not awesome, Until now.

His laughter heightened.

"Glad my parent's twisted sense of humor amuses you," she sniped.

Gaze pulsing seriousness, he rolled back to his side. "You might be reluctant to dream, but it's a cryin' shame to keep others from enjoying Moreland. Why invest in her restoration, then refuse to keep and protect her? Particularly when you've got your momma's chosen commander at the helm."

A fact that would end once he'd been paid in full.

"How about this. When you're all done here, I'll sell Moreland to you. Fair market value." She poked his chest with a finger. "And you can bring all the life and laughter into it you want."

Humor rushed back in. "Can me and my wife make babies here?"

A treasonous blush flamed her cheeks. "You, sir, may do whatever it is you like in this place with whomever you choose."

Last thing Gabe wanted to be doing on a Saturday morning before meeting Randy at Moreland to tackle roof work was trek over a golf course hauling clunky clubs to maintain the charade that he was a fan of the sport.

Feet a shoulder-width apart, weight evenly distributed, body parallel to target, easy grip on the driver and ... upswing. Hand to his forehead, Gabe followed the dumb little ball, ego sinking along with it into the lake in hard *kerplunk!* Realizing, too, how incredibly ineffective those online golf tutorials were.

And ... a driving iron? The only iron he wanted to be driving was an electric drill.

Behind him, Warren's teasing gruff frayed his nerves.

Play along. "Rustier than I thought."

Because I hate the sport. How long could Gabe keep up appearance otherwise?

As long as it took.

"We're all set for Saturday evening, June sixteenth, at Hilton Riverside Hotel?"

Four weeks and counting.

A booby-trapped question if ever Gabe heard one. "Yes, sir," he said, both hands now wrenching the driver, palms aching for the familiar feel of a sledgehammer.

Warren snagged a ball from his shorts pocket and leaned with practiced flair to set it on a tee. "Paulette, my administrative assistant, has booked banquet space in the business complex. As far as I can surmise, Carmen still believes it's a gathering of family, friends, and business associates in honor of my birthday. Your proposal, then, will be the crown jewel of the evening."

Nodding minimally, disquiet fossilized in Gabe's chest. "And then ..." Hard cough. "You announce we've been awarded the contract."

Hesitation hovered in Warren's gaze. "Right." He landed two stiff pats on Gabe's shoulder as he stepped past him and assumed a ready stance near the ball.

Gabe tugged on his ball cap to shade indifference. Sweat mingled with his hair, itched along his neck, and sluiced down his back, the moisture-wicking polyester failing miserably.

Studied gaze drawn from the sunny fairway back onto the ball, Warren's arms raised high behind his right shoulder, a hard upswing and ... *smack!*

A hole in one.

"Paulette has arranged for media coverage, submitted invites to the entirety of my network. Naturally, you'll want to forward your client contact list to her, too."

Angst hissed inside Gabe's chest, guilt widening the divide between ethics and climbing a proverbial—and increasingly wobbly—ladder. This upscale shindig was acres from the forefront of his brain, most of the mental space having been occupied by Hollywood's next intrusion at Moreland first week of June.

Moreland was progressing, but he saw no way to complete her by September, Everley's frequent reference to Gabe as the manor house whisperer upping his pulse. He'd exhausted himself going over contractor work, assuring all hands were working to spec.

"You've secured a ring?"

Gabe turned an awakened glance at Warren.

"Carmen prefers a marquis." Warren's tone was devoid of question.

"I've given them a look, yes."

He had—an investment of funds that would be made possible, in part, by Everley's first payment.

The irony.

Eager to take Gabe into the family, Warren had offered to front the cost. Gabe respectfully declined, though he'd have had little spending strength without Moreland, the Cantrell project nearing completion, limited by budget restraint.

Gabe's phone alarm sounded. He released a relieved breath and silenced the phone. "Hate to say it, but that's a wrap for me, Warren. I'm due to meet my partner over at Moreland."

"No one understands the demands of work better than me. We've got a lifetime of games ahead of us."

A lifetime.

Leaving the course, Gabe drove to Moreland to meet Randy. The two sat shoulder to shoulder atop the pitched roof, a far more suitable playing field.

He trekked his gaze from the tips of the great oak to a snoozing Champ and surveyed the sun-kissed landscape. Hugged by sugarcane fields in the distance, Bayou Lafourche's winding waters were streaked by a ribbon of sunlight.

With a hard twist, Randy uncapped his water bottle. "You returned your father's call yet?"

A hard shake of Gabe's head left no room for chastisement.

Late last evening, he willed himself to listen to Dad's latest voicemail. This time his voice was pitiful, rife with defeat. Probably a string of restless nights, having kept company with Crown Royal.

There'd been no emergency. Dad simply wanted to reconnect. Adding a God mention. Apparently, he'd been following Gabe's progress—commented on the film gig. "For what it's worth, I'm proud of what you're doing. Hope it works to your advantage. Can't say things always do. But I figure you know that. Uh, love you, son. When you're able, call me ... please."

Where did Dad live anyway? An unwelcome rep, the result of faulty and unethical business practices, had a way of chasing a man out of town.

All Gabe knew was that the proverbial hammer had come down when he—merely a misguided young boy—had cut the wrong piece of lumber. The mistake resulted in a loss of business for Dad, another week of meager rations, and a widening blight on the Bellevue name.

But it was Mom's words that'd seared Gabe's soul.

You're a no-good Bellevue just like your daddy and don't fit in anywhere. You'll never see one day of success.

And off she went. For the last time.

Gabe shook his head, attempting to dislodge the memory. Because maybe she was the object of his resentment, not Dad.

"You restore things, Gabe. Best there is," Randy said. "Might be time to reconcile. Let God restore your heart."

Guilt squeezed his chest, soured his stomach, the past threatening to rot the present.

"Carmen's happy with my heart the way it is."

The achievement of success had enabled him to scale the social ladder, Carmen Murdock being an added reward. An incredibly beautiful woman, she came prepackaged with a coveted invitation to join Murdock's enterprise at the top rung. Even though Gabe sucked at golf and was coughing up many a sunny weekend driving over an endless green obstacle course.

That and he'd yet to determine where God fit into Carmen's life.

Randy vented a noisy exhale. "It's not her opinion of your heart that matters most. And the fact that Champ's hackles rise in her presence is a red flag in my book." His cocky assertion toted a bitter edge.

A poster child for a happy family man who enjoyed a wife named Summer and two kids, Randy lived in a restored house rimmed in a white picket fence. But property ownership depended on Gabe's ability to pay his people.

"I'm giving Carmen a ring."

In a hard flinch, Randy fired a glare, nearly losing his balance. "You can't be serious."

Champ jumped to all fours. Barked. Twice. Added an unwelcome snarl.

Of all the rescue dogs in Louisiana, he picked one with strong opinions.

"She's game. I'm game."

"Game? You make marriage sound like you're going to the movies." Randy's tone went hard. "Like if either of you don't like it, you'd just walk out."

"Mom did. Dad no longer suited her after his failings led to the loss of nearly all they owned."

Possessions that included Gabe's first and only pair of brand-name basketball shoes that hadn't been purchased from a thrift store.

Worth eighty bucks and sold without consent for fifty cents.

"Just because your parents didn't love each other well doesn't justify a fair-weather attitude about what you know is a sacred union."

A mild tremor shuddered beneath his skin and singed his heart.

"You've built this company on the unwavering principle that once a historic is restored, it must be maintained. That requires two equally committed parties."

A beat of silence. The thud of his heart slashed at his reasoning.

"And dude, there's Everley."

At the sound of her name, her image flashed. Shifting emeralds ignited with desire after she kissed him. She'd held his stare like she might finally consider letting go of reluctance—Gabe being the prime reason. An awkward laugh erupted. "What about her?"

"Spare me the feigned look of disinterest, boss. You've never stopped loving her."

"She's my client."

Randy's eye roll worsened Gabe's effort to keep any emotional distance from his red-haired crush.

"That kiss was nothing more than a tactic to calm me down so I wouldn't plant a fist in Alex Coleman's jaw."

A kiss Gabe had longed for since the age of seventeen. Way better than he'd imagined. Matchless, even, the desire for which being the sole reason he excelled on the court. A kiss he wanted to wake up to every day.

"And you kissed her back."

Elation fluttered down Gabe's spine at the image of Everley's satisfied smile in that moment when the earth stilled in its orbit. He scrubbed a hand along his bristled jaw. Against the pull of gravity, he draped arms atop bent knees, toes flexed, heels digging in.

"You went to great lengths to light up the place so the two of you could share time alone," Randy added.

"I was merely casting a vision." Savoring Everley's reaction to those fries, drizzled with ketchup the way she'd eaten them in high school ... oblivious to the fact he'd studied her from a safe distance in the cafeteria.

"Tell me, Gabe. Just how much vision did you show her?"

"Nothing happened," Gabe spit out, clipping false ideas before they blossomed. "She's so hardheaded about this house, refuses to see its potential. Every house needs a chance to fulfill its purpose. It needs an advocate."

"Preaching to the choir here." Randy's gaze went pensive. "Maybe you've been chosen to show her that. God doesn't work singularly. What's he's doing in one life fulfills his purpose in another."

He let the wisdom settle while a rumbly chuckle sounded in Randy's throat.

"Sure doesn't hurt that she's a God-fearing, intelligent woman who looks to be saving herself for the right guy. Rare find these days."

"And beautiful."

Somebody's dream girl.

"If you build a house on a cracked foundation, no amount of exterior paint will spare its demise," Randy said.

Gabe knew. He'd spent years sidestepping faulty workmanship, his aim for perfection the bedrock of his success. Was the Murdock matchup nothing but a zero-sum game? His gain, her loss?

Answers went missing.

CHAPTER FOURTEEN

Bryson's call on the first of June created an undesirable rift. No thanks to unprecedented rains in southern Louisiana, MidDay bowed their strict schedule to the forces of nature, bringing their caveat into play.

"Based on the prediction of Gulf storms in August and September, we'll need to double up in June and July, possibly extend the succession of film days when we've got cooperative weather. As a result, footage of construction is ahead of narrative again, and we're lacking owner perspective, particularly how you believe G&R has met your mother's expectations."

Ah, yes. Mom.

"Could we have you here Monday, June 4th through, say, Wednesday?"

Mediate. Problem solve.

"I'll see what I can do."

Ending the call, Everley sighed. How will this affect Gabe? Soggy weather had already impeded his crew's progress. Executives were giving off vibes of dissatisfaction and still butting heads with him on occasion.

Any hint of unrest threatened an undoing she couldn't afford.

To satisfy production demand, she delegated tasks where possible, rescheduled on-site client visits, and booked a flight to New Orleans, arriving Sunday. She'd spend the next several days with Serenity in her private apartment above her bakery.

Unsurprisingly, Phillip bristled at the news. "I'd already assigned you to conduct accounting software systems training for the new hires next week."

"Then let's reschedule for the second week in June."

His chest caved in a puff of condescension. "It might be best for me to pass this on to Tyler."

She flipped a hard stare at his stony veneer. "I know the software far better than he does."

"Which is why I assigned you to conduct training in the first place."

"Short of untimely death, I'm under contract to cooperate with production. I own the house. No one else can fill in for me."

"Your job here needs to take priority. Particularly when an offer of partner has been granted."

Thrust into a cosmic game of monkey in the middle, Everley's conundrum fortified the reason a girl of sound mind should not reach for the stars. But, hey, if Tyler choked, it'd swing favor her direction.

Her chin firmed in resolve. "Best if you go ahead and assign the task to Tyler."

May he crash and burn.

In her condo Friday evening, Everley turned toward the window to see a marred view of Lake Michigan, its magnificence blurred by drilling rain. Per routine, she and Tyler should be eating at Milano's, but ...

"They went out of business," Tyler had said earlier. "We'll need to find a new place."

New meant different. And different meant unpredictable. Unpredictable brought chaos. Thus, here she sat beside Tyler while he threw a fist in the air at the flat-screen, barking at the refs.

Side-by-side. Worlds apart.

The scent of Chinese takeout curdled her stomach. She hated Chinese takeout. Friends should know each other's likes and dislikes.

Drizzled fries, please.

And then she'd gone and let talking heads of a sports network preempt the latest episode of *Fixed Up Right*.

A sudden urge to push back the walls nearly overtook her. But she'd chosen her parameters, the high-rise Gold Coast property a supremely genius investment. Until life intruded, coaxed a girl's longing, and shrunk her previously generous square footage to that of a matchbox.

Unbidden, biblical truth surfaced, rustled the edges of her heart.

I am limitless in creativity. The Giver and sustainer of dreams, your ever-present help in times of trouble.

"Help I need in large doses," she quipped.

"Huh?" Tyler's gaze flared while glued to the screen, jaw tight and intense.

"Nothing."

Everything, really.

Thoughts of Gabe set her heart to thundering a nervous rhythm. That kiss. She swiped at her lips as if to erase its impact. Three weeks later, and it still felt fresh, moist, tingly. Right and wonderful. Somehow even long overdue.

Sensuous kisses should be shared between lovers, committed until death. Like it'd been with Kyle.

Gabe's felt ... perfect.

Reckless imaginings floated through her mind's eye, Gabe and she together, breaking bounds of mere client and contractor. One to manage and market the place, open it to the public. Another to maintain its value.

Laying a foundation together.

Reach for the stars, Everley Orion!

The team of two made sense. Created order.

He was the reason she'd even consider the idea of selling her condo and disrupt her plan to accrue several more years of appreciation.

No way. Would she?

At halftime, Tyler silenced the game, splintering her thoughts. He draped an arm about her shoulder. "Game two for Warriors and Cavs is Sunday. Let's move Monday's pizza night to Sunday."

"I'll be out of town."

"Where?"

Three, two, one ...

"Louisiana."

"Again?" He twisted her direction. "Who's doing the software training?"

"Phillip said he would assign you to take my place."

"I object, Everley," he said, finger raised in protest. "I'm not your client."

You big baboon CPA-lawyer.

She stood, cupped her elbows, crossed to the window. A chill emanated off the glass and bored into her bones. Flickers of industrial light were barely discernible within the inky blackness filling a retrofit, fixed window.

"We've seen each other once since you got back."

She spun to face him. "I can count, thank you very much. And correction. You watched the Cubs while I studied home improvement DIYs on the internet."

Also checked Moreland's website, dictated emails, and responded to a burgeoning number of social media followers, the endeavor a bit euphoric, particularly since she'd topped Serenity's followers.

Lewis spirit at its finest.

"That's how we roll." Tyler's tone languished, a tendril of desperation curling around his eyes.

Right. Easy and uncomplicated. Someone to keep her warm when snow piled high. Someone with whom to share Monday night deep dish while he updated her on sports stats.

Someone to keep her life ordinary. Routine.

Boring.

The way they rolled was beginning to make her dizzy.

"Yes, but a little dialogue would be nice."

Raking hands through his hair, he unleashed a frustrated sigh. "So I score minus five on that account."

But no good would come from sniping at an agitated lawyer with impressive verbal defense skills who'd been left to conduct software training while she ...

Admit it.

Pursued a dream.

A muggy June hovered over Napoleonville as Everley drove her rental to Moreland. Easing up the drive, she parked behind the imposing MidDay van situated beside the G&R van. Gabe's white truck sat to her left. She let her eyes rest on it. Noting—and memorizing—its detail. Fitting for a guy like him. Unfettered and wild, scratched in places.

The sheer fact Gabe had agreed to cooperate with MidDay's unforeseen intrusion was astonishing. Maybe he'd sensed the impending storm clouds, a rumble of production's discontent that could topple the investment for both of them.

The crystal blue sky that'd touched the horizon earlier, sunbathing the landscape in mellow gold, was awash in dingy white clouds. Faint sounds of thunder gurgled. Through Gabe's driver's side window, a guttural snore clawed the air. Inside the passenger seat, a gaunt, older man sat with his head lolled against the glass, jaw unhinged like a baby bird in what appeared to be an inebriated doze.

No, no.

"He did *not* bring that drunken war vet along."

Oh, but he had.

"Later. I'll hog-tie him later."

She ditched aggravation and directed the little energy she had into concealing the haggard appearance of a girl who'd had no more than three hours of sleep.

A quick rearview mirror check exposed evidence of having eaten one of Serenity's latest cupcake creations. She wiped the buttery gloss from her mouth and finger-brushed her hair. The mid-thigh denim skirt and pearl and sequin encrusted jacket over a teal, scoop neck shirt should satisfy wardrobe guidelines.

Near the drive, a low buzz sounded from the woodworking tent erected in front of the house.

The sound of Gabe and his crew hard at work.

Minding ruts, she trod over the lawn and peeked inside to see Silas running a weathered plank against a table saw, creating a clean new edge.

Standing upright, Silas raised his goggles. Chocolate eyes twinkled, framed by smile lines, gaze tender and welcoming. "How-dee, Miz Scott."

She returned his smile. "Hi, Silas. How are you?"

He glugged from a thermos and set it down. "Better than I deserves."

Attitude is everything, Everley Orion. Choose a good one.

Even in this.

Being the oldest, she'd been hardwired to take care of things. Stopping short of overwhelming her heart.

An unsettling quiet of inactivity overtook her. "Where is everyone?"

Okay, *him*.

"Takin' a recess, I believes he say."

She cocked a stern brow and tensed her smile, restraining a huff.

Outside the tent, her eye caught an object flying over Moreland's imposing roof. Nicking the tip of the pediment, a neon green frisbee hung in the air, then glided a distance before landing in an easy slide on the lawn.

Jovial laughter sounded from behind the north wing. Alex emerged, balancing his shoulder cam, slow-stepping backward. Production kept pace, hoisting a boom mic from an elongated pole.

Quinton dashed across the lawn and scooped up the frisbee, Alex tracking his stride. Champ bounded behind him, barking after it.

Completing the three-ring circus, Gabe appeared in jeans and those careworn boots. Shirtless, for crying out loud!

Quinton gave the frisbee an impressive fling back to Gabe. Arms pumping, Gabe chased after the disc, bent to snatch it off the veranda, and flung it to Quinton, who leaped to snag it mid-air and attempted to fling it back.

But the frisbee took flight and landed with a *pop* several yards ahead of her feet.

What clause in Gabe's contract allowed for foolishness?

When she caught his eyes, he sprinted her direction, oblivious to the daggers in her gaze. Oblivious to the darkening, rumbly sky.

Champ outran his rascally master, dashing toward her. He came to a halt, sat on his hind legs, and pawed her shirt, streaking it brown before slobbering a tongue over her cheek.

She muffled a growl, dusting dirt off her shirt.

Champ circled her twice, rolled onto his back, and whined. All four legs bent and parted, unashamed. She stooped to oblige the irresistible dog with a tummy rub and murmured, "Bet you learned this from your master."

Speaking of ...

"Hey there, Orderly!" A smile to rival the stretch of the mighty Mississippi widened across Gabe's face. She'd like to drain the life out of it.

He eased to a slow trot across the lawn, the vision of his well-defined features now coming into focus. A trimmed auburn scruff dusted his jaw, drawing upward along his cheeks. Chiseled biceps hinged beneath solid shoulders. The look of a man who worked hard. Skills unmatched. Highly sought after ... weakening her resolve.

But little good would come to her heart by adding more layers of irresistibility to his résumé.

Champ scrambled to all fours, those pitiful, shifty eyes taking on the look of a kid caught making out on the front porch. Something else he'd learned from his master?

MidDay kept pace, nimbly sidestepping at his approach, exerting effort to make themselves scarce.

Lids lowered to slits, she struggled to summon ire. If nothing else, to minimize the beautiful view of his solid upper body, glistening in invitation. God help her—it took all she had not to inhale his masculine scent, catalogue the scene, and tuck it away in her memory for retrieval once she returned to the Windy City.

She interlaced her arms and tapped her toe like a jackhammer.

Encircling them, Alex inched around in easy steps.

"I didn't get the memo," she said.

"Wh-what memo would that be, Orderly." The breadth of his shoulders heaved as he sucked in air, playful gaze searching her face for clues.

"About recess taking priority over work."

Humor drained from his eyes. "You're questioning me?" He angled his head, brows pinched above darkened gaze, mouth held in a disbelieving smile.

"Once again, I've disrupted my work to fulfill an obligation. You, on the other hand, are out here tossing a frisbee."

He took steps closer, glare scalding. "I *have* been working. I've been bringing joy and life back to your momma's place. Do you not see the thirteen thousand square foot evidence of that?" Targeting the house, he gave a backward sweep of his arm.

Memories of the basketball superstar had surfaced. "It's no wonder you were suspended in high school."

Years spent hiding in shadows, she'd never dreamed someone of his status would've given her a second glance. Then again, except for a failed attempt at being a cheerleader, she'd never really dreamed … anything.

His jaw clenched, tone softened by what had to be injured pride. "There's good reason for that, Orderly."

In the silence, she moved her gaze in effort to avoid another incriminating once-over. Fighting against images of him offering his heart, endearing eyes … an offer she might not be able to refuse. The two of them forever invested in this place.

Stupid, stupid!

Dreams don't pay the bills.

Dreams are costly.

And trouble follows a dreamer.

The darkening sky grumbled. One raindrop smacked Everley's cheek, another spit in her eyes.

Maintaining a close distance near the great oak, the production crew gathered beneath the canopy and murmured in feverish pitch in front of monitors.

"Look, all I see is you—*half-naked*—goofing off with Quinton, leaving work to Silas when it's you I'm paying to renovate this mess."

In response to her testy stance, a tick rumbled along his jaw. Nostrils flared—his eyes a stony gray above thinned lips. Raindrops dotted his chest and dampened his hair.

Neither of them looking or acting polished for the show.

He stepped close. "I don't appreciate your questioning my work ethic or how I conduct my business."

The bloodthirsty look in his eyes suggested she'd stepped out of bounds.

Eyes jagged glass, he paused to graze her face, stretched the length of his stare before taking a slow turn in a hard trek across the lawn.

Don't leave.

She scuffled behind and caught him on the arm, a subtle awareness that MidDay's interest had piqued, their steps nearing and purposeful.

He freed his arm from her grasp. Hastened his stride.

Quelled by regret, she kept to his heels. Another choked attempt at apology softened her tone. "Gabe, I'm ..."

Rain fell faster, saturating the lawn. He stomped into a muddy puddle, dotting her legs a thick, oozy brown.

Her heart wrenched in contrition. "Gabe, please hear me out."

At that, he slowed and turned to face her like one of those western films where the cowboy's rifle peeped beneath his poncho, eyes steeled in defense. He shifted his stance. Rain trickled off his nose, his jaw.

Pain registered on his face.

"My father came up short, as did his father before him." Teeth clenched, he glanced away, thumb and forefinger pressed to his eyes before he turned back. "And so help me, God, it ain't gonna happen to me, and it'll darn sure never happen to my sons," he thundered, thumb jabbing his chest.

The punch of having unknowingly tripped a wire inside him surged in explosive heat, plumes of confusion clouding her brain. The revelation nearly choked her speechless. Regret coursed through her veins—for having let herself care and allowing him to show her the value of this stinking place. Disrupting her ordered existence.

For kissing him and liking it so much.

And now—

She cupped her cheeks, the heat of her palms matching the air swirling around her. "Y-y-you have … sons?"

A resigned grin tipped the corners of his mouth. He shook his head slowly, her skin burning hot as his assessing gaze drew down her front and back up. "There was a time when I'd hoped you'd be the one to help me out with that."

At her gasp, he started for his truck, mud spurting from the back of his boots. Breathless, she fixed her gaze on his shrinking image. To think, for three agonizingly long milliseconds, Gabe was a father. Then discovering he was not. And then smacked with the not-so-subtle confession that he'd once desired her to be the mother of them?

God, how do I reconcile that?

On the heels of unscripted, MidDay exchanged energized high fives.

"Brilliant."

A renegade smile tugged at Alex's lips. "A few more delicious scenes like that, and we'll have H2H eating out of our hands."

If she'd learned anything, it was that 'cut' meant nothing.

CHAPTER FIFTEEN

A dank scent wafted off the pavement outside the Pear Tree following last night's fast-moving storm. Inside the bakery, a swoosh of air cooled Gabe's sweaty brow. He inhaled the tantalizing scent of pastry, coffee, and welcome.

"Morning, Gabe," Serenity said. "I'll get your coffee and muffin in just a sec." She hoisted a painting against the back wall, angling her head in scrutiny. "Not sure if I like this or not. Whatcha think?"

The piece resembled an abstracted depiction of stick-figured zoo animals juggling rotten apples. "If you're looking for a modern psychotic vibe, then I say keep it. Otherwise ..." He pursed his lips and gave a thumbs down.

Sounding an exasperated sigh, she set that ugly junk down and dusted her palms. "Aw, who asked you anyway," she chuckled.

In minutes, she handed him a lidded cup of coffee and a warmed, jumbo muffin on a plate. Fragrant lavender roses graced the counter near the glass case. He sat by the window and set to task, first checking texts and email on his phone.

Until Carmen called. Make that, wife-to-be.

She pecked his brain with questions related to Saturday's gala, an event for which he had no opinion.

The real issue was where she stood in her relationship with God. Because when a guy builds on a poor foundation, the structure is destined to collapse. But following a few attempts to unearth her world view, he'd come up empty. She'd shrugged at discussing anything related to God or spiritual subjects. No concern about eternal security. Hers or anyone else's.

An unequally yoked couple will only postpone the inevitable, Gabe. Because as you set to furrow the field of your marriage, one of you is gonna be pulling in the opposite direction, and your relationship won't withstand the pressure. Both eyes need to be fixed ahead, stepping in pace with God.

Adam Carmichael's wisdom returned, a gale-force wind against Gabe's heart. Looked as if he'd be carrying sole responsibility for the spiritual discipline of his sons. Had the pursuit of success cost more than it promised?

Walls closed in.

Randy's incoming call spared him further questions.

"Boss, you won't believe what I'm seeing over here at Moreland." An ominous tone seeped into his voice. "Measurable amount of water took a fancy to the place after last night's storm."

At the news, his ear burned against his phone. Water and house in the same sentence didn't bode well.

"Inside the master, the plaster is bulging, and there's a sizable hole in the ceiling, hardwoods damaged. Worse than when we started."

Disaster. Gabe's heart seized in his chest.

"Apparently, the roof wasn't sealed properly. I dunno. We'll have to clean up and begin fresh."

The tick of a time bomb pinged in Gabe's brain. He stood, chair screeching across the floor. "I'll come check it out."

Though Randy acted as foreman for this project, effectively relieving Gabe from extensive travel to and from Napoleonville, the involvement of a production company interested in capturing his interactions with Everley had upset the natural order of business.

Serenity gestured from the counter. At his approach, concern deepened the lines around her eyes. She put her hand aside her mouth and whispered, "I thought you should know, our buddy Merrill got beat up last night. He was found near Jackson Square."

Rage sizzled low. Gabe curled fingers around the counter's ledge. "Where's he at?"

"University Med Center."

Turning toward the door, he patted the counter. "Headed over now."

"Wait, before you go …" Serenity used a tong to pinch three muffins and popped them into a brown paper bag. "Tell my jazz pal these are from the bakery girl and that I'm praying for him."

Arriving at the emergency room parking lot, Gabe read Randy's text.

RANDY: Worse than I thought. Things heating up at Moreland. Get here ASAP.

GABE: On my way.

Which he was, only Moreland would have to wait behind Merrill.

People first.

At the emergency department, Gabe dashed to the admissions window, bag of muffins in hand. "I'm here to see a Merrill Downing."

The attendant checked the screen. "He's been taken to surgery. You won't be able to see him."

"What's his condition?"

"HIPPA rules prohibit me from sharing information without patient consent."

Gabe tightened his grip on the paper bag. "What's his condition?"

Eyes flaring a bit, her brow lifted. She glanced left and right, returned to meet his stare, and held her voice in check. "Fractured jaw. Possible heart attack. He'll likely be transferred to surgical intensive care."

Backstepping, he returned a minimal nod of thanks. The sound of misery in the lobby caught his attention. A middle-aged man wrenched a handkerchief in his fist. Three others gathered around. Relentless sobbing saturated the room.

"My son ... my only son." The man rocked in his seat, chest heaving as he choked on tears. Agony marked his profile. Slowly, he tipped his gaze and raised his palms—a gesture of surrender or disdain. Gabe didn't know which.

Stepping lightly, Gabe wandered over to see the man's red-streaked, searching gaze.

He offered the muffins and turned for the exit. Having sustained a fractured jaw, Merrill wouldn't be enjoying them anytime soon.

Mounting his Harley, questions riveted his soul. Whose only son was Gabe? What would it have been to have a father who held such love for his child?

Consider the cross.

Yes, but why did that degree of love come packaged in trouble and heartache?

Embrace emptiness as a gift. Your success is measured in Me.

The truth stoked embers in his heart, the rumble of his engine fanning it to robust blaze ... awakening something in his soul.

Arriving at Moreland, Gabe was greeted by what amounted to a highly combustible foreman.

Scrambling to regroup, Alex directed the crew to huddle around Gabe and Randy as they discussed the situation. Great. The appearance of substandard workmanship caught on film slashed at his ego like a saw sash. But then, no better time to let a viewing audience know he was the man who could fix anything. Assume the role of the guy Everley had come to believe he was. Or at least she had before their last encounter that left him wondering if she might not have considered concealing an explosive somewhere on the property.

Boooom! His dream job, her mother's dream ... ashes and rubble.

Over and done.

The ominous scent of moist, musty air in the entry hung in a thick drape, clung to the walls, stole the air from Gabe's lungs.

A dry house is a happy house.

Tripwires anywhere?

As MidDay closed in, Gabe squared his shoulders as though the magnitude of the situation was no worse than a misplaced nail hole. "All righty, what are we looking at here."

Randy's countenance hissed white-hot heat, a targeted glare to turn concrete to dust. "I told you in no uncertain terms this was urgent. Since we spoke, more issues have arisen. Where have you been?"

Warning drew at Gabe's brow. "Seeing about a friend."

Business partner and life-long friend, Randy knew when to shut it.

"In addition to electrical outages, we've discovered some of those little historic house ghosts behind the walls and beneath the floor." He gestured as Gabe walked in step, working to sustain an unruffled air.

Upstairs, he followed Randy down the shadowed hallway toward the back of the house. Pale sunlight fell on the floor and drew Gabe's gaze upward. Light shouldn't be streaming in.

"For starters," Randy said, stopping in place, "we've discovered there's more rotted wood behind these walls than we thought. The result of years of slow leakage in the pipes."

Disbelief weakened his stance.

"Next, the contractor you hired to install the antique door we restored and customized to fit this doorway cut the opening too wide." He traced the gaping space with a pointed finger that screeched in Gabe's head like a freight train braking on its tracks.

Fear shot nails into his heart. He rubbed his bristled chin.

Randy handed him a retractable tape measure.

Gabe stretched it across the width and length of the opening, the dimensions off on all three sides by nearly six inches—the gap between amateur and professional narrowing to paper-thin.

Workmanship that looked like someone he'd never hire, much less to handle a treasure of Moreland's magnitude. Bigger issue was that he'd failed to lay eyes on the workmanship of his crew and give it his approval.

Bumbled the project of a lifetime.

"Not only that, but the stone foundation beneath this monstrosity may not be holding up against the assault of jackhammers and backhoes. I noticed several doors that won't open or shut without effort."

Production's jarring light targeted the wall and hungrily widened in scope around the miscalculated mess and fixed on Gabe whose gaze darted left-right, wishing he could start all over.

A rookie mistake.

You're a failure ... just like your ole' man.

With a toss of his head, Randy directed Gabe toward the master suite, production scrambling behind as though tethered to his ankle. "Here's the real issue."

Real had about taken him under.

Entering the room after Gabe, the light technician took to one corner, amply illuminating the room while Alex adjusted his position to avoid unwanted shadows.

Threads of cracked plaster on the ceiling and along the adjoining wall took on the look of gnarled fingers reaching to take him by the neck. A blackened hole of about two feet diameter at its widest stared him down. His stomach clenched, threatened to unload the contents of his lunch onto the now warped hardwoods, a precious and costly delivery that'd traveled from overseas.

"Some idiot exercising shoddy workmanship thought it'd be okay to work the front section of the roof with a fast-moving storm on its way."

Last night. Brief, but fierce.

"Along the gables, the felt paper was nailed down over the drip edge rather than beneath it. Now we've got trapped moisture making contact with fascia."

Yeah, some idiot ... hadn't bothered to sign off on the work of his crew ... racing against time alongside them ... not thinking things through. At times, hustling alone after hours, chasing the sunset. Muscling through with the strength of three men.

Impress the girl. Preserve his status and single-handedly blot out family failure.

Gabe squeezed his eyes shut.

How, God, how?

Panic swooped through his lungs. He diffused it. "I'll take care of it. No problem."

Randy flicked an open-mouthed glare at Gabe. "Do you know what it's going to take to rework the rafting and roofing components up top, replace the hardwoods ... get this place dried up and replastered?"

He knew.

With the drain to his bank account, paying contractors in monetary gifts to speed things up, he couldn't make last month's construction loan payment. He'd exhausted favors with people. And now, he'd need to place another nonrefundable materials order. The 50 percent Everley owed wasn't due till the end of June.

A custom mold of the six-foot section of original crown molding in the master would have to be made. At best guess, a month to replace. For a season, Dad had been the man to call for specialty work like that. But faulty practices—made worse by Crown Royal—shot holes in his reputation.

Shame tugged his gaze to the ground, out of the line of taunting camera lenses. He sanded the floor with the toe of his boot.

"Hey, boss." Contempt soured Randy's tone. "Is this *your* mistake?"

Slowly, Gabe raised his head, squinting under the blaring light burning his cheek.

The nonanswer betrayed him.

Randy shook his head and fired deadly rounds at Gabe's ego. "You're so driven to succeed you've let your standards slip. Make that *our* standards." He slapped a hand to his chest. "And hooked yourself to a woman you don't even love."

"I love Carmen," he shot back.

"Uh-uh." He dared jab a finger at Gabe. "You love what she *and* her daddy can do for you, a means to secure success that's confused your heart for your head."

From the shifting silhouette behind the camera, a guffaw pinged against the wall and ricocheted a nasty slap across his face. He turned to see Josiah, expression plastered in amused derision.

Finger raised, he shuddered his eyelids to slits. "Turn that thing off *now*—you got that?"

Undaunted, Josiah stood motionless, a hint of the devil in his eyes.

Alex moved into position, arms crossed, daring Gabe to carry on.

Heat climbed into his neck. "Did you hear me, Spielberg? I need you to delete that segment and turn this thing off."

The brim of Alex's cap shadowed his steely gray gaze, his brow a deep furrow of storm clouds. Inner conflict registered on his face as though contemplating a hazardous decision. "Mr. Bellevue, per our contract, you don't tell us what we can and cannot film. This is *my* project, one in which I've invested thousands of dollars. You hammer at things, I direct. Now, if you can't see reason, we'll secure a double to take your place."

Alex turned toward the crew, seemingly in slow motion, and parted his hands like a man who'd been pushed beyond his limit.

Detailed cumulative general ledgers, income statements, depreciation schedules, and inventory listings for Louella's Boutique awaited scrutiny, presently splayed like a game of cards across the screen of Everley's laptop situated on a desk in an angular back room near a sagging clothing rack.

"If their accounting records are every bit as organized as their merchandise, this should go well."

Her cell buzzed aside her laptop. "Hello."

"Everley Scott? This is Chuck Eisendrath, H2H network."

Not every day a girl gets a call from a cable network executive. Surely, he intended to contact some big wig on production's end of this financial enterprise. But ordinary Everley Orion Lewis—offspring of the eccentric—now stood on the precipice of becoming a household name.

She'd created a virtual feeding frenzy each time she'd posted images of the house, production crews ...

Him.

And them. *Mostly* them.

She blinked to attention. "What can I do for you?"

"A lot, actually. Issues have been brought to my attention. Irreconcilable ones."

A jolt fired through her chest. Shifting in her chair, she steadied her voice, prepped to reconcile. Everley, Queen of Reconciliation.

She clicked the end of a pen. "Such as?"

"Word from production is that Alex Coleman has threatened to drop the project. In the interest of all involved, you'll have to let Mr. Bellevue go and find a replacement, or we'll have to reconsider taking this on as a network offering."

Click, click, click.

"I'm bound by contractual agreement with him."

"As you are with MidDay Media. And while H2H and MidDay are separate entities, we do own first rights of refusal. Their financial investment is based largely on our willingness to give the manor house restoration idea top consideration. Being familiar with things of this nature, you can understand the risk they've undertaken."

"Yes, but—"

"It's in our best interest to ensure that MidDay is able to produce a quality product, and from the sound of it, things are unraveling on the set."

A silent pause stretched long. The cloy of disaster prickled moisture along her forehead.

"I realize your decision to contract with Mr. Bellevue—"

"Gabe."

A sharp cough. "The decision to contract with *Gabe*, then ... was based on your mother's desire, but the fact is, you're the owner and are, therefore, free to find a replacement."

Desperation shuddered through her heart. "That's just it. I'm not free. He's the one. It has to be him. His scrupulous attention to detail is the reason my mother specified that no one else was to handle the house. The reason clients wait months for him." Pulse ticking faster, she jabbed a finger on the desktop. "I repeat, he's the one."

He's the reason.

The sentiment reverberated through her. Shot wonderful doses of unforeseen satisfaction down her spine and filled her thoughts with a colored, three-dimensional perspective.

But there she went, standing in the gap for the wild card contractor and speaking up for a house she'd despised for years.

A widow-maker.

"Be that as it may, Gabe's method of operation has cost scads of time and expense and put production woefully behind. And, if I may be candid, this project has turned into a nightmare."

Eyes stinging, she turned from her phone and sniffed.

Quiet boomed against the walls, pounded inside her chest.

She drew in a long breath and returned to Chuck.

"From the beginning, Gabe was upfront about how long it could take to complete the job. He's worked till his fingers bled to satisfy unrealistic demands, up against strict production schedule."

"Are you aware he's responsible for damage following that storm? Through Alex Coleman's lens, the house looks worse than before he started."

"Damage?"

"Ah. You haven't seen it." His voice went flat before he unleashed a smug laugh. "Have your boy send pictures. I think you'll agree. The place is looking beyond help."

Defeat weighed heavy. Her shoulders sank as she expelled a long stream of air. And pictures never did justice. Instead, she'd see her house, er, Mom's house, firsthand.

Hardly a sacrifice. It seemed Moreland ... and Gabe ... needed a champion.

Chuck's breathing rang like a raging bull pawing the dirt. "You are aware MidDay initially considered other houses to produce a rock-solid pilot for our consideration."

"None to match Moreland's stately vision and charm or render you breathless when your eyes gaze across the façade. None with the same degree of picturesque appeal. None holding my unique story."

None touched by the hands of Gabriel Michael Bellevue.

Lengthy pause, the stir of hot breath. "Get back with me, Ms. Scott, and we'll discuss how to proceed. Have a nice day."

Why on earth did people think it was acceptable to make a bloody mess of someone's day and follow with the shallow platitude to have a nice one?

If the place was as awful as Chuck had said, Everley would make a clandestine, firsthand assessment. Alone.

Sparing Gabe from witnessing her response. Refusing to bother him for pictures in advance.

Any story Moreland had to tell would be told soon enough.

CHAPTER SIXTEEN

Due to Saturday's soaking rains, Everley delayed the site visit to Moreland and, instead, cozied up to the storefront window in Serenity's bakery, sipping coffee, processing audits while Serenity worked the counter and Lettie baked. In the afternoon, Kourtney breezed in and served as barista through closing.

Sunday afternoon, an evaporating heat bore down on Everley's bare shoulders below a sleeveless, cotton dress and warmed her sandaled feet. Standing on the drive, she brushed a sentimental gaze over the property and stroked it across Moreland's balcony and pillars.

"Hmmm. On the contrary, Chuck. She's looking exceptionally lovely." Her assessment drifted skyward, carried along by a gentle summer breeze.

Though still weak under the weight of sawing and hammering, Moreland's former smile had surfaced. The one Howard Gallagher intended in his supreme design. A smile multiple families must have enjoyed long ago. Before trouble visited, and her countenance drew lines of sorrow.

Absent construction and film crew, the property was wrapped in a pleasant hush, an eager bride awaiting processional cue.

A breeze sang from the great oak as Everley eased over sprigs of new growth on a revitalized lawn. Through the threshold, she smoothed her hand along the railing and made her way upstairs.

The musty scent of wet plaster, pinewood, and dust wafted down, assailed her senses. Pricks of natural light dotted the steps. She tipped her gaze to its source, assaulted by holes.

Tiny, yes, but ... holes?

Ire plumed. "What a godforsaken mess."

Her heart lurched at the sound of shuffling steps.

There'd been no sign of anyone else on the property, but she hadn't thought to check behind the house. The buckled surface of warped wood squeaked in places as she rounded the landing toward the open bedroom door.

In the far corner, topping an extension ladder, Gabe's gaze collided with hers. Through the blur of his goggles, she detected shock in his eyes.

Scratch that. A hardened glaze of shame.

A ridged hard hat domed his head, pressing his jagged hairline against his neck.

He removed his goggles, let them hang at his neck. A weighty tool belt over a waistline harness, he dressed to tackle even the most impossible job. And yet, a pitiful glance swallowed his typical confident grin. "They told you."

The Gabe she knew—and admired—bore an unfamiliar countenance.

"I thought it would be best to see the ... uh, *this*, firsthand."

A thick mental fog encroached, blurred the finish line on this project. Her lungs sank in a slow exhale. She circled a scrutinizing gaze around the room, the sight smacking her senseless.

"I'm taking care of it."

On a Sunday. Alone. Either because he refused to assign any of his contractors to work on the Sabbath or shame had him working in isolation. From the look of defeat in his somber eyes, she'd wager it was the latter.

An impressive mix of hardware clanked about his waist as he took tense steps down the ladder. Slowly, he turned and faced her. A tremulous smile quirked the edge of his mouth, withering hope fraught with desperation.

She averted her eyes, taking the hard news with her. "Alex's dissatisfaction has reached network execs at H2H. I'm being pressured to let you go, Gabe."

At this juncture, it was all the truth she could muster.

"No way you'd do that, Orderly." He grasped her wrist, placed it against his chest, let her feel the thud of his heart.

Ardor circuited through her frame. It was becoming increasingly brutal to refuse partaking of the scent of industry, stroke the swath of fine stubble along his jaw, and indulge in the essence of who he was.

"Believe in me." His brow angled down over a pained expression.

Oh, heavens.

And ... *I do.*

Okay, light-years from firing the guy. She placed a hand atop his, their hearts thundering in rhythm. "I just need you to work that historic house magic that's made you successful."

"That's the reason I'm here, working to right this mess. I'll have to wait for material delivery before I can replace the flooring, and—"

"How'd this happen, Gabe?"

Uncharacteristic humiliation played over his countenance. He scratched the side of his head, mouth parted ... the explanation snagged on something. "Contracted roof work wasn't to spec. It rained cats and dogs. Water got in, cracked the plaster."

She folded her arms at her waist. "Whoever is responsible for this negligence needs to be fired. You know that, right?"

He shifted his gaze, lagged a stare, then drew it back to her. "I'm the cause of this. I didn't double-check the work up top ... among other things. Just been trying to get ahead of the game, keep Hollywood happy."

A tic moved along the firm set of his jaw as though making a herculean effort to hold back a wash of emotion, defeat filtering into his eyes. In a fragile breath, he handed down the verdict. "I'm a failure."

The jut of his chin provoked her to agree.

That she'd never do, weld his actions to his worth.

Here stood another man who'd fearlessly scaled heights to achieve big things. And at some point, she'd let her frozen heart crawl out of hibernation and warm to the idea of caring for him ... beyond final payment.

To let him go would crush him. Maybe crush her.

Compassion swept strict adherence to her agenda under the rug. "So, you made a mistake." She shrugged. "It happens."

He scraped a wry glare over her face. "I don't make mistakes."

Everley tunneled through the rubble of self-loathing to patch the fissure of theological divide. "But you did."

"I shouldn't have."

"Well, then, I'm honored to meet you, your holiness." Posture straightening, she proffered her hand.

Confusion knit his brow. His gaze drained of humor. "What are you talking about?"

"Being one without error makes you God. Which necessitates the reverent greeting on my part." As though on holy ground, she slipped out of her shoes, dipping her head in an exaggerated bow.

Meeting her gaze when she straightened, he returned an irritated glare. "This is no time for jokes, Orderly."

"All right, then, tell me something, Gabe. Are you in this business to prove something, or do you really enjoy the work? Because I can't afford to have you chipping away at my house if you have ulterior motives. Moreland can't be some means to prop your ego or keep you bubble-wrapped in success."

Gaze adrift, he shook his head and shrugged.

"By God's design, you are who you are, a fact you made crystal clear months ago. Heaven help us if we're defined by our performance, success measured by the world's standards."

Resisting no longer, she cupped a hand to his stubbled cheek and fingered the ends of his hair. The soft cotton of his collared shirt shivered through her while his lonesome smile crept past the wall of shame. A glimmer of desire magnified in his eyes.

"I see, not what you could be, but the man God has already made you to be."

With any hope, the stamp of approval might seal cracks in his heart. No doubt, verbal affirmation had been sadly lacking in his family. Created space for the insidious notion that he was defined by what he did. An exhausting, futile exercise.

Head cocked, a boyish grin played on his lips, honey-soaked gaze sparking amusement. He moved close, threaded hands behind her waist. His warm breath collided with the heat climbing into her cheeks. "Whose house did you say this was, Orderly?"

It was true. She'd claimed Moreland as her own. A house that needed more than one pair of hands to manage it. His scent of cotton and sweat ignited a desire for their shared project.

A divine whisper swept across her dizzied brain.

Keep me.

She inched a grin, flattened hands to his muscled chest. "What'd you say?"

Denial marked his brow. His shoulders heaved in a muffled laugh. "M'lady, I think all this steamy southern exposure has gotten to you."

Quite right. Only the steam that'd gotten to her wasn't due to the sun.

Forefinger to her cheek, he tucked her hair behind her ears and caused a rapid-fire tingle to travel to her bare toes, zip up her spine, and poke at embers of longing. An intensifying heat she'd tried to douse for several weeks. Undeniably, she'd grown to love his charm, charisma, genuine concern for people no matter their station in life—the small and large acts of kindness and investment in others.

Untamed as he was, he never came up short on southern gentleman.

Intrigue played in his gaze. "You hear the widow calling?"

"Maybe." An urge to care for the place, to keep Moreland's life aflame.

"Sounds like Marigold left you with more than a house." He circled a glinted gaze around her face, the look of a man admiring art.

Twining two hearts ...

She blinked to attention. "You know, we really need to stop meeting alone in the master suite." Her directive, weakened by the rise of a smile, lost all effect against his lopsided grin.

"Actually, I'm kinda partial to this room." He roved his hands up her back and massaged out every trace of reluctance. Her chest thudded in wild rhythm as he feathered her lips in gentle strokes. Engulfed in his strength, heat coursed through her bones.

When she loaned him a key to the place, it wasn't so he could unlock her heart.

"It's been so long ... since I've felt this," she rasped, nearly breathless.

In one hungry rush, his kiss deepened, covering the full of her lips with purpose, then softer, slow and teasing. Chin tipped, she made room as he buried his face in her neck, placing easy kisses along her ear. The feel of his strength seeped into her pores and enabled her to remain standing when the rush of euphoria buckled her knees.

The notion of falling in love again clawed through the hard earth of her heart—created furrows of fertile soil. Thoughts she'd buried upon the third volley.

Crack!

Crack!

Crack!

Heaven cried that day, sky as charcoal. Raindrops beaded a customary black dress as the bugler played taps, unhindered by incoming showers. The American flag they'd draped over Kyle's platinum casket was meticulously folded thirteen times by honor guards and presented in solemn silence, stars pointed upward to honor sacred, unchanging truth ...

In God we trust.

Accepting the weighty memento, she'd pressed it to her chest, stained it with tears. A sorry substitute for her husband.

Did she? Trust God?

Was he the master engineer of her circumstances? A means to break free from the oppression of routine and see the world in color?

Infuse life.

And here was Gabe, rapturously masculine and capable, the guy divinely appointed to fix the broken. The reason she was here, surrounded by his fingerprints of restoration. Maybe those of his ancestors.

The reason her goal to abandon this place in pursuit of partner status had become as appealing as a picnic of day-old bread and sour grapes on Lake Michigan's frozen shore.

On what should have been a routine Friday morning trip to the Pear Tree, Gabe ignored his stomach's nagging growl, the result of a blood sugar plunge after a spike from sharing a pint of ice cream with Merrill this morning. With few teeth to spare, it's a good thing the salty old war vet loved ice cream.

After Merrill's assault, Gabe took the pliable apprentice in as a roommate. He'd proven a good companion, sharing war stories until late hours, but the provision of shelter came with the firm condition that he stay dry. "One drop and you're out, pal."

Merrill snapped a wrinkled hand in a sloppy salute off his temple. "Yessir, you mean ole' fart." And then, his faded, gunmetal eyes misted. He'd chewed on his lip as if fighting against the swell of gratitude.

Because when had anyone ever taken him in, erected proper boundaries, cared enough to teach a marketable skill, and treated him with dignity?

"It ain't like you got any booze in this swanky place of yours anyhow," Merrill had muttered.

"I wouldn't share a drop of it if I did."

Because Gabe loved the old man that much. An exterior in need of fresh paint, an interior that would grow priceless with age.

"While I'm gone, and you're here healing, do something useful. Like … take a bath."

Power washing might do it.

A flash of dull blue through lowered lids peered back at Gabe. "In that floating silver cruise ship you call a tub? You got it anchored, heaven only knows why, right smack in front of floor-to-ceiling windows, my muscular form on full display for all of New Orleans."

Hiding a smile, Gabe left the vet at home to heal and, more importantly, keep an eye on Champ. Over the past week, his furry pal had lain lethargic in his plush dog bed beside untouched food and water bowl. Either he'd come down with something or was suffering from heartache at Gabe's pick of brides. Maybe missing the only one he'd favored.

To date, Carmen hadn't earned Champ's favor. The dog's pouty, languid state over past weeks suggested something was amiss.

A thorough dissing from man's best friend he didn't need.

As Gabe's truck idled, thoughts of Everley hummed over his engine. He marveled at the way she balanced her job with overseeing her momma's house. The loyalty to family despite the cost—including the willingness to tear the lid off her private life. He'd even grown to love the way fire sparked in her eyes when she was in a snit over something.

Regret tumbled like jagged stones inside Gabe's stomach. Why hadn't he made an acquaintance of his high school crush when he had the chance? But now … she'd communicated an undeniable message last Sunday—the longing in her gaze when they'd kissed inside Moreland's inner sanctum reading like a Vacancy sign over her heart.

A lonely young widow willing to welcome him inside.

Add to that, there'd been evidence of a heart shift in Moreland's favor, its heiress claiming ownership. But what would it take for her to upend her orderly life to oversee proper care of it? Would she take the broad road and pay someone else to do it? Worse, remain adamant about selling?

Jaw clenched, he let the idea of a future together evaporate. Because G&R's stability hinged on a proposal. Doubt gnarled fingers around his brain like the spindled branches of Moreland's ancient oak. Echoes of Adam's wisdom resounded in frothy waves, truth crashing against his soul.

Integrity waits for the right match. Honors God with a covenant that'll go the distance.

"God, I don't want to end up alone."

Like Dad.

In the natural, he wanted to go after Everley and build a family on a solid foundation. One built by God. She was like a perfect plane of fresh-cut, old-growth cypress, strong and sweet—the ideal wood to assure longevity.

Only a low-life jerk would bust up a relationship at this juncture. But the alternative? A life of misery. Vowed in marriage to a woman who, being honest, really only cared about what he could give.

He called Randy. "You at Moreland?"

"I am. Currently staring down several buckets of exterior paint."

"Good. Remember to thin it with the additive before you start. It'll slow the drying down a bit—give it time to lay down."

"Proper painting 101, boss."

"White, right?"

"I thought you said peach."

A ball of lead formed in his stomach. "What?"

"Relax. It's white as snow. Just trying to lighten the mood."

Relief gathered into a weak laugh. "Do it at someone else's expense. I about had a stroke."

"You deserve it. You're past due on my payment. The girls will have to quit ballet if we don't cover this month."

"Just give me a little more time to move numbers around."

Like ... a year.

Due to the storm fiasco, he'd drawn from the construction loan to place another sizable material order, leaving him to cut his losses and Randy to accept delayed compensation.

"Time is the one thing I'm running short on, Gabe."

Gabe's heart thudded in the silence.

"How far out are you?" Randy said.

His truck hadn't moved. "En route. But, uh ..." If ever a man needed a dad in his corner, the wisdom of a godly father ... "You were right. I can't do this."

"What?"

"Marry someone I don't really love."

Truth surged. The hesitant, fervent love for his high school crush had sprouted through the soil of his heart. Matured by time and watered by kisses, it'd begun to bud after he'd recklessly made Carmen the object of his affection.

"You know I've been against the alliance all along. Murdock stands little to gain from it. But this far in, I feel like you've got to, or he'll crush us, boss."

"I don't think so. He's an opportunist. Beneath that rough, shrewd, and unyielding exterior lies a tender-hearted guy in pursuit of mutually beneficial, long-term business relationship."

Trepidation marked Randy's words. "I can only hope your optimism saves the day. Because the Murdock I know will eat you for lunch. As for Carmen, if you're confident that busting things up won't result in disaster, then I say follow God's lead. I'll be praying you have the strength to carry it through."

"Thanks. That means the world."

"Bryson and his subordinates are far more interested in reviewing footage over here with Everley anyway."

Everley.

A woman who, exacting little effort—and sometimes without a word—owned and ignited a room. Back in town, ahead of next week's film schedule, overseeing progress. The picture of irresistible shyness ensconced in calm confidence. A red-headed wonder with endless creativity who needed a place like Moreland to unleash her to dream beyond all she could ask or imagine and a capable someone to maintain it.

Gabe took a calming breath and phoned Carmen.

"Hi, handsome," she said.

Her voice all smiles, he shut his eyes, drew in a long breath, released it. "Hey. I need to see you for a little bit before I get to work."

"Sure! Meet me after rehearsal at the theater. I should be finished by 11:30."

"Rehearsal?"

"*Hairspray*, babe. I play Velma Von Tussle, remember?"

Uh-uh. Being honest, he really hadn't cared.

Parked on a side street, Gabe entered the theater through the backstage door. It shut with a screech and a—*slam!* Cutting through the darkness, he found Carmen standing in a spray of stage light, one arm outstretched in dramatic flair, practicing her lines, voice throbbing with enthusiasm.

Meeting his gaze, she scrambled down the side steps. He turned his cheek, trading her offer of a kiss for a hug. Her heady, lemony scent—reminiscent of chemistry class— suggested recent application.

She invited him to sit beside her on the edge of the stage, her mismatched curves pressing close. The fit was all wrong. Shrouded in lowered house lights, the abysmal auditorium nearly engulfed him, stage light blinding. Conditioned air breezed along the beads of sweat at his neck.

Nuzzling close, she hooked her arm through his. "You sounded concerned on the phone." She puffed out a gentle laugh. "If it's about Mom's spur of the moment luncheon tomorrow, no worries. She understands you're a busy man."

Geez. He'd forgotten about the luncheon, too. Fingers clamped to the stage, he turned to meet her enthralled gaze. "Carmen, I've been thinking. Praying, actually. And I believe it's best if we, you know, take a break for a while."

Not quite to the finish line.

A frown disfigured her face. Her posture slackened, and she withdrew her arm. "Why postpone the inevitable?"

In a concerted effort to dislodge the boulder in his throat, he brought a fist to his mouth and coughed. "I'm not making myself clear."

So, say it already.

"Carmen, I can't ... be with you anymore ... beyond just friendship." The words crashed onto the floor like cinder blocks, ricocheted inside his lungs. He swallowed hard, fighting to expel a breath.

Straightening, her chest lifted with an influx of air, her tone a mix of derision and panic. "What do you mean?"

"It's not right."

Desperation marked her pouty gaze. The squeeze to his upper thigh felt like a barb. "What's not right about mutual attraction?"

Nothing. And everything.

"Ours isn't the kind of relationship that goes the distance, a till-death-do-we-part kinda thing." Nerves had him gesturing with his hands, moist with sweat. "I've let it become one of convenience, a means to prop up success, and I can't continue to dishonor you like that."

Score one for Spirit-led words, empowered by prayer.

Her eyes darkened to deep ocean blue, the color of an impending storm. A feel not unlike verbal demolition—busting, pounding, and ripping.

Shoving from the stage, Carmen landed on the floor and spun to face him. Stage lights washed over the fullness of her body, her frame pinned against a hollowed auditorium. Until now, he hadn't noticed she'd been in costume—a royal blue, satiny dress, snug at the middle. A string of ugly beads slung near her neck.

Thrusting one foot forward, she clamped arms to her chest. "Daddy won't like this."

Now, if that proclamation didn't strike fear ...

But he'd resolved to trust God no matter the outcome. *Short of ruin.*

With the flair of an actress, she stalked the space in front of him like a cougar, hips pitching left and right. A murmured warning pecked like Morse code before she halted and concentrated her gaze. "What about the dinner party for Daddy tomorrow night? He's expecting you and me to be there. As a *couple.*" Her show of crossed fingers matched the twisted knot in his throat.

Thus far, there'd been no mention of her devotion or respect. Fear of losing him ... expression of need. Nothing.

Just a wild smattering of inconveniences, never more evident she didn't really love him.

Gabe probed past the fire in her gaze. "What bothers you more, the fact that I'm breaking up with you or that your daddy will be ticked off?"

In one swift movement, she lifted a palm mid-air, prepped to strike. He held air in his lungs, steadied his stance, refusing to retreat—accepting consequences. Because Love had done far more on his behalf on the cross.

And then she froze, slowly lowering a fist. A nondescript smile drew across her lips and her tone went all breathy. "You know, babe, you're right." In easy motion, she stroked the planes of his cheek, traced a finger down his chest. Her gaze roved to his waist and back up, undressing him. "Sure do hate I couldn't get you into bed with me."

Definitely made the right call.

She dusted palms together in a show of absolution. Setting the captive free.

Whew. That went well.

"Thanks for understanding, Carmen. I'm really sorry about this." In truce, he placed a kiss on her forehead ... which she accepted, posture easing.

He stepped back. "I've got to work as late as possible tomorrow. It'd be best if I just met you at the hotel."

Brow pinched, she regarded him coolly. "The gala."

"I realize it'll be a little awkward between us, but your dad is offering me one whale of an opportunity."

Nodding a couple times, a hint of impending surprise clouded her eyes. "I look forward to a memorable evening."

CHAPTER SEVENTEEN

Disgust for having twined himself to Carmen turned to sawdust in Gabe's mouth. But he was grateful she'd relented, the squall in her eyes weakening to stiff wind, the threat of landfall diminishing to zero. Leaving the theater, he sped toward Moreland and begged God's mercy and grace.

"Not trying to whitewash my mistake here. It's you I've sinned against, God. I know that full well."

I restore your soul. Mercy and grace are yours for the asking.

An undeserved and freely given sacrifice completed on the cross. A person's means of restoration.

Released from duplicity, a bounce returned to Gabe's step, a hot air balloon freed from its cabled ropes. He arrived at the manor house to find crews on scaffolding on the front and sides of her. The sweet taste of progress eased the burn of Priscilla's scalding texts pinging in rapid succession on the drive over.

If profanity could kill …

But it was Murdock's incoming call that had him shaking in his boots. No surprise, Carmen had already informed Daddy Murdock.

He answered, working steel into his voice. To no avail. Fear liquidated it.

"I understand you've broken things off with Carmen." His tone was determined, urged explanation.

Gabe gathered defense, toe on the line. Backboard and rim in sight. "It's unfortunate, but yes, that's right. I'm really sorry things didn't work out. But it'd be wrong to enter into a commitment I didn't think I could keep."

An implosive silence ticked.

"But, hey, I'm on my way to a job site, a debrief with a film crew. Can I give you a shout in about, say, an hour, and we'll discuss?"

"Now works for me, considering your decision has forced my hand to redefine the nature of our business alignment."

Oh? "And how do you see it now?" The quaking in his voice equaled the strength of a wilted daffodil up against a Sequoia.

Don't mess this up, Bellevue.

Warren gave the wheeze of heated breath. "On second thought, Gabriel," he said, voice lilted, purposeful and strategic, "all that needs to be said can wait until tomorrow evening." Like an aircraft recovering from a tailspin, Murdock's tone finally leveled out as though cruising safely over a stretch of flatland. "We all make choices that define our future, position us for greatness, and at times force us to cut losses. Far be it from Warren Murdock to stand in the way of that."

The favorable turnaround was surreal. Crash and burn avoided. First, he'd averted what would have been a devastating fallout if Alex made good on his threat to quit. Then Murdock retreated from what had the makings of an unrecoverable blow.

As favorable as things looked—bullets safely dodged— God hadn't promised anything but more of himself. But obedience to a good God–should be satisfying enough, even if God's very best didn't include his high school crush.

Ending the call, he reached the top of Moreland's drive to see the uncharacteristic form of said crush dribbling a basketball beneath the rim in a two-man game with Quinton.

Third miracle of the day.

"Wonder of wonders," he whispered, clucking his tongue. "Just look-see at Ms. Responsible goofing off over there."

And so dang cute in her cuffed denim shorts, tank top, and tennis shoes. All trace of calculating numbers girl replaced by one who'd loosened herself from confines of a strict schedule. Properly working a bit of rest into the spreadsheet of her day.

Raw authenticity right there—an uncut, unedited glimpse of who she really was. Someone should draw out that playful side more often.

For now, he'd teach the able CPA a proper pump fake, jab step, and slam dunk.

He sauntered over, muffling a laugh at her less than admirable skill. She held her tongue between her teeth, lids narrowed in concentration as if the world championship was on the line. Good thing it wasn't.

"Looks like city gal needs someone to demonstrate the proper technique."

She spun, tipped a haughty chin, and released the ball with a wild toss toward the hoop. It ricocheted off the backboard and smacked her on the head, the hard bounce sounding a twang.

"Ow!" she sputtered. Her feigned pout weakened his knees. When she massaged the top of that nice head of hair, sunlight caught the strands and turned them gold.

Full court press.

Gabe bent to scoop the ball, dribbling it around her. She reached her hand in to slap at it. Too late. He snapped the ball to his chest, faked left, spun in a smooth glide movement, then raised one long arm for a dunk into the net.

Clean swish. The audience roars to its feet.

"Think you're so cool, huh?"

"I think nothing, Orderly." He tossed the ball between open palms. "I *am* the reason our high school won the state championship my senior year."

Stealing a glance at you, hoping you'd cheer me on.

A piercing whistle and swirling hand gesture from James hailed Quinton back to work. "Next time, Mr. Gabe, it's you 'n me."

"Count on it, my friend."

He turned back to Everley, whose cheeks were flushed red, breathing labored. No longer that freckle-faced, straight-A wallflower.

To some, Everley Lewis was a girl for a guy who couldn't get a better girl. Gabe saw unmatched beauty. Top prize. Like that one rare find in an antique store—someone's perfect treasure.

Far unlike other women, she stood on her own merit. Independent. Intelligent. He loved the fact that she didn't need him yet was willing to defer to him.

A renewed glimmer twinkled to life in her eyes.

Dear God, I can't imagine life without her.

If only he could scoop her into his arms, kiss her, give voice to his love. Beg her to stay. Because he'd done the hard thing and released Carmen to find another man. Placing trust in God's greater purposes eased the weight off a man's shoulders, making him a success.

Behind him, Randy approached, pants dusted white. Head angled, he moved his eyes to Gabe's cheek. Likely looking for signs of a blow.

A touch of playful candor seeped into Randy's tone. "The, uh, meeting with—?"

"It's over."

"The proposal or the relationship?"

"Both." A renewed deluge of relief and impending doom nearly toppled him to the ground. The burn and scrape of Everley's scrutinizing stare clawed like a baptized cat.

"We're still in good standing with Murdock?"

"We agreed to discuss things tomorrow. From what I could discern, he didn't want any of this to ruin the evening."

"Best news I've heard all day."

Taking a step back, Randy switched his gaze between Gabe and Everley. "I guess I oughta leave you two to do ... uh, whatever it is you're here to do. Which is anybody's guess at this point." A ribbing grin bloomed on Randy's face before he headed back to the house.

A hint of indignation wrinkled over Everley's brow, her gaze demanding disclosure.

"I can explain." He raised palms to shield against her laser stare.

She assumed the bearing of a Supreme Court judge. "What's to explain?"

Here comes the gavel.

"Being that you were embarking on a proposal, it would have behooved you to maintain your distance and keep my heart out of what would have amounted to a wicked relational triangle."

He nodded, letting the sting of truth penetrate. For now, he tabled the mention of her heart's involvement, a brutal test of fortitude not to cling to the hint of promise it offered.

Ball in hand, he fired a shot at the hoop in an arching, one-armed swoop. It swished through, bouncing along the drive. His gaze followed its path as it settled on the lawn.

"About Carmen—"

"Ah. The brokenhearted girl has a name."

"I ... I should have told you."

"You shouldn't have kissed me." She winged a brow, hands stuffed inside her pockets.

He took two steps closer. "After you kissed me first ..." He scrubbed a finger and thumb along his stubbled jaw, eyes drifting upward in a feigned recall. "If memory serves."

Her jagged glare smoothed over a little, suggesting she hadn't really minded. Closer now, the fire in her tone reduced to a sultry warmth. "Don't make resistance so difficult."

This close to her soft, ivory arms, he ached to stroke them. "Magnetism comes natural, Orderly. The pull is powerful."

Annoyance pursed her lips. She lifted a hand, reaching back to swing.

He ducked and crossed his arms in front of his face. "All right, all right. Have mercy. I've narrowly escaped one slap already today."

She clenched and unclenched her fists, a precious frown to tempt a die-hard monk to reconsider his vow of chastity.

But then her ravenous gaze glistened, and anguish flooded his heart.

Given their kiss, it was only fair to extract detail about what led to the breakup. "Carmen's father, Warren Murdock, is among New Orleans' business elite. My willingness to marry in exchange for padding success ... kidnapped by plans of my own making ... at the expense of a woman's heart ..." He averted a moist gaze. "It was wrong."

Her exhale blistered his conscience. But he rallied, concentrated his gaze, tone firm and intent. "I'd rather die single with honor than married with shame."

What to make of her softened lips turned up on the edges, countenance ringing admiration?

"I could have resisted your kiss. I chose not to. And for what it's worth, I'm sorry about you and Carmen." She released a sympathetic sigh.

"I'll bet you are."

"No, seriously. The death of a relationship ranks right up there with paying ten years' back taxes."

Easy laughter sweetened the shrinking space between them.

"In exchange for my husband's choice to join the Marines, I was handed a properly folded American flag, a war widow's consolation."

He attempted to dispel images of Everley in the arms of another man—a darned lucky one—and smoothed over raw confession with the standard answer. "Sorry for your loss."

The return of a weak nod suggested she'd had a fair share of standard answers.

But it left him wondering. "Why'd you tell me that?"

As clouds parted overhead, pale sunlight drew across her cheeks, falling in patches on the ground. "I guess I thought you ..." She jerked her glance away, voice trailing as she drew her lower lip between her teeth.

"Cared?"

She returned a pointed gaze. "Well, sure. I mean, how readily do you kiss a girl, Mr. Bellevue? Because, in my book, a kiss is deeply significant, despite what current culture dictates."

Mmmm, the way her face wrinkled in deep concentration as she ordered her thoughts. He loved to listen to her reason through things, sort out arguments, weaving in threads of spiritual truth.

"I do," he finally said.

"What?"

"Care."

Very, very much.

From Everley's perspective, Moreland stood poised as a reigning monarch. A supreme visual for progressive transformation.

Both wings lifted in a brightened smile behind tailored shrubbery. Pleased to be doted on. Dauntless despite the weight of June's moist, sultry heat.

If the house could communicate.

If it cared.

If it was more than an ordered construction of hand-fashioned brick, mortar, cedar, pine, and plaster.

But it was.

Sure enough, Everley had broken the code and coaxed the dream, verged on being a crazy, free-thinker.

Her mother's daughter.

Overcoming adversity, Moreland's restoration had moved forward under Gabe's skilled hand and direction. A house that was nearly two centuries old and still stood strong. A testimony to the beauty of resilience, an insatiable desire to be enjoyed.

"Maybe I'll cradle the dream awhile, see how I like it."

It didn't hurt to hear Gabe's confession that he cared, delivered with utter seriousness. When he drew her close, flames of desire set her heart to rabidly expand and quiver.

But deeper still, she felt the smile of God enlarging the space of her heart. And at the end of the day, that was worth investing her undivided attention.

What had she just read on her Bible app? "Give me an undivided heart that I may fear your name."

Images of her life in Chicago surfaced, rendering her life a slab of unformed, cold, black marble. The drag of routine, predictability, and status quo pulled her beneath the surface of a frozen lake.

Lifeless.

Entrenched in heightened media attention, public appearances, local and remote radio and TV spots, Everley had shed layers of unease and become pegged as the heroine of historical landmark restoration.

Was God chiseling a new purpose out of her? Establishing a mandate to embark on a new venture, instilling a different desire? One where her savvy for checks and balances would add value?

Because maybe living out of shadows a little bit would be ... fun.

With plans to return to Moreland later, Everley left to work at Serenity's bakery. Between influxes of patrons, they connected over coffee and taste-tested another of Serenity's cupcake originals.

Breezy and hopeful, Serenity presented a cupcake topped with a swirled mound of frosting. "I'm thinking about adding this little darling to the menu. Tell me what you think."

"I need more carbs like sandals in the snow."

"Taste." She slid the plate closer.

The scent of decadent chocolate curled at Everley's middle. "Is this the same recipe you used when you had those baking battles with Owen?"

"Cupcake wars and, no, this is different." At the mention of Owen, Serenity's attempt at indifference was quickly betrayed by the wanderlust climbing into her countenance. The fearless dreamer that refused her heart the one thing it still desired.

As Everley bit into the cupcake, a rush of sugar and creamy goodness chilled her cheeks. A delicate balance of flavor, texture light and moist, a pleasing mouthfeel. A product offering that didn't edge near too bitter or sickeningly sweet. "Perfection. A sure-fire award winner, Sis."

"Want me to box something up for you to take to Moreland's crew?"

"They'd love it, thanks." Everley stood and slipped her laptop into her tote. "In fact, I'm heading over there now."

"Say hi to Moreland for me."

Everley returned a crooked grin, thinking for a blink of a second that Serenity might include one jumbo cupcake for the house to enjoy.

Leaving the Pear Tree, nostalgia washed over Everley. Meandering thoughts sent her on a detour to Dazzle Me Art in the northeast part of New Orleans. In the adjacent gallery, an original oil painting featuring potted marigolds caught her eye. The hearty flowers sprang from a bed of dark, rich soil inside a cracked terra cotta pot. Set on a rustic table coated in chipped white paint, the vibrant gold, red, and yellow petals persisted beneath a full sun and gave reason for the name of the piece. Persistence.

"Mom would have loved this."

So she purchased it.

But ... where would she hang it? It certainly didn't fit the look of her midcentury condo. Even if it did, the possibility loomed that she'd be unable to pay off the loan, forced to sell, and search elsewhere.

North of the firm, Margot's apartment at Wellington Place apartments had vacancies. But why incur monthly rent—and thus no return on investment—when she'd enjoyed a mortgage-free status for close to a year? The truth was, the search for an ideal living space anywhere on the planet was futile.

Because none included him.

At some point, Everley had fallen for the one guy she'd refused to love—despite fierce determination otherwise. The realization struck like a comet, its tail illuminating what she could no longer deny.

Reach for the stars? Maybe they'd reached down to her.

Establishing a friendship with Tyler had only served as her heart's placeholder, a means to fill a space hollowed of its courage to love again. Safe distance without sacrificing relational connection. How unfair was that? Cruel, really.

Up ahead, Moreland consumed her field of vision, an iridescent pearl beneath a drape of ivory linen sky. She parked beneath the south side grove, lowered the window, and took in the buzz of activity.

As it should be.

Saws hummed and electric tools whirred. Country twang colored the air, attempting to rise above her mantra ...

Fix it. List it. Go back home.

The production crew clustered in front of the main house near scaffolding. Annoyed voices at the front door snagged her attention toward Alex, who'd shoved a light stand aside and sent it crashing onto the veranda.

"That hothead," she muttered.

She stomped across the lawn with the stride of an angry momma prepped to put a petulant child in time out.

Though Alex's words were indistinguishable, his arms flailed like an angry bird in flight. As she neared, he whirled and jabbed the air. "No further negotiating, Ms. Scott."

She halted.

"This entire project has been an epic waste of time and money for me, my crew, and a host of formerly confident investors." His arms lifted in frustration then slapped at his sides.

The man knew drama.

"I don't care if he was appointed by God himself. Either you get rid of him, or we're walking."

This spelled trouble. Her heart thrummed behind her ears as she circuited a gaze along the veranda, then back to Alex, whose face now held the look of a stewed tomato.

He gave his head a sideways jerk, thrust a stiff arm the direction of a hard gaze. "Over there."

Gabe appeared from the far side of the house and ambled over. The embodiment of temptation with his golden, sculpted arms hanging from a sleeveless black T-shirt. Burnished bronze hair, carefree movements to match his stride. Tools swung and clinked at his waist, wholly equipped to fix things.

Stopping, he took a booted stance, parted his feet, crossed his arms—the picture of a restrained bull, horns locked with Alex.

Rumbles of war quaked beneath Everley's feet.

Beneath a stormy brow, Gabe's lips thinned with purpose. His nostrils flared. They always did when his patience had run dry.

It took a lot.

A lot must have happened.

Waves of worry crashed inside her chest.

She released a slow breath.

Gabe shifted a subtle, pleading look at her, then fixed it back on Alex.

"I've asked him nicely *three* times if he'd please turn his attention to the south wing of the property so I can capture the crown molding installation, being that it's taken weeks to complete."

"And?" She postured to fit her role as the lady of the manor. Because she was. And, at that moment, chose to brandish it like a sword.

"He refuses. Claims there's settling in the main house, still searching for signs of water damage, creaking floorboards ... says that takes priority over the pretty stuff. I don't know." His voice trailed to a vapor.

"Then film the process in order, as events unfold organically, not how you want it to be," she said. "Otherwise, you've got contrived footage viewers won't buy into, which results in net financial loss."

Right. Assume the sale.

In what appeared to be slow motion, Alex faced her, a glare throbbing beneath his cap. Something like restrained fury belied his effort to gather his senses. "I'm sorry, but are you under the mistaken impression you're my creative adviser now, Ms. Scott?"

Bowing to grace, she bit her lip, nearly choking on the double-edged rebuttal clogging her throat.

"Repetitive and boring doesn't sell. Your contractor has kept at this task for far too long."

In two steps, Gabe entered the ring, a slit-eyed gaze fixed on Alex like a lion ready to pounce. "The work isn't done until it's done right."

A faint pulse of sunlight weakened behind a shroud of gray sky. Volcanic ash gathered in Alex's countenance, his eyes now fully fixed on Everley while he aimed a finger at Gabe. "This will no longer include both of us. If you want me to bring the project to completion, your contractor needs to be gone by the time I return."

CHAPTER EIGHTEEN

Leaving Moreland late Saturday afternoon, Gabe sped home to shower. He'd replayed yesterday's encounter with Alex numerous times.

Fueled by dauntless determination, Everley had spoken on Gabe's behalf and offset potential disaster. Every word a nail securing him to the project.

"Like it or not, Alex," she'd said. "Gabe is the whole reason for—*and heartbeat of*—this project, and I don't appreciate being cornered into what will only amount to a reckless decision. It'll kick up a storm of media backlash that'll do none of us any good. We've all invested time and effort to see this house to completion, and I, for one, refuse to let anything stand in the way of that."

Nice work, Orderly.

How he would have loved taking her in his arms and stoked that passion into flame. If it wasn't a rotten thing to do on the heels of breaking up with Carmen, he'd have asked her yesterday to accompany him, Randy, and Summer to tonight's gala. To enjoy her company as he shored up the Bellevue reputation. To celebrate the wisdom in her decision to stick her neck out, effectively broadening the gap between winners and losers.

Outfitted in a tux, he zipped to the Hilton, paid the valet, and texted Randy.

GABE: Here. U?

RANDY: Summer and I already seated. Hustle.

Within the center lobby, water trickled from a sculpted fountain ensconced in marbled tile. A chandelier and inset lighting illuminated the expansive space. Impressive art deco lined the walls. Gabe took a moment to draw in the heady scent of success. Dad's dealings never afforded him the opportunity to partake in such a sheer spectacle of wealth.

With its eighteen-foot-high ceiling, the grand ballroom was a suitable atmosphere for those who'd made it big. Beside one of the draped, round tables, Carmen stood dressed in ... what else ... a satiny red dress, hair styled in a relaxed braid updo. She nuzzled against a guy whose cool bravado exuded steely determination and opportunity. Ideal makings of Murdock son-in-law material, looking like he'd already been groomed for the part.

Amazing how truth allows a blind man to see perfectly when looking through a clear set of lenses.

How very desperately a guy needed God's grace.

Grace. Truly amazing.

Of no surprise, seating assignments had been switched up, docking him to a table on the far-right side. Summer sat to his left and Randy on her other side. Gold and white balloons floated from the center of every table above elegant floral arrangements.

"I'm excited to meet the lucky girl," Summer whisper-shouted as she leaned in. "Carmen, right?"

"Yes, but ... things have changed."

Randy turned to Summer. "He busted things up yesterday. Wants to take a chance on Everley Scott."

Eyes rounding, Summer forgot her inside voice. "Moreland's heiress? The one who lives in Chicago? How in the world do you expect—?"

Gabe tapped a finger to his lips and wrinkled his brow.

Summer turned a horrified glance at Randy, who breathed reassurance. "It's all good. He's going after the one his heart loves."

When Randy leaned in and kissed her temple, Summer quirked a grin. "If Everley is as set on selling Moreland as Randy tells me, you're putting your heart at risk. But then again, it's your heart."

Offered many years late in the game. But it'd be offered to the right girl.

He swept a gaze over the crowd and found Murdock in tux and tails, ensconced with the elite. The man of the hour. Years of experience marked the lines around his eyes, pooled in the contours of his face.

Their gazes locked.

Breaking free, Murdock jutted his chin and cut a straight path to Gabe, circular saws for eyes.

His proffered handshake was remarkably stiff. He turned a calculating gaze toward Randy, taking his hand. "You must be Randy Severson. The partner."

"Yes, sir. Great to meet you. Honored you've chosen to align with G&R. We'll make you proud."

Reservation claimed Warren's gaze. The hint of unfinished business gathered in his countenance. Disquiet clawed at Gabe's spine. Had he missed something?

"Well, gentlemen," Warren said. "Tonight will be one for the books." He alternated his gaze between them, lips forming a thin-lipped grin. Sincerity hadn't yet reached his eyes.

The man who held the power to elevate—or destroy.

After a feast of blackened steak or Atlantic red snapper with sides of au gratin and roasted asparagus, Carmen stood and led the gathering in singing a hearty round of happy birthday.

Afterward, Warren stood at the lectern, quieted the applause, and commanded attention. "Welcome all. Many thanks for joining me tonight. It's a pleasure to share this evening with my wife, Priscilla, and lovely daughter, Carmen, and those who understand the value of hard work and greatness. Sacrifice."

Applause washed over the room.

Warren's formidable gaze swept the room, landed momentarily on Gabe, then rotated away. "As many of you know, I've acquired several blocks of underutilized, historic property in greater New Orleans and seek to refurbish it, stimulate growth of small business. In considering which company to award a contract for the work, I chose one with an unstained reputation, unmatched in quality. In my opinion, the finest in the industry."

A swirl of pride wound through Gabe. He straightened his posture, glanced at Randy, and raised a thumb. "Here we go, partner."

"And tonight, I'd like to take this opportunity to announce Murdock Enterprises's chosen recipient ..." His breath held, a slow gaze settling at the opposite end of the ballroom.

Wrong direction.

"Cline and Company House Works."

Warren led the gathering in robust applause. Shrill whistles rifted across the room, pulled at Gabe's insides like a pry bar. Digging behind his heart, plucking it out of his chest.

Randy burrowed fingers into Gabe's arm. Shock gathered in deep lines across his face.

Words jammed in Gabe's throat, a hard tick working along his jaw.

A devilish grin claimed Carmen's expression. She followed with a dissing shrug.

Taking purposeful steps, Warren wandered over, image hazy through clouds of defeat. He glanced at Randy like a rifleman assessing his kill before he settled a steely stare on Gabe, tongue swiping across his lips.

Gabe shot to his feet, spewing through clenched teeth. "Murdock, we had a deal. You and I shook on it."

"Now, Gabriel. You, of all people, understand a person's right to change course when there's uncertainty about a relational alignment."

The sting of double meaning finger-pricked along his spine. "Yeah, of course, but …"

Pawing at the slaughter of Gabe's expectations, Warren closed in, a lion sniffing torn flesh. "No one reaches the level of success I've achieved by engaging with folks who walk away when their feet get cold. Guess I mistook you for a ruthless, can-do guy who has what it takes. Misjudgment on my part."

The false humility only sandpapered his ego.

From behind Summer and Randy, a photographer slunk close, camera slung about his neck that held the impact of an assault rifle.

Murdock turned to go then paused, drawing a finger to his temple. "Oh. One more thing. I stumbled upon a story about faulty business practices of yours, contacted H2H top executives and the Senior Producer of MidDay Media, made sure they were aware."

Stumbled upon? More like exhumed.

Was there any place on earth Murdock's vast network didn't reach?

The twisted article published in the business section of NOLA's paper two years ago—and long since buried—now breathed sulphuric flames and threatened to rock Gabe's empire. All because of the drive to outsmart paternal failure. Now that he'd fallen from Warren's good graces, the past had him walking the plank over stormy seas.

Carmen joined the fray, hips pitched in purpose. She stroked a palm along his starched shirt, ravenous gaze intent on finishing off the remains. "I'm a far better actress than I thought. Had you believing your breaking up with me was harmless when really ..." In a millisecond, she raised her hand and struck his cheek. "It wasn't."

Stunned, he captured her fiery gaze, the sting of impact burning hot. A second strike sent him staggering backward. He crashed into the nearby table, the blunt force of the edge connecting with his ribs. Fractured glass sliced his cheek as a cacophony of shattered china and glass resounded around him. Champagne soaked the front of his tux.

Cameras flashed. Guests crowding around gasped, snickering. The murmurs of crass commentary bulleted his chest.

What was supposed to be an evening to celebrate God's good gift ended in the rubble of loss.

Ripping off his bowtie, popping buttons on his shirt, Gabe tore through double doors, down to the concierge, and demanded valet retrieve his truck. Igniting the engine, he sped along double lanes, the murky, choppy, coiling Mississippi shrinking in the distance.

He slammed a fist on the steering wheel, pressing hard on the pedal. Headed ... where? If only emergency technicians could repair a heart slashed by humiliation. It'd take all he had to bear up under this, claw his way back to the top.

But at least he was free. Free from chains of obligation to a woman he didn't really love to pursue the heart of the one he did.

No one was Everley. No one ever had been or ever would be.

He still had her and her house.

Moreland. Contract of a lifetime.

But one and done.

And then the crazy beautiful heiress—and her house— would be gone.

Unless that kiss held a promise that she'd claim responsibility for Moreland and allow him the honor of maintaining her smile.

Maybe ...

"Think about it, Orderly," he'd said. "Would you rather have a house that'll succumb to decay if left incomplete and, for darn sure, can't be sold or one that'll still be here for another hundred years?"

Having lost track of time earlier that afternoon, Gabe left Moreland in a rush to get ready for the gala. Had he secured it? Packed up his equipment, eliminated hazards? The urgent need to satisfy nagging questions and a holy nudge had him following the Luling Bridge toward Napoleonville.

Leaving the stench of disillusionment miles behind, Gabe pulled into the drive, still chugging out hot breaths. Moreland's imposing white grandeur glistened through watery eyes, the mossy scent of oak and earth and wood quieting his soul.

Here. This place, warm and breathing again, bandaged the hemorrhage.

The glow of artificial light in the entry and upstairs was as he feared. He'd failed to shut it off, adding financial burden to the owner who'd committed to keeping up the utilities for a house she'd claimed she hated.

The knob gave no resistance when he turned it, his easy access to the place accompanied by the lonesome whine of the door. "Way to leave Moreland to thieves, Bellevue. Add negligence to a tip-top evening."

Crossing the threshold, the sound of footfall at the landing had him turning with a start, eyes landing on the deliriously beautiful form of Everley.

She grinned, fanned a wave, looking altogether like she awaited—and welcomed—his arrival. "Hi."

No cameras in sight. Just them.

"What are you doing here?"

Uttered in synch, the question amplified within the entry.

She laughed. A balm to his wound.

In the months they'd spent together, he'd come to appreciate and love her laughs. Particularly the teasing banter about the right way to eat french fries and ketchup ...

"Drizzled, Gabe," she'd quipped.

"Uh-uh. Dunked, m' lady. Like so," he'd retorted, raising a ketchup slicked fry to his mouth.

And then she'd shook her head in girlish defiance and giggle.

Drizzled, Dunked. No matter.

She was here. She was beautiful. And looked like hope. *My crush.*

The very last person he expected to see amid swirls of dust and the stench of unfinished. And, man, if she didn't look good in fitted jeans, a flouncy white shirt, and sandals.

He loved her in white. Fresh and clean. A picture of grace and strength, pillars carved to adorn this historic treasure. Strength he needed in large doses after tonight's fiasco, soles sticky and tux reeking of champagne. Not looking at the prize but his heart's eye fixed on one ...

Curiosity—and that gardenia—had him ascending the steps toward the only one who could calm his nerves, salvage disaster. Tonight held success after all.

"Pleasant surprise, m'lady."

She returned a nod, her gaze bobbing somewhat aimlessly, arms now limp at her side.

Huh.

Apprehension moved in waves over her face.

The travel, the heat, missing work—it all must be getting to her. What was it, a mere seventy-five degrees or so in the Windy City? Here it'd reached a stifling ninety at high noon.

The press of silence tightened his stomach, churning tonight's salmon and potatoes. "MidDay didn't change film schedule again, did they? Or ... you've found something that's not to standard?"

Bearing an expression that begged to unload burden, she shook her head, the opinionated homeowner suddenly mute.

"Then to what do I owe the pleasure of your presence?"

She answered in a hard exhale, releasing ... something.

Stepping close, he gave her upper arms a gentle squeeze, her soft skin soothing his wound. He angled his gaze. "You all right?"

Her face turned away, she curled her shoulders inward, and shivered—in a giant of a room wielding a temperature in the eighties. Slowly, she returned a disparaging stare.

"Bryson Cox called me. It's bad news." Her voice went weak, eyes dimmed to a drab shade of olive. "For one of us anyway."

Ah. He should have known. At some point between breakup and this evening, Murdock—or his henchmen—had already set Moreland's heiress up against him. Gaze ripe with pity, she scraped it down the length of his frame and back up again.

Heat flooded his cheeks. Gabe planted his boots and prepped for defense. "What'd Hollywood say?"

"MidDay was made aware of unethical business practices from a couple years back that's cast doubt. Referenced an article published in an elite business circular on G&R, the testimony of a client who claimed you'd not completed work he'd paid for. Accusations about price gouging, substandard ratings by Home and Hearth Adviser."

"Vicious slander. All of it. Never made it to court."

Toe on the line, eye on the basket, Gabe pressed Everley for a response.

"All mischaracterizations. You know that."

Didn't she?

Believe in me.

"I say we refuse to play Murdock's childish game and let me finish what you've paid me to do."

"The media hype this house has already stirred, add to that the rumors that we're, you know, involved off the set ... has created concern."

Full court press. "I'm not doing this to please a film company, much less a network, a fact I made clear from the get-go. As for you and me, let the media make of us what they will."

A happy couple. *Please?*

He brushed past her, entered the master suite, trekked a lonesome gaze along the cracks in the plaster.

She followed him, maintaining distance like he'd carried a virus, the timbre of her voice tinged with finality. "It gets worse."

Impossible.

Rapid thudding behind his ears reverberated in his chest, lungs thinning to paper.

"MidDay is refusing any association with G&R. They'll uphold their obligation for remuneration but have reworked storyboards to make way for another contractor who'll explain the change."

Edit him out of the picture.

The threat of her fadeaway jump shot inched in.

Constantly seek out the best offensive players and challenge yourself to play great defense against them.

Yes, sir, coach.

"Not gonna happen," he fumed. "I'm the one for the job. My guys stand behind me."

He awaited a light to flicker in her eyes, hand raised in oath she'd stand by him.

Instead, silence ...engulfing ... heart crushed to gunpowder, threatening to explode inside his chest.

"I suggested to Bryson this was predictable behavior on Warren Murdock's part. He's obviously acting out of retribution, a brazen attempt to destroy you for breaking his daughter's heart. But he's beyond negotiating. Says this is indefensible."

She expelled a fragile sigh, chewed on her lip, eyes drawn upward ... shifting as though contemplating which side to take.

"You can't believe any of it, Everley."

He stepped close. "Please, tell me you don't."

I've lost all respect, Dalton. Don't believe in you anymore!

Believe. In. Me.

"Doesn't matter what I believe."

"To me, it does."

Her chin quivered, and her chest sank with hard breaths. "I'm ... letting you go."

Jump, swish, and opponent scored.

Desperation had him reaching in to block the ball. "You can't." He hitched a thumb. "I've got materials on order, my electrician conducting a post-storm assessment. I need time to get Moreland safely habitable." He took a step. "You *need* me. The chosen one, remember?" He gave his chest a vigorous slap, all trace of composure evaporating on wings of heated breath.

"Mom was left to do the work alone. I'll figure things out." Dread and uncertainty filtered into her determined gaze and sagged her brows in a downward angle.

Sympathy failed him. Like a drill, his words bored holes. "What do you know of demolition, plastering eighteen-inch-thick walls? Of environmental and electrical codes, OSHA safety requirements, bricklaying, carpentry, operating power tools?"

She turned a conflicted, misty gaze away. Strength drained. Angst played havoc with her face.

Bellevue, basketball is a game of inches. Maintain defensive stance and distance when in possession.

He sounded a withered humph, head shaking slowly. "Orderly Everley, always assuring everything lines up in neat little columns."

Even if it means ruining a man.

Fists balled at her side, arms ramrod stiff, pain bleeding into her tone. "I never meant it to come to this."

A swift evening breeze rattled the sashes. Heat radiated off the walls. After the tick of several agonizing seconds, she broke the silence, voice as glass. "Mom asked me to fix this place up, to dream big. In the process, I crushed those I care about."

"It's a little unclear who or what you care about."

"You *know* I care about you, Gabe." Her tone held a sliver of desperation, an ache over an impending fate meant to bust up two souls.

A fragmented laugh rumbled in his chest. "Thing of it is, I don't fit into one of your spreadsheets, or you'd send MidDay packing and let me do my job."

"You don't fit into anybody's spreadsheet!"

Ego crushed to dust, his head sank. He balled a fist inside his palm. Moisture blurred his vision.

"Okay, listen ..." His voice carried on a wisp of a breath, throaty and wind-whipped like the squall in his soul. "Let me go if that suits you but know this. I'm just as committed to you *and* this house as I was from the beginning. You can choose to trust my word or not, but that's all I have to offer." He glanced away, raised and lowered a limp hand. "Send payment when ... or if ... you can."

Leaving the room a mess of tools, drying plaster licked by swirls of dust, he brushed against her shoulder toward the open door, refusing to take in her scent.

"Wait. Gabe. Please?"

Darn that irresistible begging. One boot near the door jamb, he stopped mid-stride, managed a partial turn.

Agony filtered into her glistening emeralds. Voice withered, she said, "If I mattered enough for you to vote for me in high school, then ... why didn't you make an effort to meet me?"

Gaze clouded with a tender fragility, he shook his head, confounded that, in this moment, she'd thought back that far. Or cared.

Stark truth surfaced, tumbled out. "I was afraid you'd reject me."

CHAPTER NINETEEN

The following morning, Everley attended their family church in New Orleans, seeking answers, seeking reassurance. Seeking the ever-present help of God.

For a girl who'd prided herself on punctuality, she'd arrived late to answer God's calls, consult him for direction amid the conundrum. But the weight of impossible had gathered upstairs at Moreland like wicked storm clouds and gained strength, sapping the last of hers.

Despite numerous attempts to erase last evening's abrasive scene, it'd pestered like a fly on a fresh-cut watermelon. A vortex of insufferable heat had intensified in the room, whipping the air from Everley's lungs. Fighting feelings for Gabe had exhausted her. Like holding back a river with her hand, it was equally futile, illogical.

Reckless.

For all her effort to assure order, her life had become one big, unreconciled mess. Defeat tugged her shoulders. She'd sunk with her back against the wall. Gabe, a statue, had stood near the open door, nearly catatonic at her decision to let him go.

Unable to bear up, her chest heaved as tears throbbed behind her eyes, streamed down her cheeks, dribbled off her chin. This far in, it made no financial sense to end the relationship with MidDay. She wouldn't. Involving the iconic production company equaled credit to her account. Gabe equaled debit.

His ragged breathing warred with a disturbing stillness as he'd heroically made the valiant effort to hold himself together. It'd threatened to dismantle her resolve.

The manifestation of Mom's sorrow balled inside Everley's stomach. One widow to another. Restoring life to Moreland required more than one person could reasonably handle. And now, she'd been strong-armed to fire the one Mom implicitly handpicked to do the job.

Could a momma's heart, swollen with hope for her daughter, bleed disappointment after death?

Heaven held no room for sadness. Maybe now it did.

The girl who'd refused to put herself out there now a familiar face, followers rising daily. Awaiting Moreland's grand restoration ... perpetually making a match of her and Gabe. A life far more suited to Serenity, who'd unabashedly challenged a mammoth of a man to engage in baking contests.

Serenity. The sister who dared to chase her dreams, taking risks to materialize them.

Tears had continued to flow ... sorrow staining Gabe's handiwork. Her breath raspy, heaving, and shallow, she'd murmured. "Moreland, you've ... brought trouble and heartache to yet another widow."

Absent parting words, Gabe left, gutting her soul.

Dream box, Mom?

While the breezy Sunday afternoon had come to a pleasantly slow crawl, Serenity's verbal wallop had not.

"I just can't believe you let him go." The unsolicited rebuke vented over the hiss and sputter of the coffee machine. Hushed clientele made an audience of themselves, postured as though watching a movie.

A very sad one.

Serenity gave the silver handle a downward jerk, dark roast filling a cup. Capping the steamy brew, she turned and set it on the counter. Serving a smile, she called over Everley's shoulder. "Delisa, latte's here."

In short order, her countenance went dark, and she returned to battle stance. "I can get over the sad fact you've let the film thing fall apart, ruining our shot at being famous, but dropkicking Gabe? The one guy who freed you to dream again and made you laugh? He's your perfect match."

He had. He was.

Defenseless, Everley withered as Serenity continued her oratorical massacre. "I do hope you're wise to the fact that he suffered significant fallout from Carmen's wealthy father, all because he's deeply in love with you, Evers."

At the hole in Serenity's argument, Everley sat straight. "He's never said that."

"Maybe not to you." Expression awash in guilt, Serenity bit her lip.

"Spill the tea."

"He told me. Shares lots of things when he comes in."

"You're lying."

"Exaggeration may be one of my specialties, but not in matters of romance. Prince Charming said he's loved you since high school."

A labored exhale left her lungs. "All the media attention, incessant inquiries … it was becoming too much to handle."

Clientele dipped gazes, feigned disinterest.

Serenity snapped a dishrag then folded it several times over. "*Laaame* excuses. I think you love being the center of attention. Why else would you have created a website and worked double time to solicit subscribers, surpassing the number of followers I have—a feat worthy of a gold medal, I might add."

Being honest, maybe she'd pleasured in the task. At times, found aspects of design, scheduling, and effective solicitation downright thrilling.

"You'll never convince me your life in Chicago rivals what you've got going on here. The potential has no limits."

Practicality had Everley identifying reasons to return home. Fear had her justifying the foolishness of it.

"I don't suppose you'd ever part with that fancy condo you've got." Serenity's voice withered, a heated exhale singeing the counter.

"No, no. I'd consider listing it."

Mouth agape, Serenity skirted the counter and gave Everley the once-over. Suspicion hovered in her eyes. "The mere fact that you didn't balk at my suggestion to try an iced chai latte and a different pastry is one thing, but the willingness to let go of your place and hint at coming back home confirms that you're tripping on something, or you're ready to set your heart free."

Everley laughed, secretly thrilled to have been introduced to new items on the menu.

"I'll be sacrificing a valuable asset with years of appreciation left, but I could allocate profit to debt reduction."

"Whatever that means." Though her gaze was tinged in hope, Serenity's voice held trepidation. "And what about Moreland?"

The million-dollar question. Literally.

"If I keep it just for the sake of sentiment, I'll lose over two million on a sale."

"Only if it's fully restored."

Truth jabbed.

Hammer in one hand, paintbrush in the other, Everley wouldn't get far.

But sometimes, God called a girl to take forward steps with no clear picture of tomorrow. To trust God to guide her through the dark unknown, walking unafraid. Because he wasn't losing sleep over what the future held.

Take my hand. Do what I've called you to do.

"Hey, Evers. I completely sympathize with the gravity of your decision, the fear that everything will fall to pieces if you decide to let loose a little. But for what it's worth, I've always believed dreaming is part of what it means to be human. It imparts a moral obligation to act and makes room for God to do supernatural things. To show himself capable of providing the stuff we need in life. And in love."

To be honest, Serenity had it right. Particularly in matters of the heart. Because if Everley was willing to trust God to manage her future, she could keep Moreland, finish what Mom and Dad had started, and begin life anew. Of course, it was only logical for a Bellevue to oversee the restoration ... if he'd be willing.

If her stupid decision hadn't pummeled the life out of him.

In the last twenty-four hours, many disgruntled followers begged to know why she'd fired Moreland's hunky hero. The one who smelled of cedar, persona wrapped in temptation.

Keeping to hard, cold facts, her answers had been weak and unsatisfying.

Drawing from her loan, she sent Gabe a certified check two weeks ahead of the due date to clear the 50 percent owed by month's end. Maybe it'd enable him to pay down his construction loan. Or ... feed the poor.

The fact was, no price could be put on the work he'd done. Nor the cost her decision may have exacted from his heart.

Great Scott!

Monday afternoon, during another shoot with MidDay before Everley's return flight that evening, a wicked heat scorched the property. The buzz of cicadas sawed at her conscience.

Dressed in a wrinkled and frayed Commanders shirt, faded jeans ripped at the knees, and hair drawn up in a messy knot, Everley fanned moist air from her face. She ached for the shade of Gabe's presence. Because without her creative counterpart, she really had no talent—zero reason to engage a notable production company.

She felt utterly stupid out here, her heart without zeal.

For the sake of the contract, she'd have to muster a smile beside a ghost of a contractor and endure the weight of Moreland's tortuous silence, somehow refusing to behold evidence of Gabe's workmanship everywhere. Both wings completed, main house kitchen and bathroom upgrades preserved—old style and fully functional—modern plumbing and electrical passing safety standards. No longer a fire hazard.

Safe, beautiful. Very near ready to welcome inhabitants.

"If you'd give us a little smile ..." Alex stepped forward, strained a grin. "Show some enthusiasm."

Behind her, Moreland languished like a dog missing his master. Alex and crew scrambled, looking less hopeful with every attempt. He scanned a disconcerted glance around the place, sounding a withered sigh.

"I've looked for suitable replacements, Alex. There are none," Everley asserted.

Who knows what havoc Moreland might play if she'd hired a different contractor?

"We'll, uh, get our creatives on what we've got in post-production, see what they can do, but I'm afraid it'll fall short of H2H expectations. Might give credible reason to exercise their right of refusal."

"You pressured me to fire him. If you or the network—*any* network—isn't satisfied, that's not my concern." Arms tight at her waist, she left him to sink or swim in the mire.

Two weeks later, Everley received an email from Bryson, the stale Chicago evening mirroring the mood of the notice.

"Effectively immediately, MidDay has exercised its right to terminate the contract."

With the final location fee drafted to her account, the fanfare of 'lights, camera, action' was over. Like a disgruntled boyfriend, MidDay wasted no time posting images of a potential alternative, a pitiful little estate in Savannah.

To be sure, the estate was a beauty but, compared to Moreland, it lacked the pulse of story behind its aged exterior.

Mom would scoff.

And yes, Everley lost the project that'd generated revenue to skim the surface of her loan, but in reaching for the stars, she'd already lost that which money couldn't buy.

While flat on her sofa that evening, Everley pinned her gaze to the ceiling and assessed options, detailing pros and cons. First, Tyler. She had him like a girl had a stuffed animal. Cuddly, loyal. Though his crazy talk of future plans had been laid to rest, she suspected for weeks he'd been waiting for an opportune time. And partner? A lucrative career move that'd begun to shackle her to a formerly colorless life.

One without … "Gabe."

Taking herself in a hug, she missed the strength of his arms, skilled hands stroking her back, his touch tender and hungry. The effortless way he made her laugh. His stare held such adoration and intensity like she belonged in the Louvre. No one had ever considered her that way.

Gabe saw and dignified people the way God did, chiseled potential out of them. That and sheer grit, a refusal to fail.

Qualities that made him late for appointments. Qualities she loved.

Needed.

But there was more ...

Gabe's heart to rescue a stray, play frisbee with an adolescent kid, and house a war vet. Even Carmen was someone he'd rescued after a date gone wrong—or so said Serenity, who'd had the pleasure of Gabe's company when he came in every Friday. Paying more than owed. Just to bless her.

Who does that? Loves so fully and generously?

A holy presence drew near, whispered over her soul ...

Trust me. I will equip you to do what I've called you to do.

The wisdom fell in cottony layers, deepened the regret of losing a man whose love for people was God-sized. The man who'd taken the key to her heart and unlocked it.

The same guy she fired.

Status quo had robbed her of the abundant life Jesus died on the cross for her to enjoy, muting God's call on her life.

Head buried in numbers, heart shielded by predictability, she'd missed it.

Shoot for the stars, Everley Orion!

A girl can't see the breathtaking spectacle of heavenly constellations if she's striving for brilliant light of perfect order.

She'd released a man she loved. And that left Moreland unfinished. She hated unfinished.

So had Mom. Even in death.

Hence, the letter.

The ring of Everley's cell yanked her thoughts to present. It was Lettie.

"Miz Everley?" she said over the clatter of equipment in the background.

"Hi, Lettie. How are you?"

"Better'n I deserves."

"How's Moreland?" she said in hopeful falsetto.

"Empty as a fool's brain and sorrowful as a homesick chile. When you comin' home?"

"I've exhausted most of my vacation days—"

"Naw, naw, Miz Everley." Two scathing tongue clucks. "When you comin' home where you belongs?"

Oh, sweet Lettie.

During Gabe's last night at Moreland, dust whirled in angry circles and threatened to choke. In the sickening silence of Everley's decision, angst had claimed her face. Back to the wall, she'd sunk to the floor, hugged knees to her chest, and cried like a baby.

The heat of his own breath fogged the dark tunnel of space around his heart.

He wasn't sure who'd suffered the heavier blow.

Maybe it was the wrong move, but he'd left Everley to sit in the wreckage.

Hers and his.

The first of July, dark whispers of evening settled inside Gabe's condo. Unadorned walls stared back. In the aftermath of having been ousted, his rep had come into question. Murdock's toxic slander caused former and potential clients to retreat. He'd managed to acquire a few jobs. Little ones. Things easily learned if a guy simply watched a YouTube tutorial.

Installation of a period piece transom window at the Fontenot House was not the stuff of stellar business reviews.

The 50 percent Everley had paid a few weeks back enabled him to pay off his construction loan and debts outstanding to various contractors. To stave off being hauled to court by others, he'd agreed to work for free and bartered where he could. Income generated by online training videos had come to a slow drip. Big Ben, Charlie, and Ryan found other opportunities, leaving a meager crew of Randy, Silas, and Merrill.

A weak morning sun peeped past palm trees outside his windows. He flipped the switch in the kitchen, spilling light from pendant fixtures over stone countertops, stainless steel appliances, and marbled flooring.

For someone who'd built a thriving business out of creating better living spaces, Gabe's felt cramped, dark, and insufferably lonely.

Home to a defeated man, his dog, and his sidekick—a recovering alcoholic.

Merrill had scribbled a note and left it on the kitchen counter.

With Arthur at AA.

"Good." A silent prayer of gratitude for Arthur Durant glittered among the ruins. A fellow vet boasting twenty years sobriety, the man had invested in Merrill since the first support group meeting and agreed to keep him accountable.

Nothing in the refrigerator appealed to Gabe. Mostly the fact that it was barren. The milk had to be sour. Those limp fries only reminded him of the last time he'd surprised Everley with an order, the two of them seated beneath the oak during a film break.

Before handing the carton over to her, he'd drizzled them in ketchup. Because that's how she liked them.

"Makes no sense," he'd goaded her again.

"You're wrong," she'd insisted, fingertips coated red. "With my way, each fry is covered *and* visually appealing."

"They're fries, Orderly, not museum pieces. You dunk 'em. Like this," he'd said, demonstrating.

She'd returned a playful eye roll, mock annoyance in her tone. "They're fries, not a basketball."

At her wink, sweetened by an irresistible giggle, his breath caught.

The ache of missing her smile, the tease of her laugh ... the way it was before she'd cut him loose. It all just made him sick.

Last week, further discovery in K's research had the whimsical college student bewitched. A remarkable awe claimed her gaze. "I'm so going to ace this class. The fact that you were chosen to fix it up is nothing short of delicious irony."

That particular day he'd had no patience for her yammering. Still didn't.

And why'd he care about her grade? Her whole future lay ahead. Today, his looked bleak.

Time to lose himself in TV.

In the main room, he slouched in his recliner, boots slung on the footrest. "C'mon, Champ. I need company."

Silence nagged. He twisted at the waist to peer into the open laundry room adjacent to the kitchen where Champ was napping and lifted his voice. "Champ, ol' buddy. Daddy's home."

No response.

"Get over here, you lazy canine." He popped his hand against his knee.

He'd started to dig himself out of the chair when his phone pinged voicemail.

Dad again.

This time, his voice was clear. It held authority laced with wisdom gained by experience. And this time, Gabe determined to sit a spell and listen.

"Gabe, it's Dad. Been following your situation. Sure hate you lost the house deal. Media's no friend of a fella, is it?"

That stony laugh.

"What you build in years, people can destroy overnight. But the work you do isn't between you and them. It's between you and God. Anyway ... just wanted to see how you're handling things. Wondered whatever happened to the girl. She's sure pretty. Proves you got that gift, you know, a built-in ability to see beauty and potential in people. Give them a helping hand. I've always admired that about you. I hope you'll trust the good Lord to open the right doors. In due time, he'll work things out so long as he's the reason behind all you do. Anyhoo, just felt led to share. Take what you will. Leave the rest. I ... I love you, son. Call if you can."

Crazy for sure, but the timely message sealed cracks in Gabe's soul. It was only right to take a minute to express appreciation. Because it might do the same for Dad.

Gabe retrieved Dad's number and added it to his contacts just as Randy called.

"Yup."

"Where are you?" Randy snapped.

Slouching, Gabe balanced his phone on his shoulder and fumbled for the remote. "That's no way to speak to your partner."

"I'm at the Lipscomb house. You. Are. Not."

A single day's job that pretty much required a few twists of a screwdriver.

"I'm at home with my family." A man and his canine, awaiting the company of a recovering alcoholic.

Phone drawn from his mouth, Gabe released a shrill whistle. "Champ!"

"Partner?" Derision marked his tone. "That means we've got each other's back, neither one looking out for his own interest."

"I've got a lot on my mind, Randy, so I'd appreciate a little grace. As in unmerited favor ... or so says the good book." Emphasized during last Sunday morning's message. That made twice he'd gone to church in one month. Matched the sum total of the last five years.

This time, though, he'd resolved to incline his heart back to unchanging wisdom. To leave a legacy beyond being the guy who could get new business with a smile and an impressive collection of tools. To tunnel back to the truth of who God said he was and rebuild from the inside. Maybe even patch things up with Dad, add him to payroll.

But nothing could repair the crushing blow of being fired by the beautiful red-haired girl, the whole of his heart ripped apart like demo day. At times he'd even summoned the austere gaze of Brigadier General Edmund Bellevue, lead-heavy disappointment registering at his bushy brow. Gabe, a Bellevue baton bearer hopeful who'd bumbled the pass.

Randy's audible sigh slithered through the phone. "It's bad enough that Everley let you go,"

The pain of her rejection stained crimson on a thick veil of sarcasm. "As they say, 'You're fired.'"

"Look, Gabe, I've got a family to feed."

Gabe craned his neck Champ's direction. "Same."

"I'm serious. We passed up thousands of dollars because of that plantation gig, overworked and undercompensated our guys. The roof mishap that could have been avoided if performed by professionals on their game set us back several weeks."

It was true. The drain on Gabe's business account was evidenced by fast food and rationed dog food. He hadn't tasted Bryan's elite fare at Ben's Seafood and Grille in over a month. And he needed new work boots. Duct tape wrapped around the toe to hold the sole in place proved ineffective.

"It kills me to say this, but I've gotta get out of the partnership."

Scrambling out of the recliner, Gabe tiptoed toward the laundry room, stopping midstride at the sight of outstretched paws lazily draped over a dog bed.

The form of a peaceful canine.

"Atta boy. Napping through the storm." He took quiet steps backward to avoid rousing his pal.

He sidled back to the main room—attention full on Randy. "Okay, so what exactly are you saying?"

"I love you like a brother, Gabe. You know I do, but I need a steady income. Something me, Summer, and the girls can count on."

You're an unreliable fool, Dalton Bellevue.

Gabe's heart thudded in wild rhythm, breath thickening in his throat. "We're G *and* R," he said with unrelenting fervor. "You're the R."

"Believe me, I've given this a lot of prayerful consideration, but I need out. Sorry, Gabe. Really, I am."

With that, Randy ended the call.

The ministry of failure. The gift of emptiness.

He expelled a heated breath, lugged himself over to the sofa. Sinking into it, he tunneled fingers through his hair. His cell slipped from a loosened grip and fell to the floor. Moisture stung like bees, blurred his vision.

Sobs held on lockdown for years, crashed through him and racked his upper body in violent waves. Tears pooled at his feet. Strength drained, he crumbled onto the floor in a heap.

YOU ARE THE REASON

Hard as he'd tried to dodge the bullet of father-failure, he'd hadn't ducked, his pierced heart now a slow bleed of despair.

CHAPTER TWENTY

Throughout July, Everley strove to keep pace at work, but a life divided against itself shredded a heart's true desire into pieces and resulted in an exceptionally lonely woman.

Keeping an ever-watchful eye on social media and tabloids, Everley had learned the full scale of the disaster that'd fallen on Gabe at the gala, his reputation on the chopping block at Murdock's hand ... something about Randy walking away.

Her decision to fire him that same evening? Way to shoot the wounded.

The bottom line was—she'd miscalculated. She hadn't factored in the most essential variable, which was doing what God had called her to do, trusting Him to equip her and fulfill the longing of her heart.

Gabe.

At some point, Everley's reluctant heart had slid open a crack. It was Gabe who'd raised the sash and stood in all his rugged charm on the other side.

He'd even cared enough to notice how she preferred to eat her fries.

In ways she'd never thought possible, he had her believing two plus two equaled five. Because love couldn't be forced into columns and reconciled. It had taken up residence in her heart and become profoundly impossible to ignore. It'd spun desire and reality into a wonderful, dizzying dance.

Gabe was the reason she'd decided to make the monumental move back to New Orleans. The reason her condo now belonged to Marwan Eid, a wealthy young entrepreneur who'd had no interest in haggling. Paid in cash.

Because it wasn't the force of unpleasant childhood experiences and the sudden death of a husband that'd held her captive. It was memory's false interpretation of those events, plot points in the story God was actively writing in her life. What God deemed art, she'd deemed trash. And maybe Gabe and Everley were the main characters, a means to grant Gabe his big dream and offer her a reason to dream.

"I'm super proud of your courage and excited for your new adventure," Margot said. "Give hot reno guy a hug for me, heh?"

"For you, I'll suffer through," Everley chuckled.

Parting ways with Tyler, however, proved far more difficult than she'd anticipated. For all their routine and uncomplicated ways, he'd fastened his heart to hers and rallied hard to keep her in Chicago. Promising more.

"We could be great together." Brows pleading over gray eyes, he'd taken her hands, clutched them to his chest. "I had plans."

His ability to entice fell flat. She returned a sympathetic smile. "Ty, I can't neglect my responsibility to Moreland anymore. I miss my sister ... I miss ..." *Don't. Say. His. Name.* "We'll keep in touch."

Friends did that.

Submitting two weeks' notice was received by Phillip with all the welcome of a flu epidemic.

"This is not a job. It's a commitment."

A point Phillip had hammered home with such predictable frequency she mouthed the words while he spoke, wishing she had a penny each time he'd said it.

"You've been considered for partnership. Vance, O'Connor, and *Scott*. If you quit under that condition, mark my word, you'll never find a reputable firm to hire you."

She knew.

"I'll leave the outcome in God's hands."

He puffed out a skeptical breath. "You'd better hope that God of yours has hands big enough."

Experience told her Phillip would implode if she explained that God had called her to do this. Made no earthly sense. Which is why she'd come to trust it. Because truth was absolute, reasonable, and unchanging— regardless of opinion otherwise.

Stepping from the taxi outside the Pear Tree, the moist August heat touched her cheeks like a sloppy kiss of welcome. The bold move from Chicago eliminated the need for a rental. What furniture she hadn't sold or donated to charity for a tax write-off, she'd put in storage. She'd stay with Serenity while she determined her next steps.

"Today. I have today."

Enveloped in shade outside the bakery, she glanced down the street, the familiarity a refuge of sorts. The scent of fresh-baked goods hovered over a discreet undercurrent of alcohol, cigarette smoke, and sewage. A sleek white horse clopped past, garbed in celebration, bells jingling aside his neck. Fastened to a shaft, a white carriage cradled a bride and groom, their expressions glowing in hopeful expectancy. Traditional Dixieland jazz boomed from an open bar.

From her purse, she took hold of a small Bible. The same Mom had discovered years ago beneath a loose plank at Moreland. Its edges were worn by time. Pages crisp and smelling musty from age.

Gingerly, she opened the fragile volume. It fell open to Psalms, chapter 16. Her gaze narrowed to a couple verses circled in red.

"The Lord is the portion of mine inheritance and of my cup; thou maintainest my lot. The lines are fallen unto me in pleasant places; yea, I have a goodly heritage ..."

Houses are not mere bricks and mortar, pieced together by cypress and pine. They become homes when the breath of life is delivered.

Momentarily, she shut her eyes as a prayer fell to her lips. "Thank you, Lord, for entrusting me with Moreland."

Welcomed by tinkling bell, Everley spotted Serenity at the counter. "Antique shopping, here I come."

Serenity met her eyes and shouted into the kitchen. "She's back, Lettie!"

Patrons stilled, turned their gazes to follow Serenity as she scurried over and took Everley in a hug. "Welcome home, Evers."

"Duty calls."

Serenity clamped hands onto Everley's shoulders, showcasing a wry grin. "Your attempt to make this all about responsibility doesn't fool me."

"Maybe I could help you around here while I search for a job." An endless endeavor.

"I'm shocked you don't have one lined up already."

The thought rippled through her, caressing her heart. "God knows the when and where and how."

The corners of Serenity's mouth turned up in a playful grin. "I never thought the day would come when I'd hear such blessed nonchalance. And that blush crawling into your cheeks? Sister, you got it bad."

The warm, pink drizzle of lovesickness betrayed Everley's eye roll.

"As for help, I'd welcome it. I'll lose Kourtney as evening barista once the fall semester starts."

"How about I manage the books for you?"

"That would be fantastic. Books over there on the bookcase. One of them is a signed copy, a swoony inspirational romance written by an author in North Carolina. It's about this—"

"I meant your accounting."

Serenity lifted a shoulder. "I scribble things down here and there. Somewhere."

Everley palmed her forehead. "I beg you, let me handle your accounts."

"Have at it," she chirped.

They embraced again, this time Everley letting the lingering warmth of sunshine seep into her pores and suffuse her soul.

A hacking cough sounded in the back corner where a clean-shaven Merrill sat wearing a pressed collared shirt and khaki shorts belted at the waist. Hand steady, he sipped from a mug, set it down, and met Everley's eyes. He offered a small nod before returning to peruse his open newspaper.

Reading—a glorious display of sound mind, body, and spirit.

Serenity turned her gaze to Everley and delivered the answer to her silent question. "He's a regular customer."

The wayward drunk? "How so?"

"Gabe's taken him in as an apprentice, found an AA sponsor, has seen to his rehabilitation at The Hope Center. Given him a new start."

Eyes shuddering closed, she rolled Gabe's name around in her mind, letting its sweetness spread throughout her body, relishing the taste.

"How's *he* doing?" Her voice was timorous.

"Seems all right, considering. Still comes in every Friday morning."

Today was Friday. Being afternoon, though, she'd missed him. *Really* missed him. Her hand floated to her chest to still the beating.

Turbulence rumbled inside her soul at the remembrance of his wounded gaze that last night together, eyes tinged red as though by heart bleed.

Could he ever forgive her scathing rejection, this wild, rugged man who'd lured her out of hiding to a place she'd once labeled unsafe and illogical?

To prop a sagging mood, she asked, "Has he ... asked about me?"

"Nope." An abrupt response meant to slay rash decisions, dissuade any thoughts of love between them.

It did. The truth plunged into Everley's heart, causing it to gurgle and gasp. In increasing measure, life without Gabe wasn't adding up.

The bell dinged. At Serenity's elbow jab, Everley jolted then turned attention to the entrance. Afternoon light spilled onto the floor in a pool near Gabe's feet. He wore the overly worn pair of jeans she'd remembered, right knee exposed. His unbuttoned, blue denim shirt ... the cotton-soft one she'd remembered ... revealed a white T-shirt fitted to the musculature of one who'd worked hard. Overcome adversity. The fragments of a man who'd traversed the dark places God had seen fit to take him and let the brokenness of it all rebuild him and fill him with light.

How she'd love to lie beside him beneath the stars. Yearning for the warmth of his crushing kisses had begun to thaw her frozen heart, stubborn refusal to fall in love now splintering in shards.

The moment his gaze connected with her, he paused. Expression unreadable.

He gifted her with a slight tip of his chin. "Good to see you, Everley."

Her first name. Though the delivery was guarded and formal, she loved how it sounded when he spoke it.

Guilt chose her words as she dared to take steps closer. She felt the weight of deliberate stares at her back as onlookers watched reality unfold.

"Is it good? I mean, I did fire you."

"Hope isn't lost. I'll be all right."

Taking a glance at Merrill, Gabe stepped past, barely brushing her arm. His scent hung in the air—hard work, denim, and musk. The smell of rugged determination to push through difficulty.

Maybe even because of it.

"C'mon, big guy. We've got work to do." A gritty edge surfaced in his voice.

Merrill returned a sharp nod, snapped the paper shut, and folded it. Effortlessly, he rose, stance steady.

"Numbers lady know about Champ?"

Gabe shut his eyes, pinched the bridge of his nose, shook his head. "Uh-uh."

She alternated her gaze between them, stepped as near as she dared. "What's wrong with him?"

Gabe turned slightly. "Suffered a bleeding tumor. Had to put him down."

News delivered with stilted emotion, words monotone as if to guard his own heart against hemorrhage. Together they'd bled enough to stain the Mississippi.

Tears sprang, blurred Gabe's image. Emotion knotted at her throat, hammered against her chest. She drew in a hard gasp, one hand cupped to her mouth. "I'm so ... so sorry, Gabe."

Sorrow filtered into his eyes over a resigned grin. "Champ served his purpose. The Lord took him in his good time."

The slight ease of his guarded countenance held mystery, a touch of regret deepening the lines around his eyes.

Gabe turned to Merrill. "Got the Sinclair's house to tend to. Ready, sir?"

"Yes'r, boss." Purpose twinkled to life inside Merrill's brightened eyes.

Set to his task ... whatever that was ... Gabe brushed past again, a hint of anguish in the press of his lips.

At the front door, he turned to wave at Serenity. "Later, Hotshot." He gave Everley a kind glance. "Take care."

After an unsavory encounter with Gabe—made worse by news of Champ's death—how on earth was she to take care when a piece of her heart had died? Steeled in determination, she stomped a foot. Because Gabe needed to know she wasn't visiting, that she'd come back to stay. That she'd given up everything ... her property, her job, her friends.

Why did he need to know?

Because you want him to know.

Yes. I do.

Outside, the roar of Gabe's engine and odor of exhaust assailed her as he edged his truck from the no-parking zone and sped away. Red, beady-eyed taillights blinked back.

Too late.

But Mom had once said, in her hippy way of phrasing things, that if a man and woman are to become a thing, then a girl will allow herself to be chased. Otherwise, she'd lost nothing.

"He loves you crazy, you know?"

She whipped around to see Serenity, heated gaze burrowing beneath Everley's moist skin. "I see it in his eyes every time he comes in, looking past me to see traces of you ..."

A feeble shrug.

"For pity's sake, when are you gonna put that smart brain of yours to good use and allow that impossibly gorgeous man into your heart, Evers?"

Through the window of the Pear Tree, Gabe spotted Merrill seated near the back corner, gaze fixed on newspaper, sipping an amber liquid that'd darn sure better be sweet tea. Given his crusty exterior, Merrill would have been deemed an unlikely apprentice. But God had shaped beauty and usefulness from raw material, and as Merrill sobered, he became increasingly teachable—and reliable.

Very little evidence remained of the man who'd once been flattened with a piercing blow to the face.

"Guess that'll teach me to keep my mouth shut," Merrill had muttered, stroking and rotating his swollen jaw.

"Been telling you that for months now."

"I suppose those who think they have it all figured out don't listen to reason so good, do they?"

Merrill's cockeyed retort had suggested deeper meaning.

After Randy's decision to part ways, Gabe was more intent on forging an able-bodied assistant out of the old guy. Prime among the skills Gabe had learned from Dad was resourcefulness. Gabe vowed to utilize it for mutual benefit. To honor God with his abilities rather than use them to bolster his résumé. To boldly be who God created him to be and leave all glory to the one who was worthy of it.

And maybe, in due time, he'd figure a way to restore the crumbling walls of heartache.

Lord, restore my soul.

Gabe had lagged in responding to Dad's call to let him know that, despite fumbling and failures, his greatest success was having been a father who cared. Maybe God meant for Gabe to dignify Dad and work toward reconciliation.

To be an agent of restoration.

Despite a dull, achy place in his heart, he determined to remember what he had, refusing to lament over loss.

God was more than enough.

Which meant ... Gabe was enough.

A pleasant and distinct floral scent inside the bakery turned his attention toward the counter. To the unexpected—and ever more beautiful presence of Everley Lewis Scott. Why here? Why now? It sure wasn't to film. From his interactions with Serenity, he'd learned MidDay ended their dealings with her, cut their losses.

He let his gaze linger. Slain by an attraction he couldn't deny, heat infused his cheeks. The copper taste of fear landed on his tongue, rattling a mental toolbox of painful memory.

Her countenance held no trace of haughtiness. Softened, instead, by what looked to be regret. Emotionally parched, he lapped at the serene demeanor in her eyes. Gaze roaming along the bright fabric of her dress, he enjoyed how it fell along her body in perfect symmetry. It spoke of a woman no longer restrained by strict agenda, willing to invite spontaneity. His heart stepped up a notch in—*tha thump, tha thump!*

Just like it had in high school. A reticent basketball star gazing at his heart's delight from a safe distance, mind bursting with sappy sentiments he'd wanted so badly to voice.

Like now.

In all that'd transpired between them, nothing had changed. The essence of Everley Lewis still fanned flames of interest. Best to douse the passion before it set him ablaze.

Offering Serenity a wave, he then turned to Everley and tipped his head, summoned polite greeting. "Good to see you, Everley."

Really good.

This capable woman had been hiding in wintery shadows, perpetually resistant to consider the unpredictable, dogged by the need for practicality and order. He'd wanted to be the one to draw her out. The reason she'd dream of endless possibilities and make something special of Moreland. To be the one to help her carry the weight of it all.

Years back, he'd even hoped she'd be the mother of his sons.

What a team they'd have made. Win-win.

Though his business teetered on bankruptcy, his greatest loss stood right over there. A pleasing centerpiece inside a lively French Quarter bakery.

How easy it would have been to blame-shift when she'd challenged the sincerity of his greeting ...

"Is it good? I mean, I did fire you."

She offered up full blame like a signed check.

Rising above the rubble of demolition, he carefully selected his words. "Hope isn't lost. I'll be all right."

With or without you, Crush.

That stung. But nothing in their contractual agreement stated their hearts had to be sealed. Because, in large part, it was despair and heartache that'd devoured Dalton Bellevue, a man who'd had no one to shore him up in hardship. Failure had tried to entice another Bellevue offspring to play its wicked game.

Gabe had refused. Unlike Dad, Gabe had God.

More accurately, God held Gabe in his mighty grip.

Up against Murdock's character assassination, lucrative contracts lost due to ill-informed and twisted tales of why Randy Severson *really* left the partnership, Gabe experienced genuine empathy for Dad with a renewed vigor in Everley's presence.

Because she was the reason God demolished the lie that'd turned his heart to stone and had begun to rebuild a new man on the foundation of truth—the cornerstone upon which the integrity of the building depended.

Your value isn't found in what you do. In God's eyes, you are worthy apart from your performance.

Could God heal the humiliation of being ousted by the one woman he'd ever really loved?

What idiot signs up for that?

He had.

Love did crazy things. Love took risks.

Love gave all.

Somehow this fiery damsel in distress had sawed through his hardwood surfaces and got his heart ticking again. And there she stood in her sister's bakery, the lady of Moreland Manor, in all her unmatched beauty and finesse, radiating the irresistible confidence he loved.

But she'd let him go.

A gentleman knew when to bow out.

Against his better judgment, he took a final whiff of her gardenia as he offered high school crush a kind goodbye and ushered Merrill out the door.

CHAPTER TWENTY-ONE

In time, the tabloids had moved on to play havoc elsewhere. A faithful few begged to know more about Gabe's ancestry, some touting him a modern-day hero—the one fate had chosen to restore his ancestor's house.

Crazed viewers persisted in pairing him with Everley, creating a sure-fire romance.

"That part hadn't been staged," he mused as he motored on his Harley to meet Merrill and Silas at the Sinclair house.

And just why had Everley been in New Orleans a week ago? Was she making arrangements with a realtor? Torching her estate?

Dang. What would it have been like to exercise his superpower and breathe life into Moreland again? A resilient structure that'd survived war, outbreaks of yellow fever, and deadly Gulf Coast hurricanes. To reflect the lives of generations before Marigold and Pete Lewis owned it. Bellevue men, lucky lords of the manor, secured behind Moreland's twenty-four-inch exterior wall. Seated in the parlor, sipping drinks from crystal goblets, talking strategy and profit.

Edmund Bellevue must have been mighty proud to acquire such vast acreage—all the more valuable shared with the woman he loved.

Gabe had so looked forward to escorting Everley over the threshold to show her around and bask in her satisfied smile. He'd imagined it often. If only she'd not clung to pre-determined boundary lines and refused to consider a partnership with him.

Why hadn't the vision he'd cast that night reached her heart? Because last time he'd checked Moreland's website—a few days after MidDay ended the contract—she'd continued to persist in selling it. Went so far as to suggest she'd sell 'as is,' Moreland bearing the unfinished mark of his hands.

Arriving at the Sinclair's, an incoming text pinged.

EVERLEY: Can you meet me today at City Park?

Was she back in town and needed to borrow a blow torch? Trying to assuage her guilt? He'd typed an impulsive response ... I don't want your pity.
Don't be a jerk.
Delete.

GABE: Sure. Time?

EVERLEY: Around 4:00-ish? Or whenever ... by the Singing Oak, City Park?

A twenty-five-acre recreational attraction, restored after the devastation of Hurricane Katrina.
What's a guy to do?
Go to her.
Be punctual.

GABE: 4 is good.

EVERLEY: Great. See you then.

That afternoon, Gabe left the Sinclair project in the hands of Merrill and Silas and sped to City Park. Hazy heat touched the trees lining the paved road that led to the Singing Oak. The acclaimed, mature tree stood apart from the shaded path that rimmed the vast urban oasis. Its seductive melody amplified as Gabe reached the southern end of Big Lake near Bayou St. John.

Gabe eased off his Harley.

Right at 3:58.

Ducks, swans, and geese honked as they glided across the surface of the lake, rippling the water and pulling the reflection of sunlight out of shape.

Memories bubbled up. Fishing with Dad at Bayou Metairie behind the Casino on the south end, a young boy of maybe ten or eleven. The one time his catch was large enough to filet, grill, and eat. Even Mom approved. Every affirmation counted to build a man—until she'd torn them down. Married to a woman who'd refused to believe in her husband, no wonder failure had seeped in, rotted Dad's insides.

Wind swished through the leafy canopy of the famed oak, the air sweetened by the lyrical pings of windchimes. The effect wasn't enough to still his drumming heart.

Because … why'd he sign up for another beating? What shortcoming had yet to be pointed out? How much did love have to sacrifice?

GABE: Here.

The scent of gardenia wafted from the lake, tugged at places meant for lovers. Turning, Gabe narrowed his gaze to the shoreline to see a woman facing the water. Snug jeans, a cuffed ivory top, and sandals.

Unmistakably, Everley.

Moisture formed in his palms.

Sun glinted off the lake. She tipped her chin, wind brushing red-gold threads from her shoulders. She shaded her eyes and slowly rotated with a searching gaze.

Champ would have already bolted her direction, reminding Gabe of God's holy purpose in gifting him with his best friend. Poised and purposeful, there she stood. The unequivocal Champ test winner. Highest honor a dog could give.

Sadness of loss pressed in.

Gabe took steps toward her. At the crack of acorns beneath his boots, she turned. Caught his gaze. And smiled.

Fragile hope teased insufferably, lodged in his chest.

The light of early evening outlined her darn-near flawless face. Her scent penetrated his pores, pried at need.

"Champ would've knocked you over by now."

For a moment, sorrow drew at her lips. She turned a pensive gaze away then brought it back. A hand came to her chest, and she bowed slightly as though she'd received an award.

She had.

"I'm flattered."

Closer now, his voice a hard whisper. "You should be."

You really, really should be.

"I've missed him."

"He loved you."

Identified my intended bride.

A young couple intercepted their cautious advance. The woman's pasted her gaze on Everley. "Are you Everley Scott, the owner of the manor house on Bayou Lafourche?"

Great. Fandom had followed them.

Everley's shoulders slumped minimally. She released a slow, controlled breath as though weary from unsolicited attention. Still, she produced a kind smile. "I am."

The girl moved a finger between them—stopped at Gabe. Joy alighted on her face. "And you're Gabe Bellevue, the YouTube contractor who's restoring it?"

No mention of MidDay—the house, its heiress, and her contractor the sole objects of interest.

He turned a sidelong glance at Everley. "I was."

Truth was truth, and past was past.

And ... this was now.

Guess they didn't know Gabe had failed. He thanked God for the ignorance of a few.

After a brief photo op, the couple left, likely scrambling to feed the image to any number of social media shark tanks. Fuel for viewers to make Gabe and Everley's story read the way they'd wanted.

Everley chugged a low laugh, cheek crimped in a sidelong grin. "Guess we'll have to get used to that."

We? Could have been.

Nerves knotted Gabe's tongue, shooting electricity down his arms. "You wanted to meet?"

"Thanks for taking the time."

An awkward silence hung in the wispy air, gained amplitude as each second ticked. Lowering her gaze, she drew a line in the grass with her shoe, tucked hands in the pockets of her jeans. Wholly looking the part of a shy schoolgirl.

"I made the wrong decision to let you go," she said, barely meeting his gaze. "I placed my own interests above yours and deeply regret it. I've come to ask your forgiveness." A raw confession uttered without pretense. She sniffed and glanced away.

The rush of moisture to his eyes threatened to betray his heart. Darn gardenia. The scent nearly hijacked all reason.

When she turned and faced him, the brilliance of her eyes held the sheen of sunlight.

A call would have sufficed. Maybe an email or simple text. She'd come a long way to set things right, so ... "Forgiven."

Desperation made his voice go all raspy. He cleared the knot at his throat and summoned a sliver of courage. "How long you stayin' this time?"

Recovering composure, she shook her head and cut him a sideways, provocative glance. "I'm not going back to Chicago."

Shock straightened his frame. He searched her face, wondered at the grin that broadened beneath a slow sweep of her lashes. An inebriating insistence that he decipher her meaning.

"Your condo, your job—"

"Sold it. And quit."

Despite Gabe's herculean effort to restrain elation, a silent squeal eked out like a kid on Christmas morning with a new bike.

Shiny and red. Construction sturdy and beautiful.

For you, son.

He worked nonchalance into his tone. "That's pretty extreme." His statement came out punctuated and cheerless, inviting explanation.

The smile she delivered set longing ablaze. A girl unaware of her ability to incinerate a man.

"Turns out, God's provided plenty of home down here."

An unfinished one, a pitiful monument to a failed enterprise that'd marred the Bayou. At Serenity's urging—and promise to keep the endeavor off radar—he'd gone out on multiple occasions to tinker around, assure safety. No cost to the family.

Occupying the space in front of him, she captured his eyes. Stroked his bristled jaw with the palm of her hand. Her touch shimmied through him, igniting a fire. "I've always been partial to warm, southern skies."

Color blushed her cheeks. Desire filtered into her countenance, her tone soft and enchanting.

His temples pulsed and heart thumped.

Passion surged from his feet and hung momentarily at his middle before traveling to his chest. He took her in an easy embrace. She didn't resist.

He pulled back and studied her gaze, found it wanting ... her breathing shallow, matching the rhythm of his. Her lips, full, raised ... and ready.

Hold up, tool guy. Yes, he wanted her. Unhindered. But he refused to light passion's fire in the absence of a commitment that honored God.

They'd parted ways. She'd *fired* him, for Pete's sake.

At the root of it, they'd been no more than client and contractor. Or so he'd thought. Instead, the broken relational boundaries had left him emotionally and mentally depleted.

Despite her beckoning—the glisten of ardor in her gaze creating a tornadic force inside him—holy reason overtook the ache to claim her lips. Exercising immense effort, he leaned in and merely kissed her gently on the forehead.

Sounding a resigned sigh, she turned her cheek to his chest, sinking against him in an easy embrace.

"I've missed you, Gabe."

Like a girl missed her goldfish or ...?

"I'm still here. Told you as much."

"Is he the real reason you left Chicago?"

An unfamiliar baritone voice struck Gabe aside the head like a nail gun. He turned to see the form of a polished professional in tailored dark pants, a crisp dress shirt beneath a blazer, and what had to be high-end, designer shoes. Despite the *dress for success* appearance, the guy toted a none too happy countenance beneath a stern brow. In one hand, he gripped a collection of red roses wrapped in green tissue.

"Tyler?" Everley gasped. The color drained from her face as she untangled her arms from Gabe's and turned to the intrusive stranger. "How'd you—?"

"I met your sister at the bakery. She talks a lot."

One arm fell limp at the guy's side, the roses now dangling from a loose hold. Standing askew, he alternated a challenging glare between them. "It's evident that my reason for being here doesn't really matter anymore." Defeat pinched his mouth into a tight line.

Everley crossed over to Mr. Slick and took his hands with all the comfort of a bed-warming lover. "This isn't what you think, Ty. He's just the contractor."

Her fumbled explanation jackhammered Gabe's heart and made dust of his ego. He wasn't sure which of the two men had sustained greater injury.

A dot of rain stung Everley's cheek. Then a few more. the Singing Oak defied the shove of stiff wind and silenced its song.

Great Scott!

She whirled to face Gabe. In his presence—solid and handsome in his dusty blue work shirt, jeans, and untamed hair, one toe of his boot wrapped in silver duct tape—she hadn't noticed the gathering of pewter clouds that'd thickened like lava. Sunlight trimmed its billowed edges in jarring, white lines.

Raindrops speckled Gabe's shirt. Pain hung like a marred painting across his conflicted face, the gravity of her reckless statement palpable. "I'll leave you two to work this out." His words were icy against the balmy air.

He pivoted hard.

Everley caught him on the arm, the flex of his muscle an iron bar. "Gabe, please. I didn't mean that. I ... I ..." Heart's ramblings short-circuited her brain, made worse by the twitch along his jaw. The slight flare of his nostrils was weakened only by the anguish registering in his dark gaze.

He paused, then turned slowly. The desperate fury over his brow wound her into a knot. "To the gentleman's question, what *is* the reason you came back, Everley?" Hand to his chest, he leaned in, red-ringed gaze tinged with force and vulnerability. "Because if I'm any part of your decision, now would be the time to stake your claim."

At his thunderous entreaty, she squeezed her eyes shut. Fisting her hair atop her head, she clawed fingers through and let the whole mess of it fall limp around her face.

Suddenly caught in a wicked triangle. No place for a reluctant widow.

Except that Gabe was the reason she'd come. The reason she'd chosen to stay.

But her fumbled intent to give voice to her heart had only shot the wounded. Again.

Tears pooled in her eyes and threatened to overwhelm her. The urge to unleash a torrent of sobs burned inside her lungs. Drawing her gaze to meet his, her heart spoke in a delicate whisper. "I'm back ... because ... I love you." Her ragged confession caught on the air and floated between them.

There. She'd said it. Nothing logical or orderly about it, bearing all the marks of unpredictability. Yet so right somehow.

Because here she was, a girl who saw no way to live without the man who unknowingly held her heart in his hands.

Oh dear God, what would he do with it?

A weight-bearing exhale rifted the air. She felt Tyler's retreat and turned to see him plod toward the lake. He leveled a vacant stare and stood motionless. But she knew him well enough to decipher his cocked-hip posture. The skilled lawyer had gone the distance to track her down and was mentally regrouping. Strategizing.

What though?

Raindrops mingled with an errant tear and pricked along Everley's cheek.

Gabe's voice held fumes of frustration. "You love all your clients?"

All right, enough! She swiped at her tears, squared her shoulders, and matched his steely glare. "Tyler isn't my client. *You* are."

"Was," he bit back, the jagged edge of correction shredding seams. His mumbled response trailed to a pained hush. "You cut me loose, remember?"

Gross misjudgment.

"I told you I was wrong."

At her confession, he fixed his gaze, a speculative brow pinched over a shifting gaze. He softened his tone. "You hired me to make Moreland pretty again so you and your momma could rest in peace. With one regrettable exception, I did my best in the time I was given." He tossed a feeble glance at Tyler then leveled it back to her. "And now that Prince Charming has arrived, you're free to go your way."

"That's just it. I am going my way. The work isn't finished. Moreland has more story left in her."

The hope of partnership wriggled into her heart, fixed itself to desire. Way beyond what Vance and O'Connor could offer. "I'd like you to consider—"

"What, barter? In kind? Make myself available for more superficial kisses?"

"Nothing in those kisses was superficial. At least not at my end." They held a fire she'd never known, sizzled inside her soul. Blossomed into a love she could no longer ignore.

The grimace didn't wear well on his beautiful face. His flared nostrils were a sure sign she'd brought him to the edge of insanity.

"My request for restoration funds from the National Registry of Historic Places was approved. The status will save us taxes. MidDay's final remuneration will cover utilities, homeowner's insurance, and the end of year property tax."

Angling a stare, he stepped closer, dimples deepening with the slow rise of a hopeful grin. "Us?"

Nothing of question rang in his tone.

"I'd almost be inclined to believe you'd taken a liking to the place, Orderly."

"I have. Very much, in fact."

"Then you're gonna keep her?"

"Yes."

Definitely. Giving voice to the resolution filled crevices in her heart—gave it purpose and intention.

Sorrows become beauty in the magic of the morning, Everley Orion. No sense stifling the abundant life God called us to enjoy.

Bouquet in hand, Tyler lumbered over from the shoreline and stopped a few yards short. One hand firm at his hip, he splayed his jacket open. "I didn't fly all the way from Chicago to witness you groveling over someone else."

Gabe moved in beside Everley—fixed his stare on Tyler. "If I may, why *did* you come?"

Releasing a sigh, Tyler produced a ring box from inside his jacket. He pried it open and flashed an impressive diamond ring, adding a sour smile no doubt meant to sear her heart.

Waning sunlight brushed the facets of the glinting solitaire. She cupped her cheeks, found them warm, and shook her head.

"Plans, remember?" He snapped the box shut and jerked it back with fierce possession. "Can't blame a guy for going after a woman."

"A woman ... what, Ty?"

Love. The operative word. The essential foundation upon which marriage was built, enabling it to stand strong.

For better, for worse.

For richer, for poorer.

In war and peacetime.

Being someone's priority—their best interest placed before self.

An empty grin suggested Tyler's underlying purpose in going after her was merely a show of prowess. Achieving the next level.

Shattering untoward silence, he blew out a prolonged, ragged breath. He stuffed the ring box in his jacket and scrubbed a hand through his hair.

A diamond of any size does not a marriage make, Everley Orion. You'll find your true love in the one who unleashes your heart—inspires you to dream impossible things. Find you a man who isn't afraid to shoot for the stars and take you with him!

"Truth is, you deserve what I can't give," Tyler finally said. "Just thought I'd give it a shot." He turned to Gabe and cuffed his arm. "Guess the best man won, eh?"

He shifted a defeated gaze to Everley, ambled toward the embankment, and slung the roses into the air with an impressive arc. The blood-red blooms broke free and floated on the water like rubies on inky velvet. Ripples from a passing paddle boat distorted the streak of metallic sunlight and scattered the bobbing heads.

Without a glance, Tyler walked away. At his shrinking form, the rain slowed. The stark contrast between the two men utterly quaked through her.

A glimmer of sunlight peeked through parting clouds. Feathery wind cooled Everley's skin and orchestrated the oak's tinkling melody.

Everley felt the burn of Gabe's stare against her profile, surely wondering if she'd chase after Tyler.

She wouldn't. There was no need. The one she loved stood only a few feet away, looking more tortuously handsome and irresistible than should be considered legal.

Raw. Strong. Unpolished. Unbridled masculinity. A treasure worth keeping.

"He's leaving, Orderly."

"I see that."

"Totin' a mighty impressive solitaire meant to adorn your hand."

Slowly, she turned and fixed her gaze. "What logic is there in accepting a ring from someone I don't love? Who's incapable of helping me manage my inheritance ..." Closer now, she stroked his jaw that sported a day's worth of growth, let her gaze linger at the glint in his eyes. "And who doesn't have the key to my heart?"

Desire crashed inside her lungs, shortening her breaths. A soul roused from years of spiritual paralysis.

A low laugh eased tension between them. The dwindling daylight brushed facets of gold into the enigmatic sheen of his eyes.

He offered his arms. She sank into him, swallowed by his strength, and inhaled the mild scent of pine and sweat on sun-dried skin. Accompanied by the song of the oak, they swayed easy, the throb of his heart thudding against hers. Two formerly warring parties at peace.

How she desperately wanted to add his bravado, compassion, and capability to her monochromatic, one-dimensional, and—yes—mundane life.

Because divine appointments were a thing. An unpredictable, God-ordained thing.

CHAPTER TWENTY-TWO

At her soulful confession, Everley interpreted a look of perplexity skidding over Gabe's face.

"Never thought you'd be rendered speechless, Gabe Bellevue."

When she gave his hands a squeeze, the leathery feel of his skin curled about her middle. She leaned in to kiss his dusted, moistened cheek and snuck a whiff of his scent.

Gabe tightened his grip, and it'd suddenly become uncertain who was steadying who.

A remarkably roguish charm defined his expression. The dimples aside his mouth deepened. "Only one girl has ever had that effect. Just one." When he drew her closer, an endearing nervousness blazed in his eyes. "I love you, Everley Orion. Always have, always will."

Pulse thumping in wild rhythm, her brain exploded when he crushed her to his chest and pressed his hands to her lower back, fisting the fabric of her shirt. What little breath she still had nearly left her at the feel of his thudding heart. His hold like a steel casing, he drew back and kissed her full on the mouth. Heat surged through her and melded her agenda to his.

Mmmm. Wasn't the Scripture promise something like ... where you go, I will go?

After Mom's death, Everley had disregarded the iconic letter, its message muffled beneath the dusty lid of a

Dream Box. Nothing but a mix of sappy sentiment and foolish notions.

Or so she'd always believed.

Somehow Mom had seen past a mere internet search to find sentimental strength and God-sized benevolence behind Gabe's rough exterior. A gem among the ruins. The same way she regarded Moreland, sadly abandoned for years before she'd come upon it.

Undesirable to others. A treasure to her.

As Moreland's heiress, Everley was the recipient of the power of transforming love—an unmerited gift delivered right to the door of her heart. In death, Mom had successfully evoked a homesickness for what she'd had.

Before the chaos of packing, storing, and selling things had ensued, Everley carefully wrapped the Dream Box and shipped the insured package to Serenity for safekeeping. Because now it held great value.

In Serenity's guestroom the following day, Everley pondered her deeply enlightening interaction with Gabe. The Dream Box she'd set on the dresser came into focus. She took it in hand, sat on the bed, and eased it into her lap.

"I knew you'd never get rid of it." Serenity's declaration in the open doorway lanced the silence, nearly causing Everley to fumble the box.

She pressed it in firm possession against her middle. "I can be sentimental."

Seated beside her, Serenity scooted in close. When Everley lifted the lid, Serenity made the impulsive mistake of reaching beneath Mom's letter. "What are these?"

Everley caught her wrist and drew it away. "Nothing."

Everything. Thirty-six handwritten sentiments. Clipped together in the order in which she'd received them. One inked note secretly delivered to her locker each week. Initially, they were words of encouragement. In time, the messages deepened in intimacy, the author admitting romantic interest. Masterfully drawing her in ...

The rectangular edges were trimmed as though measured by a ruler.

Meticulous.

Being numbered, she'd expected other notes would follow. And they had.

She'd memorized them, recited in order, breathy whispers against mirrored reflection.

The first note. *You are smart. Smart is beautiful.*

The second. *You and me could be like magnets. Opposites attract.*

Number nineteen. *If I had a rocket, I would fly to the stars and take you with me.*

She uttered the last note—her favorite—on a wisp of a breath ... "You are the reason for everything, Dream Girl."

No one had ever called her that. Prophetic almost—as though someone saw past her attempt to confine her life to the parameters of a ledger.

"Wow, Evers. What hunky hero wrote these?"

"Gavin, in math club."

Who else knew her love of numbers? Or cared?

Whoever it was, they'd managed to tease a girl into falling in love and gave her reason to fuss with her appearance. Caused her to glance over her shoulder at lunch when she felt the weight of a stare, certain she was being watched. Wondering ... who?

Eyes afire, Serenity urged, "Read Mom's letter again."

Skipping over sentences, Everley skidded to a stop at Gabe's name. Paper raised to lamplight, she read ...

"It is my express desire that you will see to its complete restoration and that you contact Gabriel M. Bellevue of G&R Historic Restoration Specialists to handle any and all needed repairs. He is a New Orleans local, highly sought after, and has received numerous recognitions in the industry. Perhaps you've heard of him?"

Ah. There it was. Everley could almost see the puckish look in Mom's eyes.

Tranquility registered in Serenity's expression, her voice laced in reason. "I don't believe faith in God can be fully realized when we're trying to figure things out on our own."

"Meaning?"

"I think we're meant to trust God for things that are way beyond the bounds of our imagination or thinking."

Beyond the stars.

Unpredictable, far from routine.

Like Moreland. Like ... Gabe.

"Dreaming isn't fanatical or foolish," Serenity said. "It simply requires great big faith."

Everley could dream. Maybe even reach for the stars. Because she trusted the one who made them.

Possibilities spilled into her brain.

She returned Mom's letter to the box, closed the lid. "I could use a break from submitting my résumé, searching for a reliable car, and juggling social media inquiries. So if you can get away from the bakery, let's visit Moreland and do some brainstorming."

Serenity hopped off the bed and stood in front of Everley, her eyes happy dancing over a brilliant smile.

"Maybe we could open it up as an art gallery or a restaurant."

"Or a bed and breakfast."

Everley walked to the dresser. She popped a ball cap on her head, threaded her hair through the loop at the back, and assessed her appearance in the mirror—denim shorts, T-shirt, and tennis shoes. "With all the rain we've had, the lawn has got to be a disaster."

Moving to stand over her shoulder, Serenity's reflection stared back. Fingertip between her teeth, her expression held secrets. "Moreland may not be as bad off as you think. And maybe the view is far better than before. And maybe you'll be pleased with what you see."

Everley had no energy to mine for meaning. It was oddity enough that Marigold Lewis's daughters were working in tandem, opposing strengths bound by common purpose.

Score another for Mom.

Nearing Moreland, the familiar flash of white peeked through oaks guarding its treasure. The sight of Gabe's truck at the head of the drive triggered Everley's pulse.

Parking to the left of it, Serenity shut off the engine and joined Everley aside the car. Sporting a grin that smacked of covert operations, Serenity filled in the blank. "I'd asked him if he would lend a hand."

Flanked by two columns near the steps, Gabe sat in casual posture, arms resting on his knees as though he owned the place. Everley fixed a lidded stare from beneath the shade of her cap. In an attempt to overcome the erratic thudding in her ears and rush of adrenaline, she folded her arms and worked up a look of frustration. "You do know this is trespassing."

"Then go chase him off the property."

Chase him, yes.

Everley stole another glance at the guy who'd unearthed hidden gems—in people and in things—where others only saw rubbish. Wrung out to dry, yet here he sat gracing her property, comfortably perched on the ledge of the veranda, lighthearted as a bird before flight.

The one who'd delivered white-hot kisses.

The one my heart loves.

"How much is he charging you?" Everley said.

"Nothing."

Naturally. Benevolent Bellevue saves the day.

She became keenly aware of her appearance. Ideal for the cover of a woodshop magazine. Then again, this was the look of unpredictable. Spontaneous. Light-years from ordered.

Someone who might be a good fit for a guy like Gabe.

Owing to Gabe's resourcefulness, cedar woods to the northwest side had been gently thinned and cut for lumber to replace damaged flooring where sanding and restaining weren't possible. In so doing, he'd kept true to Moreland's history and saved unnecessary costs. Eased Everley's burden.

Flecks of gold, pink, white, and red lantana and peonies brocaded each wing near the windows. Mixed in among them were heat-loving marigolds of yellow, orange, and rust.

Fresh paint brightened the elevation, a perfect complement to the restored black shutters. She drew her eyes to the delicate lace balustrade around Moreland's neck.

Gabe had forged a rich elegance.

Mom would be pleased.

You're pleased.

Yes, God. Very.

Moving in easy steps beside Everley, Serenity paused and gazed long at the house, hypnotized by the view and awash in thoughts known only to her.

Tuning in to an inner voice.

Nearing Gabe, Everley attempted to hide apprehension behind a cool smile. To no avail. Fake emotion she'd leave for film stars. And honestly, he simply set her ablaze.

When they reached the steps, he stood and tipped his head in a slight bow as though in the presence of his sovereign. "Everley."

Good gracious, that matchless dimpled grin.

In a fluid motion, she tugged off her cap, letting her hair fall loose over her shoulders, giving her head a shake. Did he register the joy in her eyes, coursing through her like wild rapids?

Sparrows fluttered in the oak, swapping melodies in repetitive trills.

Gabe's boots peeped beneath the frayed and gently rumpled hem of his jeans. One toe was still wrapped in silver tape. His tender gaze penetrated her skin and hugged her heart.

For a moment, he broke her stare and glanced away.

And when he did, she contemplated his rock-solid profile, one that looked like a man his ancestors would have been proud of. Someone Moreland needed to maintain her inner and outer workings.

What only a trained eye could discern.

The truth was, Mom hadn't lost her marbles to insist on the likes of Gabe Bellevue. Because depth and value lay beneath his rough exterior.

Everley, baby, judging on outside appearances is the ultimate act of dishonor.

Holy heavens, did former lords of Moreland set a lady's heart to pound like this, knees weakened in shallow breaths?

Did the matrons of Moreland praise God for His lavish provision—like her soul was doing now?

There she stood, Moreland's dauntless owner. To date, no woman had bothered to see past Gabe's wounds and into his soul.

Everley had bothered. And succeeded.

Months before, Champ had chosen her the winner.

As Everley glanced around, an affirmative smile broke across her mouth. "The landscape. It's better than I imagined."

Hmmm. She'd imagined.

"I got Silas to assist. We seeded and clipped the lawn, built up the beds, placed the shrubs."

He stepped down to the hard earth and claimed the space in front of her. Sunlight played in her eyes, ringed them gold. He mustered strength not to get lost in them. "You'll want to keep it maintained, of course. If Silas don't suit, I can give you other recs."

"I don't need to search for the right guy ... if you're available."

At the offer, Gabe's heart lifted. Desperation churned along his spine like a Gulf storm threatening to make landfall on his face. She didn't need to see that.

Directing a thoughtful glance off to the side, he nibbled on his lower lip as though contemplating whether or not he could spare the time. He rubbed at his sandpapered chin and slowly returned his gaze. "I do still have a butt load of customized paint with no house for it."

Standing before this woman he loved, he praised God for Dad's tutelage on lawn care, proper painting, and all things handyman. For a short season, Dalton Bellevue had been the one who people called and who had income enough to sustain the house payment. But by that time, Mom had up and left.

Sometimes God sees fit to bless a man with the ministry of failure, the gift of emptiness.

Maybe so, Adam.

Gabe had been the latest recipient of emptiness, a heart hollowed of self-destructive vanity and restored by the power of Jesus's measureless love.

"Hey, while I'm here, I've got a question about the master," she said. "Mind checking it out with me?"

A coy smile claimed her face, lashes fanning over pinked cheeks as though rehearsing their dazzling night together. Then those highly charged kisses. *Mmmm.*

He loved the way her hair—open and long—framed the masterpiece of her face.

The haze of romantic tension lifted when Serenity smacked her hands together and dusted her palms. "Pretty sure this is my cue to pick pears or sweep or ... something."

No doubt, Serenity's mischievous grin was meant to razz big sister before she turned a one-eighty and disappeared around the side of the house.

Gabe made room for Everley to step past him over the threshold, brain dizzied by her scintillating scent. She could have carried the stench of a barnyard, and it'd still smell good on her.

Despite the brutal encounter with unfinished labor inside the grand hallway, the smell of dust and pinewood filled his soul.

The scent of hard work.

Skilled hands in worthy service to another.

The honor of preserving the past and securing a foundation for the future.

Gabe paused between the columns, inclining his ear to his ancestors. The echo of voices scratched behind the walls like mice.

Before Moreland, he'd never had attachment issues with his projects. Then again, no other historic came with his paternal fingerprints all over it and came packaged with an owner to whom he'd given his heart.

Focus!

Skirting the landing, he entered the bedroom behind her.

She directed a finger along the wall near the ceiling. "There's still that section of molding to be replaced, right?"

"That's right. But to match the original, I've got to get someone out here to take measurements, create a custom mold."

"Know anyone?"

"Yeah."

Dad. The holy prompt to reconcile sawed deeper. Maybe father-failure germinated from the seed of pride and choked success from future generations. Stolen what he'd rightly earned. Regret threatened to slice Gabe into pieces. Because unresolved issues stood in the way of pursuing Everley's heart.

Guilt thundered, clogged his throat. He'd given an unknown war vet a leg up but refused to engage his own father.

For the love of Pete, failure didn't have to be the death of a man.

Call Dad.

"Replacement could take months 'cause it needs to be done—"

"Right."

When she finished his sentence, she seemed to be pleased with herself.

He loved that.

"Since we're no longer shackled to production schedules and the all-seeing eye of media, take all the time you need." Her tone held refreshing ease.

Stepping through a geometric patch of pale afternoon sun, Gabe broke her stare and crossed over to one of the restored double-sash windows and peered through wavy glass. Down below, the distorted view of moss-ladened oak mirrored his thoughts.

Seemed he'd been viewing life through cylinder glass, the truth bent and twisted.

He loved this woman in his midst. Always had. In fantasy, he'd told her so over and over. She was the perfect fit, tongue and groove.

Ravenous desire swooped in. God help him. It was all he could do not to let his inner-predator override restraint and have his way with her. But he knew all too well the failure rate of quickly harvested wood, mechanically stapled together.

Hasty decisions only robbed a person of God's very best.

And he sure couldn't offer Everley a future when pieces of his own heart were disjointed.

Maybe the way to reclaim and uphold the Bellevue name had nothing to do with public opinion but everything to do with letting God make whole that which was broken. A good historic contractor never tossed out what could be salvaged, repurposed, and given new life.

"Son, lemme bust a myth for you. You gotta measure your life by loss, not by gain. Do that, and you'll find your hope and help come from God."

Dad's voice mail sermonette from last week.

Everley joined him beside the window, shattering his thoughts. He turned to face her and drowned in a delicious mixture of muted green and gold eyes.

"You okay?"

"Just thinkin'." He fingered the silken, coppery strands of her hair, running the pad of his thumb along her jawline. "You drive me crazy, you know that?"

Always have.

Chin tipped toward the light, her mouth parted, lips moistened and inviting.

"I gotta go take care of something." Stepping back, he turned for the door, paused at the jamb, and fixed his gaze on her. "Pray for me?"

Emboldened by Everley's nod and affirmative smile, he double-skipped down the bare staircase to his truck, the elegance and sophistication of Moreland and her heiress—who'd followed him outside—diminishing in his side mirror as he drove away. The vision had him believing he could conquer the world. But first, he'd start with a return to his childhood home. Because if that's where wounds of youth were inflicted, it might also be where they could be healed.

In a recent voicemail, Dad had confirmed he'd still lived there. He'd shared the address again, a pitiful assumption that Gabe would have long since forgotten.

He hadn't.

Gabe parked his truck across the street, the distance to the old front door an unnavigable chasm. He assessed the structure like a house doc. The wood-sided ranch style sat lifeless on a slab foundation moderately shaded by a low-sloped hip roof. Fractures from expansive tree roots had buckled the cement drive.

Disjointed memory stung all over. Family belongings being hauled off in full view of mocking observers.

At the drum of his heart, his placed a hand to his chest and held his cell to his ear with the other. "God, have your way."

Dad answered quickly, tone brisk above the clang and hiss of machinery. "Hullo? Gabe, that you?"

"Yes, sir. It's me."

"Real glad you called. Real glad. Say, I'm working a job right now, but when's a good time to call you back?"

"Anytime, really. I thought we could meet, catch up ... tonight if you could. Maybe grab a beer."

"That would be great, only I'm dry now."

Hallelujah. "A burger, fries, and soda works for me. Would you be free by, say, 6:00?"

"I've taken a temp assignment here in east Texas, but it'll finish up in a week or so. Welding a gas line."

The man welded, too.

"Oh, okay. Well, we'll connect later then. For now, I wanted to thank you for the words of encouragement. And to ... apologize for not returning your calls." For being a crappy, selfish son who held you at a distance like you carried a disease. For shutting you out of my life, believing you to be a loser beyond redemption. "I'd like to rebuild if possible."

A long pause, a weighty breath. "I love you, Gabriel. Just haven't known how to show it. I couldn't be more proud of the man you've become." His voice cracked. "It would mean the world to rebuild. I'll call as soon as I get back."

"Love you, Dad. Talk later. Bye."

Thank you, Jesus.

Sometimes restoration required nothing but a thorough sanding of the heart, particularly one that'd been roughed up by pride.

CHAPTER TWENTY-THREE

"For starters, we want an extension to our front porch and a breakfast nook and island," Kenneth Sinclair had explained to Gabe when he called to inquire about updates to his house.

"Trust me, Mr. Sinclair, I'm your man. I employ top-notch contractors and have a reliable crew that works closely alongside me."

No, Gabe, Merrill, and Silas did not a complete crew make, but a man in company with those who believed in him was capable of anything.

"I contacted several people—forgotten their names—each said you could be trusted to do the job right. Cost is no concern."

God be praised for those forgotten someones.

The following week at Kenneth and Barb Sinclair's home, Gabe clamped a thick slab of pre-measured red oak near the blade of the circular buzz saw while Silas advanced the piece.

"I had this awful crush on Barbie back in the day." Kenneth snaked an arm around Barb's waist as they stood looking on, sunlight dappling the lawn.

"We still get a kick out of spreading the rumor that Mattel named their famous dolls after us," Barb chuckled, turning a crinkly-eyed smile at Kenneth.

"We met in grade school. When our paths crossed later in life, boy if I didn't muster the nerve to ask her out." Kenneth traced a loving gaze over Barb's frame, the admiration of a man looking at the Mona Lisa. "Can't imagine life without her."

Gabe could. It'd be empty. A heart void of a rich interior. Cracked and rotting. The very opposite of success.

As it turned out, success wasn't circumstantial or about how gifted or resourceful a guy was but about who he'd become in hardship. Loss. Mistakes.

A dearly loved, chosen child of God.

Gabe's cell vibrated in his back pocket.

It was Everley.

He readily excused himself and stepped away.

"Hey, girl."

"Hey, Sir Fix-A-Lot."

He loved the playfulness in her voice, the buoyancy in her demeanor. Would love to be waking to it each day.

"Serenity said she's arranged for Lettie and Brooke to manage things here at the bakery and wants us to meet her over at Moreland. Overtaken, it seems, by an urgent desire to start casting a vision."

"Far be it from me to let her down, considering how long she's been casting."

Just before noon, Gabe and Silas completed work at the Sinclair's and drove to Moreland. He met Everley out front. Kissed her temple.

Serenity joined them and let out a huge breath. Exhibiting pronounced distraction, she frequently flitted attention to her cell ... feverishly returning texts.

Answering a call, Serenity pressed her phone to her ear, voice peppered in secrecy. "Yes, they're here. Finally. That's right, Highway 308. Can't miss it, a mammoth white house just beyond a line of tall trees that run along the drive."

"You expecting someone?" Everley said.

Lips pinched in a grin, Serenity shook her head and slipped her cell into her back pocket as though concealing evidence. "Nope."

A rumble of engines sounded along the main road. Gabe followed Serenity's sparkling, delighted gaze, hand raised to her forehead.

A caravan of cars, trucks, and vans appeared in stacked formation. Doors opened in succession and out spilled people dressed for work.

Lots of them, toting shovels, power tools, drills.

"You said you weren't expecting anybody, Hotshot."

"I'm not. I'm expecting a multitude."

In the lead was salty old Merrill. Hair combed in place and toting an auspicious grin inside a fresh face. He roved a twinkly gaze between the house and Everley. "Ewwee. She's a mighty beautiful thing."

It wasn't clear which was the object of his attraction, the house or its heiress.

In clustered formation, men, women, and youth trekked forward.

One who looked to be in his fifties stepped even with Merrill and met Gabe's stare. "Mr. Bellevue, I'm Leon McCullough. This here is my son, Charlie."

Familiarity rustled.

"If you hadn't taken us to the emergency room that day, Charlie would have died. He's in law school now, married with three kids. Happy and healthy and smart. I'll always be indebted to you."

A simple act of kindness. A life forever changed.

"I'm good for painting, planting, and sanding and can handle a power drill like nobody's business."

The sentiment rippled through Gabe, swelled inside his chest.

Another man proffered his hand. "Name's Wallace Conway of Conway Clips 'Em Right Lawn Service. When my mower broke, you donated a brand-new riding mower. Tried to keep it anonymous. But folks talk. Mighty grateful to you. Saved my business, enabled me to pay my wife's medical bills."

Right. He remembered now. His throat squeezed shut, he swallowed back the boulder. "Sure."

Weak response, but it was all he could muster.

A man and woman joined the lineup. "Hi, there, Gabe." The man smiled, his straight set of teeth matching his stance. "I'm Sheldon. This is my wife, Betty. Years past, we begged on the streets, held cardboard signs out front of St. Louis Cathedral. You bought us a hot meal, purchased things we needed, brought us to a shelter."

From the patch pocket of his shirt, Sheldon slipped out a small black Bible and opened it. "'The poor man called, and the Lord heard him. He saved him out of all his troubles,' Psalm thirty-four, verse six."

Sheldon lowered the Bible, fixing his stare.

"Today, Sheldon and I run a halfway house and manage a nonprofit to feed the hungry and offer them job training skills," Betty explained. "All thanks to God's mercy and your generosity."

Shovel raised, Sheldon said, "When Miss Serenity called to say you'd fallen on hard times, we wanted to lend a hand."

Stories continued to roll out. Recipients of what, to Gabe, had been nothing more than inconsequential acts of kindness. Long since forgotten on the road to success. To see a community rise in his favor, hail him a hero, nearly undid him.

Gabe's vision blurred. Gratitude tumbled around inside him, nearly buckling his knees to the ground.

Taking his hand, Everley tightened her grip and infused strength.

In the back, one man stood alone. Unassuming and quiet.

Heads turned as Merrill broke from the line and ushered him forward. "Now, I know you know *this* man."

"Dad."

Robed in sunlight, steady on his feet. The color of good health.

Gabe's pulse hammered behind his ears, eyes stinging moisture. Words as cement on his tongue.

"I about fell outta my chair when he introduced hisself to me as Dalton Bellevue after an AA meeting," Merrill said in a rusty chuckle.

Words sputtered. "I'm ... Great to see you, Dad. Meant to call and—"

Palm raised in staying gesture, Dad's pale blue-gray gaze ripened in grace. "You did call. Now, I'm here to help you and the lady out."

Yes, yes. The jack-of-all-trades.

Releasing Gabe's hand, Everley stepped onto the veranda and faced the gathering. Poised, assured, intelligent. What—*just what*—must this outpouring have done for her heart? The reluctant lioness who'd refused to accept rights to the house, fearful she'd be left to do it alone?

"Your sacrifice of time and willingness to put abilities to use out here are an immeasurable blessing. The sweat equity it took for my mom to restore Moreland nearly crushed her, but she was determined to breathe life into it and showcase it to the world. I have no doubt she's swinging from star to star, joyful to know her house—" Wrought with emotion, she pursed her lips, hand to her heart. "—*my* house—is being well cared for."

Applause and cheers erupted.

Everley stepped down and crossed the lawn to Gabe. Admiration throbbed in her gaze. "You are the best to oversee Moreland's care. But not because you know historic houses. Your integrity of character testifies against those that attempt to destroy."

Best. Customer. Review.

Desire for his high school crush threatened an unstoppable inferno. Lost in the moment, he returned a kiss, soft and easy, then hard and crushing. She drove him wild, nearly making him forget they had an audience.

A voice broke in. "If y'all need to go find a room, you've got plenty to choose from right there behind you."

Laughter cut through the air. Her cheeks went all pink and rosy aside a crazy beautiful, modest smile.

"Now that all these folks are here to lend a muscle," Merrill said, "I suggest you get to delegating tasks. As for me, I'm good with turning a screw, so if you'll pardon me, you old fart, I'd like to make the best use of the day before the sun takes a dive."

Gabe grinned and saluted off his forehead. "Yes, sir."

Dad ambled over, toting what looked to be a brand-new pair of work boots. Same color and brand Gabe had always worn. His uncompromising choice—that which a good father would know. "Word has it you're in need of a new pair." He glanced at the tattered tape, a hint of tease in his smile. "Size eleven and a half, wide."

Perfect.

Moisture pooled in Gabe's eyes. Fingers to the bridge of his nose, he shook his head. "God, You're so good to me."

He felt the cottony softness of Everley's smile beside him, the warmth of rugged breaths.

Dad set the boots down. Put his hands in his back pockets. "Your grandpa Bellevue used to say hardships may drain a man's account, but they build his character."

At that, Gabe took Dad in a hard embrace and let redolent grace soak into him. He smelled like Gabe remembered, a man doing all he could to rise above his messes.

The darker side of failure was to have never tried.

Adding to the blessed sound of progress, Special K arrived, her junk heap car sputtering at the end of the driveway. The precocious little keeper of historic secrets marched over, chin taut in purpose, dressed in olive green pants and a custom, pink bakery T-shirt.

"Hi, Ms. Scott," K said. "I called before I came, left a message on your cell."

"You're always welcome, Kourtney."

"Thanks." K turned to Gabe. "First off, I've got great news."

"Lemme guess, the new website is up and running. Techno bugs eliminated."

"Looks fantastic. Love the popup window on the landing page and earthy color palette. The new name rocks."

Bellevue Historic Restoration Specialists.

"I made an A on my research paper. Highest in the class." At that, she waggled her head.

"Congrats. Remind me to give you a raise."

Irritation sputtered through a weighty exhale. "If I had a nickel for every time you've promised—"

"No way you trekked all the way down here to regale us with your favorable report card."

"No, I have new discoveries about Moreland. For one, something about Edmund Bellevue, but … it's kinda scandalous."

Fear quaked through, clenched his gut. The afternoon sun licked at his neck. A round of cicadas sawed through the air.

For someone who'd just been awarded an A, she looked like she'd just left a funeral. Bringing the stench of death.

Please. Don't. Humiliate. Me.

Whatever the insidious nature of said Bellevue scandal, it held little hope of being eradicated. An unwelcome guest who wouldn't leave. "Seems this new discovery is troubling enough for you to waste precious time and fuel to tell me directly, K."

"I'll leave that to you to decide."

Gabe's muscles tightened from the strain of prolonged concern.

"Rumor has it that Edmund Bellevue fathered a child by a mistress while married to Anna. Given his standing in society, it's possible he used service in the war as a means to flee controversy."

A guttural moan chugged up. His arms slackened. "Give it up for rock-solid legacy."

Dad caught his gaze then lowered his head.

Intention surged in Everley's eyes. "Look, Bellevue, I've already lost one man I love to war. I won't lose another."

"What war?"

She placed a palm to his chest. "The one raging inside you, sniping at your soul, trying to take you out by way of corrosive self-hatred."

Dribbling from mid-court, she pressed in. "Your paternal ancestors weren't failures. They sacrificed for the good of others. Angels on the battlefield, benevolent to society, and wholly color blind. Men who dared to act. The flip side of that is passivity. *That's* failure, Gabriel Bellevue, and you are none of that."

Her words penetrated bone and marrow, coursed through his veins, and warmed his soul.

As pieces came together, watery eyes warped her beautiful face.

"Don't you see? Compassionate sacrifice runs through your family like a cord of three strands. Not easily broken." Leaning in, her voice swept low, feathered soft against his heart. "And that is one of the many reasons I admire you."

She'd made a list?

Heart raw and exposed, Gabe was uncertain what to do with her words. Because not every guy who'd scaled the wall of success believed himself worthy of it.

Skepticism pestered. "How do you figure Edmund's illegit child into your reasoning?"

"Operative word, rumored." Righteous fury rose in her countenance. "It's unsubstantiated. And even if he *did* father a child out of wedlock, people make mistakes, and no one who asks for God's forgiveness is denied."

The biblical wisdom slicked over his brain like wood putty, filled spaces rotted by untruth. He stole a glance at Dad, both of them nodding like they'd woken from tortuous slumber.

For all the wrong reasons, Gabe had poured energy and resources into claiming top spot in the eyes of people, and it'd hollowed him. Emptied, he'd come to the end of himself, a heart ripe to receive the truth.

"There's nothing new under the sun. Murdock slandered you, attempted to tarnish your reputation. All because you dumped his daughter."

He raised a palm in defense. "Take it easy now. I'd like to think I set her down gently."

Fists on her hips, she sounded a humorless laugh. "Trust me, any girl who loses you won't recover easily. If ever."

How'd she do that? Fit him back together and stretch his stature with mere words?

A conduit for restoration.

From his periphery, several gathered near, breaths stilled.

"I don't need Mom's letter to hire you. A guy with your DNA is outstanding among all others."

Dauntless before an audience, her proclamation was beautifully resolute. Matched her face.

"Your worth is found in God whose image you bear. It isn't measured by status, the ownership of things. Acquiring more ... land."

Moreland.

In all her grandeur, Moreland filled his scope of sight. He slid his gaze to the vast acreage beyond the home. A fragmented laugh rumbled inside his chest. He lolled a weary glance in Everley's direction. "Now ain't that an irony."

CHAPTER TWENTY-FOUR

A black SUV emerged from the highway and rolled to a stop along the property line. Hand to her brow, Everley peered long at the dark-haired driver who stepped out. He looked to be in his early thirties with a solid build, some type of dark utility pants and jacket, eyes concealed behind aviator shades. Given the distinct buzz cut, he pulled off the look of secret service.

Owen Walker, the NFL's latest recipient of the Man of the Year award, unfolded from an elegant interior.

A small entourage of men and women, athletic and exuberant youths joined Owen in a surprise convergence onto the property. The austere driver held back, gaze slowly roving the scene as though on the lookout for combatants.

Serenity's gaze collided with Owen's. She went rigid and sucked in a hard gasp of air. An altogether stupefied look claimed her face. Mouth agape, she let the sack of freshly plucked pears she'd cradled in her arms thud to the ground. Fruit rolled over the lawn like billiard balls struck by a pool cue.

"No, no, no. This is all wrong."

Despite Serenity's adamant refusal to admit that she and Owen were once *a thing*, the electricity surging between them could light Moreland's interior. To date, she persisted in brushing *the thing* off like cupcake crumbs.

Though Owen possessed status and charm en masse, he'd yet to win Serenity's heart. No amount of muscle had proved capable of such a feat. Since he'd signed with the Commanders, the star athlete had been jubilantly celebrated by the whole of New Orleans.

Save one. Serenity.

Frustration simmered in Serenity's eyes. "I specifically asked for Callahan, the QB. Not, him."

"Well, *him* is here," Everley said.

"A man of his notoriety couldn't possibly have any interest in fixing up a dumb old house."

"Ha. Rattled by the presence of your college crush and, suddenly, the house you fought tooth and nail to save—the reason you assembled all this help—is now dumb and old. And since you've been blowing up social media on Moreland's behalf, a guy who's earned Man of the Year wouldn't overlook an opportunity to lend a hand."

And a good bit of muscle.

Owen jogged over wearing dark track pants and a black and gold football jersey, a pure specimen of athleticism and power.

Serenity tensed.

Several youths lowered their tools, wandering near, eyes rounded in awe as though the president had arrived in his state car. Owen stopped to meet and greet, signed their T-shirts, shoes, ball caps ... anything.

Making his way over to Gabe, he offered his hand. "Finally meeting the infamous handyman I've heard so much about."

"Pleasure's mine." Gabe returned a vigorous handshake.

A show-stopping smile inched across Owen's face as he turned to Everley, nearly crushing her in an easy hug. "It's been a while. Great to see you again."

"You, too." She patted the musculature of his back though he probably didn't feel it.

In cautious movement, he turned to Serenity and held her gaze hostage for a second. He gave a wolfish grin that suggested he enjoyed the sight of her squirm.

"Where's Callahan?" Serenity's tone was none too kind.

"Asked me to step in."

"Well, then, thanks. I guess."

Owen switched glances between Everley and Gabe. "If you'll shoot me a list of materials needed, I'll foot the bill. Money's no object."

A good person to have in your corner when you've chosen to embrace what felt like endless square footage.

I am your ever-present help.

Wide hands low on his waist, Owen let his eyes linger over Moreland. "Beautiful place. Pictures don't do it justice. Bigger than any house I've owned and a lawn about the size of a football field." He turned to Everley and scrubbed a hand along the scruff of his chin. "My sports camp kids would love it out here. Any possibility you'd consider hosting a Walker sports camp fundraiser in the spring?"

"Sure," she said. "Give us a call."

In mere words, a partnership was established. An exceptional one.

The sudden rush of elation in Gabe's presence, partnering with this capable someone, caused her heart to skip-hop. It rendered her brain useless and coated her insides in a river of melted chocolate.

Blessed symptoms of lovesickness. Dream chasing, maybe?

Kourtney leaned in and waved a hand in front of her face. "Um, Ms. Scott, I've got something else to share. It's a big deal, the main reason I drove out here."

Lids blinking alert—and spared from drowning in Gabe's gaze, a tortuous ache for him to whisk her over the threshold—Everley turned to Kourtney. "Big deal you said?"

"A new acquisition by archives at the university this morning." Intrigue tinged Kourtney's tone. The rise and fall of her chest suggested she'd held this inside longer than she could stand. "I was at the special collections department when a document was donated by a man named Oscar Bishop, a university alum. He told the repository clerk that his mother Ruth lived at Moreland as a foster child in the '40s. While there, she'd discovered a metal missionary box used to collect funds to support Protestant missionaries. When Ruth died, she'd left the box to Oscar. He'd been following Moreland's story and felt led to donate the box."

"What's special about the box?" Everley said.

"It's not the box that's special. It's the letter inside it." Kourtney drew in a long breath. Wonderment infiltrated her gaze. "It was written by Anna Thompson Bellevue to her husband, Edmund."

Warmth enveloped Everley, swirled down her spine.

"The clerk said she blushed when she read it. Even teared up."

Anna's letter. A war widow, one calling to another.

Heavenly sweet wonder suffused her senses.

"Anna's letter was discovered in Edmund's uniform after he died. It was returned, along with his personal effects. I've got a high-res scan of the original." She slipped her phone from her hip pocket and fingered the screen. "I could read it aloud. Or ... maybe you'd like to read it?" Kourtney extended her phone.

Useless appendages.

A brief glance at Gabe—who returned a prodding wink—and she managed to summon strength. Taking Kourtney's phone, she thumbed the screen, cleared her throat, and read aloud.

YOU ARE THE REASON

April 4th, 1863,

My brave and honorable Edmund,

Though my heart aches for your return, I applaud your gallant sacrifice, unyielding resolve in matters of principle, fervent desire to bring unity to a splintered nation. I await word of your welfare and pray continually for angel armies to guard you on all sides. Your sons set to task daily to care for the needs in and around Moreland. William, prime among them, often co-laboring alongside the Negros. Unhindered by youth, he sets a fine example for his brothers, and remains committed to home studies.

Our Lord says, A wise son bringeth honor and joy to his father. My Edmund, you would be proud indeed!

I pray this dreadful conflict will come to a swift and peaceful end and that Providence will secure your return to Moreland and the wedded passion of our bed chamber. To enjoy again arduous abandon beneath the stars, the deaf and dazzling celestial beings our only witness. But if it be the Lord's good, pleasing, and perfect will otherwise, I shall entrust my cares to His ever-present help, seek His strength in heartache, and endure with greater fervor to keep its fires burning and fill its walls with merriment and song.

Future generations will receive as heir that for which we have toiled. The book of Psalms, chapter 105, verse 44.

To that, I pray our beloved Moreland will be properly cared for by those to whom it will be entrusted and remain a beacon of light to hearts in search of home.

Yours in eternity,

Anna

With that whispered end, tears sprang.

Choking sobs rumbled in Everley's chest.

Anna, a widow who'd kept her hopes and dreams alive, unleashed her heart-felt need. Fanning the flames of family inside Moreland's walls and refusing to leave it to ruin. Whispers of her heart scripted long ago, a message divinely preserved.

Moreland was no longer the widow-maker Everley had deemed it to be. And Gabe no longer the rogue contractor Mom assigned to bring it back to life.

Anna's entreaty broke the bounds of time and fell on Everley's heart—a space previously numbed by assault and rendered lifeless prior to meeting Gabe Bellevue.

Moreland's purpose, it seemed, extended beyond being a family's manor house, an architectural achievement, and the object of online viewers. It had the power to move her relationship with Gabe from attraction to committed love ... if she dared.

Beneath the weight of unflinching stare, she drew a dazed stupor along the pillars to the fanlight winking within the protruding pediment.

Dear God, please equip me to care for this great gift. And its capable contractor.

A little bit of life began to pump and course through Everley's veins. "The widow's calling," she said, barely above a whisper.

Cupping her cheeks, Gabe pinned his gaze. "Question is, how will Lady Everley answer?"

She had no need to reach for the stars when heaven had come to earth ... looking in every way like Gabriel Bellevue. She sank into his arms and turned her cheek to his chest, felt a booming *tha thump, tha thump*. Drawing in Gabe's strengthening scent of leather and sandalwood, the last bit of reluctance drained out of her.

An abrupt laugh sounded. "How about that. Momma wins."

Everley eased out of Gabe's arms and turned to Serenity. "And what, pray tell, is the grand prize?"

"For pity's sake, Evers, are you blind?" She clapped a palm to her forehead then swept it Gabe's direction like a game show host standing before a parted curtain.

Hands gripped about her waist, Gabe rotated Everley back to him—the fetching look of a grand prize for a girl in want of an able handyman. He bumped his forehead to hers. "I think she means to say your momma would rest in peace if she knew that her oldest had chosen to embrace the possibilities of this place."

Held fast by his delicious embrace, the eyes of Everley's heart opened. "And fall hopelessly in love with the 'G' of G and R in the process."

A steely seriousness fell over Gabe's expression. His gaze lingered on her eyes, moved to her lips, and back up as though surveying her like the project of a lifetime, eager to demolish the old, restore the new.

"Did it work?" he said, voice throaty and deep.

She teased her fingers through the strands of his hair along his neck. "Yes, Lord Bellevue. It did."

He stood motionless as though processing deeper, richer layers of his ancestry. He had to be wondering at God's intent to bring more of his own past to light.

"Do I have what it takes to maintain the legacy of my forebears?"

"Gabe Bellevue, because you've chosen to come under God's authority, there are no limits to what you can do. I wouldn't entrust Moreland to anyone else."

White gold sunlight blanketed the expansive lawn, a surreal glow framed by the overarching balcony. He stepped back and claimed her hands. "I love you, Everley Orion."

His rock solid confession suffused a tingling warmth into her cheeks like she'd bitten into dark choclate. The last remnant of haunting memory vanquished.

"What do you say to today's lady of Moreland Manor hooking up with a Bellevue?" A tortuous mix of trepidation and fortitude tinged his tone.

Love swelled in gentle waves inside her chest. Pity the girl who'd been blessed with a house this size but disregarded the one who could help her maintain it. "I say that makes incredibly good sense," she managed to eke out.

His hands cupped her face and stroked out tension. "Guess that's my cue, Dream Girl."

In slow motion, the earth sank beneath her as Gabe lowered to one knee. He took her hands and caressed her skin. "Everley Orion, will you—?"

"Wait. Back up." She blinked and narrowed her gaze. "What did you call me?"

Concern skidded over his brow. "Everley Orion. That's your name, isn't it?"

"No. I mean, yes. But *before* that?"

Amid the rift of collective and amplified murmurs beside them, he rose slowly and met her gaze, then took a small step back. "Dream girl?"

Note number 36.

In only two words, the veil of confusion lifted. She pressed a palm to his chest—felt it thudding. "The notes in my locker. Each one numbered. It was ... you." Her whispered breath lifted in buoyant, airy waves.

A crimson blush bloomed across his face. He circled his lopsided gaze away then brought it back. A boyish grin laid claim to the truth. "Being a numbers girl, I thought you'd appreciate them in order."

"One through—"

"Thirty-six."

Finally. The secret admirer she'd fallen in love with a thousand times over. Never dreamed it'd be him. Because she'd stopped dreaming.

He narrowed the distance between them and caressed her lips with kisses. "I should have gone after you when I had the chance." Awash in a sensuous whisper, his tone was hoarse with emotion. "If I had a rocket, I'd fly to the stars and—"

"Take you with me. Number thirty-two."

He quirked a brow, penetrating her gaze as he played the game.

"I kept them," she said.

A throb of gratitude swallowed his easy grin. The grooves in the planes of his face deepened, the set of his jaw firm. Need unleashed over his features.

Shadowing her, he reclaimed her hands and took a knee again. "Let's get married and have us a house full of sons. In proper order, of course."

Euphoria shot through her and crushed the last trace of fear on its way down to her toes. Awakened from a catatonic slumber, her soul floated into some sort of ethereal and celestial dream. Only this was real. Sweet, wholly satisfying.

Reality took on the form of a rugged, capable, larger-than-life handyman. DNA rich with history. Generous, heroic, kind, and sacrificial. Far from punctual but oh so wildly handsome and toting a camera-ready smile. Unhindered in his worn jeans and boots. The man Moreland needed who was down on one knee.

Gaze hopeful ... breath suspended ... her awaited her answer.

"Lord Bellevue, I happily accept your offer."

EPILOGUE

Spring the following year, Moreland shone like a pearl. What had been an abandoned eyesore now boasted a seven-figure value and was coveted by many.

Only she wasn't for sale.

Polished and pretty and pleased, Moreland welcomed the pulse of life. Mom's oil paintings hung in bedrooms throughout. Gabe had outfitted an unused space off the rear of the north wing into an expanded office. In weeks to come, Gabe and Everley's wedding portrait would grace the front entry.

Refinished floors were protected by period area rugs. Plush burgundy carpet paneled the grand staircase. The fully functioning and updated kitchen and bathrooms maintained the original feel of its beginnings. The front parlor and main dining halls were encapsulated in the richness of yesteryear and furnished in period antiques.

Seated in folding chairs aside a card table, Gabe and Everley's first meal together had been grilled cheese sandwiches, french fries—hers amply drizzled in ketchup—and sliced, fresh pears from the tree out back.

She'd discovered that dunking her fries alongside the guy she loved tasted just as good. Better, in fact.

On the long-awaited afternoon of their wedding and reception, the sun shimmered over the lawn that'd provided a picture-perfect setting. Hundreds of twinkling white lights were strung around the arching limbs and trunk of the great oak, the base of which would mark the procession.

Everley swore she'd detected a knowing smile on Moreland's face as though the house had expected this day.

Word of their engagement and April wedding date spread quickly, the power of hashtag originality ...

Moreland makes memories.

CPA plus contractor equals love ever after.

Blissful Bellevues.

When asked, Everley had permitted select cable and local media personel to attend, limiting their intrusion to one interview each. A few days before, a former client in Chicago, Stuart Ormond, a producer of feature films and documentaries for a small start-up company, had contacted her. Stuart's younger sister Adelyn had recently married executive chef, Bryan J. Carlyle, who'd chosen Gabe to be his best man.

"Heard your network deal fell through." Stuart's voice sagged. "But listen, don't sweat it. I've got a guy who's interested in the production and distribution of a split-time feature film depicting the 1800s and a contemporary time and wants to film on location. Wouldn't turn down a proposition like that, heh?"

For a millisecond, Everley nurtured the possibility. Until saved by a sound mind. "Love that Moreland is so highly favored, but ... her—our—film days are over."

Custom-ordered from Marina Mosteller, proprietor of Inner Princess Boutique in Laurelton, North Carolina, Everley's full-length gown featured a stretch French lace, fitted bodice, off-the-shoulder neckline, and mermaid skirt. It exuded modern romance, femininity, sophistication, and fun. Perfect for a girl who'd embraced her inner dreamy romantic, now married to the one who was the reason she had.

At the reception, a distinguished couple approached Everley and Gabe near the linen-draped cake table that held Serenity's three-tiered wedding cake. The man shook Gabe's hand. "Congrats to you, Gabe."

"Thanks, Kenneth." Hand to Everley's back, Gabe made introductions. "Kenneth and Barb …" He turned to her. "I'd like you to meet Mrs. Everley Bellevue, the love of my life."

The sound of her name blushed pink from her middle, exploded inside her head, and drew a shy smile.

"Very pleased to meet you, Everley," Kenneth said, coming up on his toes.

"The wedding was sensational," Barb said.

"We'd secretly hoped to make an offer on Moreland, especially considering Gabe was your contractor. He's done impeccable work for us."

"Thanks much, Ken."

"You're welcome out here anytime," Everley offered. "I'll most likely be running accounts, paying bills." She turned to Gabe, flutters expanding in her chest. "Staring at my contractor." A lot. She raised a palm to stroke Gabe's bristled jawline.

"Will Moreland be open to overnight guests at some point?" Barb said, eyes pleading.

Um.

The electric bill had arrived. It'd exceeded $1000, half that of the summer months. Everley took her lower lip between her teeth, crunched numbers. She hauled in a breath. "Actually … yes. A full-service bed and breakfast. In the parlor, you'll enjoy a wine and cheese reception to mingle with other guests, followed by a tour of the house and its history. For supper, your choice of shrimp or chicken pot pie and traditional sides ... served by candlelight in the dining hall. In the morning, we'll treat you to a hearty breakfast buffet of scrambled eggs, salted ham, hash browns, and fresh-baked muffins and coffee from the Pear Tree Bakery."

At the slow, angular sweep of Gabe's cocked brow, elation zipped through her.

"Sounds heavenly," Barb said.

"How much do you charge?" Kenneth said.

Numbers, crunching. "$250 per night. Two-night minimum."

Covered half the bill.

"You plus me equals a wildly successful team." Gabe's breathy whisper tickled her ear.

In one swift movement, he scooped her into his arms. Her shoes dropped like two ripe pears as he hefted her from the cake table and crossed the lawn. Stepping onto the veranda, he pivoted to face the guests engaging in happy chatter.

Curled against Gabe's chest, Everley fisted his silk vest and squealed in feigned helplessness.

Casting his voice over the property, he made a quick audience of them, their gazes rapt and stilled. "Y'all just keep enjoying yourselves."

A tighter curl of his biceps clamped her squiggling form closer.

"Seeing that Lady Bellevue now bears my name and a ring to show for it, we're going to disappear inside for a bit and enjoy the place. Resurface in, say, an hour. Or so."

Hearty laughter bubbled up. A teasing grin swept across his face, his grip intensifying against her futile wriggling. He turned a seductive gaze on her lips, traced her bodice, and slid hungry eyes to her bare toes and back to her slackened jaw. "No use fighting the obvious. We're crazy about each other. Just made this love affair an official till-death-do-we-part union in the presence of God and these fine witnesses, and, frankly, I've waited for my dream girl long enough."

"Waiting a little longer won't kill a guy." She exerted effort to hide an electrifying smile, the strength to fight waning in his grip.

"Unless he's waited since high school. Do the math."

The thought of his forbearance drained the last ounce of defense from her limp frame.

Beneath the spell of his wink and a feathered kiss, she nearly lost all breath. Her head spun in a free fall as desire coursed through her body. "I surrender." Her words thinned to a raspy, fainting whisper.

"'Bout time, Lady Bellevue," he said, tone low and ravenous.

In a cool one-eighty, he pivoted toward the partially opened door, heeled it open, and held his prize at the threshold.

Their threshold. Perfectly restored.

The photographer scrambled up the steps and voraciously snapped pictures. Gabe twisted and flashed a ready smile. Whoops and cheers erupted. Camera crews scurried over, stopping at the base of the veranda. Guests clustered near the steps.

Breaking through the lineup, Serenity raised a champagne flute. "Here's to shooting for the stars, Evers!"

Chiseled chest fitted inside a crisp suit, Owen kept to Serenity's shadow and clinked his flute to hers.

Gabe wore the irresistible smile of a man who'd lost everything and created space in his heart to receive the fullness of life. For all his rugged edges, he chased after the staunchly predictable Everley Orion and turned her orderly world upside down. The only man who could set her heart free.

She grounded him. He kept her spontaneous.

And all along, Mom knew. Her true heart's desire existed outside time and space, beyond mere wood and brick. She'd left Everley the very best inheritance a girl could receive—the need to trust God in all things and follow his call wherever it led.

Just as the evening primrose flourished when shadows of night fell upon it, neither of the widows' letters suggested the investment in Moreland would be free from trouble. Because all good things came through the dark of struggle and gave way to soul-satisfying joy.

As for Everley's tomorrows? No matter. God was already there.

ABOUT THE AUTHOR

Mary A. Felkins is an inspirational romance author, blogger, and contributor to writer's blogs and online publications. Her debut novel, *Call to Love*, is set in Hickory, North Carolina, where she lives with her husband. They have four young adult children. She is a member of ACFW (American Christian Fiction Writers) and My Book Therapy, a writer's coaching group, and an active participant in a writer's support and critique group.

The unmerited gift of a large, unopened bag of Peanut M&Ms® or an episode of *Fixer Upper* will lure her from her writer's desk. A surprise appearance by her teen idol, Donny Osmond, would also do the trick, although she'd likely pass out.

If, upon introduction, she likes your first or last name, expect to see it show up in one of her novels.

To receive Mary's story-style devotions via email, along with a quarterly author newsletter offering book-related giveaways, subscribe on her website www.maryfelkins.com.